KT-134-083

THE DOWNSTAIRS MAID

She is a servant girl... When her father becomes ill, Emily Carter finds herself sent into service at Priorsfield Manor in order to provide the family with an income. **He will be the Lord of the Manor...** Emily strikes up an unlikely friendship with the daughters of the house, as well as Nicolas, son of the Earl. But as the threat of war comes ever closer, she becomes even more aware of the vast differences between upstairs and downstairs, servant and master... **If you like Downton Abbey you'll love this!**

h
√
22

Powys
Digital
History Project
37218 00441882 3

THE DOWNSTAIRS MAID

THE DOWNSTAIRS MAID

by

Rosie Clarke

Magna Large Print Books
Long Preston, North Yorkshire,
BD23 4ND, England.

British Library Cataloguing in Publication Data.

Clarke, Rosie
    The downstairs maid.

    A catalogue record of this book is
    available from the British Library

    ISBN   978-0-7505-3993-7

First published in Great Britain in 2014 by Ebury Press,
an imprint of Ebury Publishing
A Random House Group Company

Copyright © 2014 Rosie Clarke

Cover illustration © Birgit Tyrell by arrangement with
Arcangel Images

Rosie Clarke has asserted her right to be identified as the author of
this work in accordance with the Copyright, Designs and Patents Act,
1988

Published in Large Print 2014 by arrangement with
Ebury Publishing,
one of the publishers in the Random House Group Ltd.

All Rights reserved. No part of this publication may be reproduced,
stored in a retrieval system, or transmitted in any form or by any
means, electronic, mechanical, photocopying, recording or otherwise
without the prior permission of the Copyright owner.

Magna Large Print is an imprint of Library Magna Books Ltd.

Printed and bound in Great Britain by
T.J. (International) Ltd., Cornwall, PL28 8RW

This novel is a work of fiction. Names and characters are the product of the author's imagination and any resemblance to actual persons, living or dead, is entirely coincidental.

Part One

1907–1914

Chapter 1

'Under there and hide quick!' Emily's mother pushed her towards the kitchen table. A heavy chenille cloth hung down over the sides, almost touching the brownish red of the polished quarry-tiled floor and, once hidden beneath its folds, Emily could not be seen through the window. She hurried to obey, knowing that such a warning could only mean that the tallyman was on his way to collect money Ma didn't have. 'Don't come out until I tell you – and keep quiet.'

Emily scuttled into safety beneath the faded cloth she knew had once been her mother's pride and joy. Bounded by the four legs of scarred pine, she felt safe, securely hidden from the enemy, her senses alert to danger. She heard Ma walk quickly into the pantry and held her breath. The tallyman wasn't easily fooled. He would guess that they were hiding and he might bang at the door for ages, shouting threats through the letterbox of the ancient thatched cottage that was their home. Emily trembled at the thought, waiting for the ordeal to commence.

'Mrs Carter, I know you're there,' the tally-man's voice was pleasant at the start, coaxing and friendly. 'It's silly to hide, because you know the debt isn't going to go away. All I'm asking is that you pay a shilling every week.'

There was no answer. Emily's mother never

answered him, even though she could hear him perfectly well in the large, cool pantry. Whether she was as frightened of him as Emily was, Emily could not tell, because when Ma had a few pennies to offer she opened the door and invited him in for a cup of tea and a bun, but too often the jar on the mantel was empty and they had to hide and wait until Mr Thompson gave up and went away.

Emily hated having to hide under the table, because it was stuffy and airless beneath the cloth. Sometimes she felt as if she couldn't breathe, especially if the tallyman kept on banging at the door and she had to hide for ages. It was during these times that she would try to block out what was going on around her and think of nice things – like the day she'd been taken to see Pa's rich uncle, Albert Crouch.

Albert Crouch was as old as Methuselah, so Ma said, and when he died he was going to leave them a fortune. At least that's what Pa had promised her years ago when Ma married Pa, but Uncle Albert didn't seem to want to die. Ma said he'd taken against them because Ma hadn't provided him with a male heir to follow Emily's father. Pa said he could keep his rotten money and didn't care whether his uncle left him a penny – but then, he didn't have to hide from the tallyman.

Emily had liked it at Uncle Albert's house, because it was filled with pretty things, like the clock on the mantelpiece, which Pa said was French and bronze, and the cranberry epergne on the sideboard (Pa had one similar in his barn, but that was cracked, while Uncle Albert's was perfect). For tea

12

they'd had cakes and jelly with ice cream, as well as ham sandwiches.

Uncle Albert had a housekeeper with a sharp tongue and she'd warned Emily to keep her feet off the antique furniture, because she didn't want it kicked or scratched. The dining chairs were made of a dark polished wood. Pa had told Emily later that day that the wood was mahogany. The legs were curved inwards in a strange way and the back was square with bits of brass inlaid into the wood. Pa said they were called sabre-legged chairs, Regency, and worth a lot of money, which was why Miss Concenii thought them too good for children to sit on. Ma had taken exception to her speaking to Emily like that and they'd had *words,* which was perhaps why the invitation for tea hadn't been repeated.

Emily had thought how smart Miss Concenii was with her long dark hair swept high on her head and fastened with shiny combs. Her ankle-length dress was a pale silvery-grey and made of much better stuff than Ma's Sunday-going-to-church dress. Her shoes were black and shiny with shaped heels and she wore a huge sparkly ring on the third finger of her right hand. Emily thought it looked pretty and on the train taking them home later that night, she'd asked her mother what kind of ring it was. Ma had sniffed and said it was a diamond and then she'd muttered something strange.

'She's no better than she ought to be and he might think he's fooling us by calling her his housekeeper but we all know the truth.'

When Emily asked Ma what she meant, she shook her head and looked angry. She'd refused

13

to answer even when Emily repeated her question so she'd given up asking. It was just one of those things people thought a nine-year-old child shouldn't ask. Emily was ten now and she still didn't know why Miss Concenii was no better than she ought to be.

The tallyman had started banging on the door and shouting at them. Emily put her hands over her ears to shut out the words, which she knew were abusive. Mr Thompson always started out by being polite but then he ended by yelling and swearing. Emily didn't know what all the words meant, but she knew they were rude. She was trembling and feeling sick but she hunched her knees to her chest and kept as still as she could. If he saw the cloth move he would guess she was under the table and then he would just keep on and on banging. She forced herself to think of other things.

Emily liked being ten. She was ten years old and the year was 1907 so she'd been born in the sixth month of the year 1897; the figures had a sort of ring to them and she was good at sums. She could add up in her head faster than Pa could with a bit of paper and a pencil. It was early October now and she ought to be at school, but her mother often kept her at home to help her, because she said she was having another baby. Emily had noticed she was getting fatter, but she wasn't quite sure what *having a baby* meant.

The vicar, who ran the Church school, charged the families of people who could afford to pay, but took poor children for free. There was a school in Ely that was entirely free, and all

14

children under the age of thirteen were supposed to attend, but it was nearly four miles to walk and the bus fare to get Emily there every day would have been too expensive. Because Pa had a smallholding, he was supposed to pay three pennies a week for her to attend the vicar's school, but sometimes he didn't have enough money. If Emily didn't attend, her father didn't have to pay the three pennies, so when money was tight, Emily stayed home to help her mother. She wasn't the only child to be kept off school to help out at home or in the fields, but most of her friends didn't care; they would rather be at work earning a few pennies than at school.

Emily hated it when she had to miss school. She liked the vicar's house, which was almost as big as Uncle Albert's. He had a lovely parlour with green brocade curtains at the windows. His furniture was shabby and old, but it was comfortable and Emily was sometimes invited for tea after school. The vicar's wife was a plump, friendly lady who had three sons but no daughters and she always made a fuss of Emily. Emily often wished she could live in a house like Mrs Potter's, but of course she always had to go home to her father's cottage. She wouldn't have minded that so much if her parents hadn't quarrelled most of the time.

Emily didn't remember it happening so often when she was small but of late they always seemed to be at each other's throats – and it was always over money. Joe Carter wasn't much of a farmer, so Ma said, and she let him know he was a failure in her eyes. Stella Black had come from better things. She was the daughter of a Fen farmer. His land was in Chatteris and, according to Ma, much more fertile than the few acres Pa had inherited from his father.

Pa's smallholding was situated between the village of Witchford and Ely, a small market town, with the status of a city, and famous for its wonderful cathedral and rich history. At the vicar's school they learned about Oliver Cromwell, who had cut off King Charles's head in the name of democracy and then become a sort of king himself.

'He allowed his men to destroy beautiful stonework in the cathedral,' the Reverend Potter told them in accents of utter disgust. 'The cathedral was begun in the time of Saint Etheldreda, and is one of the finest of its period. Cromwell was a bigoted man and though he may have been just in many ways, I cannot forgive him for his wanton destruction of such beauty.'

The vicar knew a lot of stuff about history and books, and Emily enjoyed listening to him. Sitting under the kitchen table, waiting for the tallyman to stop banging at the door, she wished she was in class learning about history and sums and all the other things Reverend Potter taught them.

The banging had stopped now. Emily was tempted to peep out from under the cloth, but she knew it wasn't safe yet. The tallyman was crafty. He would make out he'd gone and then sneak back as soon as they came out of hiding. Emily counted to ten and then twenty. She could scarcely breathe under the table. Surely, it was safe to come out now? He must have given up and gone away, because she'd been here ages.

Unable to bear the tension a moment longer, she crawled out from under the table and stretched, easing her shoulders. She went over to the deep stone sink with its one tap. Pa said they were lucky to have running water in the house rather than having to fetch it from the well. In Uncle Albert's house there was a bath and a proper toilet with a chain that you pulled to flush it with water, instead of the wooden seat out in the privy that had to be cleared from underneath and stunk something awful in the summer.

Emily thought that if you had to be *no better than you ought to be* to live in a house like Uncle Albert's she wouldn't mind being like Miss Concenii and having fancy chairs to sit on and a diamond ring to wear on her finger.

As Emily turned on the tap to get herself a drink of water, an angry face appeared at the window and the tallyman banged on the glass.

'I can see you, Emily,' he shouted. 'You tell your mother I'll be back next week and if she doesn't pay up, then I'll take something from the house to cover what she owes me.'

Emily shrank back, frightened by the red, angry face that glared at her once more before turning and stalking off. She filled a cup of water and was drinking it when her mother came from the pantry. Her face looked like blue thunder and she grabbed Emily by the shoulders, shaking her until her teeth rattled.

'Why won't you ever do as you're told?' she demanded. She suddenly let go of Emily and then slapped her across the face, making her stagger back and crash into one of the assorted chairs at the table. They had six wooden chairs, none of which matched the other. Pa was always buying things cheap from the cattle market in Ely and sometimes from other people. He said the things he bought would be worth good money one day, and now and then he sold something for a few bob or even a pound or two; those were the good times, because he would have money in his pocket and Ma could fill up her jar on the mantelpiece. She could pay the tallyman what she owed then and Emily didn't have to stay off school or hide under the table.

'It was hot under there and I couldn't breathe,' Emily said, her eyes smarting with the tears she was too proud to shed. Ma didn't often hit her, but when she did it hurt. 'I wanted a drink of water.'

'You should have waited a bit longer. Now he'll know I was here and next week he'll ask for double.'

Emily stared at her. Her cheek stung from the hard slap and she felt like crying but if she did Ma would shout at her again and call her a silly little girl. Emily wasn't a silly little girl and she didn't want her mother to be angry with her. So she just stood looking at the floor saying nothing, until the door opened and her father came in. Pa was a tall man with dark hair and broad shoulders. She thought he was handsome, even though her mother didn't seem to like him much. He had a lean, craggy face and Emily adored him. She wanted to run to him and bury her face in his body, inhaling the scents of the horses, hay, cowsheds and milk, but if she did that her mother would accuse her of being her father's spoiled baby.

'What's all this then?' Pa asked and looked at Emily. She hung her head and didn't answer.

'I told her to hide from the tallyman but she came out too soon and he saw her – now he'll ask for more next week and how am I to pay?'

'I saw him on my way through the yard just now and gave him five shillings,' Pa said. 'I was lucky today. I sold an old lead pump for scrap and a set of chairs for twelve shillings.'

'You should have given the five shillings to me,' Ma said, looking annoyed. 'I would have paid him two next week and kept the rest. How do you think I'm going to manage if you give all our money away?'

Pa didn't speak immediately. Emily wondered if he minded Ma nagging at him all the time. He never seemed to get cross and she knew he never raised a finger to his wife, which a lot of men did. She knew that because her best friend, Polly, told her that her father gave her mother a black eye most Friday nights, after getting drunk on his wages.

'Well, maybe things are going our way at last, lass,' Pa said. 'I've heard from Uncle Albert's lawyer. He passed away last week and I'm to go into Cambridge when it's convenient and he'll tell me what's been left to me.'

'Thank God!' Ma cried. 'I thought the old goat would go on for ever.'

Pa looked at her as if he didn't approve of what she'd said but he didn't answer her back. He just sat down in his chair by the fire and unlaced his boots, then took his pipe down from the mantel-piece. His tobacco jar was empty, because there was not often money enough to fill it, so he just sucked at his empty pipe and looked at Ma.

'Pop upstairs and fetch me my Sunday coat down, Em love,' he said. 'I want a few words with your ma.'

Emily nodded and shot out of the room. She closed the door on the stairs leading to the landing above, but even with it closed she could hear the raised voices and she shivered. Sticking her fingers in her ears so she couldn't hear what was being said, she ran up the remaining stairs and down the hall to her parents' room. She found Pa's coat immediately but lingered a while so that they could get their argument over before she returned.

Her throat felt tight and she wanted to cry but she knew crying wouldn't do any good. She loved her father and her mother too, in her way, but it seemed that neither of them loved the other.

Emily felt sad that Uncle Albert had died, even though she'd only met him once. He'd smiled at her, patted her head and given her two toffees wrapped in gold paper from his pocket. She'd liked him, even though Miss Concenii was no better than she ought to be, had a diamond ring Emily coveted, and didn't like children sitting on her chairs.

Emily was sorry that she wouldn't see Uncle Albert again. She knew what it meant to pass away, because they'd buried Grandfather two years earlier and, although Emily hadn't been taken to the funeral, she'd visited his grave with

20

Ma since to place flowers there and say a little prayer. She couldn't remember much about Grandfather now, except that he'd smelled peppery and had whiskers that scraped her chin. He'd left Emily his silver watch and chain, but Ma said it should have been Pa's and she'd sold it when she needed some money. She didn't even give Emily a penny for sweets; though Pa had brought her a packet of Tom Thumb drops a day or so later.

'I'm sorry your ma did that, Em,' he'd told her. 'Your grandfather wanted you to have it to remember him by but it's my fault for not giving your ma the living I promised her.'

Pa always made excuses for Ma. He would stop her hitting Emily if he knew what happened, but Emily never told. She knew that if she did her mother would get her own back eventually so she just accepted the slaps and harsh words and got on with her life.

She wondered if Uncle Albert would have left her anything, then decided it was unlikely. She'd hardly known him, whereas she'd been her grandfather's little pet. Even if Uncle Albert did leave her a silver watch, her mother would take it away and sell it.

Emily rubbed at her cheek, which was still stinging and walked back down to the kitchen. Her father smiled and thanked her, then took the coat, slipping it on without a word. He was wearing his best boots too and picked up a hat rather than his old working cap as he left. Emily looked at Ma fearfully as the door shut behind him. Would her mother have another go at her for letting the tallyman see her?

'Get the cake tin out, Emily,' Ma said. 'I'll put the kettle on and we'll have some tea. If your father has the money you'll be going to school next week and we shan't have time to indulge ourselves.'

Obviously, Ma's mood had improved. Emily sensed that she was hoping for something good to come out of Pa's trip to the lawyer. If Uncle Albert had left Pa his house, they might go and live there. Emily remembered that it was at a place called Hunstanton in Norfolk, at the seaside. Her visit to Uncle Albert had been her one and only trip to the sea and she remembered it as being the best day of her life. Pa had carried her on his shoulders along the seafront. He'd bought her a stick of peppermint rock and some cockles at a little stall close to the sea; she'd loved the rock but hadn't liked the cockles much so Pa had finished them up, because you couldn't waste good food.

Sitting at the table, from which the precious cloth had now been removed, Emily munched her seed cake and looked about her. At the far end of the kitchen was an oak dresser; its shelves were cluttered with bits and pieces of china her mother had collected over the years and prized above anything. Pa had given her a few pieces of blue and white, and they were all perfect, unlike the things he sometimes gave to Emily. He could never afford to give anything away that might sell for a few shillings – but perhaps things might change now. She wondered what the future might bring. Were they going to be rich?

Emily could hear the row going on downstairs and she stuck her fingers in her ears, burying her head under the pillows to shut out the angry words. It was warm in her bed, because she had two wool blankets and a thick eiderdown filled with duck feathers, and the sheets smelled of lavender. At night when it was cold out, she liked to burrow right down into her soft mattress, pull the covers over her head and disappear into her own world. In Emily's secret world she could be whatever she wanted to be – a princess living in a castle with jelly and cake for tea every day. Or a lady in a fine house with a big diamond ring like Miss Concenii had – or … there Emily's imagination ran out, because she knew so little of the world. The vicar spoke of foreign lands sometimes, but the stories he told seemed more like the fairytales in the old books Pa sometimes brought home for her to read. Pa was always bringing some treasure home for Emily, although the bits of glass and china were usually chipped or cracked.

'I can't sell them like that, Em lass,' he would tell her, taking her on his knee to explain that the latest find was Derby or Coalport or Worcester porcelain and the glass cranberry or Bristol blue or perhaps a very early Georgian wineglass with a spiral stem. 'If they were perfect they would be worth money – this scent bottle has a silver top, see – look at the hallmarks; that little lion means it's proper English silver and the leopard's head means it was made in London and that one is the date letter. See those four letters; they're the maker's marks but they're a bit worn and I can't see, but there's a feel to this piece. That was made by a good silversmith that was and I'm not going to scrap it even if it would bring in a couple of bob. If this was perfect it would be worth at least two pounds, perhaps more – but the cap is dented, the stopper is broken and the glass is chipped. I wouldn't get more than a shilling.'

'I don't mind,' Emily said and hugged him. 'I love it, because it is pretty and I don't care that it's damaged.'

She thought she would like to learn all the silver hallmarks but Pa didn't know them all. He needed a reference book, so he'd told her. Emily decided that one day, when she had lots of money, she would buy him one, to say thank you for all he gave her.

Pa nodded and kissed the top of her head. 'That's right, lass. Always remember when you buy something to buy quality. If it's damaged it will come cheap and that way you can afford things you'd never otherwise be able to own.'

In Emily's eyes the fact that her father had given her the treasure and took the time to explain what it was, where it was made and what it was for, meant more than the item itself. She liked to be close to Pa, to smell his own particular smell and feel safe in his arms. Emily knew her father loved her. She wasn't sure if her mother even liked her, though sometimes she would smile and tell her to fetch out the biscuits or cakes, though she more often received a smack on the legs than a kiss.

The row seemed to go on for longer than usual that night. Driven at last by a kind of desperate curiosity, she crept down the uncarpeted wooden

24

stairs, avoiding the one that creaked, to stand behind the door that closed the stairs off from the kitchen. Because it wasn't shut properly, Emily could hear what her parents were saying.

'But you're his only relative,' Ma said and she sounded almost tearful. 'It isn't fair that he should leave everything to that woman.'

Pa's tone was calm and reasonable, the same as always. 'Miss Concenii has been with him for years and nursed him devotedly this last year. The lawyer said he changed his will two months ago. I was the main beneficiary in the first one – most of the money and the house and contents ... but then he changed it.'

'And we know who's behind that, don't we?' Ma said in a sullen tone. 'She must have guided his hand. I told you to go and see him. I would have had him here and looked after him myself if you'd bothered to do something about it – but you're always the same. You just leave things and now we've been cheated out of a fortune.'

'You don't know that,' Pa said. 'He probably thought she deserved the house and money for putting up with him all those years.'

'She guided his hand that's what she did. You should go to court and get your share.'

'He left me fifty pounds, a set of chessmen in ivory and ebony, a mantel clock and a Bible – and he left Em a ring. I've got it in my pocket...'

'She can't have that, it's too valuable,' Ma said. 'Give it to me. I'll look after it for her until she's older.'

Emily wanted to call out that the ring was hers. She was frightened her mother would take it and

25

sell it, but her father was speaking again.

'I'll just keep it for her. Albert left you this, Stella...'

Emily heard her mother give a squeak of pleasure. Obviously, the bequest had pleased her. Emily craned forward to peep round the door and have a look. She could see something on the kitchen table. It flashed in the light and she thought it must be diamonds, though there were blue stones too.

'That's sapphire and diamond that is,' Pa said. 'It's a brooch, Stella – and worth a few bob.'

'I can see that but it's not worth as much as a house – and three hundred pounds. Think what we could have done with all that, Joe. You've been cheated of your fortune but you haven't the sense to see it.'

'Even if I have there's no proof,' Pa said. 'She made sure of that – the doctor signed to say Albert was in his right mind when he made his last will...'

'And what did he get out of it I wonder!'

Ma was in a right temper. Emily turned and went back up to her bedroom. She ran across the stained boards and jumped into bed. Her feet had turned cold standing on the stairs listening to her parents and her mind was full of pictures that troubled her. What had Miss Concenii done to poor Uncle Albert to make him sign his house and most of his money and possessions over to her?

Emily's eyes stung with tears that trickled down her cheeks. She didn't mind much that they wouldn't be rich. Fifty pounds sounded a lot to her and she was curious about the ring Pa was keeping for her – but she hoped Uncle Albert hadn't been made unhappy when he was ill. She felt sad for him having his hand guided and she felt sad for her father, because he'd lost his fortune.

Joe Carter worked hard from early in the morning to late at night, mucking out the horses and the cows, milking and watering and feeding the stock. His was only a small farm and he eked out a scarce living from his pigs, cows, ducks and chickens. He had one ten-acre field put down to arable, which he alternated between barley, rye, wheat and potatoes, with a patch for vegetables for the house. He worked alone most of the time, though there was a lad of sixteen who came to help with the jobs he couldn't manage alone. Bert was a little slow in his head but strong and a good worker. No one else would employ him, because he couldn't be left to do a job alone, but Pa gave him a shilling now and then and he was always hanging around the yard, grinning at nothing in particular and eager to help. Because he was harmless and would do anything, Ma tolerated him and if there was nothing else for him to do she asked him to chop the logs for her.

When Pa had nothing much to do on the land he went out buying the things other people threw away. He had a barn filled almost to the rafters with old furniture. Ma said it was all junk; but Emily had seen some things she thought looked nice.

Pa had shown her some chairs, with turned legs and a wide carved splat at the back, which he said were Georgian. He'd told her they were quality when new, but he'd only got five of a set of six and two of them had broken legs. One day he hoped to mend the legs but he was always looking for a single chair that would match the set – because a set of six was worth a lot more than five.

Best of all Emily liked the selection of silver bits, china and glass that Pa kept in a cabinet in the barn. She liked the delicate silver jug with a shaped foot Pa also said was Georgian, the little enamelled snuff or pill boxes with pictures on the lids – and the silver box that opened to reveal a singing bird. That was lovely and Emily would have loved to own it, but Pa had to sell his nice things because there wasn't enough money coming in from the land. He'd talked of having a shop in Ely one day, but Ma told him he was daft because he could never afford to pay the rent.

If Pa had got Uncle Albert's house and money he could have bought a shop. Perhaps then Ma and Emily wouldn't have had to hide from the tallyman ever again.

It was quiet downstairs now. The quarrel seemed to have finished. Emily supposed Ma had given up. Whatever she said, Pa wouldn't go to a lawyer and challenge his uncle's will; he wasn't that sort of man – and perhaps he thought Miss Concenii deserved the money for looking after her employer so devotedly. Besides, he had a few things to re-member his uncle by – and fifty pounds was more money than he usually got for the harvest.

Turning over in her warm bed, Emily tried to stop thinking and go to sleep, but she couldn't forget what Ma had said. Until now she hadn't realised there were people who would guide an old man's hand just to get his money. It struck Emily as being more than unkind; it was wicked and Pa ought to do something about it, because Miss Concenii shouldn't get away with it.

Yet in her heart she knew that Pa was too gentle a man to do something like that and she felt sad again. If people didn't stand up for themselves, others just walked all over them. Uncle Albert had been kind to Emily and he'd thought enough of her to give that ring to the lawyer for her – and she hadn't liked Miss Concenii, who was *no better than she ought to be.*

Perhaps she was a bit like her mother, Emily thought, because if she'd been in Pa's shoes she would have gone after that woman and made her admit what she'd done.

It was too difficult a problem for a ten-year-old girl to work out. Sighing, she closed her eyes and drifted into sleep.

Chapter 2

It was nearly three weeks after the quarrel over Uncle Albert's money when Ma had the miscarriage. Because Pa had money in his pocket, Emily was at the vicar's school and the first she knew about it was when she arrived home at half past two in the afternoon, to find there was no sign of her mother and the kitchen looking a mess. She called out a couple of times and heard sounds from upstairs. She was just clearing some dirty dishes into the deep stone sink when her father came downstairs. Emily turned to look at him and was disturbed to see how drawn he looked. He saw her but didn't smile in his usual way, just sat down in his old wooden rocking chair next to the stove and buried his head in his hands.

Emily felt a thrill of fear. She took two steps towards him and then stopped uncertainly.

'What's wrong, Pa?' she asked. 'Where is Ma – is she ill?'

'She's not feeling very clever at the moment,' he said, looking up at her. She was stunned as she saw the expression of despair in his eyes. Pa never looked like that no matter how bad things were. 'Your Ma's lost the baby, Em. It was lucky I was here to get her upstairs. I sent Bert for the doctor but he was out visiting another patient. By the time he got here, three hours after Bert went for him, it was too late... He was sorry but there was nothing he could do...'

'Oh Pa...' Emily's throat was tight and she was sad that her mother had lost the new baby. How could you lose a baby when it wasn't even here? At least, Emily hadn't seen it. 'I don't understand properly...'

'Come here, love,' he said and opened his arms. She crawled on to his lap and he kissed the top of her head. 'It's time you understood these things, Em. The new baby was in your Ma's tummy – or her womb, as it's properly called. It shouldn't have come out for another four months.'

'Is that why she looked fatter?' Emily asked and he nodded. 'How did it get in there?'

'Your Ma and me, we made the baby between us. It's called loving and you'll understand that bit when you grow up and get married, but you need to know that losing the baby has made your Ma ill.'

'I'm sorry Ma is ill. What can I do?'

'You were starting to clear up when I came down. You'll have to do that for a while, Em. It means no school for at least a couple of weeks, perhaps longer.'

Emily's heart sank but she didn't let her father see she was upset. It was her place to look after her mother while she was ill and she would. Besides, she would have done anything to take that sad, defeated look from her father's face.

'It wasn't your fault, Pa. You didn't make Ma lose the baby.'

He was silent for a moment, then, 'In a way it was, Em. You see your Ma could have married anyone. She was pretty the way you are – all dark hair and eyes too big for your face. I promised her I'd be rich one day and she believed me, but all I've done is disappoint her.'

That was the first time anyone had told Emily she was pretty and she would have been pleased if Pa hadn't been so sad over Ma losing the baby.

Emily puzzled over the rest of what he'd said. How could Ma be disappointed in him when he worked all hours for them? It wasn't his fault that it rained and the wheat went down in the fields and was half ruined; he didn't rule the low price of potatoes when there was a glut – and he couldn't help it if a cow died in calf.

Thinking about the cow that died, Emily remembered the farmer bringing the bull to her some months earlier. She'd hidden behind the barn and watched what happened ... it was sort of awful but fascinating to watch at the same time. Now she wondered if that was how Ma and Pa made the baby but it seemed improbable and unpleasant so she decided it couldn't be the same for people.

'I'd better get on,' she said. He nodded and let her go. For a moment he sat in his chair and then he took down his pipe. His tobacco jar was filled, because he'd allowed himself a little money from Uncle Albert's bequest, and he lit the pipe, smoking as Emily cleared the table and washed the dirty dishes. She looked round and saw a pile of ironing waiting to be done. The flat iron was near the range so it looked as if Ma had been about to put it on to heat up when she lost the baby.

Emily stuck it on the range, which was hot. Pa must have made the fire up at some time during the day. As Emily was putting the old sheets on the table in readiness for the ironing a woman came down the stairs. Her name was Granny Sawle and she lived with her husband in a cottage at the edge of the village.

'She's settled now and will sleep,' she said to Pa. He nodded and took some coins from his pocket, offering them to her. 'I don't need paying, Joe. Stella has been good to me. She helped me out last winter when my Tom was down with the agues. I'm sorry we lost the boy but it was much too early. Even if the doctor had got here sooner I doubt the babe would have lived.'

Pa nodded but didn't say anything more. She gave him a pitying look and then turned to Emily. Her dress was black and she had on a plaid shawl over her shoulders, her hair rolled tight into a bun at the nape of her neck. Emily could smell carbolic soap on her hands.

'Your Pa's upset over losing his son and heir,' she said. 'As for your Ma, she's devastated. You've got to be brave and look after them both, Emily love. If you need me – or you're worried – just send young Bert to fetch me.'

'Thank you,' Emily said. 'Is Ma all right?'

'She will be. All she needs is rest and looking after,' she said and went out without another look at Pa.

Emily carried on with the ironing. Her mother didn't normally allow her to do it, because she said Emily might burn herself on the iron if it was too hot and she liked her things just so. Emily couldn't put as much pressure on as Ma but she could make these towels and her Pa's long-johns and shirt look all right.

Her father didn't look at her. He seemed lost in his thoughts and after a few minutes he got up and went outside. He didn't speak to Emily and she knew he was too upset, but she missed his smile and hoped it wouldn't be long before he would be back to normal. Clearly he was upset about losing his son and heir, like Granny Sawle had said, because he always had a smile and a word for Emily.

She finished the ironing and was wondering what to do when the door opened and a young man entered. Emily frowned, because she didn't like her uncle very much. He was her mother's

33

brother and Ma thought the world of him, but there was something about the way he looked at Emily that made her feel he wasn't to be trusted.

'Been doing the ironing, Em?' he said and she scowled, because that was her father's pet name for her. 'Where's Stella?'

'My name is Emily. Ma is upstairs sleeping – she's lost the baby.'

Derek sat down abruptly, the colour washing from his face. 'I told the stupid woman not to do so much. She ought to have had help while she was pregnant. If your father had anything about him he would have got a girl in to help out.'

'I help sometimes.' Emily was defensive, because no one was allowed to find fault with Pa.

'What can you do? A bit of washing up or ironing? What about making the butter, scrubbing floors and all the rest of it? Stella works too hard and always has done. She should never have married that loser.'

'Don't talk about Pa that way...' Emily was furious. She had the still-warm iron in her hand and without thinking just threw it at him. It missed and fell a few inches short but it shook him up. For a moment he stared at her, his eyes narrowed in anger.

'You want to watch that temper, girl. What you need is a good smacking...'

'You're not my father.'

'You little bitch...' Derek lunged at her, grabbed her by the arm and hauled her across his knee. He slapped her hard several times and she gasped with pain but struggled and then nipped his leg through his trouser. He yelled and hit her harder.

'Beast. I'll tell Pa...'

'Hurts your pride does it?' he said and then his hand caressed her backside through her knickers. 'Rub it better shall I?' His hand had slipped beneath the cotton drawers and he was caressing her bottom. She felt a surge of revulsion mixed with anger and bit his bare arm hard. Derek shouted with pain and jerked. She rolled off his lap and ran across the kitchen, pulling open the back door and making a run for it. Her heart beat wildly as she made her escape, fleeing through the yard and out into the fields beyond. The air was cold and damp but she hardly noticed in her panic.

Derek was horrid! She hated him now. What did he think he was doing, pretending to make it better after he'd hurt her? The thought of him touching her made her feel sick and dirty. She didn't know why, but it had seemed wrong and nasty and she would have done anything to get away.

Emily knew that she would have to be careful when her uncle was around in future. He was mean and spiteful and he would get his own back one of these days.

If Emily had dared to tell her father he might have sent her uncle packing but she couldn't do that, because it would cause another quarrel between her parents. Ma thought the world of Derek. He could never do anything wrong in her eyes and she was always telling Pa how much better her brother was at farming than he could ever be.

All Emily had done was to throw the iron at

him in a fit of temper, because he'd been rude about Pa – and he'd punished her. Pa never hit Ma whatever she said or did. He just looked at her in his hurt way and went out without speaking. Derek was a bully and he made her feel uncomfortable whenever he touched her.

She wouldn't tell on him, because Ma wouldn't believe her and if Pa did there would be a row – so she'd keep it to herself, but she wouldn't give him a chance to touch her again like that...

She made a bolt for the open fields. Ma was sleeping and if Derek woke her up she wouldn't want Emily around. All Ma really cared for was her brother and money – and, apparently, the son she'd lost. The son and heir that had made Pa lose his smile.

The tears building inside her, Emily ran and ran. She climbed the stile at the edge of her father's meadow, where the cows were feeding on the meagre grass, raced across the dividing lane and scrambled over the stile into the next meadow, where she threw herself down on the damp grass and wept. The ground was soaking wet, because it had been raining and heavy clouds scudded across the sky even now. It was getting darker and turning much colder. Emily was too miserable to notice. She didn't know why she was so miserable but her life just seemed to get worse and worse. She'd always been able to run to her father, but now suddenly she felt alone, forced to stand up for herself.

She couldn't ever tell what Derek had done so she would just have to keep her secrets inside her head.

Emily cried for a while longer and then sat up and wiped the tears from her cheeks. She was chilled because she didn't have a coat but she didn't want to go back to the house in case Derek was still there. Instead, she stood up and looked about her. She saw a youth riding on a pony and there were two smaller girls with him. It was almost dark now and she couldn't see them properly until they came closer. Until this moment she hadn't realised that she was on private land, but she remembered now that these fields belonged to Lord Barton. Pa had warned her not to play here but she hadn't thought about it when she jumped over the stile from her father's land into the lane and crossed it.

She wondered whether to run away but curiosity made her stay where she was a little longer. Emily liked horses, but Pa just had a couple of heavy horses that pulled his plough and the wagon, Saracen and Whistler. She could see that the ponies the children were riding were beautiful; a grey with a silvery mane and two chestnuts. For a moment she felt a pang of envy as the well-dressed children rode up to her. The girls were both wearing riding habits, short jackets over long, divided skirts under which were some kind of trousers. The youth had tight-fitting breeches, long brown boots with the tops turned down and a tweed jacket that fitted to his shoulders and waist. His stock was white and he wore a black velvet cap on his head, his gloves of tan leather; in his hand he carried a riding crop. Emily had seen people dressed like that riding through the village now and then, and also on the road when Pa took her into Ely on the wagon, and she knew they were rich. Her head went up and she stared at the youth boldly, expecting to be told she was trespassing.

'Hello, little girl,' he said and to her surprise his tone was gentle. 'Are you lost?'

'I'm not a little girl,' Emily said, her eyes sparkling with ire. 'I'm ten and I'm not lost – I live just across the lane.'

'She must be the Carters' girl,' the elder of the two girls with him said, looking at Emily curiously. 'Have you been lying on the ground? Your dress is muddy and so is your face.'

'She's been crying,' the younger one said in a tone similar to the youth, who Emily surmised must be her brother. 'Are you in trouble, girl?'

'I'm Emily. I just forgot where I was. I'll go now.'

'It doesn't matter,' the youth said. 'I'm Nicolas. My father owns these fields – at least Granny does. Father had his own estate until we moved here.'

'Why are you telling her that?' the elder girl asked. 'She's just a common farm girl and nothing to us.'

'Do you have to be rude, Amy? I'm just being friendly. Emily is clearly upset about something.' He gazed down at her, kind but autocratic, seeing her as the common little girl his sister thought she was. 'Is there anything I can do to help you?'

'No thank you, I can manage.' Emily looked at him proudly. She didn't want anyone to feel sorry for her, even though she'd been feeling sorry for herself a few minutes earlier. 'I'm sorry to have trespassed...'

She turned and ran back the way she'd come earlier. She was cold, dirty, humiliated and envious. The clothes those girls were wearing and their ponies told their own story; they were gentlefolk and she was a common farm girl. Emily had always known there was a difference but it had never been brought home to her in that way before.

Nicolas had been kind and the younger girl might have been, had Emily given her the chance, but she didn't want their kindness when she knew what they must be thinking of her. Looking down at the dress her mother had washed and patched so many times that it was little more than a rag, Emily felt ashamed. Most of the girls in her school had dresses their mothers had mended more than once and she'd never really bothered what she looked like before, but the look in that posh girl's eyes had made her squirm.

Wiping the dirt from her face with the sleeve of her dress, Emily made a vow. One day she would have proper clothes – not the shapeless things her mother made on her treadle machine, out of remnants from the market or the cut-down dresses that came from second-hand stalls, but stylish clothes – like Miss Concenii had worn that day they visited Uncle Albert. She would have a big diamond ring too, though she loved the pretty, daisy-shaped ring of different coloured stones that was her bequest from Uncle Albert. Her father had shown it to her, telling her that it was a keepsake ring and had belonged to Uncle Albert's mother. All the stones were a different colour and the first letter of each stone spelled the word

Regard. 'That's a ruby, emerald, garnet, agate, ruby again and diamond,' Pa had said, pointing to each stone in turn and then he locked the ring in a tin box in his rolltop desk with his other papers and important things. She could have it when she was seventeen but not before because it was too precious for a child to wear.

The thought of her ring comforted Emily. At least she had something of worth, even if she did have to wear shapeless old clothes.

She saw Bert coming towards her as she approached the farmyard. He was grinning in his vacuous way, heading towards the barn, but stopped when he saw her, lifting his greasy cap to scratch his head.

'There you be, little miss. Your Pa be looking for you – and he bain't pleased. He bain't pleased 'cos you ran off and left your Ma alone in the house.'

'Derek was there,' Emily muttered but ran across the uneven cobbles towards the back door. The black paint was peeling off in lumps and it looked dilapidated in the fading light, as did most of the sheds and the house itself. Emily hadn't realised how poor they were until now. She was used to the shabby interior and the chairs that didn't match; they hadn't mattered but suddenly they did and she felt resentful. How dare that posh girl look down her nose at her!

As she opened the door and went in, she saw her father come downstairs with a tray. He'd taken some food up to her mother but by the looks of it she hadn't eaten very much.

'Your mother wants a cup of tea. Do you think

you could manage that or will you run off again as soon as I've gone?' The tone in his voice was one that Emily hadn't heard before and it stung her.

Pa was cross with her. He was never cross with Emily usually, but he was now. She felt as if she'd been beaten black and blue as she stared at him.

'Derek was here. Ma wasn't alone. I didn't mean to leave her alone.'

'Well, if he was here he didn't stay long. Why did you run off – he didn't upset you?'

Pa's eyes were narrowed and angry. Emily was shivering inside but she lifted her head and gave him a proud look, then shook her head. She couldn't tell him about that humiliating episode with her uncle.

'I'm disappointed in you, Emily,' her father said and his look of hurt bewilderment stung worse than anything that Derek had done. 'I thought I could trust you to look after your mother while I'm working.'

'You can, Pa. I promise I shan't leave her alone again while she's ill.'

He looked at her for a long moment and she'd never seen him so stern. 'Well, I shall trust you this time, but I've got my eye on you, miss – let me down again and I shall have to punish you, Emily.'

He never called her Emily. The name was a reproach, because she'd let him down.

Her cheeks were flaming but she didn't answer him back. She couldn't tell him why she'd run off like that because it would cause more trouble in the house – and perhaps he wouldn't believe her.

Emily had always felt secure in her father's love,

but now she wasn't quite sure. Ma had lost the son he'd wanted – Granny Sawle had told her so. Perhaps he was so disappointed that he no longer cared about Emily in the same way.

Choking back her hurt, Emily went to fill the large copper kettle and set it on the range to boil. The outside of the kettle was blackened by use but the inside was clean because her mother scoured it out to keep it shiny. Emily hadn't truly realised how hard Ma worked to keep things right, but in the next few days she was going to learn.

She would learn to do everything Ma did, because she had to make Pa smile at her again. If he didn't love her in the same way, Emily still loved him and she wanted things to be as they were before it all started to go wrong...

Chapter 3

Lizzie Barton listened to her mother and father having an argument. Lord Henry Barton disliked having had to come to live at his mother-in-law's home and was unsympathetic when his wife complained about the way Lady Prior dictated to her.

'If you hadn't been such a fool we should never have had to sell the estate,' Helen Barton said. 'I don't see why you should complain, Henry. I am the one who has to put up with Mama's demands.'

'Will you never allow me to forget? It isn't as if I threw the money away at the card table. I was told the investment was sound...'

Lizzie crept away, going up the magnificent carved mahogany staircase to the rooms she and her sister Amy shared, which were close to the schoolroom. Amy was two years older than Lizzie and she too resented the move to Priorsfield Manor, complaining that the house was old-fashioned and over-crowded with too many knick-knacks.

Lizzie, by contrast, didn't mind that they had come here to live at the manor, and she liked her grandmother, who seemed very old, the backs of her hands blue-veined. She wore lots of rings on her fingers, which flashed fire in the candlelight when they gathered in the big drawing room at night. The room was crowded with bits and pieces Granny had collected over her long life, but everything meant something to Lady Prior and she sometimes told stories about the curios that fascinated Lizzie.

They often sat together in the afternoons, when Miss Summers, their governess, had finished lessons and gone home for the day. Miss Summers was a pretty young woman and her father was a farmer, quite prosperous for a man who worked the land, so Papa said when talking to Mama. She didn't live in as the governess usually did, but cycled back and forth each day. She'd been away to a good school and Granny said that if she'd been a man she would probably have been a politician or a lecturer – but of course ladies didn't do that sort of thing.

Lizzie felt it was a pity that Miss Summers couldn't be a politician if she wanted to be, but she

wasn't sure that she did, because she was wearing
a ring on her engagement finger. Amy said she was
going to be married soon and that, when she did
marry, both Amy and Lizzie would go away to
school instead of being taught at home. Lizzie
wasn't sure what she would feel about that, because although the boarding school was only in
Cambridge, just over twenty miles away, they
wouldn't come home very often.

Lizzie would miss her grandmother and the
stories she told. She wouldn't miss hearing her
parents argue, but she'd begun to feel at home in
the big, rambling old house.

Of course Nicolas and Jonathan had both been
away to school and Jon to college. He was the
eldest and he would be finishing at college next
year. Amy said that Jon would run the estate for
Granny. Emily wondered why she didn't ask
Papa to do it for her, but perhaps she didn't trust
him because he'd lost most of his money in that
silly bubble, as Mama called it.

Papa wasn't usually silly. In fact he was stern
and whenever Lizzie did something wrong and
was called to his study, she quaked in her shoes.
Nicolas was always being called to account for
getting into scrapes, but he didn't seem to mind
Papa's temper – even when he got the cane.

Lizzie loved Nicolas the best of all her family.
She sometimes wished that she could live with
just him and not see any of the others, but of
course that wasn't possible.

Nicolas was so kind. He'd been kind to that
poor little girl they'd seen in the fields. She'd
looked so awful, her face streaked with tears and

44

her dress filthy where she'd lain on the muddy grass. She'd seemed so very poor to Lizzie, her boots scuffed and her dress patched so many times that it looked a mess.

Mama complained that they were poor, but Lizzie had lots of pretty clothes in her wardrobe. For a moment she wondered if Emily would accept a dress from her, but then she remembered what Amy had said about giving things to the poor.

'They only take advantage if you're not careful, and if they don't do that – they resent you for offering charity.'

Amy had been so rude to the poor girl. Lizzie had felt ashamed for her sister, but Amy was always like that, thinking she was above everyone else.

'Lizzie, dearest, will you do something for me please?'

Lizzie forgot about the girl in the field as her grandmother called to her and she ran to her grandmother's side. It was probably best not to send the girl a present, she had decided, because she would only think Lizzie was being condescending.

She would probably be going away to school in the autumn and then she wouldn't have much chance to go riding with Nicolas – and she wasn't likely to see the farmer's girl again.

Chapter 4

Emily was at the kitchen table baking, her mother upstairs seeing to the new baby. It was six years now since Ma had lost her first son, because the doctor had been late in coming and the birth too hard. Granny Sawle had done all she could for Emily's mother, but she had not been able to save that baby, because it had come too early. This time, however, the doctor had been present and she'd given birth to a healthy boy. Ever since the birth Ma had been walking about the house looking like the cat that got the cream, a huge smile on her face. Her hair was still as dark as it had always been and a slight plumpness in the face suited her. Emily had expected her father to be delighted with his new son, but to her surprise he'd seemed distant and, as far as she knew, he'd hardly touched young Jack.

'I'm going into Ely this afternoon, Em,' he said. 'Do you want to come with me on the wagon? I have to pick up some bits I bought last week – and I've got a surprise for you.'

'For me?' Emily felt a warm glow inside. Sometimes her father seemed just as he always had been, before that day she'd disappointed him, but at others he sank into himself and didn't speak for days at a time. 'What is it?'

'It wouldn't be a surprise if I told you, would it?'

Emily shook her head. Pa got to his feet and

placed his paper on the table. She glanced down at it and saw the headlines concerning the death of a woman who had thrown herself in front of the king's horse at the Derby. Miss Emily Davison was a martyr to the cause and her fellow Suffragettes were mourning her.

'They've buried that poor woman then,' she said. 'She was very brave to try and stop that horse...'

'Brave or foolish,' Pa said. 'I don't say her cause isn't just, because it is – but there's better ways than disrupting a race meeting. These Suffragettes are making a nuisance of themselves everywhere. If you read the paper you'll see there's too much trouble going on already. It seems harsh but the police have no choice but to lock them up.' He pulled on his jacket and went out, saying he'd be back later.

Emily nodded agreement, because she'd already read every single word of the paper and knew that some of the women she considered brave had been starving themselves in prison as a protest.

It was yesterday's paper and she'd taken it to bed, reading until her candle guttered and went out. Emily read everything she could get her hands on these days. Pa brought a paper back if he drove into the market in Ely, or if he found one when he went to view stuff people wanted to sell. And he bought any books he came across in case Emily wanted to read them before they were sold on as a job lot.

He was gaining quite a reputation for buying the junk others didn't want and he now had two barns filled to the rafters. Ma still thought it was junk but with the prices for wheat and milk down again, it was the occasional sale of Pa's 'junk' that kept the wolf from the door. They hadn't had to hide from the tallyman recently, though the jar on the mantelpiece was empty more often than not when he called. It wasn't Mr Thompson now, but someone called Eddie Fisher. He was a tall blond man with blue eyes and a nice smile. Ma usually sent Emily out on an errand to her father when Eddie called, and she always answered the door to him, even if there was no money to pay him the two shillings owed each week.

'Where's your father?' Ma asked as she came downstairs, after tending to the baby. 'I thought I heard his voice.'

'He was here for a while. I made him scrambled eggs with toast and a pot of tea, and then he looked through the paper. He's taking me to Ely this afternoon.'

'I suppose he's going to buy more of that rubbish...' Ma grumbled. 'You'll get your chores done before you go.'

It was an order not a question. Emily didn't bother answering. She'd known her mother would find as many jobs for her as she could. Emily had left school the previous Christmas, because Ma said she'd learned all she needed to know.

That wasn't true, because the vicar had been Emily's window on the world. She would have known nothing of the Olympics that happened in London in 1908, had the vicar not asked the children to do a project about it. Emily went home in tears because she didn't even know what it was, so Pa went out and bought a souvenir newspaper with lots of pictures of the competitors. Someone from America won the 1,500 metres final but second and third went to British men; they won medals in swimming and rowing and all kinds of sports Emily had known nothing about. So she cut out all the pictures and pasted them in her scrapbook – and she won the prize of a penny bar of chocolate from the vicar.

When in 1909 Bleriot flew across the English Channel, it was the vicar who told Emily about it. He told his class that the brave ladies of the Suffragettes were being force-fed in prison. As the weeks and months passed, he told them of the miners' struggle for an eight-hour day and of the wonderful X-ray machines that were helping doctors to improve people's chances of surviving an operation. He told them when the wicked Doctor Crippin was caught and of the terrible disaster when the Titanic was sunk and so many people died in the icy water.

Leaving school for Emily was like being torn apart. The vicar had tried to tell Ma that Emily was bright and could go a long way given her chance. Emily had had vague hopes of becoming a schoolteacher herself or perhaps a librarian. Her favourite treat was to slip into the library in Ely while Pa was busy at the market and borrow some books, but she'd known from the look in her mother's eyes that she had no chance of choosing what she wanted to do with her life.

Ma wanted her home to help with the heavier chores, like butter making and scrubbing out the dairy, because she was busy with caring for the new baby. Jack cried a lot and seemed to pick up chills easily. Emily gave her father a hand with the milking too, because he'd increased his herd to ten recently and was hoping the price of milk would increase, though with his luck it would sink like lead or the cows would get some dreadful disease. Milking was a chore she didn't mind, because she liked the warmth and smell of the cows and each one was an individual; you had to watch Bella, because she kicked, while Bess was as docile as could be.

Being at home wasn't too bad these days, because Emily had learned to turn a deaf ear to her mother's nagging. She supposed that was what Pa did too, because he ignored Ma more often than not and just went out to the yard or the barn. However, Pa took Emily with him to Ely on most market days. Going to Ely market was a treat for all the families from the fens, and those who could manage it went in as often as they could. A few weeks back they'd bought a box of day-old chicks for a shilling in the cattle market. Emily had kept them in a little shed at the back of the barn; she put down old newspapers for them to run about on inside the pen she'd built and she'd fed them on hard-boiled egg and soft scraps. They were already growing well and Pa had told her they were hers to sell or rear for the eggs the hens might lay. She'd given them all names and loved watching them scratching about in their pen.

Emily wasn't paid a wage for her work, but Pa slipped her a few shillings when he had some to spare. She liked to spend her money on the market in Ely, because she could get good bargains there, and shops were too expensive. The stall selling

50

remnants of material was her favourite. She could buy a pretty length of cotton or wool and a pattern and make her own dress in the latest style. Once in a while she bought a fashion magazine, and the previous week she'd bought a little box of face powder and a lipstick from Woolworth – though she hadn't dared to wear them yet, because Ma would have given her a good slap.

It was Emily's secret but one of the nicer ones – not like the dark one she'd buried deep in her subconscious. She'd never told anyone about the way Derek had humiliated her as a ten-year-old child, but she hated him more every time she saw him and his expression whenever he looked at her made her curl up inside. He might be handsome, as her ma was fond of saying, and he might have the girls running after him, but Emily couldn't bear him near her.

She finished all her baking, and then went upstairs to make the beds and polish the furniture, glancing in at Jack as he lay in his crib sound asleep for once. In her parents' room there was a rather nice mahogany chest – or a tallboy, as Pa called it. He'd bought it with some money he'd got from selling the chess set Uncle Albert had left him; it had turned out to be a good one and Pa had bought something decent for once, which he'd given to Ma as a present. Their bed had a brass and iron bedstead but the mattress was soft, made of feathers and covered in striped ticking. When Emily removed the sheets for washing once a week she thought how soft and nice it must be, because her own was lumpy and she needed a new one, but a new mattress was expensive.

Having made the beds and polished the floors and the furniture, Emily had a strip wash in her room, using a blue and white Mason's Ironstone jug and basin set her Pa had given her for one of her birthdays. Then she dressed in her best skirt of green wool, the hem of which finished just above the top of her black button boots. Emily had made the skirt herself, stitching a band of black brocade about six inches from the hemline. With a white, starched cotton blouse and a coat that came down to about twelve inches above the hemline of her skirt, she looked fashionable – though if you looked at the quality of the material and the slightly uneven hemming on the skirt you could tell it was home-made. However, with a wide-brimmed straw hat trimmed with a black silk ribbon she looked smart – and, her Pa said, pretty.

Emily glanced at her boots. The toes were scuffed and the heels worn down, giving away the truth of her situation. It was Pa's job to mend her boots and he would when he had time, but he was always so busy that she didn't like to remind him. Everything she was wearing was cheap, even though the skirt was her best and she'd given two shillings for the coat from a stall selling good second-hand stuff.

She was still the common little farm girl that snooty girl from the manor had said she was, even though she'd tried to improve herself. She knew a lot more these days, because of all the reading she did – but sometimes she despaired of ever being more than she was. How could she be when Ma insisted she stay at home and help with the chores?

Occasionally, she thought about those children in the fields. She knew now that they belonged to the family at the manor. Priorsfield Manor was the property of Lady Prior, so Pa said, but her daughter was married to Lord Barton, who had lost most of his money in some kind of scandal, and the family had come to live at the manor. Since that day in the fields, Emily had not spoken to them again. Emily had seen the family occasionally in a carriage on their way to church, and she'd also glimpsed the youth riding his horse. Of course he wasn't a youth now but a young man. Through listening to her father talking to friends, Emily knew that there were four young people at the manor, two boys and two girls. They all went away to expensive schools so were only at the manor during their holidays.

Pa was waiting for her when she went down to the kitchen. He looked at her and gave a nod of approval, but didn't look at Ma. Emily noticed the atmosphere of strain between them. It was there most of the time now but she didn't know what was causing it. She thought she preferred the old way, when they were shouting at each other instead of this cold politeness. At least then they had made up their quarrels and she'd heard them laughing together sometimes. Now they were just silent – distant.

'Come on then, Em,' Pa said. 'I've got the wagon hitched and I want to get going.'

'I'm coming,' she said and laughed at his impatience. This surprise must be something special or he wouldn't be in so much of a hurry to show her. 'I've finished upstairs, Ma. I'll do the parlour tomorrow.'

Her mother nodded but made no reply. She was looking a bit chastened and Emily wondered what had been said between her parents before she came down, but she wasn't going to ask. Pa was in a good mood for once and she didn't want to spoil it.

'Well, there it is – what do you think?' Pa asked as he pulled the wagon to a halt near to the pub across from the marketplace in Ely. If you walked through the brick and stone archway you could get to where the cattle market was held on a Thursday and on the following day there was always a faint whiff of horse or cattle droppings from the pens. She could smell it now but she was used to worse, the cowsheds being situated so close to their cottage at home.

Emily looked about her, trying to see what he meant and then she suddenly saw the shop window with a set of chairs and a rolltop desk set out. In the forefront was a blue and white earthenware jug that she was sure she'd seen before and also a brass fender and fire irons that had been in Pa's barn for ages. Someone had cleaned them up so that they shone like gold.

'You've got a shop,' she said and looked at him in delight. Emily knew that it had been Pa's ambition to have a shop for his second-hand goods for years, understanding now the suppressed air of excitement about him. 'I'm so pleased for you. It's a lovely surprise, Pa.'

'It's our shop, Em,' he told her with pride. 'I'm

going to have Joe Carter & Daughter painted on a sign over the top just as soon as I can afford it – and when it starts to make a profit half will be yours. One day it will belong to you – and all the stuff in the barns. I've been hoarding for years now. Your Ma thinks it's rubbish but one day it will make you a fortune – you see if I'm not right.'

Emily smiled at him, happy because this meant that Pa did still love her. She thought he'd stopped the day she disappointed him, but he cared underneath, even though he was often grumpy these days.

'Oh Pa, that's wonderful,' she said. She would have said a lot more but he had started to cough. It took a few moments for him to stop and she looked at him anxiously. She'd heard him coughing in the yard a few times, but this time he'd been red in the face and looked as if he were in some distress. 'Where did that cough come from, Pa? Have you been to the doctor?'

'It's nothing, Em, just a bit of a cough,' he said. 'Come on, I want you to meet Christopher. He's going to be looking after the shop for us. He's an intelligent lad, good with his hands. I think you'll like him.'

Emily would have liked anyone her Pa told her to at that moment but as soon as she saw Christopher she took to him. His hair was a sandy brown and his eyes were hazel, his brows darker and somehow startling, and he had freckles all over his nose and cheeks. He was wearing dark trousers and a blue shirt with a leather apron over the top and his hands looked grimy, as if he'd been cleaning something with brass polish. She thought he must be about seventeen but she knew he was clever, because Pa said so, and the moment he spoke to her, she was sure they would be friends.

'I've seen you in the market a couple of times,' Christopher Johnson said and grinned at her. 'My father is the head carpenter up at Priorsfield Manor. He wanted me to work for Lady Prior but I was looking for something else – and then I got talking to Joe.'

'And now you're working for me,' Pa said. 'And Em too. This place will be hers one day, Christopher. So you'd best keep on the right side of her.' Christopher laughed and winked at Emily. 'I'll do my best, sir.'

'None of that,' Pa said. 'I'm Joe to you, same as always, and Emily is Em. We're relying on you to run this right for us.'

'I'll do that, Joe. I've been mending a chair this morning. That yew Windsor armchair was a bit rocky, but I've glued the stretcher at the bottom and clamped it together and it will be as right as rain.'

'Good. Put it in the window and charge two pounds ten shillings for it.'

'I think it might make a bit more than that,' Christopher said. 'I'll see who asks after it before I tell him the price.'

'There...' Pa said beaming at Emily. 'Didn't I tell you he was bright?'

'You did,' she agreed and laughed. 'This was a wonderful surprise, Pa – the best ever.'

'Well, you deserved it.' The smile left Pa's face.

'I'll leave you to look round where you like, Em – but meet me here in an hour.'

'Don't you want me to help carry some stuff?'

He shook his head and went off without another word. Emily frowned, because she felt that he was hiding something ... but Christopher was talking and she turned to him with a smile.

'Shall I put the kettle on, Emily?'

'No, thank you,' she said. 'I want to pop to the library while I've got a minute and then I'll see if there's anything cheap in Woolworth that I fancy. I'll be back soon and we'll have a cup of tea then.'

She was feeling pleased as she went out. She might buy a fresh cake from the baker's when she'd been to the library and share it with the young man she'd just met. Christopher was nice. She liked him and her world had just got that little bit better.

Emily borrowed the two books she was allowed – Jane Austen's *Pride and Prejudice* and a book depicting silver hallmarks. Pa was always wishing he had one, to check up on various bits of silver he picked up on his rounds. If this was the kind of thing he needed, she would save her pennies and order a copy from the bookseller in the High Street for his Christmas gift.

After leaving the library, she went down the hill to Woolworth and popped in to look at the cosmetic counter. It smelled of the loose, rose-scented bath salts you could buy by the pound and various cheap perfumes, but she came away without purchasing anything, though she fancied a bottle of eau de Cologne. Instead of spending her last sixpence on the scent, she went to the cake shop and bought three iced buns. One for each of them, to eat with their cup of tea.

As she crossed the Market Square, waiting for the brewery's wagon with its beautiful heavy horses to pass, their harness jingling like bells, she felt a hand on her shoulder and turned to see Uncle Derek. Despite the warm sunshine, a trickle of ice slid down her spine as he leered at her.

'Quite the young lady now, aren't we?' Derek asked. 'You're growing up, Em. I dare say you've got half the lads in the neighbourhood sniffing after you?'

'I don't go out with lads. I'm too busy.'

'Been to the library? What's in the bag?'

'None of your business. Excuse me, I'm busy.' She tried to dodge by him, but his hand shot out, gripping her wrist. 'Let go of me, Derek.'

'What if I don't want to?'

She was aware of the strong, sharp scent of his cheap hair oil and her stomach churned, though there was little he could do to harm her in the middle of a busy street.

'I say,' a voice spoke from behind them. 'Let go of her like a good chap.'

Emily turned and looked at the man who had spoken. He was a gentleman, well dressed and there was something vaguely familiar about him, though she was sure she didn't know him.

'And who's going to make me?' Derek muttered belligerently.

'Perhaps I shall if you force me,' the man said, slate-grey eyes narrowing. 'However, I see a police

58

officer just across the road. Perhaps you would wish me to summon him?'

Derek's face went red and then white, but he let go of Emily's wrist, turned and walked off without another word.

'Thank you,' she said and smiled at her rescuer. 'That was kind, sir.'

'Jonathan Barton,' the man said. 'I should be careful of fellows like that if I were you. Best not to give them the time of day. Good afternoon.' Tipping his grey felt hat, he went off without giving her a chance to reply.

Emily was torn between feeling grateful that he'd stopped Derek molesting her and annoyance that he should imagine she'd wanted that kind of attention. She stared after him, wishing she'd had the presence of mind to make a cutting remark – but what good would it have done if she had?

He saw her as just a common girl and of course girls like her always encouraged men to make free with them – didn't they?

Emily felt a surge of frustration and anger. One day she was going to be someone. When she married and had children they were never going to hide from the tallyman. In fact they wouldn't buy from him. Emily wanted to walk into a posh dress shop and buy whatever she liked; she wanted to be somebody – to be respected and admired.

For a moment the clouds seemed to gather about her, but then she pushed them from her mind. This was a good day and Derek wasn't going to spoil it for her – and she wouldn't let herself be affected by that rude gentleman. He had

59

been rude, even though he'd seen her uncle off.

Lifting her head proudly, Emily ran towards Pa's shop. Sunshine was hitting on the brass harness of a horse between the shafts of a baker's van. The horse lifted its tail and a stream of liquid shot out, the pungent smell making her wrinkle her nose as she went into the shop. She was going to make a cup of tea and eat her iced bun with Pa and Christopher and to hell with the rest of them!

Chapter 5

Emily glanced at herself in the dressing mirror Pa had given her recently. It was in the shape of a shield, dark mahogany with a light fruitwood stringing in the frame. Pa said he couldn't sell it, because the mirror was a bit spotty and the drawer had bowed slightly, making it difficult to open and close. The mirror was one of the best things Pa had given her and she didn't mind its faults.

'It might bring in a few bob but I'd rather you had it, Em,' he'd told her, the night he brought it home. 'It's good that – Regency or even earlier by my reckoning – and it will teach you to appreciate nice things.'

'If it's worth a few bob you should sell it and give me the money,' Ma grumbled. She was sitting at the table mending Pa's socks, a silver thimble on her finger. 'How you expect me to manage on what you give me I don't know.'

Pa looked at her but said nothing. He took three half crowns, some shillings and a sixpence from his pocket, the coins jangling into the jar on the mantelpiece. Saucepans were bubbling on the range and the enticing smell of a stew made Emily's mouth water.

Her father turned to her. 'Have you got a dress for the dance next Saturday, Em? It's the special Christmas do and the vicar gave me tickets in exchange for a goose and three ducks.'

Emily listened to the sound of a wailing cry from upstairs. Jack had woken again, but she didn't go up to him at once, because Ma said it would spoil him if he was forever being picked up.

Ma sniffed loudly and put away her darning things, getting up to move the pans off the heat. Neither Emily nor Pa took any notice of the sniff, even though it showed Ma's disapproval of Pa wasting money on the dance.

'I've finished my dress,' Emily said to cover the silence. 'Ma showed me how to finish the buttonholes.'

'Stella was always good with her sewing.'

Emily looked at her mother as Pa went upstairs, closing the door behind him. She couldn't decide whether Ma was upset or angry.

'Shall I put the kettle on?'

'Please yourself.' Ma shrugged. 'I shan't come to the dance with you. If you want to go with your father, then that's up to you.'

'Your blue dress is nice but we could make another in time.'

'It's not the dress. I don't want to come so don't ask.'

Emily had tried to persuade her. She'd made tea for her mother, reminded her that their neighbours down the road were willing to look after Jack for a couple of hours if she changed her mind but she just started setting the table for dinner and refused to answer.

Now, getting ready for the dance that Saturday evening, Emily was saddened by her mother's attitude. Why had she refused the treat offered? It was so seldom that Pa could spare the money for something special like this Christmas dance. Emily didn't understand why her parents were almost strangers these days. They hardly spoke to each other, though Pa was never harsh to her mother in Emily's hearing. He just behaved as though she didn't exist.

They had never been very loving to each other but now Emily thought they might actually hate one another.

Sighing, she fastened a string of pink faux pearls about her throat. Pa often bought job lots of costume jewellery and he let Emily pick something for herself. Sometimes he was lucky and they would find a gold pin amongst the junk, but they always had to sell that, of course. One day she intended to own a string of real pearls – or at least a good set of cultured pearls. The difference was that real pearls were formed naturally in the oyster, whereas cultured pearls came from a small piece of grit being inserted into the living oyster. Emily had read that in a book. She was fascinated by jewellery in any form and had borrowed a book from the library, tracing the history of jewellery from Roman and Greek times.

Her dress was a very special one. It had sleeves that reached to just above her elbow and the bodice consisted of two pieces; underneath was a lace panel that was low enough for her to show off her necklace, and over the top a full bolero, which she'd edged with the same lace. The skirt was long and narrow, with a straight panel at the front and gathered panels over her hips. She'd seen an expensive gown made by the dressmaking establishment of Jays' Ltd in a magazine of 1908 and copied it as best she could with two remnants and a bit of lace from the market. The front panel was plain pink, and the side panels were a kind of shiny brocade in a darker pink, which she'd thought made it look similar to the glamorous gown she'd seen in her magazine. However, when she looked at herself in the mirror, she wasn't sure that it looked right, but it was too late now to change her mind; she had nothing else fit to wear.

Ma had told her to copy a simple dress she'd had for dancing before she married but Emily had liked the elegant gown in the fashion plate. She wondered if perhaps her mother had been right after all.

She pushed the thought from her mind. It was a special night, her first dance. Pa was making a big effort because he said she was sixteen and old enough to see a little bit of life. Emily was thrilled and determined that nothing should spoil her evening.

When she went downstairs in her new dress Pa looked at her for a moment in silence. She saw the doubts in his eyes and her heart sank into her boots. Of course the dress ought to be worn with pretty shoes but Emily only had the sturdy black boots she wore for Sundays. Her stomach started to tie itself into knots.

'Do I look awful?' she asked. 'Should I put my Sunday-going-to-church dress on, Pa?'

'No, of course not. You look ... lovely,' he said and smiled. 'I was just taken back for a minute. I hadn't realised you were so grown up, Em.'

Emily breathed a sigh of relief. She'd thought for a moment that she looked silly.

The village hall was decorated with dark green and butter-cream gloss paint. At one end of the long room there were trestle tables covered by white cloths and set with plates of sausage rolls, cheese sandwiches and mince pies. There was beer for the men, sweet sherry for the ladies and orange squash for the children, some of whom were running about, laughing in excitement. At the other end of the room was the stage for the musicians and they had started to play a soft melody.

Emily felt a thrill of excitement. Looking round, she saw a couple of girls she'd known at school. Their dresses were just variations on the clothes they normally wore and Emily was uneasy again. Had she been foolish to try and copy the stylish gown she'd seen in that magazine? She was aware that a few of the girls and women turned their heads to look at her as Pa found her a seat amongst them and went off to fetch a drink for them both. Hearing a giggle from behind her, Emily flushed and felt hot, sure that the girls were laughing at her.

However, Pa was soon back from the bar. He

handed her a small glass of dark, sweet sherry and told her to sip it. She almost choked on the first sip, because it seemed very strong. She took another sip and then set it down on a windowsill. Emily didn't want to say but she would have preferred the orange squash.

Pa finished his beer, wiped his mouth on the back of his hand and looked at her. 'Want to risk your feet dancing with your old man?'

'Yes, please.'

Emily stood up instantly. She'd been watching the dancers and it looked easy enough. Pa had shown her a few steps at home and she'd practised them alone in her room. The band struck up a catchy tune for what the announcer said was a barn dance. Emily watched for a moment or two and then Pa led her onto the floor. She was hesitant at first but the steps were easy to follow and she felt comfortable with her father, but then the announcer said it was time to change partners. She felt a moment of panic, but Pa squeezed her hand and passed her on to the next man in the line, taking a new partner himself.

'You're new here,' the man said and smiled at her. He was taller than Emily but he had a friendly smile and she relaxed. 'I think you must be Joe's daughter Emily. I'm Harry Standen. I've got a farm in Sutton Fen. Your father was asking me about my bull the other day. I'll be bringing him over when your Sally Anne is in season.'

Harry Standen's natural talk of the farm put Emily at her ease. She talked to him about her father's best cow and then asked him about his own farm, which he invited her to visit soon. Her father was going to look at some old junk in his barns that he wanted to get rid of, and he suggested that Emily should come too.

Harry liked her at once and was sorry when she had to pass on to another young man. This one didn't talk much and kept tripping over Emily's feet. He mumbled his apology and said it was his first dance, but it was hers too and she'd found the steps easy to follow. After the rather uncouth youth, she passed to an older man who smelled of beer and kept squeezing her hand too tightly. Emily couldn't wait to get away from him but when she came face to face with her next partner she was almost too shocked to take his hand, because it was the gentleman who had rescued her from her uncle's attentions in Ely.

'So we meet again,' he said and took her hand, leading her surely into the dance. Emily was too tongue-tied to answer. He smelled gorgeous, of some wonderful cologne, and he was dressed in a black evening suit and a white shirt with a frill at the front where it buttoned. She was so shocked that a man of his class should be at the dance that she almost forgot her steps and narrowly avoided treading on his toes. 'I shan't bite you know.'

Emily glanced up. 'I didn't think you would, sir. I was surprised to see you here this evening.'

'My brother is home from Eton and my sisters wanted to come,' he replied. 'I think you must be Joe Carter's daughter – but I don't know your name.'

'Emily. It's my first dance. I'm sorry if I almost trod on your toe.'

He glanced down at her feet and frowned. 'It's

a wonder you can dance at all in those things.'

Emily wanted to die. She'd known her boots weren't suitable, but she couldn't afford the material for a dress *and* some proper shoes. She'd never had a pair of pretty shoes in her life; they wouldn't be much use for life on the farm.

'They're my Sunday ones,' she said and stuck her chin in the air.

'Yes, I'm sure they are. Forgive me, I didn't mean to be rude.'

The dance was coming to an end now. He bowed and thanked her, then turned and walked away. Emily's whole body felt as if it were on fire as she returned to her seat. She picked up her sherry from the windowsill and drank the remainder straight down, coughing as it stung her throat. Tears were burning behind her eyes and she was aware of female voices behind her.

'What on earth does she think she looks like?'

'Don't be mean, Amy. Her dress is pretty and the colour suits her.'

'Lizzie, you're simply too kind for your own good. You can see she made it herself – and she has no idea of what a girl like her should wear. That dress would be more suitable for Mama – or Granny.'

The girl named Lizzie giggled. 'Well, yes, it is too old and sophisticated for her but she has tried to look smart – and it makes her different to all the others.'

'Have you seen those ridiculous boots?'

Emily got up and moved away. She refused to let any tears fall. The family at the manor were stuck up and she hated them all.

Pa was at the bar. She went up and asked for an orange squash, which he gave her with a smile.

'Enjoying yourself, love?'

'Yes, thank you, Pa,' she said and drank most of her orange. She was hating every minute but she couldn't let on and spoil his treat.

Finishing her drink, she headed for the toilets. She splashed her cheeks in cold water and looked at herself in the mirror. Her own good sense told her that she looked pretty, even if her dress wasn't suitable and didn't go with her boots. Raising her head with pride, she decided to go back out there and enjoy her first dance evening. Why should she care what that lot at the manor thought – or anyone else?

As she walked back towards where Pa was sitting, a man touched her arm. At first she thought it was Jonathan Barton, because he looked a bit similar, except that he had fair hair and his brother's was darker. Emily knew him for the boy on the pony that day in the fields, and it seemed that he'd recognised her.

'I almost didn't know you, Miss Carter,' Nicolas Barton said. 'You look so grown up and pretty this evening.'

Emily's cheeks burned as she met his smiling gaze. 'Are you making fun of me? I know I look awful. My dress is home-made and too old for me – and my boots don't go with it.'

'Really? I had no idea. I just thought how lovely you look...' The music had started again. 'Would you dance with me? I'm not sure I know how to do the two-step but I dare say we can do as well as most.'

Without waiting for her answer, he caught her hand and drew her onto the dance floor. A quiver of excitement ran through her as he placed a hand in the small of her back and held her close. She wondered what he was doing and almost broke away, except she could see that everyone else was doing the same thing.

'Just follow my lead,' Nicolas whispered, 'and we'll be fine.'

Emily wasn't sure if it was the sherry that had gone to her head, but suddenly she felt like giggling. She smiled at him, relaxed and followed his every move, finding it far easier than she would ever have imagined. He was so confident, so in command that she gave herself up to the pleasure of being close to him and let her body sway with his. Music flowed about them, swirling, gathering them up in a cloud of pleasure so that she felt she was floating on air. How she managed it she would never know but she didn't miss a step and, when he released her at the end of the dance, she felt as if she were in a dream – a dream from which she did not wish to wake up.

'Nicolas, you mean thing,' a voice said and Emily saw the girl who had laughed at her earlier. 'You promised you would do the two-step with me.'

'Did I, Amy?' Nicolas gave her an odd look, almost as if he were cross with her and had danced with Emily to annoy her. He turned to Emily. 'Thank you, Miss Carter. That was delightful.'

Taking his sister's arm, he steered her away towards his brother and the younger girl. As Emily sat down at her father's side, she saw that the party from the manor was leaving.

'Fancy them being here tonight,' Pa said and looked at her. 'You danced with Mr Jonathan in the barn dance I know – but Mr Nicolas asked you for the Boston two-step. How did you know the steps, Em?'

'I didn't,' she said. 'He told me to follow him and I did.'

Pa nodded and then got up, walking in the direction of the bar. She was surprised at how much he was drinking, because he didn't often drink at home.

'Would you dance this one with me, Miss Carter?'

She looked up and saw Harry Standen, the farmer from Sutton Fen she'd danced with earlier. 'What is it? I only know a few steps.'

'It's a waltz, and as easy as the two-step you danced with Nicolas Barton. Come on, I'll show you.'

Emily accepted his hand. She was filled with confidence now. How hard could it be? All she had to do was to follow her partner's lead.

As they took their places with the other dancers, Emily smiled up at him. She no longer cared that she was wearing boots rather than dancing shoes and it didn't matter if her dress was too old for her. She was having a good time and a lot of that was due to the way Nicolas Barton had smiled at her – but it was due to this man too. He was just as pleasant in his way and she thought he liked her.

Pa was a little drunk when they left the dance at about half past eleven. Emily couldn't ever recall him being unsteady on his feet before. They'd walked to the village, because Pa had said they couldn't leave the horse standing all night. Emily had had to hold her dress up all the way and she'd wiped the mud from her boots carefully before they went into the dance. She'd managed to get there without getting her hem dirty but Pa was going to need help to get home and she couldn't see how she was going to manage it.

'Is Joe a bit the worse for wear?' Harry Standen drew up next to her in what Emily thought of as a horseless carriage. She'd only seen them once or twice in Ely, though Pa said they were the coming thing for the future. 'Hang on a minute and I'll help you get him inside. You don't want to walk all the way home with him in that state.'

Emily gave him a grateful look. Pa was in a good humour and laughing, but he couldn't walk straight and had almost stumbled twice already. He protested as he was manhandled into the automobile but was ignored by the smiling conspirators. Harry pushed him into the back seat, where he flopped over on his side and proceeded to snore happily.

Harry opened the front passenger door for Emily and she slid in. He tucked her dress in carefully and then climbed back into the driving seat. He'd left the engine ticking over so didn't need to use the starting handle again.

'This is lovely. I've never been in an automobile before.' She looked around in excitement. 'Is it new?'

'Almost. It's not bad,' he grinned at her, then glanced at her father in the back. 'He's settled. I'll bet he has a sore head in the morning.'

'Yes, I expect so,' Emily agreed sniffing the pleasant smell of leather from the seats. 'I've never known him to drink so much.'

When she thought about it, her Pa had been changing a lot recently. Not only was he distant with her mother, but he coughed a lot and didn't eat as much as he had once upon a time. She wondered if he was sickening for something and decided to talk to him about it the next day.

It was nice sitting in the car in the darkness, which was lit only by a few street lamps, the moon having sailed behind a bank of clouds. The little popping sounds made by the engine occasionally and the humming of the tyres on the road were the only sounds, except for Pa's snores. Fancy her being taken home in style! It made her feel like a real lady.

When they got home, Pa was still asleep. Harry hauled him out of the automobile, heaved him over one shoulder and took him into the kitchen. He put Pa in his armchair, stretching his legs out in front of him. Then looked at Emily.

'I'll be over to see Joe before Christmas,' he said and then surprised her when he leaned forward and kissed her cheek. 'Goodnight, Emily. I enjoyed dancing with you.'

Emily thanked him. She locked the door after him, and then looked round for something to cover her father. He was lolling back in his chair, sound asleep and snoring. She fetched his greatcoat and placed it over him, looked round the kitchen once more and turned the oil lamp down low. There was nothing more she could do, though she knew Pa would feel dreadful in the morning.

Creeping upstairs, she looked in her parents' room. It was in darkness. Emily spoke softly but there was no answer. She could hear little snuffling sounds from Jack, but Ma was either asleep or pretending to be.

Emily sighed and went down the passage to her own room. As soon as she entered she sensed something was different. It didn't smell right. There was the smell of cheap perfume but also something else – something she couldn't recognise. She lit her lamp and looked at the bed. The covers were in place but not as she'd left them. Had someone been in her bed?

Pulling back the covers, she caught the same smell only stronger – it was sort of musky and sharp, like some of the men had smelled at the dance. Her spine prickled. Had a man been in her bed? Surely not! Who would come to her room and get in her bed?

It didn't make sense, and yet she felt that both her mother and a man had been in her room. Emily pulled the covers back up on the bed, because she wasn't going to get into a bed that smelled like that. In the morning she would have the sheets off and wash them.

She undressed and put on her warm nightgown, then lay down on top of the bed, pulling the eiderdown over her.

Her senses were telling her that her mother had been in this bed with a man – and the musky odour reminded her of the tallyman's smell.

Emily frowned as the suspicion formed in her mind. Ma had hidden from the old tallyman but she always welcomed Eddie Fisher with a cup of tea and a cake, even if she had no money to pay – and she sent Emily on errands to her father when Eddie called.

Was it possible that Ma had found a way to pay her debts that didn't involve money? The thought made Emily feel sick inside. She tried to dismiss it, but the thought stayed there in her head until she finally drifted into sleep.

Chapter 6

'Well, I think you were very unkind,' Lizzie Barton said. She was in the schoolroom at the manor with her sister, wrapping presents for Christmas, which would be placed under the huge tree in the drawing room downstairs. 'I'm certain that poor girl heard you.'

'What does it matter if she did?' Amy said and tied her pink ribbon in a perfect bow before sticking on a label she'd written in her copperplate hand. Amy seemed to do everything effortlessly and sailed through life like a queen, expecting everyone to make way before her. 'The Carter girl looked awful and that dress was ridiculous. What did she think she looked like wearing those awful boots with a gown like that?'

'She probably didn't have any dancing shoes,' Lizzie objected. Her beautiful sister was always dressed in the latest styles, but she ought to realise that not everyone was in her fortunate position. Lizzie had felt very sorry for the Carter girl.

'You've been spoiled, Amy. We've always had everything we wanted.'

'For goodness' sake! She was just a common farm girl.'

Amy gathered up her parcels and flounced out of the room, leaving Lizzie to finish hers alone. Unperturbed by her sister's show of temper, Lizzie continued to cut paper and lengths of ribbon. Much as she admired and loved her elder sister, Lizzie was distressed by the way Amy seemed to dismiss the feelings of others as unimportant. It was true that Emily Carter's dress was unfortunate to say the least. She must have copied it from a fashion plate, because the style was similar to something Mama or Granny might buy in Worth's or commission a skilled seamstress to make. A gown like that would have looked perfect on either of them, but on Emily it just looked odd. The stitching had been uneven, the hem hadn't hung properly and worn with black boots it had looked ridiculous.

Lizzie had recalled seeing the girl some years previously. She and Amy had been out riding with Nicolas and it was beginning to get dark when they saw her. If anything, Emily Carter had looked even worse that day. Her dress was old and patched and hung on her like a sack, and she'd had mud on her face and hands. Lizzie had thought how poor she looked but she'd seen her tear-streaked face and felt sympathy for her. Amy had been rude but Nicolas had spoken to her nicely. Not that she'd appreciated his attempt to be kind. She'd just stuck her head in the air and looked proud.

75

Lizzie knew their father had lost his estate or, rather, he'd had to sell it after some bad investments meant that he was short of money. Their Uncle Simon had bought it, which had made Papa even angrier. He resented the fact that his younger brother had made money whereas he'd lost his, and he was annoyed because Granny had offered them a home here rather than lending him the money to clear his debts, which would have enabled him to keep his estate. Of course he wasn't poor, because he still had the London house and a few investments, but he wasn't rich either.

Granny was rich, which was why he'd accepted her offer, albeit grudgingly. He was hoping she would leave her money to one of them when she died, but Lizzie didn't want to think about that. She was very fond of Lady Prior and she wanted her to live for years and years. Granny made more fuss of Lizzie than she did of the others, though she also had a soft spot for Nicolas – but, then, everyone loved him.

A smile touched Lizzie's lips as she thought of her brother. He was home from school for Christmas. Then he had another term at Eton, after which he would come home until the following autumn when he would go up to Oxford. The thought of his being home for Christmas made her smile. She was fond of all her family, but Nicolas was special.

'Daydreaming again,' Nicolas's voice hailed her from the doorway and she jumped, covering one of the parcels quickly so that he shouldn't see his name.

'I was just thinking about something,' she said, as he entered the room and sat down at the table, stretching out his long legs. He was wearing riding breeches and they suited him. 'Have you been out on Rufus?'

'He was a bit restive so I gave him a good gallop.' He eyed Lizzie thoughtfully. 'Something is on your mind – out with it, princess.'

'I was thinking of that girl at the dance, the one you showed how to do the two-step.'

'She didn't need much showing. She had a natural flow that made it easy to dance with her.'

'Did you notice her boots? It must have been hard to dance in those things.'

'I didn't notice.' He frowned. 'I know Amy was rude about her a couple of times.'

'That's why you asked her to dance instead of Amy.' Lizzie had known it all along but his look confirmed it. 'I was thinking she ought to have some pretty shoes ... but I'm not sure what to do. Do you think she might be offended if I bought her a pair? Would she refuse to accept them, think I was being condescending or something?'

'She might ... unless...' Nicolas smiled and rose to his feet. 'Leave this to me, Lizzie. I'll see to it in a way she can't refuse.' He turned to look at her from the doorway. 'I'm shopping in Ely; anything special you would like for your gift?'

'I never mind what you buy me – but I know Amy wants the silver bangle in the jeweller's. It was right in the centre of the window when we were doing our shopping yesterday.'

'Thank you,' Nicolas said. 'The bangle for Amy and a surprise for you.' He blew her a kiss.

'Don't forget Emily Carter's dancing shoes.'

Nicolas nodded and went out, leaving Lizzie to the contemplation of her parcels once more.

Her problem over the gift for Emily Carter was solved. Now she could forget about her and look forward to Christmas.

It was Christmas Eve. The tree in the drawing room was so tall it almost touched the ceiling. Lizzie and Amy had helped decorate it, though Granny had directed them to put the delicate glass balls in a certain way, and she'd given them a silver star to place right at the top.

'It should be a fairy,' Amy had objected. 'We always had a fairy at home.'

'I think a star more appropriate,' Lady Prior replied firmly. 'Christmas is a religious occasion, Amy. We may choose to celebrate it with a special dinner, presents and a tree – but it is still Christ's birthday and the star guided the shepherds to the stable where he lay.'

'It's lovely, Granny,' Lizzie said, because she could see the storm brewing in Amy's eyes. 'I think it's nicer than a fairy – and we shouldn't forget the true meaning of Christmas.'

Amy glowered at her, but Lizzie ignored her sister. It was Christmas and she didn't want to quarrel, especially as they had guests for dinner on Christmas Eve. Lizzie didn't know all the people her grandmother had invited. She supposed that most of them would be old like Granny herself, but perhaps one or two would be younger.

Now the evening had arrived and Lizzie wasn't disappointed. Most of the guests were older, but a

78

couple of young girls had been invited – and Sir Arthur Jones. Lizzie had seen him in Ely once or twice, though he'd never spoken to them. She knew that he was very rich and had only recently come to live nearby. He'd bought a big house, not a new one but a grand house built in the Georgian era, and only a matter of half an hour's ride on horseback from Priorsfield Manor. Granny had invited him to be their guest and Lizzie liked him at once.

She supposed he must be in his late twenties or thirty at the most. He had dark hair, grey eyes and a sensitive mouth, and his face looked a little craggy. Granny had told her that he'd been to South America returning only a few months before deciding to settle here. It was said that he'd discovered a valuable emerald mine and the shares were due to be sold at the Stock Exchange soon. Lizzie thought that sounded very exciting and she would have liked to ask him about it, but Amy was talking to him and he didn't seem to have noticed Lizzie at all.

She wasn't really surprised. Lizzie was not quite seventeen and Amy was nineteen. Lizzie was pretty but Amy was beautiful. More than that, she was regal. When she entered the room everyone stopped talking and turned to look at her. Lizzie knew that she had several admirers, but they were all farmers and Amy wanted more than they could give her.

If Papa hadn't lost his money, Amy would have had her season in London the previous year. She'd been taken to local dinners and parties, but as yet the talk of Granny paying for her to have a season had come to nothing.

Noticing the way Amy was laughing up at Sir Arthur, Lizzie supposed that her sister must like him a lot. She couldn't blame her. Lizzie thought he looked nice and she liked the warmth of his laugh. She wished he would notice her, but he had eyes only for Amy.

Lizzie didn't normally envy her sister, but this time she couldn't help wishing that Amy had gone to stay with friends for Christmas, as she'd talked of doing a few weeks earlier. Perhaps then Sir Arthur would have noticed Lizzie.

'What are you looking so glum about?' Nicolas sat down next to her, and then followed the direction of her gaze. 'He's much too old for you, princess. You'll find a prince of your own one day, and he'll be the luckiest man alive.'

Lizzie giggled, because Nicolas always made her feel better. 'Let's hope Amy is away then or married, because when she's around no one notices me.'

'If they don't they are idiots,' Nicolas said and reached into his pocket, bringing out a small parcel. 'I put something under the tree for you, but I thought you deserved something special.'

Lizzie accepted the small flat parcel and opened it. She looked at the beautiful gold compact inside and gave a squeal of pleasure. 'It is so lovely, Nicolas. You always spoil me.'

'You deserve it,' he said and smiled. 'By the way, I chose some white satin dancing slippers and had them sent straight from the shop. I got a size five as you suggested. They have a strap with a button and shaped heels. Miss Carter can change them if she wants but the shop owner won't tell her where they came from, because I told him he mustn't – made him swear it on pain of death.'

'Nicolas, you didn't,' Lizzie said and her laughter pealed out. Sir Arthur turned his head and glanced at her. For a moment he looked interested, a smile on his lips, then Amy spoke and he turned back to her. Lizzie gave a faint sigh. He was clearly besotted. She would be foolish to even think of him, because while Amy wanted his attention she would have it. 'I hope Emily likes them.'

'She's bound to, isn't she? I don't suppose she's ever had anything like that – and she isn't likely to again. Only my precious Lizzie would think of such a thing.'

'No, I suppose she won't.' Lizzie was thoughtful. She had so much to be thankful for. They might have to live with Granny, who wasn't always kind to Mama and made it clear she expected them to live by her rules, but she wasn't poor like Emily Carter.

Lizzie didn't know what it would be like to live on a farm and she didn't want to. Granny's housekeeper had appeared, calling them all in for dinner. The parcels under the tree would be opened later, just before the family went to bed. Lizzie knew she would have several gifts, though nothing would please her as much as the gold compact Nicolas had given her. He offered her his arm, taking her into the dining room.

Sir Arthur was escorting Amy, of course. Granny had placed them side by side. Lizzie supposed Sir Arthur was the latest attempt on their grandmother's part to find Amy a husband without going to the expense of a London season. If Amy liked him, she might get her way, though Lizzie couldn't help hoping she wouldn't.

It was ridiculous of her to hope, because what man in his right mind would want Lizzie when he could have Amy?

Chapter 7

Christmas morning dawned fine and bright. Emily yawned, got out of bed and threw back the curtains. Early yet, the wintry sun glistened on white crystals of ice that had formed on bushes, withered flowers in wooden tubs, and the roofs of the cow byre and the milking parlour. She saw her father heading towards the cowsheds and knew what had woken her. Even at Christmas Pa had the same chores as on every other day.

Dressing hurriedly, and trying not to wake her little brother, she went softly downstairs, pulled on her old coat and shoes and followed her father to the milking parlour. Ma would need help with the dinner later but if Jack slept on, she wouldn't be up for another hour and Emily was concerned about her father. The cough he'd developed in the summer had worsened as the weather got colder and she could hear him as she opened the door and went in.

'What are you doing up, Em?' he asked, turning to look at her. 'It's Christmas morning. You should be making tea and toast and opening your presents.'

'I'll open them later, when we've done the milking,' she said, her heart warmed and filled with love. 'It won't hurt me to give you a hand. Ma won't start on the dinner for another hour.'

Pa nodded and handed her a pail. She picked up a stool, sat down at Bess's side and pressed her face into the cow's warm belly as she began to stroke her teats with practised fingers, washing her udder before starting the milking process. The milk squirted into the pail, coming easily as the placid Bess munched in contentment. Moving on from Bess, Emily tipped the milk into the churn and turned to the next cow in line. Neither she nor Pa felt a need to speak, their silence companionable and in tune with each other. It was the morning of Christ's birth and for this little moment in time all was well with their world.

Leaving Pa and Bert, who had turned up at the last moment, to put the churns on the wagon, Emily went up to the house. She washed her hands at the deep stone sink and then filled the kettle. Fire glowed red between the iron bars at the front of the range. She poked at it and then shut the door so the heat intensified. Fetching a heavy pan down from the shelf above the range, she put dripping into it and began to fry bacon, eggs and leftover potatoes, crisping them at the edges. Plates had warmed in the oven beside the fire and Emily was just loading the food onto them when her father walked in. He washed his hands, looking round at her.

'Stella not down yet?'

'Not yet. Let's have our breakfast together and then I can make Ma's toast or whatever she wants when she comes.'

Pa sat down, looking at the loaded plate she set before him. Emily brewed tea in the large barge teapot. It was colourful and her favourite, though normally more for display than use, but this was Christmas and special.

'Making a fuss of your old man?' Pa teased. 'Expecting a nice surprise, Em?'

'I don't mind what I've got,' she said truthfully. 'But I got something for you.' She placed a parcel wrapped in pretty blue paper by his plate.

'What's this then?'

'Something you need.' Emily watched as he opened the parcel and saw the little paperback copy of a book with all the English silver hallmarks. The smile on his face was her reward for not buying herself the eau de Cologne she'd wanted in Woolworth.

'Just what I've always wanted,' he said. 'Look in my haversack in the corner, Em. There's something for you and a small parcel for Stella. Fetch them out, love.'

Emily fetched out the parcels she found in the haversack. Ma's was wrapped in brown paper and felt like a box of perfume, but Emily's was smaller and she guessed it was something special from the look on Pa's face. She tore off the wrappings and discovered a small silver compact with enamelling on the lid. As far as she could see it was perfect and she looked at him in surprise.

'It's beautiful, Pa – but it's perfect?'

'Just like my Em,' he said and smiled. 'Look

84

under the cushion now. There's a couple more gifts came for you. Harry Standen gave me one when he called to have a word the other morning, but I don't know who sent the other. It came through the post and was addressed to you. I put it away until today.'

Emily was still admiring her compact. The enamelled picture was of a beautiful girl and delicately painted. Pa could surely have sold it for good money, but he'd given it to her and she would treasure it all her life.

She placed it on the table beside her plate and then went to the cushion. One parcel was quite small and wrapped in pretty Christmas paper; the other was strongly wrapped in brown paper with her name boldly inscribed in black ink and with a row of postage stamps. Emily opened the smaller parcel first and discovered a tiny bottle of Yardley perfume. She squeaked with delight and opened the stopper, smelling the scent of roses. She held it up to show her father and then read the note, which just wished her Happy Christmas from Harry.

Fancy Harry Standen sending her a Christmas gift. She hadn't expected anything from him. Christoper had given her a small box of chocolates when she saw him in Ely, and she'd given him a card and a man's handkerchief that she'd made and embroidered in the corner.

Emily ate her breakfast, because she didn't want to waste it, but kept eyeing the bigger parcel as she tried to work out who it was from. Only when her plate was clear did she pick it up and break the seals. Inside, she discovered a box. It was a shoebox from the expensive shop in Ely High Street. Her heart beat like a frantic bird trying to escape from a cage. Lifting the lid, she saw a pair of white satin dancing shoes and almost dropped the box.

Who would send her a gift like that?

'What have you got, Em?'

Emily took out a shoe and held it up for him to see. It had a rounded toe and a shaped heel, with a strap that fastened with a button across her foot – a bit like the ones Miss Concenii had been wearing when they visited Uncle Albert, but with thinner heels and more delicate.

'Very pretty. Who sent you those?'

Emily looked through the wrappings. She found a card from the shop saying they were a Christmas gift but could be exchanged if necessary. She went through it all again, thinking she must have missed something but all she could find was the shop's card. She passed it to her father, explaining that there was no other message.

'Well, there's a mystery,' Pa said. 'You've got a secret admirer, Em.'

Emily was silent. She didn't think her mother would have bought something like this, so unless Pa had wanted it to be a surprise she had no idea who had sent the shoes. Pa's gift must have cost him as much as he could spare so who had sent her the shoes and why shoes like these...?

Suddenly, it came to her. Someone had noticed that she didn't have proper dancing shoes and had sent her these as a gift – but who would do that? She would have thought it was Harry, but he'd given her perfume. The only other person she could think of was Mr Jonathan Barton, but surely

86

he wouldn't – why would he?

To make up for being rude about her boots?

He'd rescued her from her uncle in Ely and he'd danced with her in the progressive – but he hadn't sought her out for a dance; it was his brother Nicolas who had done that ... why would he send her shoes?

Emily puzzled over it. The only other person who might give her something was her uncle and he always gave her the same gift. Five shillings, which he left with her mother – and which she always put in her mother's jar on the mantel. If Emily thought the shoes had come from him she would have sent them back to the shop but she was sure they had come from one of the gentlemen she'd danced with at the village hall.

Had it been Mr Jonathan or Mr Nicolas? Emily would have liked to thank whoever it was, but she couldn't unless she knew.

Why hadn't he sent her a card?

Perhaps it was because he thought her pride might make her refuse the gift. Perhaps she ought to – if she knew for certain. Her mother would tell her to return it and her father might think it unwise to keep a gift like this from a man she hardly knew – unless Pa had sent the gift himself and didn't want either Ma or Emily to know how extravagant he'd been.

That was the sensible explanation and the one that made her feel comfortable.

Hearing her mother coming down the stairs, Emily put her gifts away and cleared her dirty things into the sink. She'd bought small gifts for her mother and Jack, and she placed them on the table, turning as her mother entered the kitchen.

'Would you like bacon and egg, Ma – or just toast?'

'Toast and marmalade as usual,' Ma said. 'Here, take Jack for me and I'll make the toast. You burn it too much.'

Emily did as she was asked, smiling down at her brother. He was beginning to make intelligible sounds and he blew bubbles at her, mumbling what might have been her name. She was glad that he seemed to be free of cold for once, because she wanted her little brother to enjoy Christmas.

'Happy Christmas, Jack darling,' she said and kissed him. Jack gurgled with laughter and held up his chubby hands. She took her parcel from the table and opened it, giving him the soft toy she'd purchased for one shilling and sixpence in Woolworth. It had been marked down, because it had a little spot on the pink fur but Emily had washed it away and it was as good as new. Her brother's hands flapped at the toy, his face a picture as he laughed. 'Look, Pa, he's laughing. He knows it's Christmas.'

Pa looked at her but didn't say anything. She waited for him to produce a gift for the baby but he made no move to do so. She thought it odd he hadn't bothered to buy his son a present and then thought he must have given Ma money to buy Jack a gift.

Ma had made a fresh cup of tea. She poured herself one and offered one to Pa but he shook his head. Ma drank her tea and then started to make her toast. She made no attempt to open either of her gifts, just sat down when she was ready and started to eat.

'Aren't you going to open your presents?' Emily asked.

'Your father knows I would rather have the money,' she said. 'What good is perfume to me when I'm stuck here day in day out?'

Emily felt hurt for Pa. She'd saved up to buy Ma a pretty scarf although it didn't matter about her feelings, but why did her mother always try to spoil everything for Pa?

'Pa thought you would like it.'

She sniffed and ignored the parcel. 'Derek left five shillings for you. I put it on the mantel. Do you want it?' Emily shook her head and her mother frowned. 'I don't know why you're so difficult. What has my brother ever done to harm you?'

Emily didn't reply. She put Jack down on a blanket on the floor with his toy and started to prepare the vegetables for dinner. Hearing his gurgles of glee, she glanced at him and smiled: at least her brother was happy. When she'd finished them, leaving the cabbage, carrots, onions and potatoes in water, she gathered her parcels and went up to her bedroom. The quarrel started the minute she closed the door to the stairs behind her.

'Damn you, Stella,' she heard her father say. 'Can't you ever let the girl have a good day? Do you always have to ruin everything?'

'What about me?' Stella said and the bitterness ran deep in her voice. 'My life was ruined the day you got me pregnant. If she hadn't been on the way I might have married anyone.'

Emily closed her eyes, feeling the sting of tears. So that was why her mother resented her so much. Now she understood. She hadn't wanted Emily. She'd only married Pa because she'd been pregnant and he'd promised her that one day Uncle Albert was going to leave them a fortune.

Emily sat down on the bed. For a moment the pain was so bad that she felt sick, but then she pushed away her own hurt and began to think of her father. Pa always bore the brunt of Ma's dissatisfaction. He tried to please her as best he could and she didn't deserve it.

Emily was certain that she was having an affair with Eddie. Since the night of the dance, when she'd smelled a man's strong scent in her bed, she'd looked for the signs and she'd seen them – a smile and a wink or a certain look in their eyes. Ma was cheating on Pa, and worse than anything was the fact that as he grew Jack had begun to look like Eddie Fisher.

Pa had to know. Of course he did. Emily understood why he was so distant with Ma now. He must have known what was going on from the start and he suspected that Jack wasn't his son.

Her little brother wasn't Pa's. No wonder there were so many quarrels. Now Emily understood why Pa hadn't bought the boy a gift himself.

Tears trickled down her cheeks. It wasn't fair on Pa. Ma's cheating hurt Emily because she knew it had hurt Pa. He hadn't hit his wife or thrown her out of the house, as most men would, but their quarrels were deeper now, bitter and resentful. Most of the time Pa just walked out on her – but today she'd pushed him too far.

Hearing a crash downstairs, Emily rushed down to the kitchen just in time to see the door slam behind Pa. She looked at her mother and saw she was holding a hand to her cheek.

'He hit me,' she said, looking at Emily in disbelief. 'He hit me.'

'You pushed him too far...'

'Take his side like you always do.' Ma glared at her. 'I suppose you heard it all? Well now you know. I never wanted to marry him and I never wanted you.'

Ma went to the hook behind the door, took her coat and put it on then turned to look at her. 'I'm going out for a few hours. If you want that goose cooked for two this afternoon, you'll have to do it yourself.'

'Are you coming back for dinner?'

'I might and I might not. What do you care – it will be just you and your father then, won't it?' Swooping on Jack, she wrapped him in a blanket and went out.

Emily stared after her, and then looked around at the kitchen. Ma's parcels were still on the table untouched. She hadn't done anything towards making the dinner and clearly didn't intend to. Emily wasn't sure whether to cook the goose or wait – supposing neither of them returned for Christmas lunch?

She would just have to put it in the oven. They could always eat it cold and she didn't know what else to do...

Emily was basting the goose when the door opened and her mother walked in with Jack, who was whimpering. She put the child down on a blanket, gave him the toy Emily had bought, which seemed to quiet him, and went to the stove, looking inside the saucepans.

'It all looks good, Emily,' she said in a tone Emily hadn't heard in a long time. 'I wasn't sure you would have it ready.'

'I wasn't sure what to do so I cooked it.'

'Let me have a look at the goose.'

Ma bent down to look in the oven. She tested the flesh with a long-handled fork and nodded as the juices ran clear.

'It's just right,' she hesitated, then, as the kitchen door opened. 'Don't tell your pa I was gone all morning – please?'

Emily hesitated, because her pa should know, but Ma's eyes pleaded with her and as her father came in she gave a slight nod of her head. Pa looked cold and ill and she went to him, helping him off with his coat.

'Do you want a drop of whisky, Pa?'

They only ever had strong drink in the house at Christmas. The dairy that bought their milk usually gave Pa a small bottle as a gift and he made it last for months. He nodded, hardly speaking and went over to the range, opened the door and held his hands to the fire.

'It's bitter out,' he said. 'The dinner smells good, Stella. Has Em been helping you?'

'She's been a real good girl,' Ma said and looked at him sideways. 'You look frozen. I ... shouldn't have been so mean this morning. I was feeling a bit out of sorts.'

'I shouldn't have hit you. I'm sorry for that.'

'I pushed you too far. It won't happen again.' She hesitated, then, looking ashamed, she said in a low voice Emily could hardly hear, 'It's over,

Joe. I'm sorry it happened.'

'Just forget it,' he muttered and started to cough. Covering his mouth with a handkerchief, he was just too late to hide from Emily the flecks of blood on his lips.

She felt a flicker of fear. Ma hadn't noticed. She was too busy seeing to the dinner, bustling about as if she hadn't just made an earth-shattering announcement.

Emily looked at her father. He sat slumped in his chair and she could see he felt ill, but he wasn't going to give in. She put the small glass of whisky in his hand and then impulsively kissed the top of his head, whispering that she loved him. He looked up and smiled but didn't say a word. He didn't need to because she knew all he couldn't or wouldn't say.

Then she knelt down on the blanket and played with Jack, until her mother called her to help serve up the dinner.

For the rest of the day Ma and Pa were carefully polite to one another. Neither of them smiled much, but in the evening Pa fetched out the pack of cards and they played whist for matchsticks. Emily went to bed at her usual time. She could hear them talking after she'd gone up but they didn't quarrel.

When she was alone in her room she tried on her pretty satin shoes. They fitted her perfectly and felt wonderful. She wished she knew who had sent them but if she did, perhaps she might feel obliged to give them back.

Two days after Christmas, Pa took Emily on the

wagon and they drove out to Harry Standen's farm in Sutton Fen. It was a long way on the wagon but a wintry sun was shining and they both had a blanket over their legs to keep them warm. The main road from Witchford led eventually into the village of Sutton and they went straight through, past the pub on the corner of The Brook and then turned left and along the High Street, down the sloping hill towards the fen and left again towards the Burystead.

Once they turned off the main road, the lane became narrow with just a few old cottages to either side. After a while even the lane disappeared and they had to negotiate the bumpy droves that led to Harry's farm. Steep ditches formed a framework, draining the fields of rich black soil, which had been ploughed and left fallow for the winter. You could see for miles across the flat fields and in places the sky seemed to touch the earth. At first the sky had looked blue with just a few white clouds scudding across it, but gradually the sun faded away and the skies darkened. It was now that the lowering skies made the fens seem a hostile, lonely environment.

It was colder once the sun had gone, but both Emily and Pa had knitted hats and scarves and their coats were buttoned up to the neck. Emily was relieved when they saw the large farmhouse come into view. A man opened the door and came out to greet them as Pa pulled the wagon to a halt.

'Nice to see you, Joe,' Harry said. 'I wasn't sure you would come, Emily.' He held out his hands and helped her to jump down.

'I wanted to thank you for the perfume. I've

never had any Yardley perfume before; it's lovely.'

'It was just a little thing,' Harry said but he looked pleased. 'Come in, both of you. My mother will make you a hot toddy and then I'll take you to the barn, Joe. We got some lovely puppies, Emily – if you'd like to see them. They're black Labradors and good farm dogs.'

'I should love to see them,' she said and smiled at him.

Harry's mother was a plump friendly lady with dark hair and eyes like her son. She welcomed them in, drawing them to the big open fire that formed a part of the modern range. Emily thought her smart oven with its enamel front was much nicer and would be easier to clean than their old-fashioned one, which had to be blacked every day.

'What a cold day to be out,' she said. 'You drink this and warm yourself, Miss Carter, and then I'll show you the pups while Harry takes Mr Carter to look at that old stuff in the barn. We were going to make a bonfire of it but then Harry told your Pa about it and he said he might buy it from us. Can't see as there's anything much good amongst it myself, but there's no sense in burning it if it will do someone else some good.'

Emily thanked her for the drink. Her father and Harry were talking. They drank their hot toddies and then went off together. Mrs Standen took Emily into a large back kitchen to see the puppies nestling in a bed of old rags she'd made for them. Their mother got up and came to meet her, leaving the pups crawling over each other.

'How lovely they are,' Emily said. 'Can I touch them?'

95

'Yes, they're old enough now. You have to be careful at the start or the mother might eat them, but she's over that stage now. These are five weeks old now and will soon be ready to leave home.'

It was on the tip of Emily's tongue to say that she would love one, but she didn't, because she knew what Ma would say. Even if Emily could afford to buy one, she couldn't afford to keep it. Puppies were sweet but they grew into big dogs and would need a lot of food. They didn't have enough scraps to feed a dog like this, so despite falling in love with one of the pups that had a white patch over its eye, she kept her feelings to herself. Ma had been easier to live with of late and Emily didn't want to risk more quarrels.

She contented herself with stroking the puppies and added them to the list of things she was going to have one day.

Emily's imaginary list grew all the time. One day she was going to find herself a job that paid good wages, and then she would be independent and could buy all the things she wanted. She would be someone and the posh girls at the manor wouldn't be able to look down their noses at her any more.

When her father came back looking very pleased with himself, Emily was ready to leave. Mrs Standen was friendly but Emily wasn't used to sitting down in the mornings and she knew there was a pile of ironing waiting for her when she got home.

She thanked Harry's mother for her hospitality, and thanked him again for the perfume. He smiled and said he would be calling at the farm one day. Emily went out to the cart with her father. She saw it was piled high with old furniture, over which he'd pulled a tarpaulin tied down with ropes. Pa helped her up on the wagon. She tucked the blanket round herself and he let the horses go.

'Did you buy anything nice?'

'I bought a couple of gate-legged tables, which I'll take to the shop tomorrow, a set of yew kitchen chairs and two sabre-legged mahogany elbow chairs. Also a couple of brass and iron bedsteads, an extending table and a couple of old wardrobes.'

'You won't be able to sell the wardrobes.'

'No, but I'll chop them up and use them for wood on the fire.'

Emily nodded to herself. Pa was making more work for himself but he'd bought one or two nice things and she supposed he hadn't liked to leave the rubbish, because that wouldn't be fair.

The afternoon was closing in around them, a light mist spreading over the fens as they wended their way back along the droves. The skies seemed to press down on them now, dark and menacing, cutting them off from the rest of the world, as if a wall of silence surrounded them. On the way to the farm they'd been able to see the dykes easily but now it was hard to distinguish anything. Emily was glad the horse walked at a steady plod, because one foot wrong and they could all go tumbling into the dyke, which was filled with icy water.

She couldn't help hearing Pa's cough. It was surely getting worse. If she'd thought it would do any good, she would have begged him to go to the doctor again, but she knew he would only do what he wanted.

When they reached the road leading back through Sutton village, Emily felt a sigh of relief. Not much longer now and they would be home. She thought longingly of her tea and the warmth of the kitchen. Her throat felt a bit sore and her nose was running. She wiped it on her coat sleeve, because she couldn't get at her handkerchief.

On days like this, she wished she need never go out on the wagon again, but she knew she had no choice. When Pa needed her she would go, whatever the weather.

'You wait here,' Pa said when they drew up outside the Golden Hen pub in Witchford one morning later that week. 'I'm going inside to take a look at the stuff Josh asked me to clear, and if there's anything I need a hand with I'll let you know. As it's so cold you can lead Spartan up and down if he gets restless.'

Josh Bracknell was the landlord of the Golden Hen, and he had a daughter a little older than Emily. She'd seen him at the door, when she'd walked into the village occasionally, but she didn't know his daughter. People said Josh was hot-tempered but Pa seemed to get on well with him.

Emily took the reins in her hands. Spartan moved his feet and tossed his head a couple of times, then settled down as she gentled him. Emily sat on the driving box waiting. It wasn't too bad at first but after a while it began to get very cold and she hugged the blanket round her. She was just wondering if she should walk the horse when a girl came out of the pub with a glass in her hand.

'My father said to bring you this,' she said. 'Can I get up and sit with you?'

'Yes, of course. I'm Emily.'

'I know – I'm Carla. It must be interesting going out with your father all the time. I get so bored stuck in the house or the pub.'

'It gets a bit cold in the winter.'

Carla nodded. Emily sipped her drink. Carla was a friendly girl and very pretty with dark hair and eyes and a lovely smile. Emily wasn't certain but she thought she'd seen her talking to her uncle Derek when she passed thc pub with Pa a few days previously.

'Have you got a feller?' Carla asked.

Emily thought about Harry, but shook her head, and said, 'I've got a friend. He's nice but I wouldn't call him my feller. His name is Christopher and he works in my father's shop.'

'I've got a lover,' Carla said and her bold dark eyes were alight with mischief. 'My father would kill me if he knew – but I'm in love and I don't care. I'm going to get married soon.' She touched her stomach, a dreamy look in her eyes. 'You won't say anything?'

'No, of course not.' Emily wasn't sure what Carla meant by a lover. And why had she touched her stomach that way? Did she mean she did things no decent girl ever did unless she was wed? Emily thought of her mother and the baby brother she suspected wasn't Pa's; Ma had only got wed because a baby was on the way. She felt confused and uncomfortable. Emily's cheeks burned and she couldn't look at the girl. Carla couldn't be more than a few months older than Emily. She felt embarrassed by the girl's confidence and thought she must have heard her wrong or was imagining more than was meant.

She was relieved when her father came out with Carla's father. They were carrying an exquisite little seat – or sofa. Emily wasn't sure what to call it because there were three seats back to back, which made a circle. As they loaded it on the back of the cart and then went back for more, Carla jumped down and ran into the pub, taking Emily's empty glass with her.

Pa came out twice more with a couple of single chairs and a round table with a pedestal and three pad feet. The table was dark mahogany and she knew it was a wine table, because Pa had bought them before, but most were not as nice as this one.

He shook hands with Josh and climbed up onto the wagon next to Emily, taking the reins from her. As they drew away from the side of the road, he turned to her with a look of satisfaction.

'That's a Victorian love seat that is,' he told her, jerking his head towards the attractive seat. 'It needs covering but then it will be pretty and worth a few bob. Might be out of fashion now, Em, but one day people will want them again.'

'Yes, I expect so,' she said, looking at him fondly.

Pa might have his moods and she got cold waiting around for him sometimes, but she loved being with him and she would miss him if things had to change.

She wouldn't want to be Carla and she was glad she didn't have a lover. She thought the girl was silly to boast about it and wondered if it were true.

For a brief moment she recalled seeing her talking to Derek as she and Pa drove by the pub, then she dismissed the thought. Derek couldn't be her lover, could he? No, Carla had too much sense to get involved with a man like that – hadn't she?

'Cat got your tongue?'

Pa's jest brought Emily's attention back to him. What did it matter what Carla Bracknell got up to? Suddenly she didn't care that it was cold and her toes felt frozen. They would soon be home and the kitchen would be warm. Emily smiled to herself; she was content as she was for the moment.

Chapter 8

Amy Barton glanced at herself in her elegant dressing mirror. It had been a Christmas gift from her mother and was set in a silver frame with trails of vine leaves and flowers embossed on the frame in art nouveau style, and bought from Asprey of London. Amy had been particularly delighted with it, because she did like nice things. Of course Grandmama had some good things, but so much of the furniture was old-fashioned. Amy longed for the modern world with all its innovations. Here at Priorsfield, convention and the tradition of years trapped her. Grandmama still clung to her carriage and the horses needed to draw it, though her father had spoken of purchasing an automobile when he could afford it. Of course Jonathan already had a car, which he'd purchased with money left him by his paternal grandfather.

Amy made a sound of frustration. If only her father had not lost most of his money. Perhaps then she would have had the Season she craved, which she felt sure would have resulted in a good marriage for her. She was quite determined to marry into money, because she disliked the idea of being poor. It was bad enough having to watch what she spent on clothes and to live in this mausoleum of a house – but to be stuck in a marriage without sufficient money would be unbearable.

If Grandmama were not so mean she would have paid for Amy to have a London Season, but she refused to give Mama the money they needed. Sighing, Amy realised that her best chance of making the kind of marriage she wanted was to persuade Sir Arthur Jones to propose to her. He had seemed taken with her at Christmas and he'd called on them quite a few times since, but as yet he had shown no signs of wanting to marry her.

Somehow, she had to make him speak, because she had settled on it in her mind that he would do. She wasn't in love with him, of course, but she liked him and she enjoyed his company. Besides, he was very rich. He'd floated the emerald mine shares on the Stock Exchange and Lord Barton said they had sold well, bringing Arthur a sizeable fortune on top of what he already had. Amy knew that stuck here at the manor, she wasn't likely to meet many men who could give her the lifestyle she wanted.

It was so unfair. She ought to have had her chance to shine in society, to have men admire her and flirt with her. Amy longed for excitement, the thrill of being courted by someone dashing and handsome ... someone who would make her go weak at the knees. Arthur didn't make her feel like that, though she'd quite enjoyed it when he'd kissed her cheek – but she wished he'd been more passionate. She wanted a man who would sweep her off her feet and carry her away on a tide of passion.

She wanted altogether too much, Amy admitted and laughed, as she fastened pearl drops to her ears and sprayed on a little French perfume. She would just have to forgo the passion, at least until she'd been married a while and could take a lover without getting caught.

Arthur was exactly what she needed as a husband and he would just have to do.

Lizzie was feeling lonely. Nicolas was back at Eton, Jonathan was out on the estate somewhere and Amy had gone for a ride in Sir Arthur's automobile. It was a De Dion, painted green with shiny wheels and a wooden steering wheel. Lizzie wished she might have gone with them, but Amy hadn't even considered asking her if she would like to go. Amy had been seeing Sir Arthur regularly since Christmas. He called at the house at least twice or three times a week and he'd taken Amy to parties and dances.

Lizzie was afraid he was in love with her. She'd seen the look in his eyes when he saw Amy enter a room and she knew her own feelings for him were doomed to disappointment. It'd be silly of her to sulk or cry over it, because Sir Arthur had never looked her way. It wasn't as if Amy had stolen her beau. He hardly knew that Lizzie was alive.

'Lizzie dearest, come here a moment, will you?'

She turned as her grandmother called to her, going obediently to her side. Granny was leaning heavily on her stick. Dressed in a dark grey gown with a high neck finished with a lace collar and a rather splendid cameo brooch at the throat, she looked like the Victorian matriarch she was. Lady Prior made few concessions to the modern era, her drawing-room a hotchpotch of styles ranging from good Chippendale chairs to heavy, over-stuffed sofas bought when she was a bride. The rooms she used were crammed with knickknacks she'd collected, because although she added some-thing every time she was given a gift, however insignificant, she never put anything aside. Price-less silver and objets d'art mingled with cheap china fairings her grandchildren had given her and an assortment of photographs in frames. She was a lady of strict morals and had a highly developed sense of her place in the world. Lizzie suspected that her grandmother suffered a lot of pain with her rheumatism, but she never complained, because one didn't if one had 'backbone'.

'I would like you to run a little errand for me, Lizzie,' Granny said. 'Would you mind having the pony and trap put to and taking a note to Rever-end Potter for me?'

'Of course not,' Lizzie felt rather pleased. She'd been bored on her own and it would make a change. 'There's no need for me to take the trap, I can walk into Witchford. It is a lovely day and I like to walk.'

'Very well, if you prefer. It's bright and dry even if cold. Wrap up warm and take this note to him. It's about the village bazaar. I have some things for him to sell for his latest good cause, but he must come here and sort through them. Tomorrow morning will do very well.'

'Yes, Granny.' Lizzie wondered if her grandmother knew how autocratic she sounded. She didn't consider that it might not suit the vicar to come the next morning. In that she was a bit like Amy, though neither of them would admit it. They didn't get on too well.

She accepted the small envelope, which smelled of Granny's lavender water, then went through to the gun room and selected some stout boots and a long, oversized duster-coat to put on over her clothes. She wound wool scarves about her neck and pushed an old hat of Nicolas's down hard on her head. Amy would never go out looking like that but Lizzie didn't care. She would be warm and no one would bother to look at her, and that suited her.

Leaving the house, she walked through the front gardens, by way of the long gravel drive. Ancient trees grew to either side of the drive, their branches sweeping down to touch the earth in places. Many of them were specimen trees and had been planted by her great grandfather. There were rose beds set into the lawns, alive with colour in the summer but in winter they looked bedraggled, the stems black and withered. Soon the gardeners would cut them down to get fresh growth but not before the frosts had finished.

The wind was chilly and the tip of Lizzie's nose

was pink by the time she reached the lane that led into the village. The old Rectory was close to the church and the vicar's garden was small but always neat. His roses had been pruned in the winter and looked like little twigs, surrounded by a mulch of leaves that had decayed into the earth. She wondered if that was why he usually won the prize for the best roses at the village fete, annoying Grandmama every time when she had to take second place.

Lizzie was welcomed inside the Rectory and given a hot drink and one of Mrs Potter's cinnamon buns. The vicar came hurrying in as she was eating it, full of apologies for keeping her waiting. He'd been giving lessons to the local children and been delayed because the curate had a sore throat and couldn't take over from him.

'I'm sure Peter will be better tomorrow, and if not Mrs Potter will sit in for me,' he said. 'Tell dear Lady Prior that I shall be delighted to call on her at eleven tomorrow, Miss Lizzie.'

Lizzie thanked him and his wife for the cocoa and bun. She pulled on the old coat again, and left the Rectory. If anything, it was even colder now, but she enjoyed the chance of some fresh air and exercise, because it was seldom that she got the chance to walk this far. It was as she was walking back through the lane, after leaving the village, that she saw the man coming towards her. He was, she supposed, in his early thirties, a tall, strong-looking man with black hair and dark eyes. His clothes proclaimed him a farmer, for he wore long boots similar to those Nicolas wore for riding but with straps at the side and heavy soles. His trousers were moleskin and fitted tightly to his thighs and he wore a tweed coat that fitted into the waist with a little belt at the back, the elbows patched with leather. He was wearing a hat but though he put a finger to it he didn't remove it as most gentlemen did – but, of course, as Amy would say, he wasn't a gentleman in the strict sense of the word.

'Good morning, Miss Barton,' he said and grinned at her.

Lizzie hesitated, because she normally didn't speak to men she didn't know, but the admiring look in his eyes made her forget her Mama's warning.

'Good morning, sir.'

'Derek,' he said. 'My name's Derek. I farm over Chatteris way – been visiting my sister.'

'How nice for her,' Lizzie said politely. She was tempted to linger but then she saw Jonathan's automobile coming towards her from the direction of the village. He slowed down, opened his door and told her to get in. 'Goodbye...'

Jonathan looked at her as she slid into the seat next to him. 'What on earth did you think you were doing, Lizzie? Talking to a man like that...'

'He spoke to me and I said good morning, that's all,' Lizzie protested. 'I wasn't doing any harm, Jon.'

'*You* might not have been but he was eyeing you up and down.' Jonathan frowned. 'What on earth are you dressed like that for?'

'I thought it would keep me warm. I've been on an errand for Granny to the vicar.'

'Well, be careful Mama doesn't see you like that

– and take my advice, Lizzie. Stay away from men of that kind. I don't know him by name but I've seen him before. He isn't a gentleman and I don't want him hanging around my sister.'

Lizzie felt chastened. She'd only spoken a few words to the man and she couldn't see what the fuss was about. She'd liked the way he looked at her, making her feel she was a pretty girl and not just Amy's little sister. She wouldn't have minded talking to him some more if her brother hadn't come along – but she would probably never see him again.

Sometimes she thought she would be a child for ever. Would her family never allow her to have any fun? She wanted to be taken to dances and parties like Amy, instead of being stuck at home with her mother and Granny.

Of course the man she'd met wasn't a gentleman, but she'd only wanted to talk, perhaps flirt a little.

Surely there couldn't be any harm in that?

Chapter 9

Emily smiled as she came from the dairy and saw Harry Standen talking to Pa. She knew that Harry had brought his bull to one of their cows that morning. Emily had heard the shouts from the yard behind the cowsheds but hadn't gone to see what the fuss was all about. She had been busy all the morning, ironing and baking and polishing, and now she'd just finished churning the butter.

'Good morning, Emily,' Harry said and came to greet her. 'Your pa asked me to stop for a cup of tea before I go. I'm glad to have seen you alone – I was wondering if you would come out with me one evening? We could go to the cinema or a concert – or there's a dance on in Cambridge, if you fancied it?'

'When is the dance?'

'Not until next week.'

Emily thought quickly. She could make herself a skirt and use the bolero from the dress she'd worn at Christmas, and now she had those wonderful dancing slippers.

'Then I'd love to go to the dance,' she said and gave him a flashing smile. 'Why don't you come and have a cup of tea? We've been baking all morning – jam tarts and Ma's famous seed cake.'

'Thank you, I will,' Harry said. 'Ma told me to send you her good wishes, Emily. She liked you – thought you were a very pretty young lady. I do too...' His neck heated as he spoke and Emily felt like laughing but kept her amusement inside. Harry was nice and she liked him.

Emily hadn't thought about getting married yet. She was far too young and her ambition was to make something of herself before she settled down to marriage and children. Of course a man like Harry would provide a much better life than Pa had been able to give Ma, but Emily felt she wanted time to grow up, time to learn things and see a bit of life.

Not that Harry was thinking of marriage, of course. He just liked her – and it would be nice to go out with him sometimes, if her mother and Pa agreed.

When they went into the kitchen, Emily's heart sank because Derek was sitting there already, having a cup of tea. He looked at them, his eyes narrowed and calculating, as if he were weighing Harry up and wondering why he was here. Emily felt his eyes on her as she took the can of milk she was carrying into the cool pantry and poured some of it into a jug. She brought it back to the table just as her mother poured fresh water into the teapot.

'Well, this is nice, Mr Standen,' Ma said. 'How did things go in the yard?'

'Very well. I'm sure your Annie will provide a decent calf for you in a few months.'

'It was good of you to bring the bull yourself rather than just sending your stockman.'

'I like to see a job done myself,' Harry replied. 'Besides, I have to admit that I had an ulterior motive. I wanted to see Emily – and to ask her out. She has said she will come to a dance with me next week – if that's all right with you and Mr Carter?'

Ma looked at him, and then sent Emily a coy glance. 'I'm sure I've no objection. We can trust you to look after Emily, Mr Standen. Joe won't mind, as long as you have her back by eleven.'

'I'll do that,' Harry said and sipped his tea. He'd accepted a piece of cake and ate it with evident enjoyment. 'If Emily is half as good a cook as you, Mrs Carter, she'll make someone a good wife one day.'

'She will indeed,' Ma said and preened. 'I've taught her myself.'

Derek made a snort of disgust and pushed back his chair. 'I'll be off, I've got work to do,' he said and shot a look of anger at Emily as he passed her. He slammed the kitchen door as he went out, but Emily ignored him.

Jack was whimpering in his playpen. Emily went over and picked him up, wiping his running nose with a handkerchief. She didn't know why he seemed so vulnerable to colds and illnesses, and sometimes she thought he wasn't just as he ought to be – a little slow or backward perhaps – but she hadn't said anything to her mother, because she didn't know for sure. Perhaps a lot of babies were this way.

She could hear the murmur of voices as Ma quizzed Harry about his farm and his mother, and then the scrape of a chair as he stood up.

'That was very nice, Mrs Carter,' he said. 'I need to get on, but I'll call for you Saturday next week, Emily.'

'I shan't forget. Thank you.'

Jack had stopped crying. She put him down and fetched his bottle of juice, watching as he sucked at it for a moment before turning away to clear the table.

'You'll need a new dress,' her mother said.

'I thought I would make a skirt and use the bolero I had at Christmas.'

'You can borrow my best silk blouse,' Ma said. 'I've got a pattern. What you need is a nice bit of black wool or heavy satin to make a skirt. I'll help you get it ready if you buy a length when you go to the market tomorrow.'

Emily was surprised, but there was a gleam in

her mother's eyes. Now what was she thinking?

'I should like a pale colour rather than black,' she said, thinking about her dancing slippers. 'But I'm sure I'll find something and I've got three shillings saved.'

She smiled to herself as she went upstairs. She hadn't expected Harry to invite her out so soon, and she was excited – but she hoped Ma hadn't got silly ideas that she was serious yet.

Emily did her mother's shopping first that morning, and then headed towards the stall selling lengths of material. She had a good idea of what she wanted but wasn't sure whether she would be able to afford the quality material she'd envisaged in her mind. At first glance everything she liked appeared to be too expensive, but then she discovered a length of fine cream suiting. With a pretty blouse it would do for dancing but she could also use it for church on Sunday.

She asked the stall keeper to measure it and there was just enough. The price was two shillings and sixpence, which meant she couldn't afford a new blouse as well, but she could borrow Ma's or wear her own best blouse and trim the high neck with a piece of lace.

She was turning away when she saw Christopher walking towards her through the market. Waiting for him, she greeted him with a smile.

'Is this your lunch break?' she asked.

'Yes. I don't often close the shop but I saw you so I thought I'd come out and have a word. I'm going for a pie and chips – would you like to come?'

Emily hesitated, and then glanced at the clock on the market square. Pa had gone on an errand and told her he would be back in an hour. She had half an hour left.

'I have to meet Pa soon, but I might have a glass of lemonade and pinch one or two of your chips.'

Christopher laughed and agreed, offering her his arm. They crossed the market square again and went into the café. Christopher directed her to a table and ordered their meal. He ordered her a pie and chips too, because, as he said, it didn't matter if she didn't eat them all.

Emily nodded, feeling pleased with the unexpected treat. She hadn't expected to see Christopher unless she popped into the shop. He told her that he'd been busy. He'd sold several small things that week and also the set of yew chairs Pa had bought from Harry Standen.

'I was wondering if you might like to go out sometime,' Christopher said just as their food arrived. 'Just for a drink or a concert or something.'

Emily considered. Harry had asked her out and she'd said yes, but she liked Christopher too, and surely there was no harm in going out with friends? She wasn't actually courting anyone. She nodded but when he suggested Saturday of the following week, she told him she already had an engagement that night. He looked crestfallen, but she said she would meet him for lunch on the following Thursday and he cheered up.

Emily found him easy to talk to and enjoyed her meal. She thanked him and left when she spotted Pa's wagon draw up near the shop.

'I'll see you next week,' she said and ran out to

meet her father. He turned his head to look at her, arching one eyebrow.

'Where were you, Em?'

'Having pie and chips with Christopher. I'm going to do it again next week.'

'He's a nice lad,' her father said and nodded. 'Ready to leave then?'

'Yes, thank you. I've got all I want...' She looked in the wagon and saw some scrap metal. 'Did you buy what you wanted?'

'Some of it. I had another errand...' He shook his head when she arched her brow at him.

Emily wondered where he went when he left her to shop alone. He wasn't seeing another woman? No, not Pa. He might not love Ma but he wasn't a cheat. Still, there was some mystery, unless ... she wondered if he'd been to the doctor. Glancing at his coat pocket, she saw the bulge and knew she'd solved the puzzle. Pa had been to get something for that cough.

It was spitting with rain as they left the market and drove past the shops in the High Street. Emily caught sight of Derek. He was talking to a young girl, arguing with her. She couldn't see the girl's face but she was almost sure it was Carla Bracknell...

'I like Christopher,' Pa said. 'He hasn't got much to offer yet, but one day he'll do all right. You'll see, Emily. He's a bright young man.'

Emily smiled and nodded. She liked Christopher too and she was glad she'd arranged to meet him again.

Chapter 10

Derek Black was in a temper. He was helping out at his brother-in-law's farm, as he often did these days, replacing a rotten fence. He hammered the wooden fencing stakes into the ground with a fury that almost split the thick wood. If that stupid girl opened her mouth he was going to be in trouble. She'd loved what they did together at the beginning and vowed she would never tell another soul, but the little bitch was getting greedy, always demanding more and more from him. She was always at him, wanting him to give it to her. Not that he minded that, but she'd been dropping some worrying hints recently ... asking what he felt about being together for always and putting her hands on her stomach suggestively. He'd tried to buy her off with presents, giving her a silver locket she'd coveted in the window of a jeweller in Ely, and some chocolates, but the previous night, when they'd met outside her father's pub, she'd whispered something in his ear that terrified him.

'I'm having your baby,' she'd said. 'My da will go off his head when he finds out – so you'd best think on what we're going to do.'

She'd broken from him then before he'd had a chance to question her and had run across the road to her father's pub. He would have followed her but the door opened and a group of men came out, laughing and calling to her. Derek had held back because he didn't want anyone to know he'd been seeing her.

Josh Bracknell was a big, strong man with a fearful temper and Carla was only just eighteen – seventeen when Derek had first had her. If she was telling the truth, Josh was going to knock his head off – worse than that, he might be forced to marry the girl.

In a way that wouldn't be so bad, because her father owned the Golden Hen pub in Witchford and that must be worth a bob or two, but Carla was greedy and demanding and he'd already begun to tire of her. Besides, he wasn't ready to marry yet. He wanted to travel a bit. His small-holding brought him in a decent living for a single man and his brother-in-law paid him a few bob for helping out at his farm, though Stella thought he did it for free. He'd had his eye on a nice motorbike, green it was with big shiny wheels. That would be a thing of the past if he were forced to marry the girl – and if her father turned ugly and refused to give them anything he'd be stuck with a wife and kids and nothing to show for it.

There were a lot of pretty girls. Derek's expression lightened as he thought of the girl he'd met coming from the village a couple of weeks earlier. Her clothes looked so odd that for a moment he'd thought it was Emily and his heartbeat had gathered pace as he anticipated seeing her. His niece avoided him whenever she could and he knew she was seeing someone, which made him angry. When he'd realised the girl was the youngest of Lord Barton's daughters, he'd been amused. She was pretty and though he didn't find her as

116

sensual as Emily, he'd been conscious of his dick stiffening in his breeches. Yes, there were a lot of pretty girls about and he wasn't about to get caught by that scheming bitch Carla.

Swearing, Derek hammered the last of the thick wooden stakes into place and then turned in time to see Emily enter the dairy. The thought of his niece made him harden instantly. God, how he would like to stick it into her! He'd only taken up with Carla because the thought of Emily haunted him day and night. Stella would have him boiled alive if he touched her daughter, but he couldn't help the way he felt.

He was torn between remorse for having feelings for his niece, because obviously he couldn't have carnal knowledge of his own sister's daughter, anger because of the scorn in Emily's eyes as she looked at him – and regret that she was such a close relative. If Emily had not been forbidden to him, Derek knew he would have tried to court her – he might even have married her. There was something about Emily Carter that turned his guts to water, making him ache with need. It might have been her dark eyes, which sparkled with laughter or the thick luxuriant hair that tumbled over her shoulders when she let it hang loose. He thought his feelings for Emily came closer to love than anything he'd ever felt for anyone else and it tore him apart, knowing that he would never be able to have her.

He moaned with need, closing his eyes as he thought of having her in his bed all night, of being able to turn over and touch her – have her every time he wanted her. Once a night would never be enough. He thought he could be at it all night with her.

'Damn and blast...' Clenching his hands at his sides, Derek forced his tormented thoughts to the back of his mind, as he finished his work for the morning. Time for a break and a cup of tea in his sister's kitchen. He'd better stop lusting after a woman he could never have and think about what he was going to do about Carla.

He didn't want to marry her. She would just be a millstone round his neck, tying him down. Surely she was lying? Girls didn't get pregnant every time they did it and he'd only been with Carla a dozen times or so, because she couldn't always sneak out to meet him. He'd done it with tarts in Ely on scores of occasions and none of them had claimed to be pregnant, though he'd once caught a dose of the clap. That had been damned painful and the treatment even worse; it had cured him of going with tarts, which was why he'd snapped up the chance to take Carla down. She'd been a virgin but ripe and ready for the taking.

'Stupid bitch,' he muttered as he approached the dairy and glanced in. Emily had taken off her coat because she was warm churning the butter and her washed-out green dress strained against her breasts, outlining the nipples. He was so hard he could burst his breeches. Against his better judgement, he went into the dairy, swallowing the saliva in his throat as it tightened with lust. 'Butter taking its time to come? Want a hand there, Emily love?'

'No thanks, I can manage,' she said, her eyes

sharp and suspicious.

'No call to be like that,' he said. 'I was only asking.'

She set her mouth and didn't answer.

Derek felt the anger surface. She was proud but so beautiful and so desirable. She didn't flaunt herself like Carla but the sex appeal just oozed out of her – even in those dreadful old clothes she was forced to wear. Her lovely dark hair smelled like flowers and her skin was as soft as velvet. If Emily were his he would dress her in silks and satins. God, how he wished he could have her for his own!

'Suit yourself. I was just being friendly.'

Turning, he left her at work and headed for the kitchen, where his sister would have the kettle on the boil and fresh cakes waiting on the table. Derek was twelve years younger than Stella and he'd always looked up to her, which was why he would never dare to step too far out of line with Emily. If Stella guessed what was in his mind she'd throw him out and never speak to him again.

Derek's temper wasn't improved when he went up to the house only to discover Harry Standen already there, sitting with his feet under the table and drinking tea.

He scowled into his mug of strong tea as he listened to the lively chatter around the large pine table with its eclectic mix of odd chairs, some oak, some elm, others pine like the table. It was like the rest of the stuff in this house, old rubbish Joe Carter bought cheap; the things other people threw away. As if the old skinflint couldn't afford to buy Stella a decent modern set the way other men did! Derek knew he'd got a few bob put away even if Stella didn't.

Rage was boiling up inside him and it was all he could do to keep it inside. What was Harry Standen doing here, poking his nose in where it wasn't wanted? Damn the man! Just because he owned one of the largest holdings in the district, apart from Sir Arthur Jones's estate, so he thought he could lord it over the rest of them. Now he was after Emily and the jealousy inside him was so bitter that Derek could taste it on his tongue. He wanted to take the rotter by the throat and squeeze until he choked to death.

'Something wrong with your tea?' Stella asked. 'I made that seed cake special for you, Derek, and you've hardly touched it.'

It would choke him to get a morsel down, Derek thought. He was holding his temper by a thread but he couldn't raise an objection to the idea of Emily going to a dance with Harry Standen. Stella was smiling and looking pleased. She'd got her best blue and white cups down from the dresser for the occasion and that showed what was in her mind. She was already making plans for her daughter's wedding, down to the hat and shoes she would wear.

'Well, I mustn't take up any more of your time,' Harry said and stood up. 'That cake was delicious, Mrs Carter – the best I've tasted in an age. Don't tell my mother I said so, but her cakes are not a patch on yours.'

'Emily is just as good a cook as me,' Stella said,

giving her daughter a coy look as she came in from the dairy. 'I've taught her all she needs to know about cooking – and looking after a house. She's a bright girl our Emily.'

'Ma don't,' Emily begged and blushed. 'I'll see you out, Harry.'

'I shall call for you on Saturday, Emily. I enjoyed myself so much last time we went dancing. Don't forget to tell your father I'll send over that harrow I promised him tomorrow.'

'You want to watch that one,' Derek said darkly as the door closed behind Standen and Emily came back to the table.

'Well, Emily,' her mother said as she started to clear the table. 'He must be keen, because that's the second time he's asked you out since Christmas. Dancing again, is it? You are a sly cat! When should we expect the wedding?'

'Nothing like that is going on,' Emily denied, her cheeks warm. 'Mr Standen is always friendly when he calls in to see Pa, and yes, he's asked me out again – but he's never said anything about us getting married...'

'He doesn't need to say. You can see what he thinks by the way he looks at you. He likes you, Emily. Play your cards right and you could end up being Mrs Harry Standen.'

'I wouldn't count my chickens,' Derek said harshly. 'A man like that has his choice of all the girls. You be careful, Emily. Just keep your legs crossed and you'll be all right.'

'Derek! Don't be so crude,' his sister rebuked. 'She knows better than to allow any man liberties. Besides, I think Harry Standen has marriage on his mind. Well, well, I never expected a chance like this, Emily.'

'I'm off.' Derek scraped back his chair. He couldn't listen to this. If he stayed another minute he would wipe the satisfied smile off his sister's face. How dare she push Emily at that bastard Standen when Derek was sick with love for her? Getting up, he left, slamming the kitchen door behind him.

Emily was a fool if she settled for that bastard. Derek knew he could never have her but the thought of her with another man turned his guts to water.

Derek waited across the road from the Golden Hen. The pub was busy that evening, noise and laughter spilling out as the door opened and a group of farm workers went in. It was bitter out here, his breath making little clouds on the frosty air. Carla was taking her time about coming out to him and he was frozen. He ground his teeth in frustration, because he didn't want to be here standing in the dark with his balls nearly frozen off. It had been dripping wet earlier but now the paths were getting slippery and the trees were coated with tiny icicles. What the hell was he doing here? He would much rather be at home in his own kitchen in the warm. Why he'd ever got involved with the greedy little bitch he didn't know. He must have been drunk or out of his mind. Seeing Carla slip out of the side door, glance back and then run across to join him in the shadows, he felt no sense of satisfaction or pleasure. He was bored with her. The prospect of taking her down had lost its appeal and he was damned if he was going to be stuck with her for the rest of his life.

'You took your time.'

'Pa was in and out of the bar all night. He kept asking me to fetch things for him and I couldn't get away. I had to pretend I had a headache and then he told me to go to bed. He'd kill me if he knew I'd come out to see you.'

'Why bother then?' Derek's manner was rough but he was past caring. 'It was a bit of fun for a while but it's no fun standing here in the cold. We'll call a halt to it and then your pa needn't know what we've been doing.'

'Don't be like that,' Carla said and pressed herself against him. She smelled of some cheap perfume that made his nostrils sting. Emily always smelled like flowers. Why wasn't she Emily? It was Emily he wanted. 'I love you, Derek. I'm sorry I kept you waiting. You know all I want is to be with you. You love me too – leastwise, you said you did when you wanted me to let you do it.'

'It was all right for a while,' Derek said. 'It's over now. We've had our fun and we'll quit while we can. Besides, I'm going away for a bit...'

'Take me with you,' Carla begged, clinging to him. Her lovely face was pale in the half-light, desperate. 'You can't leave me here alone – my pa will kill me when I start to show. I told you I was having your baby.'

'That's rubbish,' Derek said but looked at her uneasily. 'You can't be pregnant yet. It doesn't happen that quick. We've only done it a few times.'

'I don't know how long it takes but I'm sure I'm having a baby. My courses haven't come. I'm a week late and I feel different.'

'That doesn't mean anything. You've probably just got a chill or something. You'll start tomorrow and everything will be all right.'

'No, it won't if you're not here.' Carla's eyes filled with tears and she rubbed at her cheeks. 'It isn't fair. You promised you loved me. You kept on until I agreed to do it and now ... you don't want me any more. You're a beast, Derek Black – and I shan't let you leave me like this. If you go off without me I'll tell my father. He'll come after you and knock your head off.'

Her expression now had changed, becoming angry and spiteful, her mouth thin with temper and her eyes sharp like a cat's. He thought she looked ugly and wondered why she couldn't look more like Emily.

'If he can find me,' Derek sneered. 'What makes you think I'd want to marry a cheap little tart like you?'

They had walked away from the pub and the houses, towards the field, which was sheltered by a high hedge, and the barn where they'd met to make love in the shelter of the straw bales the farmer stored there. It would be warm inside, away from this bitter night, but they didn't get that far. Carla whirled on him, pulling at his coat lapels in a frenzy. She was crying and hitting at him, spittle on her mouth as she accused him of never caring for her.

'You're hateful and I'm going to make sure you suffer now,' she said and she suddenly ripped the front of her dress. 'I'm going back to the house and I'll tell my father that you raped me. He'll come straight after you and he'll kill you. You won't have a chance to get away.'

Derek was certain she was right. He stared at her for a moment and then grabbed her by the throat. 'You little bitch. You just keep your mouth shut, do you hear me? Breathe one word of this to your father and I'll make you sorry you were ever born.'

Derek had lost his temper. He was no longer thinking clearly. She was the cause of all his troubles and if the little slut thought he was going to be blackmailed into marrying her, she had another thing coming.

Her fingers were clawing at his hand as he held her by the throat, her nails scraping the skin. She was gasping something, her face turning red and then purple. He shook her once by the neck, lifting her off her feet, and then let go. She fell to the ground like a stone and just lay there not moving, her long hair spread out on the ground. For a few seconds Derek stared down at her in disbelief.

'Get up you silly cow. Keep your mouth shut and I shan't hurt you. I was just teaching you a bit of a lesson. Get up now...'

Carla didn't move. Derek caught his breath and dropped to one knee, bending over her. He turned her and her head lolled to one side. Her neck was broken. Derek didn't know his own strength. He glanced at his large hands, as if he hadn't known what they were capable of. He'd killed her. He hadn't meant to do more than give her a scare, but she was dead. He was a murderer.

Derek could feel the cold sweat trickling down

his spine. What was he going to do? Standing up, he looked about him. Had anyone seen him waiting for her? Had they been noticed as they walked to the field?

It was a cold night, too cold for folk to be standing about. He'd only seen those farm workers go into the pub and they hadn't noticed him in the shadows across the road. Maybe he could get away with it – if he ran now. No, he mustn't panic. If he was seen running people might put two and two together when her body was discovered. He must walk. He must go home and stay there – pretend that he'd been there all night if anyone were to ask him.

Who would ask? No one knew he'd been seeing Carla. She'd kept it secret because her father would have thrashed her if he'd known. All Derek had to do was to keep his nerve. Just go home and carry on as usual. After a few weeks he'd sell up and leave the area. He'd been thinking that it would suit him, to travel for a while – and he couldn't live here now. It would haunt him, what he'd done ... murdered a girl...

No, it wasn't murder; it was an accident. Derek fought the panic that was rising inside him. He hadn't meant to hurt her, not really. He didn't know his own strength. It was her fault for struggling like that ... if she hadn't pulled away from him it wouldn't have happened.

Derek had been walking for a few minutes. He was away from the site of his wicked deeds and now he couldn't stop the panic. He began to run as fast as he could, across fields, scrambling over stiles and gates, avoiding the roads. The clouds had rolled across the sky and it was pitch black. From time to time he stumbled and once he fell face down, grazing his cheek, but he got up at once and kept on running, heading for home. He ran and ran and ran until his chest burned and he had to stop. Then he began to think. No one was going to suspect him. Why should they?

If he held his nerve he would be in the clear. He began to walk more slowly across the fields, and then he smiled. He'd shown that little bitch who was the master – and now he was free.

Derek spent the night hanging on to his nerves by his fingernails. He kept thinking the police would come and arrest him, but when morning came and still no one arrived, he began to relax. He worked on his farm, as always, speaking naturally to his neighbours and behaving as if nothing had happened.

No one could know he'd been seeing Carla, because she'd been too frightened of her father to tell anyone.

As the day wore on he began to feel safe. By evening he was sure he was going to get away with it and he laughed inwardly. He'd shown that little bitch! He was too clever to get caught and he decided that he wouldn't run away, because that might look suspicious. If the police had any idea he'd been meeting Carla they would have been here by now.

He decided to walk to his sister's home and see if Emily had come back from her night out with Harry Standen yet. If she were in her bedroom, he would stand in the yard and watch her undress.

Emily always drew her curtains at night but the material was thin and if she had the light on he could see the shape of her body ... he licked his lips at the thought and smiled.

He saw them standing outside the kitchen door smiling at each other. Derek couldn't get close enough to hear what they were saying without risking being seen and he didn't want anyone to know he was there. As he lurked in the shadows he saw Standen reach out and draw her close; their kiss was deep and intimate and it sent Derek wild with jealous rage. His hands balled at his sides and it was all he could do to stop himself going after Standen right then – but he had to wait until Emily went inside.

After she closed the door behind her, Standen stood outside grinning. Derek gritted his teeth. He would soon wipe the smile from that bugger's face. He followed silently as Standen went off whistling.

Lost in his own thoughts, Derek's victim didn't realise that there was someone behind him until Derek jumped on him. In the dark Standen couldn't see who was attacking him and he got little chance to fight back, because Derek struck him a blow on the side of the head with a brick he'd picked up. As Standen lay on the ground half conscious, Derek went in with the boot as hard as he could.

Derek was panting when he stopped kicking his victim. He'd lost his temper when he saw the damned scoundrel kissing Emily. If she'd pushed him away or smacked the rogue round the face

Derek might not have been so angry, but to see her giving the rotten bugger what she had denied him made his guts boil with rage.

She was his! If he couldn't have her he wasn't going to let someone like this idiot spoil her innocence. Was she daft enough to think he would marry her – a man like Harry Standen? With all his money he could have anyone. He would take Emily down and then desert her – the way Derek had Carla.

The memory of what he'd done to Carla sent a chill down his spine. So far he was in the clear but for how long? He certainly couldn't bring himself to visit the Golden Hen and hear the talk about Carla. Because he'd seen hardly anyone all day, he wasn't sure if her body had been discovered, though he was sure it must have been. He'd left her lying where she fell and someone was sure to find her pretty quickly.

Derek's throat went dry. He ran his tongue over his lips. In his fury at seeing Harry Standen kissing Emily he had forgotten he'd already committed one murder. Had his temper led him to kill again? He was about to bend down and examine his victim when he heard a groan. Harry Standen was still alive, though he would be black and blue from his bruises in the morning. Served him right for trying to turn Emily's head. Well, Derek certainly wasn't going to hang around and ask if he could get home on his own.

Setting off at a good pace across the fields, Derek felt pleased with himself. He'd shown that little bitch what he thought of her and now he'd given Standen a good hiding. The fool didn't have a clue as to who or what had attacked him. It was like taking sweets from a baby. No one was going to come after him. He could do what he liked...

His feeling of invincibility began to grow in his mind as he strode through the darkness and he laughed. He was too clever for the law, too clever for Standen – and if he got a chance he'd show that stuck-up little miss where she stood too.

Emily wasn't the innocent he'd thought her. To think he'd felt ashamed of what he'd thought about her that day in the dairy. She was just like all the other cheap tarts, gagging for it with the first man to notice her.

A smile touched his mouth. He wasn't going to stay around here much longer so he didn't give a damn what Stella thought. He'd bide his time until he was ready, but before he left he'd show Emily who was the master...

Chapter 11

The local papers were full of the murder of Carla Bracknell and the story made a few of the nationals too. Emily was so shocked she couldn't believe it had happened. People didn't get murdered in their little village. Pa came home from Ely market the following Thursday shaking his head over the fact that something like that could happen to someone they knew.

'I went to see Josh at the pub. He's devastated,

Em. You remember Carla, don't you? She brought you a glass of lemonade out when I bought that Victorian love seat from her father.'

'Yes, I remember,' Emily said. She felt an icy chill at her nape as she recalled what the girl had said to her when they sat on Pa's wagon outside the pub. 'Do the police know who did it?'

'They're making inquiries. Apparently, Josh thinks it might have been a gypsy. He had a gang of them making trouble in the pub a few nights earlier and he sent them packing – but what he can't understand is why she went outside at that time of night. Also, the police said the gypsies had left the area.'

'Perhaps she went to meet someone – a man?' Emily said. Ought she to tell what she knew? Her conscience nagged at her, because it might help find the killer, but Carla hadn't told her much – just that she had a lover. But if she told her father it might stir up a hornets' nest. Josh would be angry if anyone suggested his daughter might be no better than she ought to be. What good could it do to distress him further when Emily didn't know the name of the man his daughter had been seeing?

Emily turned away to clear some dirty plates into the sink, feeling deeply troubled. Something else was nagging at the back of her mind but she didn't know what it was. If she'd thought she could help the police it was her duty to speak up, but she might just be wasting their time. She decided that she would do better to keep her mouth shut on this occasion, because she didn't really know anything.

131

She listened as her parents talked about the terrible tragedy. Ma was anxious and Pa was upset for his friend. Carla was only just eighteen and Pa was troubled as he looked at Emily.

'It might have been anyone's daughter ... even you, Em.'

A pot was hissing on the stove. Ma made a dash to move it before it boiled over. They all looked at one another uncomfortably, the sense of menace close and frightening for a moment.

'Emily doesn't go out alone at night,' Ma said, breaking the silence at last. 'Harry Standen is a decent bloke. If I didn't trust him I wouldn't let her go...'

'Yes...' Pa nodded but still looked troubled. 'Harry was attacked the other night but he's all right. When I saw him in the market he said it was nothing ... seemed a bit embarrassed over it.'

Emily frowned. Who would want to attack Harry? He was such a friendly, pleasant man. She would have liked to question her father further but the subject was closed.

'You just be careful, Em. Don't you go walking far from home on your own, until the police catch the culprit,' her father warned.

'I shan't,' Emily promised him. She felt shivery all over. Carla had struck her as being a rather silly girl, but she hadn't deserved to be murdered. 'Mrs Smith came for a jug of milk earlier, Pa. She said that Miss Amy Barton was going steady with Sir Arthur Jones. Do you know him?'

'He has been in the shop a couple of times,' Pa said. 'That reminds me. Christopher wants to know if you'll go to the tea dance on Saturday afternoon with him. I told him yes, provided he brings you home on the bus and walks you to the door. Was that all right?'

'Yes, I suppose so,' Emily said, though she felt a little guilty because she'd kissed Harry when he took her to the dance and she thought he expected her to be his girl. Christopher wanted her to go out with him too and she wasn't sure which one of them she liked best. In any case it was much too soon to be thinking of marriage.

What Emily really wanted was to do something different with her life. She wasn't sure what she could do, because she'd left school too soon to get a good certificate and she wasn't trained for anything except helping Ma and Pa. She was good at adding up, subtracting, multiplying and division. If she'd stayed on at school a bit longer she might have found office work taking care of someone's accounts – or she could have worked in a shop. Emily had tried for a position in a high-class dress shop in Ely without telling her mother but they'd turned her down. They were sorry but they were looking for someone with experience, their letter said. How was she to become experienced if no one would give her the chance?

'You be careful, miss,' Ma said. 'Harry Standen is a good catch – if he thinks you're playing around he won't want to know.'

Emily went to the sink to fill the big copper kettle. She wasn't sure how to reply but Pa answered for her.

'Em isn't seventeen until June. It's too soon for her to be thinking of marriage. Harry's all right but he's just a friend – isn't he, Em?'

'Yes,' she said without looking round. 'I like Harry but I like Christopher too. For the moment I just want to have fun.'

'I really enjoyed myself,' Christopher said as they left the hotel on Saturday afternoon. 'Dancing with you was wonderful, Emily. You looked so pretty and your shoes were lovely.'

Emily laughed and hugged his arm. She'd un-picked the dress she'd worn to the Christmas dance with Pa and made the brocade into a plain slim skirt that finished just above her ankles, wearing it with a cream artificial silk blouse that she'd edged with lace from the bolero. She knew it looked much better than the dress and this was only the third time she'd worn her shoes, twice to go dancing with Harry and now with Chris-topher. Because it was a tea dance, most people had danced with their partners the whole time and Christopher had been very careful not to tread on her shoes.

Emily had noticed a couple come in a little after she and Christopher arrived. She'd known Amy Barton and her escort at once but Miss Barton hadn't looked at her. Not that Emily expected her to – why should she?

Miss Barton was smiling at Sir Arthur and he hardly took his eyes off her. Emily had thought how beautiful she looked in a blue wool dress and light cream suede shoes. She had a double row of pearls about her throat but as yet no en-gagement ring on her left hand.

Christopher had ordered both sandwiches and cakes with their tea and, as the food arrived just after Miss Barton and her escort, Emily was soon too busy enjoying herself to notice the other couple. Even when they danced by Christopher's table, Miss Barton did no more than glance their way. She showed no sign of noticing Emily, perhaps because she was wrapped up in what her partner was saying to her.

Emily danced with Christopher several times. She thought it was a lovely way to spend an afternoon and was sorry when it was time to leave.

'We could see the new Keystone Cops film next time I have the afternoon off,' Christopher said as they waited for the bus to take them back to Witchford. 'And fish and chips afterwards, if you like.'

That sounded like fun to Emily, but she told him she would only consider it if he let her pay next time. Christopher protested that he wanted to pay, but in the end he said they would share. That having been negotiated, Emily agreed to meet him in three weeks. He ought to have an afternoon off every week, but Christopher said the shop couldn't afford it and Pa had put him on commission so if he sold more he earned more.

Emily knew her father intended to make him a full partner one day and she was glad. No one else would work as hard as Christopher and she really liked him. In fact, she thought she might like him more than Harry Standen.

For the moment she would continue to see them both – but she didn't want to think about settling down for years.

It was Emily's seventeenth birthday and the sun

was shining outside. She wished she could go for a walk to the village, because there was a bus that went into Ely in half an hour. She would have liked to catch it, but her mother had asked her to churn the butter and that would mean her opportunity would be lost, because the next bus didn't leave until half past three. That meant she would miss out on most of the market stalls, because the stallholders would have cleared their goods and be packing them away by the time she arrived and all the bargains would have gone.

That morning her mother had given her a pair of silk stockings and her father had given her a string of garnet beads that he'd bought some-where and five shillings. She'd waited for him to produce the ring that Uncle Albert had left for her but he'd said nothing of it and she thought he must have forgotten about it. She hadn't liked to remind him, because he'd been in a bit of a mood that morning and gone off straight after his breakfast. He'd looked pale and tired, his shoul-ders bent. Emily hadn't wanted to push her claim, but she did want the pretty ring she'd been left all those years ago. Pa had told her she could have it when she was seventeen, and so it ought to be hers, but she hadn't liked to ask that morn-ing.

Emily sighed, changed into the shoes she used for the yard and went out the back door. She walked across the cobblestones, which were still slippery with cow dung despite Bert washing them down with buckets of water from the well. It was cooler inside the dairy, because there was only one small window and flagstones on the floor. The counter was made of marble; it was always cold and that made it easier to set the butter. Besides, it cleaned easily with a damp cloth and some hot water and carbolic soap.

Everything had to be spotless in the milk parlour. The dairy that bought Pa's milk was becoming more and more difficult to please, because they claimed they had the Ministry on their backs. Farmers were going to have to produce more food and milk to make the country self-sufficient if there was a war. The papers were talking about trouble in Europe. Emily read them avidly whenever she could get hold of one and she knew that the situation was difficult, though she didn't know exactly what was going on. The Russians, Austrians, Germans and French all seemed to be at each other's throats. The headlines spoke of an arms race and the Balkans being like a tinderbox, ready to go up at any moment. The British were talking about treaties and responsibilities and seemed to be hanging out for peace, but the Austrians, Germans, French and Russians were more militant, according to the British press.

Bert was still flushing water over the cobbles, but unless he brushed it away it would not improve their condition. Emily thought of telling him, but she didn't have time to explain it to him slowly. Her mother was waiting for her to churn the butter.

Her father had separated the cream from the milk earlier. He sent a churn of milk away most mornings, sometimes more now. First of all he had to milk all ten cows by himself. Emily sometimes helped with the milking in the evenings, but in the mornings she was busy doing chores for Ma. Once the churn was full, Bert helped Pa load it on the wagon and he took it to the end of the lane, where the dairy's wagon came to pick it up. Some of the milk was sent straight to London on the train, but most was sent to the local dairy for bottling.

Two of Pa's cows were Jerseys and Pa kept their milk separate. He skimmed off the cream for making into butter and sold the rest to folk who came to the milk parlour with their jugs and cans.

'Jenny and Annie's milk is too good to go with the rest,' Pa was fond of saying. 'You remember that, Em. If ever I'm not around you remember to treat them right.'

Emily didn't like it when he said things like that, because he had an odd look about him, as if he thought she might have to take over from him soon. She knew his shop in Ely didn't make as much money as he'd hoped, because most people wanted to buy the more modern furniture, which was much lighter and smaller than the large, ponderous Victorian stuff that people were turning out of their houses. A lot of things now were made of pale woods like satinwood and inlaid with fancy motifs of holly wood and ebony stringing. The newer style of art nouveau was what most people liked these days, but Pa kept on buying whatever came along, because he said it was quality and quality would always sell.

Sometimes he was right and Christopher would manage to sell a piece for good money and then Pa had money to fill Ma's jar and to buy tobacco for himself. When there was money to spare, he gave Emily a few shillings or occasionally a pound for herself. She spent a few pennies each time on things she needed, because Ma never bought her anything now, but she tried to save a little too. Once or twice she'd bought something she liked from Pa's cabinet in the barn, and she'd collected some trinkets Pa said were good.

'You've got an eye for a bargain, Em,' he'd told her. 'You and Christopher will make a go of that shop when I'm gone.'

Emily begged him not to say things like that, because she didn't want him to die. In the winter his cough had been terrible and in the end she'd nagged him until he went to the doctor; it had seemed better for a while, but lately she'd noticed it getting worse again.

It was becoming obvious to Emily that her father liked Christopher far more than Harry Standen. He kept putting in a good word for Christopher, though he acknowledged Harry was a decent enough man, and if she'd wanted him her father would never have denied her, but she wasn't sure she did. Harry hadn't called at the farm so often recently and it was more than a month since he'd asked her out. Ma said she'd warned Emily and thought it was because he'd heard rumours, but Harry had never asked Emily to be his exclusively. He'd enjoyed their kiss at the end of the evening, as she did, but he hadn't tried to go further and he hadn't mentioned going steady.

Emily's thoughts kept her going as she wound the wheel of the butter churn. It was taking for ever today and Ma wanted it so that she could do some baking.

'What are you up to, Em?' The voice from the

doorway brought her out of her thoughts sharply. She frowned as she saw the person she liked least in the world looking in at her. Why did he keep coming here when he knew she didn't like him? He'd always made her feel uncomfortable but of late there was something in the way he looked at her that frightened her. He'd changed somehow and it wasn't for the better.

'You can see what I'm doing,' she said sharply, ignoring him as he entered the dairy.

'Now that's not very nice,' Derek said. 'If you asked me nicely I might give you a hand.'

'Thank you, but I prefer to do it myself.'

'Why don't you like me, Em?' He moved closer to her, standing in her way as she tried to turn the butter onto the cold slabs. She froze, looking at him hard, but he ignored her icy stare and reached out, touching a finger to the V at the opening to her blouse. She'd worn a white cotton blouse because it was a warm day and churning butter was hard work. She'd been sweating and the material was damp, clinging to her breasts. 'You've got lovely tits,' Derek said and reached out to squeeze the nearest to him, his finger rubbing over her nipple. Emily jerked away as if she'd been stung.

'What do you think you're doing?' she cried, furious with him. 'Don't you dare touch me like that! I haven't forgotten the last time...'

He frowned, looking puzzled, then grinned. 'You mean when I gave you a good smacking and then rubbed it better? You were just a little girl then, Em. You're seventeen now and I reckon you know what it's all about. I've seen Harry Standen sniffing round you when he comes here.'

'Harry is just a friend,' Emily said stung to a reply. 'You just wash your filthy mouth out with salt, Derek. If I told Pa...'

'I shouldn't do that if I were you. If I don't give him a hand with getting his corn in it will rot in the fields and then where will you be?'

'You're horrible,' Emily said and glared at him. 'Go away or I'll scream – and I'll tell Ma what you are.'

She saw the reaction in his face. He didn't like that, because Ma was the one person in the world he seemed to care for. She was glad he didn't know that telling her mother was the last thing she would ever do.

'Come on, Em,' he said. 'It was just a bit of fun like. No harm done.'

'Just keep away from me in future or I'll tell what I know.'

'And what do you know?' Derek's eyes narrowed. For a moment she thought she saw fear in his eyes and wondered if she was right in her suspicion that he'd been Carla's lover – and her murderer? – but it was gone in a flash and the cocky expression was back. 'I was just teasing the birthday girl that's all. I've brought you a present – don't you want to know what it is?'

'No, I don't. Just go away and don't ever touch me again.'

Derek gave her a look that was little short of murderous but turned and went out without another word.

Emily was trembling. He'd made her feel sick inside and somehow dirty. She wanted to run to her father and tell him, but of course she couldn't, just as she couldn't tell anyone of her suspicions concerning Carla. Pa needed Derek's help to harvest the wheat – and he wasn't well. If Emily told she would just be making things worse, and her mother would never forgive her.

No, she must keep it all to herself and try to forget what had happened. Somehow she would keep him at a distance in future.

She turned back to the task in hand, using the butter paddles to make little squares of butter, which she placed on the marble slab. There wasn't enough for Pa to sell any when people came for a jug of milk. Her mother would need all this for her baking and for buttering Pa's toast in the morning.

Thinking about her father, she remembered the ring that Uncle Albert had left her that her father was keeping for her. She would remind him that evening when he came in for supper.

'The ring...' Pa looked at her in silence for a moment, and then glanced at Ma. 'I know I promised it to you, Emily, but your mother wanted some things for Jack in the winter and I didn't have any money to give her. I had to sell it. I'm sorry. I'll get you another one when I can to make up for it.'

'It doesn't matter.'

Emily turned away to hide her disappointment. She'd been looking forward to this day for years, hoping the ring would fit when she was eventually allowed to have it. Glancing at Ma, she saw an odd look in her eyes and suddenly knew the truth. Pa hadn't sold the ring; she'd taken it to sell herself – just as she'd sold Grandfather's silver watch and chain. Pa had taken the blame but in her heart she knew he was protecting Ma, as he always did.

She wanted to shout at her mother, to tell her she was a thief and a cheat, and she wanted to tell her what Derek had done in the dairy, but if she said what was in her mind it would just cause more trouble. Emily hadn't forgotten the row between her parents on that awful Christmas morning. Ma had gone off and Emily thought she'd intended to leave but she'd come back for some reason. Since that day Eddie Fisher hadn't called at the cottage once; there was a new tally-man and Ma paid him what she owed every week, even if they went without something else.

Emily knew she couldn't just blurt out her anger or her suspicions. She couldn't say that the only reason Ma had come back was because Eddie Fisher wouldn't have her, because it was rude. She couldn't tell anyone she thought Derek might be a murderer. Instead, she held back her anger, got up and started to clear the table of dirty dishes and wash them in the sink.

She was lucky that Pa had given her the garnets and five shillings. It was probably far more than he could afford.

'I'm going to bed now,' she said when she dried her hands. 'I've got a book to read. Thank you for the presents, Pa – and the stockings, Ma.'

'Derek left you something,' Ma said. 'It's in your room.'

'You didn't let him go up there?'

'Why ever would he want to do that? I put it there myself when I took Jack up to bed.'

Emily nodded and turned away. She would

hate it if Derek had been in her room, touching her things. The thought of what he'd done in the dairy made her skin crawl. She wished there was some way to punish him without hurting others, but she couldn't think of anything she could do that wouldn't distress both Ma and her father.

She went upstairs to her room. A small parcel wrapped in brown paper was lying on the bed. From the size of it she suspected it might be some kind of jewellery but she didn't open it. Even if it were a diamond necklace she still wouldn't want to know. Picking up the parcel, she took it into her parents' room and placed it on the dressing table. Ma could give it back to Derek or keep it herself. Emily would never take anything from that man.

'It looks bad, Em,' Pa said when he came back from Ely the next week. 'There's been an assassination of a Habsburg duke and his morganatic wife.'

'What does morganatic mean?'

'That she is of lower rank than her husband and she will not inherit titles or ducal property.'

'That's not fair,' Emily said and Pa laughed.

'Mebbe not but that's not the point, Em. The paper says it was a plot by the Serbs to bring down the Austrian throne and they say there will be war for certain now. We shall have all the young men joining up before long, you mark my words.'

Emily stared at him anxiously. 'Oh, Pa, that's terrible. How could something out there cause a war for us?'

'It's something to do with treaties so they

144

reckon – but I think they're all spoiling for a fight. It's pride, that's what it is, Em. They're all afraid of losing face or influence.'

'I can't see why anyone would want to fight for something silly like that,' Emily objected, then, 'You haven't forgotten that I'm going to the tea dance in Ely with Christopher this afternoon, have you?'

'No, I hadn't forgotten. I'll take you into the village to catch the bus. I mentioned it was your birthday a few days ago, Em. It just slipped out, so don't be embarrassed if he buys you a late gift.'

'You shouldn't have, Pa. Christopher can't afford to buy me presents.'

'Well, I expect it will just be some sweets or something.' He arched his brows at her. 'He likes you a lot, you know. I thought you two might get together – but you've been out to a dance twice with Harry Standen, to the pictures and a concert too.'

'I like Harry, he's nice,' Emily said. 'Ma says he has prospects and I should try to get him to marry me – but I'm not ready to think about marriage yet.'

'I shouldn't let you if you were,' Pa said and turned away to cough into his handkerchief. This time Emily saw the blood and she grabbed it out of his hand.

'You must go back to the doctor, Pa. You can't go on like this...'

'Well, I have and he's doing some tests. If it's what he thinks, I may have to go away to a sanatorium, Em.'

'Oh Pa,' Emily caught the sob back in her

145

throat, because that sounded bad and she was afraid she knew what it meant. 'You should've gone sooner.'

'It will cost money to go away and I'm not sure I can spare the money.'

'I've got a few pounds and some trinkets you can sell.'

'No, Em. If I have to go, I'll find the money somehow – but it's how you'll manage without me, that's what worries me. Even if I put the arable land down to grass the stock is still too much for you.'

'Bert will help me.'

Pa looked at her and Emily sighed. Bert was almost useless, except for very simple jobs. It took longer to explain what needed doing than it did to do it yourself. Emily could milk, water and feed the stock but the mucking out was hard work. Bert might do it but he could wander off in the middle. She would find it hard to manage – and she wouldn't be able to help Ma much in the house.

'I'll find someone...'

'Derek has offered to help more. I know you don't like him...'

Emily hesitated. She longed to tell her father why she couldn't bear her uncle near her but she had kept the secret too long. Even if Pa believed her, Ma wouldn't. It would result in more rows – and Pa wouldn't have Derek near the place if he knew. If Pa was ill, they just couldn't manage without some help and so Emily had to keep her secret.

'I'll manage somehow.'

'If there's a war all the young men will be off. You won't get anyone of any merit, Em. It's my fault. If I'd been more successful you and Stella wouldn't have had to worry if I died.'

'I don't want you to die,' Emily said and tears caught at her throat. 'Please don't say things like that, Pa. You're going to a sanatorium if you have to, and you'll get better.'

He patted her cheek and nodded. Emily wanted to cry or scream and shout, but she couldn't change things. All she could do was to make things as easy for her father as possible.

A dray cart had just pulled up at the inn that faced the market square in Ely. The horse was sweating after its long haul, steam rising off the gleaming chestnut coat. Someone came out of the inn and offered a bucket of water to the driver, who held it for his horse while his mate unloaded the heavy barrels and reloaded empty ones. The return journey to the brewery at the bottom of the hill would be much easier for the poor beast than the one coming up. It snorted as it dipped its snout in the water, making rude noises as it took a welcome drink.

Emily helped her father unload his treasures in the yard behind the shop, carrying them into a little shed so that he could stack them high. The shed was filled to bursting, tables piled upon chests and oak coffers tucked into odd spaces, even a broken mangle Joe had bought because he felt sorry for the woman who had nothing else to sell. As they were finishing, the back door of the shop opened and Christopher looked out at her.

147

'Is it all done?' he asked. 'I'd have been out to help before but I was busy.'

'Pa said you had a customer,' she said and looked at him hopefully. 'Did you sell anything?'

'Yes, as a matter of fact I sold that silver rose vase your pa bought last week,' Christopher told her, a gleam of satisfaction in his grey eyes. Christopher wasn't as handsome as Harry Standen but he had a nice comfortable face and eyes that lit up from inside. 'It was filthy and the bottom was a bit bent but I managed to straighten it and polished it up – came up a treat it did. I sold it for ten shillings and sixpence.'

'Pa gave five for it,' Emily said. 'That was really good, Christopher. If you could do that every day we'd be all right.'

'I sold an oak stool yesterday for five bob and a kitchen chair the day before for half a crown – but that's all this week.' Christopher looked anxious and flicked back a lock of sandy hair. 'It's not very much. I tried to sell that nice roll-top desk to a farmer this morning. Your father wants six pounds for it, but the customer wouldn't give more than four. I wasn't sure what to do. Mr Robinson isn't an easy man to budge once his mind's made up.'

'Pa paid five pounds for the desk. It might as well sit there for a bit as let it go for less.'

'Don't look like that. Your pa didn't give too much for it. Mr Robinson is a mean old sod. Someone else will pay what it's worth, you'll see.'

'If you say so.'

They both heard the shop bell go. Christopher immediately went back inside and she followed, standing just behind the door that led into the little back room where Christopher made himself a cup of tea on the gas ring when he had time. The room smelled of glue and metal polish and the pine table was covered with an oilskin cloth and littered with bits and pieces he'd been mending. She examined a silver purse that had been dented when her father bought it; Christopher had managed to straighten and polish it and it was nice enough to sell for a few bob now. Tiptoeing to the door, she squinted through the crack near the hinges into the shop, and was shocked to see that the customer was a gentleman.

'Good morning, Sir Arthur,' Christopher said in the respectful tone he used for customers. 'Is there something I can show you?'

'Good morning, Christopher. Your father told me you were working here and I thought I would say hello – but then I saw that desk in the window and I believe it is exactly what my bailiff needs for his office. He has one but we are training an assistant and John must have his own desk. How much is it please?'

'My employer told me to charge six pounds for it, sir – but it came up well with some polishing and I think it's worth a bit more.'

Emily heard a muffled laugh and then the sound of drawers opening and shutting before Sir Arthur spoke again. She dug her nails into the palms of her hands, silently praying that he would purchase the desk. The money would mean so much to Pa. He really needed some good sales because so far the takings would hardly cover the rent and Christopher's wages. If things didn't pick up Pa might not have his shop for much longer.

And he needed to have the treatment for his cough.

'I think I would agree with you, Christopher. You are a good salesman and your employer was lucky to get you. The desk is worth every bit of seven pounds and ten shillings and I should be happy to pay that amount – if you will deliver it to my house?'

'My employer will do that on his cart,' Christopher replied. 'That is extremely fair of you, sir.'

'Excellent. Here you are,' Sir Arthur handed over the money. 'If you ever tire of working here, Christopher, you may apply to me. I'm sure I could find a position for a bright lad like you.'

'My father told me to come to you, sir, but I wanted to prove I could find a job for myself.'

'And I respect that in you, Christopher. However, the offer stands, should you wish for a change of employment.'

Emily entered the shop as the bell rang and the door closed behind their customer. She looked at Christopher with respect.

'Why didn't you want to work for Sir Arthur?'

'It would have meant working with my father. I think the world of him, but ... you know how it is.'

Emily nodded and laughed. She knew exactly how that felt, because although she worshiped her pa they sometimes struck sparks off each other, especially if it was cold and wet and they'd been working hard.

'I can understand that but ... Sir Arthur might have paid you more than Pa can afford.'

'I know but your pa is a fair man. He promised

me a partnership if things go well. I'm willing to work for small wages now if I can be my own boss one day.'

'You're ambitious.'

Emily had known it already. She liked that he wanted to make something of himself, to be better than his father and get on in the world. It was what she wanted too, what she was determined to do somehow. She threw a smile at Christopher and then saw her father was waiting for her by the wagon. She told Christopher she was leaving and went out. Climbing on to the driving box, she noticed that Pa had bought a newspaper and the headlines were dire. It really did look as if there would be a war very soon.

Chapter 12

'Well, I think it is appalling,' Lady Prior said as the family faced each other in the drawing room that evening. She placed her hands, one on each arm of her chair, the diamonds in her rings catching the light. Her hair had been dressed in a coronet of plaits that evening and was fastened by a comb studded with amethysts, her gown of purple silk regal and becoming despite being long out of fashion. 'We haven't had anything like this in the district for years. What kind of a world is it these days when a young girl isn't safe a few yards from her father's inn?'

'What was she doing out at that time of night?'

Lady Barton said. An attractive woman in her youth, she had put on weight over the years and looked pale and ordinary beside her mother. 'Her father should have kept a better watch over her in my opinion.'

'Young girls will slip off to meet their lovers.' Lord Barton poured himself a brandy from the crystal decanter on the sideboard. The oil lamps had been lit and cast a gentle light over the room, some of them with exquisite glass bowls that were fragile and beautiful, relics of their owner's youth. Electricity was not allowed at Priorsfield Manor and was in the family's opinion long overdue. 'She had no mother to teach her how to behave. Bracknell has been a widower for years. At least my daughters have more sense than to go wandering off to meet strange men late at night.'

'I hope my granddaughters have more self respect than to behave in such a loose fashion,' Lady Prior said. 'These common gels have no idea of what is proper.'

'That is a bit unfair,' Jonathan said. 'There are plenty of young women who come from ordinary families who wouldn't dream of slipping out to meet a stranger behind their father's back.'

'Do you think he was a stranger to her?' Amy frowned. 'Arthur was called in on the case you know, because he is a JP and he has to be informed of anything of the kind in his jurisdiction. It was his opinion that the girl knew her attacker. Her dress was torn but bruising occurred only about her throat. If she'd been attacked and put up a fight she would have been more badly bruised.'

'Please don't,' Lizzie cried. 'It is such a horrid

thing to happen – and just a few miles from us.'

'You are perfectly safe here,' Lady Prior told her and patted her hand. 'No one would dare to attack you on my land.'

'Lizzie will not be allowed to go for walks on her own until this rogue is caught,' Lord Barton said. 'She ought to be safe on our land but I would not guarantee it at the moment. No more long walks until this business is settled, Lizzie.'

'I would be afraid to go far with a murderer about,' Lizzie said shuddering. Her dress of pale lilac lace over silk complemented her grandmother's ensemble and suited her English rose complexion. 'Amy shouldn't either.'

'Arthur has already made me promise not to ride out without a groom unless he can accompany me,' Amy assured them. 'Don't be too upset, Lizzie. You would never dream of meeting the kind of man that would do this so you are perfectly safe. Besides, Arthur thinks he will be long gone; it was obviously someone just passing through.'

'Not necessarily if she knew him,' Lady Prior said. 'Now that is quite enough of all this. I think we should talk about your dance, Amy. I have decided to give it to you, as a part of my wedding gift so there is no need for your father to commit himself to finding the money. How many guests would you wish to entertain, my dear? I was thinking of around two hundred – is that enough for you?'

'Two hundred guests would be splendid,' Amy said, her face lighting up with pleasure. 'It is very generous of you, Grandmama.'

'Granny, if you don't mind. Nicolas and Lizzie call me Granny. I much prefer it.' Lady Prior's eyes darted to her eldest grandson. 'Jonathan, would you mind waiting on me in the morning? I shall receive you in my dressing room at eleven if you please.'

Jonathan had been in the act of pouring a brandy and looked startled. 'Have I done something wrong?'

'Have you?' Lady Prior arched her sparse brows. 'If you have I have no notion of it – but I do not wish to talk business this evening. We shall speak tomorrow if it suits you.'

'Well, I had arranged to inspect the rebuilding of Morgan's cottage wall but I can change that to another time. Although...' he hesitated, then, 'yes, of course. Whatever you wish.'

'Very well. I think I shall retire now. Nicolas, will you lend me your arm please? I find I am tired and may need a little help up the stairs.'

'Of course.' Nicolas had sat observing the others but taking no part in the conversation. He stood at once and went to offer his grandmother his arm as support. 'You should have asked sooner if you were tired.'

'No, no, I shall spend more than enough time in bed once I'm unable to get about. I like to sit with my family at night, though I cannot keep late hours.'

'I shall go up now,' Lizzie said and rose. She kissed her mother's cheek and smiled at her father. 'Goodnight, Papa. Don't worry. I shan't do anything stupid.'

'I have every confidence in you, my love. Sleep

tight and don't worry about this unpleasant business.'

'Goodnight, Amy – unless you're coming up?'

'I'll pop in and say goodnight soon,' Amy said. 'I want to talk to Father for a while.'

Lizzie nodded, following her grandmother from the room. She waited patiently for Nicolas to help the elderly lady up to the landing, then ran up the stairs and caught them at the top.

'Goodnight, Granny. You're not unwell, are you?'

'Not at all, my love. Run along now. I want a few words with Nicolas.'

Lizzie kissed her cheek. 'Goodnight then.'

She went past them and down the hall. What did her grandmother have on her mind? Had she decided to put Jonathan out of his misery at last? Nicolas had no expectations at all and was uninterested in the question most of the family found of such burning importance. However, Lizzie knew her grandmother's feelings too well to believe that she would not leave Nicolas some part of her estate.

Going into her room, Lizzie sighed as she sank down on the comfortable bed and released her hair from its ribbons. The style was a little too young for her but she had no maid of her own and was forced to do her own hair if Mrs Marsh was busy with her mother and Amy. Tying it back with a ribbon was the easiest way to keep her thick, ashen locks tidy for they had a natural spring and would not stay confined for long in any other way.

As she undressed she wondered vaguely what Amy wanted to say to their father that was so important it needed to be said that night.

'A maid of your own?' Lord Barton frowned at his daughter. 'You've always managed with Mary or Mrs Marsh before. Doesn't one of the parlour maids help you now and then?'

'Yes, Mary sometimes comes to help with my gown or dress my hair. Her work is adequate for when we dine alone at home, Papa, but I am going to be dining out more in the future. Mary has other duties. I need another maid. Besides, Mrs Marsh doesn't always have time for me *and* Mother.'

'It would take some time to find a trained lady's maid these days – and she would be expensive. Perhaps we could get another girl in to help with Mary's work and Mrs Marsh could give her some extra training in dressing your hair.'

Her father sipped his brandy, twirling it so that the rich liquid clung to the glass as it warmed in his hands and gave off a wonderful aroma. The glass was heavily cut and matched the others on the large silver tray. Despite the old-fashioned furniture, the room was comfortable, its colours of crimson, gold and blue rich rather than faded, the drapes having been renewed only five years previously. A jade chess set stood ready on a table made for the purpose and small pieces of silver, figurines and porcelain bowls cluttered every available surface.

'That would be sufficient for the moment. I shall of course have my own maid when I'm married. Arthur will insist on her being properly trained.'

'He will also pay her salary, Amy. You know very well I'm pushed to the limit now – and I refuse to ask your grandmother to pay for a dresser for you.'

'Then I suppose I shall just have to accept extra help from Mary.' Amy looked disappointed. 'I shall ask Arthur to advertise for a suitable girl.'

'We could do with another girl to help in the kitchen and perhaps do some of Mary's work,' Lady Barton said. 'Mrs Marsh has been asking for some help for Cook for a while now. I'll tell her to look for someone who won't mind what she does. June could move up to parlour maid, and the new girl will do the rough work.'

'If that is your wish,' Lord Barton said. 'You had best speak to your mother about her wages.'

'Mama always pays for the kitchen staff,' his wife said. 'It is the reason I suggested it happen that way. She might not be as happy to pay for Amy to have her own dresser.'

'I am certain she wouldn't. I must admit I was surprised when she came up with the idea of a ball for Amy.'

'It is as much for Lizzie's sake as mine,' Amy said and fiddled with her ring. 'Lizzie might have had a season in view this year, had things been different.'

'Lizzie can wait a bit longer. Perhaps next year, if things go well for me.'

'She told me Grandmama has hinted that she will pay for her to have her season next year. It wouldn't be a good idea at the moment because of my wedding. Besides, she may be eighteen but she is too young in her ways – look at the ribbons

157

she wore this evening. Lizzie should be putting her hair up now.'

'Yes, well, if that is all you wanted, you may as well go up now. I have some work to do in my library.'

Amy said goodnight, left her parents and went upstairs to her sister's room. Lizzie had already undressed and was perched up against a pile of lace-edged pillows reading her book. She put it down and smiled as Amy sat on the edge of the bed.

'So, Granny is giving you a grand dance for your wedding,' Lizzie said. 'Are you excited?'

'Yes, I am. I think it will be lovely to see the manor polished and shining and dressed for a ball. Perhaps we could persuade Grandmama to put some of the clutter away for a while. We shall have to think of a theme, Lizzie. If we bought some material we could make garlands ourselves. Would you enjoy that? And of course you will need a new gown. We shall be so busy planning it all and writing invitations.'

'You don't have to think of things to do just to make me feel better. I'm not a child. Aren't you just a little frightened about what happened?'

'I'm more angry than scared,' Amy said. 'I like to ride out alone – unless you come with me. Do you remember when as children at the old house we used to race the milk train on our ponies, where it passed the edge of our land near the river?'

Lizzie nodded. She plucked at the bedcover, which was green like the curtains at her windows. Unlike most of the house, her room had been refurbished recently and she'd been allowed to choose her own colours. 'Do you miss it – the old house and all the rest of it?'

'Papa is the one I feel for. The estate was in his family for six generations. To be forced to sell and come here must have been a blow to his pride.'

'We were lucky Granny invited us. Had she not given us a home we might have had to live in a much smaller house.'

'Father could have sold the London house rather than letting it out to strangers. He could have bought a smaller estate in the country.'

'It wouldn't have been like Barton Abbey, nor would it have been as large as Priorsfield Manor.'

Amy had noticed her father prowling after dinner, filling his brandy glass perhaps more often than was good for him. Perhaps it was because of losing his estate, but she'd become more aware of his unhappiness – the silent look of resentment towards his wife, and sometimes an expression of resignation. Amy was disturbed by it and knew that she did not want to end her life feeling cheated as he did.

Amy picked up a blue glass scent bottle from the dressing table and opened the silver top, sniffing it before replacing it amongst the clutter of bottles and powder jars, bits of ribbons and other trinkets littering the polished top. The perfume was flowery and young, not to Amy's taste. Lizzie was almost as bad at collecting things as her grandmother. Amy found the mess offensive; she preferred everything to match and asked Mary, the maid who looked after her occasionally, to keep things tidy.

'Perhaps you are right. Personally, I can't wait

for my wedding.'

She smiled at Lizzie and went out, leaving her to sleep.

Lizzie sat looking at the door as it closed after her.

Tears welled up inside her and a few trickled down her cheeks. She wiped them away with her hand and told herself not to be stupid. Of course Arthur would never have looked at her. She was too young. He was older and he wanted someone more sophisticated. Amy was perfect for him.

Lizzie must learn not to mind. Her feelings would mend in time. She would meet someone nice when she had her season and forget she'd ever had a crush on her sister's fiancé. It was merely a crush and this feeling that she would never love anyone else was ridiculous.

Lizzie thought about the girl that had been murdered. She was so young and she hadn't had a chance to live and be happy. Lizzie wouldn't dwell on her unhappiness. It would be dreadful if Amy guessed how she was feeling and it spoiled her wedding.

Reaching out, she turned her lamp down but not out. Lizzie didn't much like the dark. She preferred a little light in the room if she woke in the night.

Chapter 13

'They're advertising in the local paper for help up at the manor,' Ma said when Emily came down for supper that night. 'You're dressed up. You're not going out again, are you?'

'No, but Harry Standen told Pa he might call to see me this evening.'

Her mother nodded, looking thoughtful. 'You know your father's ill? He needs to go away for treatment but the foolish man says he's too busy. If you found yourself a job he could take on a man full time and then he could go to the sanatorium.'

Emily was so shocked she couldn't speak for a moment. She'd dreamed of perhaps having a job in the future, but she'd never thought her mother would allow it. Ma had always said she couldn't manage without her – now she was suggesting she take a job at the manor. The idea horrified Emily.

'Go out to work somewhere else?'

'It would be good for you, a nice little job like that up at the manor.'

'Me work at the manor as a skivvy? Why should I want to do that? I'd rather find work in a shop in Ely. Besides, you need me here and I help Pa on his rounds sometimes.'

'You mean you like being at home.' Ma glared at her and folded the paper. She got up to take a tray of rock cakes from the oven and the smell of them made Emily feel hungry. 'Your father is a fool to

161

himself. I've told him he should get a man to help him full time but he says he can't afford the wages. If you were bringing in a wage he could manage to pay a lad to do most of the work. We can't always expect Derek to help out for nothing.'

It was on the tip of Emily's tongue to tell her mother that Derek was paid for his help but she kept silent. 'Is that what Pa wants? Me to go out to work?'

'He wouldn't dream of asking it of you. I've told him he must go to the doctor and ask what he needs to do. He says he will but he hasn't been – and I don't like to see him so tired. I know he's thinking of how much it might cost for medicines and treatment. Think about taking this job, Emily – for your father's sake.'

Emily felt pressured. Her mother was black-mailing her, using her father's illness to make her feel guilty, trying to force her to take a job she would hate. She sought for an excuse.

'What about Harry? If I worked at the manor I couldn't see him often.'

'Is that more important than your father's health? There's no saying you would get the job if you tried, but it would be a help if you were bringing in some money.'

Ma's face was hard, looking older than her thirty-nine years, with her dark reddish-brown hair swept back from her face and turned under in a roll that went right round her head. It was fastened by hairpins and tidy but far too severe. Like her washed-out blue dress, it did nothing for her appearance. She could have made more of her looks but she'd stopped bothering since she'd promised Pa it was over with Eddie Fisher.

'You spend half your time with your head in a book anyway.'

Emily felt her mother's criticism unjust but didn't deny it. She enjoyed reading, especially since Christopher had found her some novels by Emily and Charlotte Brontë, and was at the moment halfway through *Wuthering Heights* with the promise of *Jane Eyre* to come. Despite her love of reading she never neglected her chores and her mother's accusations made her smart with indignation.

Just as she was about to answer back, her father came in. He looked tired, his face pale and drained. Emily's heart caught and she realised that her mother was right. If she was earning money, Pa might be able to afford to take on a labourer so that he could take the time he needed to get well.

'I shall want you in the morning,' he said to Emily. 'Be up early and don't slip off anywhere.'

'Of course I shan't,' she said. 'I think I heard Harry Standen's car. He might take me for a little drive somewhere. Is that all right?'

'Just behave yourself,' Ma said. 'I don't want you getting into trouble and bringing shame on us.'

'Em wouldn't do that,' Pa said. 'Besides, Harry is a decent bloke.'

Emily darted at him and kissed his cheek, whispering in his ear that she would be good. He grinned and gave her a little push. She went outside to Harry's little car. He was just getting out to come and call for her and smiled as he saw she'd saved him the trouble.

'I thought we might drive down by the river

163

and have a drink at a hotel there.'

It was like Harry to think of something special. He was kind and considerate and she went to put her arms around him and give him a hug. Harry hugged her in return, and then kissed her cheek.

'You're a nice girl, Emily,' he said. 'I've got something to tell you later...'

Emily felt her stomach spasm. He wasn't going to ask her to marry him – was he? She looked up at his face and thought his expression was a bit strange, almost guilty, but then he was smiling and she thought she'd imagined it.

Half an hour later, sitting in the quiet lounge of the small riverside hotel, Harry told her what was on his mind. He'd bought her orange juice and a beer for himself. He fidgeted with his glass for a moment before clearing his throat.

'I hope you won't hate me, Emily...'

'Why should I hate you?'

Harry cleared his throat again. 'I really like you, you know I do – but ... there's this girl called Christine. We used to go out and then she broke it off just before the dance last Christmas. I was a bit cut up over it that night and you were such a pretty, decent girl. I liked you and I asked you out but ... two months ago I met Christine again at a young farmers' meeting and well ... she told me she still loved me.' He took a deep drink of his beer. 'We ... we started kissing and one thing led to another. I did things I shouldn't have done. After-wards, I told her I was seeing you and I needed time to think ... but she came to see me this morn-ing. She's having my baby, Emily. I have to marry her. I don't have a choice.'

Emily was stunned. She didn't know whether she was more shocked because he'd got a girl into trouble or that he'd carried on seeing her, Emily, knowing what he'd done. Harry was right about one thing. He didn't have a choice. Her family would demand that he marry the girl and it was only right that he should.

'No, you don't,' she said, feeling let down and disappointed. The idea of becoming the wife of a successful farmer had taken root in her mind and she had thought it would be nice. She liked Harry, enjoyed his kisses and being taken out in his car, but she wouldn't marry him now even if he asked. Not after what he'd done.

'I'm sorry, Emily. I didn't know any other way to tell you.'

Emily took a sip of her orange juice. At least he had told her. He'd brought her here and let her down as easily as he could, but it didn't alter what he'd done. She wasn't sure how she felt. It was a blow to her pride, but had he broken her heart? Emily didn't think so, though she knew Ma would go on about it when she told her – and Pa would feel Harry had let her down.

'Well, maybe it's for the best. I'm probably going into service so I shouldn't have much free time to see you.'

Harry looked relieved. Perhaps he'd expected her to make a fuss or get angry, but she couldn't be bothered. She'd enjoyed his company and she felt let down, but she wasn't going to break her heart over him. After all, she'd been seeing Christopher sometimes, as a friend ... but Harry had seemed serious for a while. Finishing her drink, she stood up.

'Let's go. I wouldn't want your fiancée to think you were cheating on her with me.'

Harry looked red in the face but didn't speak. He hadn't finished his beer but he left his glass and followed Emily outside. Neither of them spoke on the way home.

Harry pulled the car to a halt outside her house. He got out and opened the door for her, looking at her in such a miserable way that her anger evaporated.

'It's all right, I shan't die of a broken heart,' she said, kissed his cheek and ran into the house.

'So Harry Standen's marrying someone else,' Ma said when Emily got back from helping her pa the next morning. 'You might have told me, Emily. I warned you what might happen if you went out with that Christopher as well as him.'

'It wasn't important.'

'Harry Standen was a catch, my girl, and don't forget it. He'd have given you a good home and a secure future – do you want to end up like me?'

Emily turned away without answering. Ma wouldn't understand that though she'd liked Harry she didn't mind that he was going to marry his former girlfriend. Nor would Ma understand that she felt comfortable with Christopher, because she wasn't ready to marry anyone just yet.

'I'm going out to see if there are any eggs,' she said and took her coat down from the peg behind the door.

Having shrugged on her coat and boots, she

picked up a large rush basket and went out into the yard. The weather had turned really hot of late. Emily thought that might be the reason the hens were not laying as much as usual. She checked the hen houses but found nothing, then walked into the paddock and started to make her way round the large field, bending down to look under the hedges. She found three eggs but was about to give up when she saw a patch of violets and knelt down to pick them with a cry of pleasure. They were always such a joy at this time of year and she picked some, holding them to her nose, to inhale the fresh perfume. They made her smile, because little things like this made her feel good to be alive.

'A penny for them,' the voice she least wished to hear was so close behind her that she jumped. 'Dreaming of your lover I suppose?'

Emily looked at her uncle as she rose to her feet. Something in his face made her shiver, her blood running suddenly cold. She glanced round, realising that they were out of sight of the house behind the high hedge. Her mouth felt dry and her stomach tightened with nerves. Why was he looking at her like that? His expression was so strange, so menacing that it frightened her.

'I don't have a lover,' she said icily. 'I was just enjoying the violets and the mild weather.'

'Don't lie to me, Emily. You bitches are all alike. I know you're giving it to Standen. You little whore.'

'Don't you dare say such things to me,' she said, anger making her forget caution. 'I don't have to listen to your filthy talk.'

'You'll do as I tell you,' he muttered and moved

to block her path as she tried to pass him. 'Always pretending to be so high and mighty. I saw you with him...' He grabbed her as she would have walked off, swinging her round to face him. 'Don't you dare ignore me. It's time you were taught a lesson, Emily Carter.'

'Let go of me. You filthy brute!'

She hit out at him but he caught her wrists, thrusting her back against the hedge and clawing at her skirt. The branches caught in her hair and scratched her cheek but she hardly noticed them. Fear was curling inside her as she felt his warm breath on her face. Guessing what he meant to do, as he released one of her wrists to fumble at his breeches, she screamed for all she was worth and, in desperation, kneed him in the privates. Derek gave a yell of pain and let go of her. Emily made a run for it across the field but Derek was faster. He caught her and brought her down with a flying tackle so that she landed beneath him on the ground. She landed with her face against a pro-truding stone, feeling a sting of pain as it grazed her cheek. Panic made her scream again and again. She fought him, wriggling, bucking and fighting to throw him off, her nails going for his face as he pawed at her skirt. She managed to claw his cheek deeply before he grabbed her wrist. Then he hit her and swore, before trying to kiss her, to force open her mouth to allow his tongue inside as his hand went beneath her skirt to feel for the tender place between her legs. She bucked and fought as hard as she could, screaming out once more, even though he hit her across the face again and warned her to be quiet.

'Scream again and I'll break your neck,' he muttered.

Emily's reply was to turn her head and bite his exposed wrist. He yelled and hit her harder. Her senses reeling, she knew there was little more she could do to defend herself when she heard a roar of rage and the next minute Derek had been hauled off her. She struggled to open her eyes and see what was going on. Realising hazily that her father had come to her aid, she was more anxious than relieved. Pa was breathing heavily, shouting at Derek, calling him a dirty bastard as they struggled.

'I always knew you weren't to be trusted,' Pa muttered as he swung out with his stick. 'Come near my girl again and I'll kill you.'

As Emily struggled to her feet, one hand to her head because she still felt dizzy, she saw Derek punch her father in the stomach and then land another in the same place. Until then Pa had been giving a good account of himself but now he buckled and she saw blood trickle from the side of his mouth. He doubled over, the thick cudgel he'd been using falling from his hand. Seeing that Derek was about to kick her father, she swooped on the stick and raised her arm, bringing the stick down against the side of Derek's head with all the strength she had left. He swore and reeled. Her blow had brought blood to the surface. He touched it with his fingers and his top lip curled in a snarl of rage.

'I'll finish that lesson...' he began but then a shout from the gateway made him pause and, seeing the man charging across the field towards

169

them, he suddenly took off in the opposite direction, a threat on his lips. 'I'll get you another time, Emily. Just wait and see...'

Emily ignored him and dropped to her knees beside her father who remained doubled over. 'Are you all right, Pa? Did he hurt you bad?'

'Be all right in a minute...' Pa said but when he tried to rise he swayed and if Harry Standen hadn't arrived in time to catch him Emily couldn't have saved him from falling. His skin was ashen, his dark hair damp where the sweat trickled down his forehead and into his eyes. He wiped it with the sleeve of his coat. 'Feeling a bit sick...'

Pa turned away and vomited a mixture of blood and some vile-smelling bile. Emily gave him her handkerchief and he wiped the mess from his mouth.

'I should have gone after him,' Harry said. 'Who was the bastard? I heard you screaming as I got out of the car, Emily, but your Pa was here before me.'

'It was...' she stopped and looked at her father. 'He's tried before, Pa – but not like this. The first time it was just a joke or so he said...'

'Your mother will have to know,' Pa said and looked at Harry. 'Derek Black – my wife's brother. I've seen him looking at Em before and wondered, but I didn't dream he would try anything like this ... filthy bastard! I've a good mind to go to the police.'

'Be careful, Pa,' Emily said. 'Are you sure you want people to know about this? Ma will be so upset.'

'I won't have the bugger here again,' her father

said and turned to Harry. 'Thanks for coming to help us. I'm not the man I was and he had the advantage.'

'You're not well,' Harry said looking grave. 'Naturally, I shan't speak of this to anyone else. It's up to you whether you report it or not – but if he tries it on again let me know. I'll take a couple of my men to his place and we'll teach him some manners.'

'Please don't do anything foolish,' Emily said, and then, without thinking, 'I'm probably going to work in the kitchens at Priorsfield Manor so I shan't be here. Derek will think twice about attacking me there. I'd go to the police myself but it would break Ma's heart. I don't think we should tell her, Pa.'

'You're wrong there, Em love. She should know what her brother is. He's helped me out on the farm a few times, I'll admit, but now I'm going to do what your Ma wants and get a man in full time. It will be a lot easier if you're bringing in a wage.'

Emily saw the pleased look in her father's eyes and knew there was no going back.

'I'll take you through to the doctor,' Harry said. 'I've got the car.'

'I'll be all right...

'No, Pa,' Emily said. 'Let Harry take you in now. I'll go and change my dress and then I'll be off to the manor. I probably shan't be the only one to apply.'

'Harry could take you as far as Witchford, if he wouldn't mind? You'll still have a couple of miles to walk even then, because the house is a bit off the beaten track.'

'Are you in pain?'

'Yes, just a bit, but I can wait while you change your dress – if Harry can?' Harry nodded. 'Hurry and change. Leave it to me to tell your ma when I get back later – she might not believe you.'

Emily had been thinking the same thing. Besides, she didn't want to throw something like this at her mother, despite their disagreements.

'Thank you,' she said, looking at Harry. 'You don't mind waiting?'

'It's the least I can do. I came to have a word with your pa.'

'I'll be as quick as I can,' Emily said. 'Thank you for coming to our rescue.'

'I was glad to help.'

Emily could see the relief in his face and knew he felt he'd made it up to her a little. Her insides were churning, because she was too aware of what might have happened if Pa and then Harry hadn't come along. Emily would always be grateful to Harry. He'd been embarrassed because of letting her down with Christine, but he was still Pa's friend and she could never thank him enough for saving her from her uncle. She brushed at her face as she walked back to the house, wiping away a tear. Her cheek felt sore where Derek had hit her hard a couple of times. She would put a little powder over her cheek; she just hoped the bruise wouldn't come out until the next day or her mother was going to ask questions she didn't want to answer.

'What experience have you had?' the house-keeper at the manor asked her later that day. 'I prefer girls with some training behind them.'

'I've helped my mother at home,' Emily replied, her heart sinking as she looked at the woman's stern face. Her grey hair was scraped back into a bun and held in place with tortoiseshell combs. Dressed in black with a neat lace collar and a silver brooch, she looked very like the pictures of Victorian housekeepers Emily had seen in illustrated gothic tales. From what she'd seen of the manor so far, it was as if the whole house was stuck in the mid-nineteenth century!

The room they were sitting in was dark, its windows small, and the heavy oak furniture solid and probably worth a few bob in her father's shop. It was the housekeeper's sitting room, but there were no personal bits, flowers or photographs, or anything to make it homely. At that moment she wished she'd never thought about applying for the job, but she was here now and she didn't like losing. The woman was waiting for her to go on, so she tried to make an impression. She explained that she was a good plain cook, could iron, wash and clean stoves, scrub floors – and had helped her father in the yard, making it clear she didn't mind hard work.

'Your standards will hardly be up to ours.' Mrs Marsh looked down her thin nose. 'However, I dare say you can learn.'

'Yes, ma'am,' Emily counted to ten in her head before speaking again. 'I am sure I can learn whatever you require of me. My mother was in service as a lady's maid for a while when she was a girl. I'm good at washing and ironing silk or lace – and I can cook most things.'

'Cook will decide whether that is true,' the housekeeper said. 'However, I think we shall give you a trial of one month. If you are not satisfactory you will have your wage and go at the end of that period.'

'I hope I shall give satisfaction, ma'am.'

'Call me Mrs Marsh if you please. Her ladyship is ma'am and the young ladies are miss to you. Your wage is fifteen shillings a week to start but if your work is satisfactory you will be given more in six months' time.'

'Thank you, Mrs Marsh.' Emily hesitated, then, 'What do I wear for work please?'

'Your uniforms will be provided. Report to the kitchen by seven, tomorrow morning. You will of course live in and you will have one day off a month. Once in two weeks you may have an evening off, but you must arrange it with me at least three days previously.'

'Thank you. Am I allowed to go to church on Sunday?'

'We have a service here in the chapel. Lord Barton reads the lesson and leads prayers unless the curate comes to take the service. If you want to go to church you will have to ask for a Sunday off.'

'I see...' Emily smothered a sigh. It sounded as if she would be living a very different life to the one she was used to, but she would be better off here. Once her mother knew what had happened with Derek, she would blame Emily. 'Thank you for giving me a chance, Mrs Marsh.'

A slight smile appeared on the housekeeper's lips. 'As a matter of fact no one else has applied. Few girls are interested in service now I fear.

Many of them prefer working in a shop or the jam factory these days.'

Emily murmured something appropriate and stood up. She was taken through a dark passage to a side door and left the way she'd come, walking back through the kitchen courtyard and past the glasshouses over gravel paths that were free of weeds, down to the stables and out into the lane that led eventually to the village. She hadn't even seen the front of the house yet, though she could see that it was huge, parts of it dating back to the sixteenth century, so a helpful passer-by had told her when she'd enquired the way in the village.

At the back of the house, which appeared to be very old, the faded yellow brickwork was crumbling, though it looked strong enough to last another few centuries. The woodwork surrounding some of the windows was rotting and in need of paint but the glass itself was spotless, as was the kitchen she'd been shown. Mrs Hattersley was the cook here and Emily had known at once that she'd want everything just so. She hadn't said much, but she'd looked Emily up and down and then nodded to the housekeeper, as if to say that she'd do.

A part of Emily felt elated to have found a new job for herself, though she suspected it was going to be a lot harder work than she was used to at home. She walked briskly until she left the estate, then more slowly across the fields. The hedges were blooming with white blossom and dog roses, and wild flowers had sprung up beneath them. She could hear birdsong and see birds flitting from branch to branch. It was such a lovely day – just the sort of day she would like to spend sitting on a rug in the paddock with a book and a biscuit to munch. However, it seemed those days were gone for her.

Emily had been lucky, because despite helping both her mother and father, she'd always managed some free time every day, but now everything would be different. It wouldn't be as easy working at the manor. Yet she'd had to leave home, because she couldn't face seeing Derek again. Her stomach, was just beginning to lurch, because her father would be home by now and if he'd told her mother about Derek there would be hell to pay...

'I know Derek,' Ma said as Pa went out to check on the stock, leaving her alone with Emily for the first time that evening. The oil lamps were lit, casting a yellow glow over the room. Outside it was pitch black, clouds obscuring the moon. 'He would never have done anything like that unless you provoked him to it. You were always a troublemaker. You've had it in for him for ages.'

'That isn't fair.' Emily felt as if her mother had slapped her. 'I didn't do anything to encourage him. He tried to touch me once before but when I slapped him he said it was a joke.'

Ma's dark eyes narrowed with temper, her pale lips thin and disbelieving. 'Why didn't you tell me then?'

'I didn't think you would believe me.'

'Are you sure you aren't making this up just to cause trouble?'

'Pa saw him trying ... he knocked me down and tried ... well, you know. Pa has told you. They fought and Derek punched Pa in the stomach

176

twice. He would have done more if Harry hadn't arrived.'

'It was good of Mr Standen to take your father to the doctor. The doctor has given him some medicine and he's going to do some tests. He has been told to rest more and he's asked Mr Baker's son Ted to come and work for him.'

'I knew he was going to ask. At least now he won't have to do everything himself.' Emily looked at her mother's face. 'I'm sorry, Ma. I know you care about Derek. I didn't do anything to provoke him, honestly. He seemed strange...'

'He has seemed a bit odd recently,' her mother agreed. She'd been folding dried washing into the big rush basket, ready for Emily to iron. 'I think I'll visit him in the morning. Hear his side of it – he may have been drunk.'

Emily didn't reply. If her mother preferred to think that her brother had been drunk she wasn't going to contradict her. Ma would find it hard to believe that Derek was less than perfect.

'At least you got the job.'

'I was the only one to apply,' Emily admitted. 'I'm on trial for a month. If I'm not up to standard they'll let me go at the end of the trial.'

'You'd better make sure you are up to it then,' her mother said. 'If you lose this job you can look for another. It's time you worked for your living, my girl.'

Emily turned away. Her eyes stung with tears but she refused to let her mother see them. Why could she never do things right for her? She did all the chores she was given and often more.

She left the room and went up to her bedroom.

The floor was just stained boards with a small peg rug she'd made from rags. There were two lamps, one on the five-drawer chest that contained her clothes, and the other on a small chest beside the large double bed. The bed was covered with a white candlewick counterpane, which had a brown stain one side that wouldn't come out no matter how often Emily scrubbed it, and above the bed hung a picture of a cottage with *Home Sweet Home* printed underneath.

Sitting on her bed, Emily wondered what to take with her to the manor. All her treasures that Pa had given her over the years were packed into a small oak hutch. She obviously couldn't take them with her just yet, but they would be safe here in her room. She was only going to work at the manor until things got better at home. Once her father had finished his treatment she could come back and help him again.

She would take her best clothes, the compact Pa had given her at Christmas and the white satin shoes, but everything else would have to be left behind. Emily felt a pang at leaving all that was familiar to her to go to a stranger's house. She would be living and working with people she didn't know and she was going to miss seeing her father every day, but once he got his appointment for the sanatorium he wouldn't be at home anyway.

Raising her head, Emily fought her fears. She'd always wanted to make something of herself and that would involve leaving her home one day. Going into service wasn't exactly what she'd planned, but she'd taken the job on and she was going to do her best to make a success of her life.

Part Two

Spring – Christmas

1914

Chapter 14

Emily could hear her mother talking to Jack as she picked up her bag and left the house. It was chilly in the early morning and she tucked her scarf tight about her neck. She'd said her good-byes the previous night and she wanted to escape before her mother found her a job to do.

She had a five-mile walk ahead of her, which was why she'd set out at half past five. The short-est route was to cut across the fields rather than going by the high road, but it had rained a little in the night, and after she'd been walking for some minutes, Emily knew that her boots were muddy and the hem of her skirt was getting wet. She stopped, hoisting it up a little so that it showed the top of her sturdy black boots. They were her best ones that she used for church but she wanted to make a good impression and wasn't going to show up at the house in her old ones. She was wearing a dark blue coat, second-hand from the market but good quality, over a dress of light grey wool and a red muffler about her throat. Her hat was grey felt and trimmed with a red ribbon and a bunch of artificial cherries she'd sewn on her-self.

At least it wasn't raining and the sky was clear. She would have found it a lot harder had the mist been hugging the land as it often did over the Fens. The droves all looked the same then and it was easy to lose your way or walk into one of the deep ditches that had been dug everywhere to drain the marshes centuries earlier. It was those ditches that had turned the Fens from a marshy wasteland into the rich farmland it was today.

She'd been walking for more than an hour before it happened. Lost in her thoughts, Emily didn't take much notice of what was going on behind her until the thud of hooves was so close that she jumped and whirled round to look at the horse and rider coming towards her at what seemed an impossible pace. He had the whole field to choose from but his course seemed to be headed straight for her. She was caught like a rabbit frightened by a stoat, unsure of which way to move, belatedly jumping to the right just as the horse brushed past her, knocking her to her knees. She heard a shout and a curse, and then horse and rider halted a little ahead of her. Emily struggled to her feet, brushing at the mud on her skirt as the rider circled his horse and came back to her. He was frowning as he glared down at her.

'Why didn't you get out of the way?' he demanded. 'This is private property, you know. Can you not read? There's no right of way across this land for villagers.'

She raised her head, annoyed that she had mud on her best clothes, and recognised the man as Jonathan Barton. 'Is that why you deliberately knocked me down? I didn't know it was forbidden to walk over the fields. I'm on my way to the manor and I wanted to be early.'

'I was in a hurry.' His grey eyes sparked with temper, his dark hair slicked close to his head and, she could see, because his hat had fallen off, parted down the middle.

'I've been hired as a maid up at the house, sir. My name is Emily Carter.'

'I know who you are,' he said. 'I'm sorry I knocked you down – but you should have got out of the way sooner.'

'Yes, sir.' She retrieved his hat, which had landed near her feet, holding it out to him. He took it and grunted his reluctant thanks.

'Right, well get on then. I don't want Mrs Marsh calling me to account because one of her girls had a foolish accident and was late for work.'

Emily sent him a speaking look but he had turned his horse and was riding away as if the devil were on his tail. What a bad-tempered man! Had she dared she would have told him he could keep his rotten job but Pa needed her wages and for the moment she was forced to hold her tongue.

Mrs Marsh looked at Emily when she walked in through the kitchen door. It was a few minutes past seven by the clock on the wall and by the expression on the housekeeper's face it was obvious she'd begun to think Emily wasn't coming. She made a show of looking at the silver watch pinned to her dress, which was different from the one she'd worn previously but just as severe and, to Emily's mind, old-fashioned.

'Well, you finally arrived,' Mrs Marsh said, a prim look on her face. 'This is Mrs Hattersley. I believe you met yesterday when you enquired for the position?'

'Yes, Mrs Marsh. I'm sorry I was late. I ... fell

183

over and that's why I have mud on my clothes.'

The housekeeper's eyes narrowed. She inclined her head but made no comment on Emily's excuse, merely giving her the names of the people she would be working with. There were three other maids, June, Mary and Anne; also two footmen – Tomas and Gilbert Phillips; Billy, the boot boy, who was their cousin; Miss Lancaster, Lady Prior's maid; Mr Hattersley, the butler; and Mr Payne, Lord Barton's man. There were also several outside men, but Mrs Marsh did not bother to name them, as they seldom came into the house. Emily was told she would meet them all in time, but they were busy and Mrs Hattersley needed her to get on with her work.

'You'll be all right once you get to know people, lass,' Mrs Hattersley said after the housekeeper departed. 'For a start you'll be doing all the rough jobs in the kitchen and helping wherever you're asked, but if you've the knack for it I'll be teaching you to cook and then you'll be excused some of the scrubbing. We ought to have a scullery girl for that, because I need help in the kitchen all the time. Now I'll take you up to your room. You can change into uniform and come back quickly.'

Emily listened but said very little as they went upstairs. She was told she was to share a room with Mary. They entered the room, which was a bit bigger than Emily's at home, but looked crowded because there were two beds, two chests and two cupboards. She was told which was hers and then left to get changed. She didn't bother to unpack, just left her things on the bed, changed into the pale pink striped uniform, tied the white apron over the top, put the cap over her hair and hurried back down the stairs to the kitchen. She was given tea in a nice blue and white cup and then set to scraping new potatoes and preparing asparagus. She'd never eaten it, but she asked and was told how to prepare it.

The servants' quarters were in the basement, though their bedrooms were right at the top of the house, but everywhere Emily had been so far seemed dark and oppressive. The furniture was heavy and ponderous, probably Victorian, but nothing of any merit found its way into this part of the house it seemed. At least the kitchen was lighter and it smelled of baking and herbs, rather than the slight mustiness that seemed to cling to other parts of the house.

Emily found the morning soon fled by. Once she'd done the vegetables she was fetching and carrying things from the huge pantry. Mrs Hattersley seemed to think several courses of food were necessary to satisfy the family upstairs and Emily was astonished at all the butter and cream that went into the fancy dishes she made. Ma was a decent cook but she didn't make things like the syllabubs, lemon mousse and upside-down apple cake Mrs Hattersley seemed to think essential for a simple lunch.

By the time the other maids came in for their meal, which was a rabbit pie with mashed potatoes, carrots and onions followed by a treacle tart and custard, Emily was feeling as if she'd been run off her feet. Upstairs was having roast chicken, fish pie, devilled kidneys, sauté and boiled potatoes, asparagus, peas and baked onions, followed by an assortment of puddings, fruit and cheese. All of which was sent up in a serving hatch to be served by June and Mary and the footmen.

'I'm hungry,' Mary said, pulling her chair up to the table as Emily served her. 'Give me more of those potatoes please. I've been on the go since six this morning.'

Emily might have reminded her that she'd walked five miles to get here and had also been working hard, but Mrs Hattersley had told her to serve the others first and then she could sit down and have her own meal.

She was hungry and could have eaten more than her share of the rabbit pie but it disappeared quickly as, one after the other, the staff came in for their meal. Mrs Marsh and Miss Lancaster were having the same as was served to the family, though only one main course and one pudding. They ate in Mrs Marsh's parlour and only came into the kitchen when they felt like it. Mr Payne and Mr Marsh could have done the same but they preferred to sit with the others.

They all greeted Emily with a smile, seeming willing to accept her as one of their own, though Mary was a little bit sharp.

'Don't take any notice of her,' June whispered when Mary grumbled about being given too small a slice of the treacle tart. 'She was in hot water with Mrs Marsh this morning so she's in a bad mood.'

When all the staff had eaten and gone back to work, Emily cleared the dirty dishes into the scullery and started to wash them in hot water and soda. It took more than an hour to finish them and her hands felt sore when she wiped them and returned to the kitchen.

'We've got half an hour to sit down before we start the dinner,' Mrs Hattersley told her. 'We make several more courses for dinner than we do for lunch so put the kettle on, lass, and we'll have a cup of tea before we get started.'

Emily filled the kettle then sank down into one of the comfortable wooden elbow chairs by the range. She could hardly believe that the family upstairs could eat all that lot and then do the same again at night.

'Do they always eat this much?'

Mrs Hattersley laughed. 'You wait until they have a big party. That was just the family. Mr Nicolas is home from Eton. He's finished there and will be going to Oxford in the autumn. The gentlemen have big appetites and Lady Prior eats a good meal herself. You'll get used to it, Emily.'

When she was finally released after supper that night Emily was exhausted. She tumbled into bed, knowing she had to be up again at five-thirty to scrub the kitchen and scullery out before Mrs Hattersley came down to start breakfast. Emily had thought she worked hard on the farm, but her first day at the manor was far harder than she'd imagined. If Pa hadn't needed her money so that he could take on a man to help with the work in the yard, she would have given in her notice at once.

It was slavery that's what it was. Emily pulled up the covers, after blowing out her candle. She was already asleep when Mary came in a few minutes later and she hadn't even unpacked her things.

Chapter 15

'Can I see your ring?' Lizzie Barton pounced on her sister as she entered the bedroom, catching her in the act of trying on Amy's clothes. She took her sister's hand to look closer, awed by the magnificence of the expensive ring. 'Oh, it's beautiful! A sapphire to match your eyes and a cluster of diamonds. You're so lucky.'

'Don't envy me,' Amy said. 'You'll get your turn soon enough, Lizzie darling. That blue suits you – why don't you keep the dress?'

'Do you mean it?' Lizzie whirled in front of the cheval mirror in excitement, the full skirts of deep blue silk swishing about her. Across the quilted bedcovers of rich crimson were scattered dresses of every hue. Amy had been going through her extensive wardrobe and abandoned the gowns in her hurry to leave, tempting Lizzie to try them on. 'Oh, you are a darling! I love it. I absolutely love it – but are you certain?'

'Of course. Mother is insisting on buying me loads of new dresses for my trousseau – of course it's Grandmama's money.'

Lizzie arched delicate eyebrows. 'You're like Mother – you hate living on Granny's money, don't you?'

'She does make one feel so obliged. It's her house and her money. All Papa has left is the London house and hardly enough income to run his stables. Mother relies on Grandmama for her clothes and everything else.'

'I don't mind and nor does Nicolas. Granny never makes me feel obliged and Jonathan earns his keep by running the estate for her.'

'I pity Mother. She has no choice but to live here, because Father barely gives her enough to manage on. I suppose Father should sell the London house but he refuses to think of it.'

'Well, you'll soon be out of it and mistress of your own house.'

'Exactly.' Amy removed the dress she'd worn to Ely that morning and selected another. 'That is what makes marriage to Arthur so attractive.'

'You do love him?' Lizzie was shocked. 'Surely you must, Amy? Sir Arthur is such a gentleman – such a lovely kind person and so handsome.'

'You sound almost as if you're in love with him yourself.'

Lizzie was only two years younger than her sister but knew that she looked younger than her eighteen years, because of the flounces on her dress and the ribbons she wore in her long hair. Mama said she wasn't out yet and refused to buy her anything more stylish. If Papa hadn't lost most of his money, Amy would probably have married ages ago and Lizzie would have come out this year. She shook her head, her cheeks pink as she looked away.

'Of course not. Besides, he never notices me. He is head over heels in love with you, Amy.'

Amy laughed carelessly. 'Of course I care for Arthur. I'm not madly in love but marriage isn't like that in our circles. You know that Mother married for the title. Grandfather was rich but he was a mere baronet, as Arthur is of course – but he has rather a lot of money. Father had the title that mattered. It's why Grandmama puts up with him and pays his expenses – because he's Lord Barton and she likes the consequence that brings to the family.'

'That's a horrid thing to say about Granny,' Lizzie stared at her, her greenish-blue eyes reflecting hurt. 'She is never unkind to you or me – or Nicolas.'

'Mother bears the brunt of her temper and Jonathan is often made to feel his efforts are inadequate,' Amy said. 'Grow up and look about you, Lizzie. Life is far from perfect at Priorsfield Manor.'

'I think you're cruel and I shan't keep your dress.' Lizzie swiped at the tears on her cheeks and ran from the bedroom, leaving her sister to gaze after her and wonder.

Lizzie spent half an hour crying in her room. She took off Amy's dress and threw it down, angry with her sister. Sometimes Amy could be such a beast. How could Arthur have fallen in love with her?

Lizzie was sure she would give him a terrible time once they were married. She could be generous when she wanted but she was often selfish and hurtful – and Lizzie would hate her if she made Arthur unhappy.

She wished she could tell him that Amy didn't love him, beg him not to marry her, but of course it was far too late. Arthur had given Amy a ring and they were already making plans for the wedding in the late summer – and it was breaking Lizzie's heart.

She looked about her. Her room had been decorated in fresh spring colours, green, white and yellow. Granny had had it done for her birthday and she knew she was fortunate to be so privileged, but material things didn't help when her heart was broken. The awful thing was that she couldn't show her feelings, because she didn't want Arthur to know she was in love with him. He would either find it amusing or be sorry for her and she wasn't sure which would be worse.

If only she could leave, go somewhere different, far away from this old house where everything seemed to go on the same, day by day. Granny ruled the house with the proverbial rod of iron and there was no chance of Lizzie escaping unless she married.

And now she didn't want to marry ever, because the man she loved was marrying her sister.

Swiping at her cheeks, she rose and went over to the mahogany washstand in the corner. She had a pretty jug and washbasin set, pink roses on a white background, and there was some cold water left in the jug. Pouring it into the basin, she splashed her face. Amy said it was ridiculous that they had to wash this way. Granny had plenty of money to have new modern washbasins and running water put in, but she refused to do it because she didn't want nasty builders making mess and noise all over her house. Instead, the maids still had to toil upstairs with water every time one of them needed a bath and that was ridiculous in 1914.

Lizzie dragged a brush through her hair, glanced

at herself in the Georgian mahogany dressing mirror and pinched her cheeks to bring a bit of colour to them. Then she put on a fresh skirt and blouse, leaving Amy's beautiful dress lying on the floor. She would never wear it now, even though it suited her and made her feel grown up. Lifting her head proudly, she went out of her room. The sun was shining even though it had rained earlier and she needed some fresh air.

Lizzie leaned against the low stone wall at the bottom of the garden leading to the orchard and watched her brother Nicolas. He had been riding and was walking back from the stables, crop in hand, his long boots and pale breeches splashed with mud. Nicolas was a wonderful rider and he took all kinds of risks when out with his horses. Generally considered an attractive man, his sister thought him perfect. Although reckless at times and moody at others, he was a gentle sweet man, a dreamer, quiet and thoughtful. Lizzie knew about his poems, though she didn't think the rest of the family was aware of how much they meant to him.

'I wish I'd come out with you,' she said as he approached her. 'Was it just too lovely?'

'Wonderful,' Nicolas said in his soft lazy way. 'You should ride more often, Lizzie. Granny has offered to buy you a horse of your own so you need not borrow Amy's.'

'Sir Arthur bought the mare for her use. My pony is too small for me now and I don't like to borrow Amy's horse, unless she tells me I may.'

'Let Granny buy you a horse. I've seen a lively little filly that would do very well for you ... same temperament, a little flighty but to be trusted in general.'

'Nicolas! That's no way to talk about your sister.'

She tossed her long hair, which fell down her back in gentle silky waves and exuded the perfume of flowers, but her eyes were mutinous and her mouth was a little sulky as she pouted at him.

Nicolas laughed as her eyes took fire. 'I love to see you when you're mad, Lizzie. I think you've spoiled me for all other women. I shall never marry because no one will ever match up to you.'

'Please don't be silly. Amy is beautiful. I'm just ordinary.'

'Perhaps that's what I adore about you,' her brother teased. 'Plain little Lizzie. I can be myself with you. Amy is such a goddess we all have to worship at her feet.'

'Oh, you wretch! I was cross with her for saying horrid things about Granny – and now you're being a beast about Amy.'

'Silly Puss! You know I don't mean anything. I adore both my sisters – but you're just you, the little sister I've always known – and she is the beautiful Miss Barton, who is going to marry one of the richest men in England and perhaps the world.'

'Is Sir Arthur really so rich?' Lizzie's nose wrinkled and the freckles she'd gained the previous summer disappeared for a moment. 'He always seems just like you and me. Amy can look ... well, regal, I suppose is the word, especially when she's dressed to kill.'

'Well, if this mine of his turns out well, Arthur

193

will be fabulously rich.' Nicolas looked at her in amusement. 'Amy does pay for dressing, doesn't she? Arthur will get his money's worth if he is looking for a wife who can hold her own in the top echelons of society – even in London I doubt anyone will outshine our sister.'

'You make it sound like a crime.'

'Do I? I certainly don't mean to criticise. I admire her for knowing what she wants and going all out to get it. I wish I had half her courage and determination.'

'You have a different kind of courage. Look at the way you ride – and the way you protected us when that man Father dismissed shouted at Amy and I...'

'That doesn't take courage; it's blind instinct,' Nicolas said and his eyes had that queer remote look that seemed to come into them at times. 'I was thinking of other things...'

Lizzie turned and walked in silence beside him as they left the orchard behind, went through an old gate and began to walk across smooth lawns bordered by deep beds of roses, flowering shrubs and perennials. In the spring, sweet blue hyacinths, yellow crocus and tulips peeped out from neat borders that were regularly hoed and weeded and high grey stone walls enclosed the gardens on either side. Now, daisies, irises, flowering shrubs and roses had replaced the glory of the spring bulbs. Beyond the flowerbeds were further gardens, including the kitchen courtyard and the glasshouses. In front of them the house rose in pure classical lines of yellow brick with rows of long elegant windows and a Portland stone arch over the impressive front door.

Glancing at Nicolas's face, Lizzie saw his frown and held her silence. She knew better than to chatter when Nicolas was in this mood. She was aware of some kind of suffering within him but she didn't understand what it was or why he should be unhappy. Nicolas was different from other people, more sensitive, introspective and, at times, almost morose. She thought that perhaps it was when his muse was on him and that he had gone to that place even she could not reach, but after a moment he turned his head and smiled at her.

'Poor Lizzie. It isn't fair on you being stuck here in the country. At least Amy had one season – and she might have married then had she wished, but she was hard to please. Granny ought to stump up the money for your season, but she's annoyed with Mother for telling her so and refuses to do it.'

'I know.' Lizzie sighed and tucked her arm through his. 'I don't really care. I'm happy here with you, but I shall hate it when you go to Oxford in the autumn.'

'Amy will be married by then. Granny may give Mother enough money to take you to London for a while – theatres and museums but you won't be able to go to all the balls, of course. You'd need to open the house, buy loads of clothes and entertain lavishly for that – and unless Granny stumps up it won't happen.'

'I don't really mind about the balls,' Lizzie said not quite truthfully. 'It's just that you will be gone and Amy – and I'll be here alone with Mother and Granny.' She squeezed his arm. 'Don't say I'll still have Jonathan because he's never around.

195

When he isn't working he's courting that awful...' she stopped and blushed. 'Now *I'm* being horrid. Mabel Saunders is a perfectly pleasant girl...'

'But very boring and plain,' Nicolas said, his eyes alight with mockery. 'I'll say it for you. Poor old Jonathan doesn't have much choice, you know. Father has nothing to give him and Granny keeps him on a string. He has no idea where she intends to leave her money or even how much there is of it, and he needs to marry money just in case. Mabel's father is in manufacturing and rolling in the stuff.'

'Yes, I know,' Lizzie said. 'Granny likes to keep Jonathan waiting – she keeps us all hanging on – but it's her money. We shouldn't expect that she will leave it to us or give us anything more than she does already. She does have other relatives...'

'Distant cousins who rarely visit. If she made it clear that Jonathan was to inherit Priorsfield Manor he could ditch the plain Jane and marry where his heart is.'

'Is he in love with someone?'

'Not to my knowledge, but he might be had he the chance,' Nicolas said. 'We're a sorry lot, Lizzie. You are the best of us. If Granny had any sense she would leave the estate to you.'

'I should share it with the rest of you if she did,' Lizzie said. She shivered as a cool wind lifted her hair and blew it across her eyes. A fine mist was beginning to settle over the lawns; it sometimes came rolling in over the flat landscape and marooned them, cutting the house off from its surroundings. 'You don't think she will? I should hate anyone to think I sit with her in the hope of it. She

196

makes me laugh – and underneath she isn't as hard as she makes out. Anyway, I like her!'

'That is why she should leave the money to you,' Nicolas said and then laughed. 'Don't worry about it, love. Lady Prior isn't going anywhere for a long time yet.'

'Thank goodness,' Lizzie said. 'I don't want her to die.'

Nicolas raised his brows. 'You must be one of the few,' he murmured. 'I couldn't care less what she does with the money but I feel sorry for Ma sometimes.'

Lizzie nodded. When Nicolas spoke of their mother in those terms she knew he was privy to more than she was aware of. Nicolas was their mother's favourite and she told him things she told no one else.

'Mother will miss you when you go to college.'

'We have the rest of the summer to get through first and Lord knows what will happen before the autumn.'

'What do you mean?'

'I mean, my sweet little innocent, that before it's time for me to go up to Oxford we may have a war on our hands. The papers are full of nothing but the trouble in Europe and the Balkans. Don't you ever read them?'

'Only the society pages. Mother never gives me the rest of the paper. She says it isn't suitable reading for a girl of my age.'

'That woman has no more sense than...' Nicolas broke off with a strangled oath. 'I love her dearly, you know that – but we shall all have to face it if it comes, Lizzie. I shan't ignore the call to arms if it happens. Jonathan may have to stay here for the sake of the estate but I wouldn't if I were him.'

'A war...' Lizzie stared. She vaguely recalled hearing her father mention something but she'd thought it would happen in Europe and would not involve anyone she knew. 'You wouldn't have to fight, Nicolas?'

They had entered the house, his boots clattering on the shining marble tiles in the hall, from which soared a magnificent mahogany staircase, beautifully carved with swags and vine leaves. It was the relic of an ancient age and she thought it beautiful, as was the rest of the house to her eyes. There might be too much old-fashioned Victorian clutter, which could be put away in the attics, but the house belonged to an earlier, elegant era and she adored it.

'Wouldn't I?' He looked at her oddly. 'I would do what I had to do, Lizzie – as we all must in such times. You wouldn't want me to be called a coward?'

'No – I don't know. I shouldn't want you to go away and perhaps...'

She suddenly felt very sick and her head was filled with pictures that made her feel faint. The idea of men being wounded and dying was so new and awful to her that she could not bear it.

'Don't please,' she begged, holding his arm tighter. 'Please don't talk about it any more...'

Chapter 16

Lizzie seized the chance to escape. She had been longing to read her book all morning but her mother hadn't given her a chance. Lady Barton complained of a headache but rather than lie down on her bed she continued to sit in her parlour and complain about everything. If her Mama was truly unwell Lizzie would have done everything to help ease her pain, but she knew it was just another attack of nerves, brought on by an argument with Lady Prior earlier that day.

'Elizabeth, spare me a moment if you will.'

Lizzie checked and turned as she heard her grandmother's voice. Lady Prior had left her apartments and was on her way down to the ground floor. Smothering a sigh, Lizzie went to her and offered her arm. Lady Prior took it and leaned on her heavily. Although in good health, she walked badly and suffered the pain of arthritis in her legs and feet, though she said little about it.

'Where is your Mama?'

'In her parlour. She has one of her headaches, Granny.'

'My fault I dare say. We had an argument this morning. Helen wanted me to pay for the wedding, which is quite ridiculous when Sir Arthur is very willing to cover all the costs. I shall give Amy a good present and I've paid for her trousseau – why should I do more? It's your father's responsibility but he hasn't the funds, of course.'

'Sir Arthur wouldn't want you to pay, Granny. He is giving Amy the wedding she wants because he loves her.'

'And what do you think of all this then?'

'What do you mean?' Lizzie avoided her searching gaze. Her grandmother had the most searching eyes of anyone she knew, as if they could see into one's soul. Her nose was long and thin, her mouth almost colourless, as was her skin these days. When Lizzie kissed her, her cheek felt papery and too soft. She was dressed that morning in a dark skirt and a high-necked lace blouse with a gold and diamond brooch pinned at the throat, her white hair drawn back into a knot at her nape. 'It has nothing to do with me.'

'You're in love with him, aren't you?' Lady Prior laid a blue-veined hand on her arm; her diamond rings were loose and they swivelled on fingers made thin by age but would not come over her swollen knuckles.

'I ... like him,' Lizzie admitted, each word causing her exquisite pain. 'But he loves Amy. Even if she'd turned him down he wouldn't have looked at me.'

'He isn't good enough for you,' Lady Prior said. 'His father was in trade – made a fortune and sent his son to Eton to learn to be a gentleman. I want at least a fourth or fifth generation lord for you, my love.'

'Granny!' Lizzie looked at her, half in indignation, half in amusement. 'Do my feelings come into this at all?'

'Yes, of course, you silly child. I think nothing

200

beneath the rank of lord good enough for you, but I want only your happiness. You and Nicolas are different from Amy and Jonathan. You feel more. Your sister thinks only of herself – and Jonathan schemes to get what he wants. That girl he is engaged to is good enough for him even if her father is in trade. Jonathan thinks like a Cit so he may as well marry the daughter of one.'

Lizzie frowned, because to call someone a Cit, or a tradesman, was derogatory and an insult in her grandmother's day.

'Granny, you are being unfair. Jonathan works so hard for the estate. He is a good manager, you know he is.'

'Yes, I'll give him that,' the old lady agreed and smiled at Lizzie. 'If he didn't make it so obvious that he was waiting for me to die and leave him my money I might like him more.'

'I'm sure he doesn't want you to die. He just wants ... a little security. I suppose as the eldest he would have inherited Father's estate.'

'If there was anything to inherit.' Lady Prior snorted her disgust. 'If he had anything about him he would tell me to go to hell and make his own way in the world. You don't see Nicolas relying on my money.'

'Father is paying for him to go up to Oxford – but he does have a small independence from Uncle Maurice. Uncle Maurice was always fond of Nicolas and I suppose he thought Jonathan would inherit the Barton estate. Papa still had some money when his youngest brother died so prematurely.'

'As he would still if he hadn't thrown his inheritance away. Barton was a fool but he's a gentleman and he puts up with your mother without complaint – and I respect him for that. Helen has no more idea of how to keep a man happy in bed than a mouse. Most men in his position would have taken a string of mistresses but Barton never did.'

'Granny!' Lizzie was shocked. 'Should you be saying these things to me?'

'You're old enough to know what's what,' Lady Prior asserted. 'If your mother had any sense she would have brought you out before now.' The old lady frowned as Lizzie was silent. 'You don't really imagine it's for lack of funds? As if I would deny you anything. You've always been my favourite – you and Nicolas. Helen makes out it's my fault when she knows she has only to ask, but she won't. She wanted your sister married first. Probably thinks you wouldn't stand a chance if Amy was still on the market, but she's wrong – and Sir Arthur is a fool in my opinion. He chose the wrong sister.'

'You mustn't say things like that,' Lizzie said. 'May I truly have a proper season?'

'Of course – if Helen asks.' Lady Prior snorted. 'You'll go another year yet. If that peahen I gave birth to doesn't come to her senses I'll arrange it myself – but although you're eighteen you're too young yet. I should hate my little Lizzie to be pushed into marriage too soon. It's just a game I play with your mother, child. All I have is for you and the others, but I'm damned if I will let Helen have all her own way. This is my home and she'll play by my rules if she wants to live here.'

'You are a wicked old thing, aren't you? Poor

Mama is terrified of you, don't you know that?'

'More fool her then. Had she stood up to me more we should have been on better terms. You're not afraid of me and nor is Nicolas. To give him his due, your father tells me what he thinks to my face, though only in private. He was far too good for Helen. She never appreciated what she had so she lost it.'

'I think your bark is worse than your bite. I'm glad you're here, Granny. I'm going to miss Nicolas when he goes up to Oxford and Amy too.'

'We shall have a ball for Amy before she marries,' Lady Prior said. 'It might be the last one I give here – unless I live long enough to see you wed.'

'You'll live to be a hundred. You know you will.'

The long case clock in the drawing room was striking the hour. In the hall they passed a footman who smiled at Lizzie and nodded respectfully to his employer as he opened a door for them to pass through. Her grandmother's parlour had a faded look, the dark green curtains long past their best, the armchairs worn and sagging but comfortable. Here the floors were of wood boards polished dark by the ages and covered by rich rugs in reds and blues on a cream background. The furniture was mostly high Victorian, bought when Lady Prior was a bride, though here and there something from a much earlier century had crept in – like the Carolean chair with a carved splat, which stood in the corner next to a huge aspidistra in a salt-glazed jardinière.

'Perhaps. My heart seems strong enough – according to that fool Doctor Morris, but the pain is hard to bear, Lizzie. He says I should take laudanum but I can't abide the stuff. Rots the mind and saps the will. I'll deal with the pain as long as I can but it may become unbearable even for me.'

'I'm sorry you're in pain.'

'Don't be, girl. I'm past seventy and I've had my life. All I ask is that you are happy – you and Nicolas. You are the ones I care for, though I know my duty to the others, so don't look like that.'

'Do you think Nicolas is happy?'

'Few of us are truly happy. Nicolas is too sensitive for his own good. He has a place inside himself that he retreats to and none of us can follow him there – but it's just his nature. I think he isn't unhappy and that may be all we can ask for that brother of yours.'

'I try to understand him but I don't.'

'Nicolas will seek you out when he wants you, my love.'

'Yes, I know.'

As the old lady settled herself by the fire, which was lit every day regardless of the weather outside, Lizzie drew up her chair. The pine logs crackled and spat, casting a pleasant aroma into the room and giving off enough warmth to make it pleasant. She held up her book so that her grandmother could see.

'Shall I read to you, Granny? It's one of your favourites – Miss Austen's *Pride and Prejudice*.'

'Ah yes, I always enjoy hearing you read and that piece of nonsense is a favourite. Where are you up to this time?'

'I've just reached the part where she overhears Darcy saying that there are no young ladies he would care to dance with.'

Lady Prior laughed. 'One of the best bits in my opinion. Read to me for a while and then we shall tear his character apart to our hearts' content...'

Lizzie saw Amy run from Mama's parlour in tears as she was coming back from her walk. After leaving her grandmother, she'd managed to escape for an hour or so, walking across the fields with the wind in her hair. The sun had come out from behind the clouds even though it wasn't truly a summer day, because the breeze was chilly. She'd been thinking about the future, about Amy's wedding, and how she was going to get through all the fuss before it happened. Since her engagement three weeks earlier, Amy had been having masses of fittings for her clothes, and Lizzie had been fitted for the gown she would wear as a bridesmaid. Amy had chosen green silk, which suited Lizzie well and they'd sort of made up their quarrel.

Realising that something awful must have happened, Lizzie stood uncertainly, wondering what to do until the door of Mama's parlour opened and Jonathan came out. He was frowning, still wearing his riding things, his boots spattered with mud. Mama would not have been pleased about that and a chill ran down Lizzie's spine as she wondered what was so important that he hadn't stopped to change his boots.

'Is something wrong?' she asked, and then, as he hesitated, 'I'm not a child. I saw Amy in tears so I know something has happened.'

'Sorry, Lizzie. I know we tend to treat you as a child, but you will have to know.' He gave a sigh of exasperation and ran his fingers through his dark hair. Like Amy, he took after his father, while Lizzie was much like her mother had been as a young girl. 'Amy is upset because Mama told her that she must break off her engagement.'

'Break it off? No! Why should she?' Lizzie was astonished and immediately concerned for Sir Arthur. 'She can't. It would be humiliating for him.'

'Amy doesn't want to. She quarrelled with Mama, but I can't see how she can marry him now. There's going to be such a scandal.'

'A scandal?' Lizzie shivered, feeling the ice at the nape of her neck. 'What has happened?'

'I'm not sure of all the details, but you knew Sir Arthur had sold a lot of shares in his emerald mine?' Lizzie nodded. 'Well, it seems that it was a fraud – at least that's what the papers are saying. The shares are practically worthless. It's something to do with the leases on the land reverting to the government over there. Apparently, Arthur neglected to renew on the right day and they lapsed so now he has no right to the mine and everyone has lost their money. Of course most people will just blame him – and at worst he could be charged with fraud.'

'No, surely not? He sold the shares in good faith, didn't he?'

'Yes, of course he did – well, as far as I know. People won't care about whose fault it was, Lizzie. If the mine has failed for whatever reason, they are going to resent losing their money. Arthur's name will be dragged through the mud. If he can prove it wasn't his fault, he may not be accused of fraud – but people will still be angry.'

Lizzie stared at her brother in horror. She had no idea of how shares worked or about leases on mineral rights, but she did know that this was serious. A lot of people had invested money in Arthur's scheme and he would be labelled a cheat or a fraud, even if it was something outside his control, which it surely was if the government out there had taken away his lease and the right to mine for emeralds. She felt a sinking inside, not because the wedding was off but because it was all so horrible and Arthur would be in trouble.

'Has he lost all his money?'

'I doubt it, because he has a lot of irons in the fire and his risk was spread, but some people have lost a lot of money they couldn't afford to lose. It isn't just the money, Lizzie – it's the scandal. Amy said she would marry him regardless but Mama said that Papa would forbid it and the awful thing is that he will. Amy would have to go against him and Mama – and Granny too. She would probably find she wasn't welcome in society as his wife. Until the scandal blows over he will be an outcast. No one will want to know him. The wedding will have to be called off immediately and Amy is going to be caught up in this scandal whether she likes it or not.'

'That is awful.' Lizzie now felt sorry for her sister. Amy had been looking forward to being the wife of the wealthy Sir Arthur Jones, and now she would have the shadow of scandal hanging over her, perhaps the chance of a rich marriage gone for ever. Yet in her heart, Lizzie felt Arthur's disgrace and the loss of his bride was more painful.

He'd been in love with Amy, but she had only wanted the money and prestige the marriage would bring her. 'Do you think I should go to her?'

'I wouldn't if I were you,' Jonathan said. 'She might snap your head off. She shouted at Mama and ran from the room, but I think she knows it's over.'

Lizzie knew he was right. When Papa heard he would withdraw his permission, force Amy to withdraw. Or more likely, he would summon Sir Arthur, demand an explanation and, if it were not considered satisfactory, he would expect Arthur to do the right thing – which was, of course, to withdraw.

Lizzie's eyes filled with tears as she turned away. Her heart ached for Arthur and his pain. Amy would be humiliated and disappointed although in time she would get over it, but Arthur had really loved her and it would break his heart.

'Sir Arthur is with Papa in the library,' Lizzie said entering her sister's bedroom the following afternoon as Amy was changing into a gown for the evening. 'I saw him arrive and smiled at him, but he looked stern and worried. I'm not sure he even saw me.'

'How long ago was that?' Amy asked.

'Just a few minutes. I thought you should know he was here.'

'Thank you.' Amy's hands were trembling. She looked nervous and unsure. Lizzie wanted to comfort her but there was nothing she could say. 'Do you think I should go down?'

'You can't intrude on them while they're talking. I don't think either of them would appreciate you being there – it's men's business, Amy. You should wait in the parlour opposite until you hear Sir Arthur leaving.'

'He will surely ask for me.'

'He might not if Papa tells him he is a disgrace and asks him to release you.'

'Father wouldn't do that without my permission ... would he?'

Amy gripped the handle of her hairbrush so tightly that her knuckles turned white. Lizzie had never seen her sister like this and her heart went out to her. Even if Amy hadn't loved Arthur, she'd liked him and she was clearly very upset.

'You know how angry Papa was when he heard the news. I heard him speaking to Granny this morning. She was advising it and he agreed with her that it was the best thing for all of us.'

Amy dropped the hairbrush on her dressing table with a little clatter. Her nervousness turned to sudden anger and her head went up, her eyes bright with pride.

'No! I won't be bullied into giving him up. It is my decision, not Papa's and certainly not Grandmama's.'

'Can you stand against the whole family? They are all convinced you should walk away from him ... except me. I think you should do what you want, Amy. If you still care for him you should stand by him.'

'As you would?' Amy smiled at her. 'It's all right, dearest. I know you are fond of Arthur. I'm fond of him too. I think I've realised it more since all this happened.'

'Go down now,' Lizzie urged. 'If Papa tries to send him away you can tell him you still wish to marry him.'

'Yes, I shall. Thank you for telling me Arthur was here.'

Lizzie watched her sister walk away. She hoped it would all turn out right but she knew it was unlikely. Their father had been adamant that the wedding could not go ahead. Whatever Amy said, he was unlikely to change his mind. The only way she could marry Sir Arthur now was to run away with him, but somehow Lizzie didn't think her sister would carry her defiance that far.

Chapter 17

Emily finished scouring the breakfast dishes, washed down the wooden draining boards and then wiped her hands on a towel before going through to the big, slightly over-warm kitchen where Cook was busy preparing food for the midday meal. At least she had been when Emily started her work, but the scene in the kitchen was very different now. Most of the servants seemed to have gathered there and were talking in an excited manner. A hush fell over them as she walked in and they looked at one another, as if wondering what to say to her.

'I've finished the dishes and I've cleaned the sinks and surfaces. What should I do now?'

'You'd best come and sit down and have a cup of

tea, same as the rest of us, Emily. We've had a bit of a shock if you want the truth,' Mrs Hattersley said and pointed to a spare stool.

Emily approached but didn't sit immediately. She looked at the faces of the other servants. Everyone seemed very serious. 'Has something happened?'

'It's terrible that's what it is,' Mrs Marsh said. 'I've never known such a scandal in the family.'

'Sir Arthur wasn't really family – yet,' Tomas Phillips objected.

He was wearing black trousers, a white shirt and a waistcoat with a striped red front. In the evenings when he was serving upstairs, he'd wear a dark coat over his waistcoat but when he was downstairs during the day he took it off.

'He was considered family being engaged to Miss Amy and this scandal must reflect badly on her. It's a tragedy.'

Mr Payne, his lordship's valet, a middle-aged man with slightly receding hair shook his head sorrowfully. Like the footmen, he wore dark clothes and a white shirt, but had kept his coat on.

'This is a very sad day for us all.'

'Has someone died?' Emily asked.

'Not died but...' Cook looked odd and shook her head. 'Well, we don't know the truth of it so perhaps we shouldn't say.'

'What has happened?'

'Miss Amy's engagement is off,' Mary said. 'They won't be getting married.'

Emily accepted the cup of strong tea placed before her on the table. She felt cold all over. Looking at their faces, she sensed there was a lot

211

more that she wasn't being told. Because she was still new at the manor, they didn't quite trust her and whatever had happened was out of the ordinary.

'Well,' Mr Payne said, placing his empty cup on the kitchen table. 'I'm sure we're all very sorry about what has happened today. I thought you should all know, but there must be no gossiping about this unpleasant business. Anyone who takes this outside the family will be severely reprimanded. His lordship is adamant that this is all to be kept as quiet as possible, for Miss Amy's sake.'

'Yes, Mr Payne.'

'Mary, you're wanted upstairs. The rest of you, get on with your work.'

Mary obeyed without question. Over the past two weeks since she arrived, Emily had noticed that Mr Payne was respected by everyone and seemed to be in charge when Mr Hattersley wasn't around, though Mrs Marsh looked after the household arrangements. It was she who asked Cook what was needed for the larder and paid the tradesmen who came to the kitchen door once a month.

One by one the maids and footmen finished their tea and left the kitchen. Emily had emptied her cup and, without waiting to be asked, she gathered the dirty cups on to a tray and picked them up ready to take through to the scullery. She felt sorry for Miss Amy, even though the girl had been rude about her dress that night at the dance, but of course she'd been right, and Emily no longer resented her comments.

'Put that tray down for a moment,' Mrs

Hattersley said. 'I think you should know it all, and then you won't do or say anything silly.'

Emily pulled out a chair and sat down, looking at her expectantly. She already knew that Mrs Hattersley enjoyed a gossip when she wasn't too busy. Emily's eyes travelled round the large kitchen, which was twice the size of her mother's at home. The range was large too and took a lot of blacking and brushing. Emily didn't enjoy that, but it was a part of her job, just as scrubbing the floor and the scullery was her work.

'Why has the engagement been called off?'

'They say Sir Arthur's emerald mine is in trouble and a lot of people may lose their money. They say he may have sold the shares fraudulently – though I don't believe that myself. You wouldn't find a more decent and honest man if you searched the country ... but mud sticks even if it isn't warranted.'

Emily stared at her in silence for a moment, then, 'That's a shame. Miss Amy must be very upset.'

'Yes, of course she is,' Mrs Hattersley agreed. 'Marriage in families like ours isn't always a love match, but I think Miss Amy is fond of him and she was happy. We'd been expecting lots of visitors, parties, dances and the like. It was part of the reason you were taken on. There's bound to be a terrible scandal whatever happens.'

'Does that mean I'll be let go?' She'd hardly got here and now they wouldn't need her. Emily was conscious of a sharp disappointment. Even though some of the others weren't particularly friendly she liked the cook and the footmen, and the maids seemed all right too. It was just Mrs Marsh and Miss Lancaster who treated her as an outsider.

'Not if I have anything to do with it. You've been a big help to me since you came. The last girl took ages to do a simple job. You just get on without being asked. Don't worry; I'll put in a good word for you with Mrs Marsh.'

'Thank you. My mother needs my wages, because my Pa isn't well.'

'Mrs Marsh told me. I'm sorry your father isn't well, lass, but I'm glad to have you here.'

'If they get rid of anyone it will be me. I'm only the scullery maid.'

'Well, if you work as hard as you have recently, you'll soon be promoted to my assistant.'

'Will that mean more money?' She frowned and Emily added, 'I only ask because it's for my pa, Mrs Hattersley.'

'I understand you want to do your best for your family at a time like this, but be careful, because they may decide they don't need you now.'

Emily was thoughtful as she went through to the scullery to start preparing vegetables for lunch. If she'd been a spiteful girl she would've thought Miss Amy had got her come-uppance for being such a snob, but instead she felt sorry for her. It was rotten luck and she must be feeling devastated, especially if she'd been in love with him.

'We shall be busy today,' Mrs Hattersley said the next morning. She was rolling pastry with a wooden pin and dusted it with flour, before turning the dough on the marble slab. 'Lord Barton decided that they would go ahead with a reception for the church dignitaries – it was planned months ago and I understand a couple of bishops are coming here. Mr Hattersley said Lord Barton thought it would occasion more scandal to cancel than to go ahead. It is more a business meeting than a party, of course – but they all have a buffet lunch here and as there are at least twenty of them it makes more work for us.'

'It may help to lift the gloom,' Emily said. Everyone was still subdued, speaking in whispers and looking anxious. 'I'd rather be busy than sit around with nothing to do.'

'Well, you won't have time to be idle today,' Cook told her. 'The circumstances have cast a cloud over things here and no mistake. We were all looking forward to the wedding.'

'I wonder what will happen to Sir Arthur – will he go to prison?'

'I should hope not. I heard he'd gone up to London.'

'I saw Miss Amy in the garden when you sent me for some vegetables earlier. I took the wrong turning into the rose garden again and she was picking dead heads off the flowers, and cutting the best ones.'

'You didn't get lost again?'

'It's just that I get muddled which is left and which is right,' Emily made a wry face. 'Miss Amy saw me and I apologised. She told me to turn right by the water butt.'

Miss Amy had been cutting flowers, placing them into a shallow trug and had seemed to be enjoying the sunshine. Outwardly, she was serene, but Emily had caught an expression in her eyes, which told her Miss Amy wasn't as calm as she appeared.

'Was she annoyed with you for disturbing her?'

'No, not at all.' To Emily's surprise Miss Amy had smiled and asked her how she liked being at the manor.

'I hope you apologised for being in the wrong place?'

'She said it didn't matter but I was not to make a habit of it because Lady Prior might be annoyed if she saw me.'

'If you've finished that asparagus, you can help me by fetching the things on that list from the pantry.'

Cook had begun to cut out fancy shapes to place around the lid of her chicken and ham pie. She didn't look up as she spoke, concentrating on her work as always. Emily had never seen things done in quite Mrs Hattersley's way and admired her skill. All the other servants respected her, because she was such a good cook and also because she'd been here since she was a girl. She had a vast repertoire of stories about the family and, some-times, when they had a quiet moment, she would tell Emily about her early years at the manor. She had been a young woman when Lady Barton was married and she'd known all the younger mem-bers of the family from the time they were born.

Emily picked up the list of ingredients Cook wanted and walked to the far end of the kitchen, opening the pantry door. She saw Tomas immedi-ately. He'd entered through the far door, which led into the butler's pantry. Tomas had obviously been cleaning silver and he was wearing gloves, carrying a tray of cutlery and fancy dishes, used for sweets and fancy cakes.

'A present for you,' he said. 'This lot needs washing. I'll take it into the scullery and then I'll give you a hand with polishing it dry. You'll need hot water and soda to get this off, Em – and a lot of washing.'

'I've got a list of things to fetch for Cook first. You'll have to make a start yourself if you're in a hurry. Cook's very busy this morning and...' Emily gave a little shriek as he aimed a kiss at her cheek when he squeezed past her. 'You watch what you're doing, Tomas Phillips, or I'll box your ears.'

'You can't blame a man for taking advantage of an opportunity. I fancy you, Emily Carter. I reckon it was a stroke of good luck for me when you came to work here.'

'Don't you believe it,' she retorted but his kiss had not been malicious and she wasn't afraid of him, as she had been of Derek. 'I've got my heart set on being a farmer's wife.'

'My father's father was a farmer, but not a very good one. They had some bad luck – three rotten harvests on the trot and then the sheep and pigs took sick and they lost everything. I've thought about going into business for myself, but not farming.'

'What do you want to do?' Emily asked. She didn't stop what she was doing, but gathered the bits and pieces she needed as she waited for his answer.

'I've thought about running a little shop – newspapers and sweets, tobacco. I think there's more to

217

be had out of working for yourself in a business like that than being in service or running a farm.'

'Not if you've got enough acres. I know a rich farmer.'

'You'd be better off with me, Emily.'

'You'd best take that lot to the scullery,' Emily warned. 'Cook will have my hide if I don't get these things back to her.'

Emily tossed her head as she filled her tray with all the spices and bits and pieces Cook needed for the next stage of her work. She liked the young footman but she had her own ideas about the future and she didn't think she would want to be stuck behind a counter in Tomas's shop. She wasn't sure what she wanted to do in the future. It was all right here for the moment, but as soon as Pa could manage things himself again, Emily would leave. She would try to find herself another job, something different – something that would get her somewhere. She saw herself working in a high class shop, wearing a smart suit and fancy shoes, but that was probably ever going to be only a dream. Maybe she would do better to be a cook like Mrs Hattersley, who was respected by the staff and family.

Returning to the kitchen, she saw that Mary was sitting by the range and sipping a hot drink Cook had given her. She made a moaning sound and held a hand to her right cheek, which looked swollen and painful.

'Why did this have to happen today of all days?'

'Is something wrong?' Emily asked.

'I've got terrible toothache,' Mary said. 'I asked Mrs Marsh if I could go off to have my tooth seen to but she said I must wait until tomorrow, because I can't be spared.'

'Couldn't June take your place for a while or Anne?'

'Anne is helping Lady Barton, because Mrs Marsh has so much to do. June and I will both be needed when the guests start arriving. The ladies will want someone to take them upstairs and to attend to their needs, and then Cook needs June to take the food from the serving hatch and place it on the side tables so that she can send up more. June will be setting out the cold dishes while the guests are arriving and then we'll both be on hand when the hot dishes start coming up.'

'Couldn't Mrs Marsh help out? Or one of the footmen?'

'Mrs Marsh will be helping the ladies upstairs, and the footmen will open the door, take the guests to the drawing room and circulate with drinks. They've all got their jobs to do. I'll be seeing to the ladies' coats and hats when they come in, taking them upstairs to tidy themselves. Then I've got to help June with the dishes. Mrs Marsh oversees it all and helps the guests if they need anything. Mr Payne will be looking after the gentlemen and Mr Hattersley sees to the wine and makes sure the table is perfect, the silver all in place. The footmen serve and fill glasses so don't ask why they can't do my job.' She moaned again. 'I'm not sure I can do it, Mrs Hattersley. I'm in too much pain.'

'I could help June,' Emily said. 'If she told me where things go, I could help – once we've finished down here.'

'You don't have the right uniform,' Mary objected. 'If you were seen upstairs in what you're wearing there would be ructions, especially when they have company.'

'I bet I could wear your uniform,' Emily said. 'If June shows me what to do and then goes downstairs to take your place I could manage until she came back.'

'Do you think you could manage?' Mrs Hattersley asked her. 'I shall need you here for a bit longer, then you can change into Mary's uniform and June will show you what to do. If Mary gets off now she'll likely catch the bus into Ely.'

Mary left the kitchen hastily, before she could change her mind. Mrs Hattersley looked at Emily. 'It will mean extra work for you. Once we've finished down here you should be having a cup of tea and a bite to eat – and I'll need you here when the dirty dishes start coming back. It's times like these when we need more help. In the old days we had six maids in the laundry room and another six in the house.'

'I don't mind going without my lunch for once,' Emily said. 'Do you need me for a few minutes? Tomas said he wanted me to wash the silver he's been cleaning.'

'No, I can manage for a while, but don't let him keep you talking. You won't have time if you're going to change into a different uniform and be ready when they all start to arrive.'

'I promise to be as quick as I can,' Emily said. 'I won't let you down, Cook. It can't be that difficult to lay some dishes out, can it?'

'Mrs Marsh likes them just so. She will come to

inspect your work, but if she asks what you're doing there just tell her I sent Mary off and told you to take her place.'

Emily had just finished washing the silver when Mrs Hattersley called to her from the kitchen, and she rushed in to discover that Anne was there looking flustered.

'Miss Amy asked for Mary,' she said. 'She wants some hot water. I can't take it because I've got to iron this dress for Lady Barton. You'll have to go, Emily. You can't make a mistake with that...'

'But Mrs Hattersley needs me...'

'I can spare you for ten minutes,' Mrs Hattersley said, 'but come back as quick as you can.'

Emily wiped her hands on a towel, and filled a brass can with hot water from the kettle on the range. She followed Anne from the kitchen, up the back stairs and along the landing to the bedrooms used by the family.

'It's just along there,' Anne said. 'Knock before you go in, and don't forget she's upset.'

Miss Amy hadn't dined downstairs since she'd been forced to break her engagement to Sir Arthur, though she did go into the garden sometimes. She'd sent back the trays Mrs Hattersley sent up to her, the food untouched. Emily knocked cautiously and then entered when she was told. She'd thought Miss Amy might be crying but she was sitting on a stool looking at herself in the dressing mirror.

'Put the water down, Mary, and then you can do my hair for me.'

'It's Emily, miss. Mary had toothache and went

221

to the dentist.'

Miss Amy turned to look at her, an expression of annoyance in her eyes. Emily thought she *had* been crying earlier, because her nose looked red and her skin was blotchy.

'I could try to do your hair, miss. I'm not as good as Mary, but I could put it up in a simple knot – if that would do?'

'Just do the best you can with it then.'

'Yes, miss.'

Emily took up the brush and began to stroke it over Miss Amy's long dark hair. It had a slight wave in it and seemed to fall into place naturally at the sides of her face when Emily gathered it into a knot and fastened it with pins from the glass tray on the dressing table.

'Be as quick as you can. I was tardy in dressing and my father will not be pleased if I'm late.'

'I've finished, miss.' She handed her the silver hand mirror. Miss Amy glanced at herself and then in the dressing mirror at the back. 'It will do for now I suppose. Can you fasten my dress at the back?'

'Yes, miss.'

Emily did as she asked and was dismissed. She ran down the stairs, knowing that the cook was rushed off her feet and that she would be needed upstairs in twenty minutes. Mrs Hattersley would not be very pleased with her, but she'd had to do what Miss Amy asked, and she'd felt a bit sorry for her. If she was forcing herself to go downstairs and greet her father's guests she must be very brave. Emily admired her for that even though she was a bit of a snob.

'There is a lot of food left over from the luncheon,' Mrs Hattersley said the next morning. 'We can eat most of it ourselves, but some is going to be wasted. Do you fancy a walk to the village, Emily? The vicar is holding a little supper at the church hall. He gives free food to anyone who attends his Bible readings.'

Emily had just finished scrubbing the pine table-top. She took the dirty water through to the little scullery at the back and tipped it into the deep stone sink, then came back.

'Yes, I know about the vicar's tea parties. Ma used to send me when I was small. We all had cakes and trifles, things most of us never have at home.'

'I dare say they were sent down from the manor. Lady Prior has always been generous that way. She may be a tartar to her family, but the poor of the village can always rely on her to send food and money when they're in trouble.'

'Shall I go alone? I can carry two baskets.'

'Pop upstairs and put your coat on, Emily. The sun is warm but you'll find the wind cold.'

'Is there anything you want me to do here before I go?'

'Not that I can think of. If I need her, Mary can help. You did her work yesterday and so it won't hurt her to do some of yours.'

'I didn't mind. It was interesting to see the lovely dishes and the silver they use upstairs all set out instead of when they come back dirty. Miss Amy's room is lovely, but a bit dark because of the colours. I enjoyed helping her, but I wasn't able to do her hair the way Mary does.'

'There was talk of Mary being Miss Amy's personal maid but I'm not sure what will happen now the wedding's off.'

'Mary would go to London and various places with Miss Amy then, wouldn't she?'

'I've got no use for travelling all over the show,' Mrs Hattersley said with a sniff. 'Don't you go getting ideas above yourself, Emily. It takes years to learn how to look after a lady's things properly.'

'Ma was a lady's maid before she married. She taught me how to care for silk and lace, even though we didn't have much, except second-hand stuff, and how to get stains off a skirt.'

Cook had finished packing the baskets. She set them down on the table with a bang, as if annoyed.

'Stop that dreaming, girl, and take these baskets to the vicarage. Don't dally on the way. I know how long it takes so no dawdling with young men.'

'I don't have any young men to dawdle with,' Emily laughed. 'Maybe I'm not clever enough to be a lady's maid yet, but I intend to be more than I am one day.'

'You'll do well enough with me. If I teach you to cook you'll be able to find a job anywhere. Take my advice and stick to cooking. Being a lady's maid is hard work and even longer hours than ours sometimes.'

Emily picked up her baskets and left the kitchen, walking through the small, enclosed courtyard and the large vegetable gardens behind it. She was glad of her coat because the wind was icy, though the sun felt lovely on her face. The weather had been cool lately, except for the odd warm day. She thought about what Mrs Hattersley had told her about working hard and becoming her assistant. If she learned how to cook delicious food the way Mrs Hattersley did she might stand a chance of a better job – perhaps in a hotel or even her own small teashop. It would be a good life, better than scrubbing the scullery floor each morning before six.

Yet her taste of waiting on Miss Amy had made her feel that she might prefer to be a lady's personal maid. Mrs Hattersley had spoken of long hours and Emily knew that was true. Her mother had told her about sitting up to two, three or four o'clock in the morning when there was an important ball. During the London season that might happen for five or six nights out of the week, but against that was the pleasure of handling beautiful clothes and seeing her lady dressed in her finery and jewels. However, Miss Amy would pick Mary unless she advertised for someone new, because Mary knew how she liked her hair.

What was Emily doing, thinking of a future in service? This job was only supposed to be for a short time, just until her father was well and able to earn a living again.

She began to whistle a tune. So far, working at the manor hadn't been as bad as she'd feared. She walked briskly because the wind was cool, lifting her hand to wave to one of the gardeners. They were all much friendlier now and Emily was used to fetching the vegetables they needed for dinner, getting to know her way about and the people who worked here. Two of the gardeners were older men with families, but there was also a young lad who was learning his trade. He did a lot of the digging and fetching and carrying; a bit like her, Emily thought. At the moment she was a maid of all work, but she didn't intend to spend the rest of her life this way. She wanted something better – and now that she'd seen a little of the house upstairs she thought she'd rather be above than below stairs.

The house was grand in its proportions with many more rooms than she'd yet seen, the windows small paned but letting in plenty of light because there were enough of them, not dark upstairs as it was in some of the rooms below stairs. The furniture was grand too – at least most of it was. Emily thought some of the wooden-seated chairs she'd seen were not much better than her Pa had in his barns, except that these were in better condition and well polished. Lady Prior seemed to be a hoarder and there were oak hutches, chairs and tables set at intervals all along the landings. On each of the tables stood a tall vase made of porcelain with odd-looking figures Emily thought might be Chinese painted all over them, and there were tall silver candlesticks and big brass bowls that she thought must be filled with rose petals, because there was a lovely smell.

It was a strange household, because everyone seemed to have their own favourite rooms and they furnished them differently. Emily hadn't seen inside most of them herself, but Tomas had told her what they were like. June did most of the polishing but Tomas helped her do the various parlours and he'd described the furniture in the grand drawing room. He'd told Emily there were far too many objects that needed dusting and June said she spent half her time polishing bits of glass and photograph frames.

'She can't need the half of them,' June had complained. 'It takes twice as long to get round as it should because of all the clutter. Some of it is precious but some of it's no more than rubbish in my opinion.'

Emily wondered what it would be like to live amongst such clutter and decided that if she were a part of the family she would sweep half of it away and have new. Laughing to herself, because it was never going to happen, she began to run.

Chapter 18

Emily realised she'd taken the wrong turning once more. After her return from the vicarage, Mrs Hattersley had sent her for more vegetables, but instead of the kitchen courtyard she'd ended up in the rose garden. The roses were not yet in flower but she could see the buds beginning to form on the bushes and guessed that they would be glorious in summer. From here she could see the house to advantage, its windows gleaming in the sunshine. The yellow brickwork looked in better condition here at the side of the house and there was something beautiful about the clean lines of its architecture, as if it had been built at a different period to the older buildings at the back. She thought this wing had probably been added on at a later date to the main wing; it looked like some of the glossy pictures of buildings in London she'd seen in books, which had been described as mid-Georgian period with a French influence. She wished there was someone she could ask about things like that, but Mrs Hattersley probably wouldn't know and Mr Payne never had time to gossip with the likes of Emily.

Dreaming again! She was in the wrong place and she wasn't sure where she'd made her mistake. When would she learn to tell her right from her left? She'd better retrace her steps and hope one of the gardeners would set her right. Miss Amy had said something about a water butt...

Just as she was about to turn back she heard a voice and halted. Someone was talking – or rather declaiming aloud. It sounded odd and Emily crept closer to the source until she could see the man walking up and down the rose arbour. It was Mr Nicolas. She'd hardly seen him since she'd been working at the manor and her heart took a flying leap as she remembered their dance. Looking at him from her hiding place, she thought he had the most beautiful face of any man she'd ever seen. Thin and sensitive and ... just lovely. What on earth was he doing?

'*Moonlight in her hair...*
I turn and she is there...
But when I reach for her she is gone...
And all the bright pleasures...'

He stopped abruptly and shook his head. 'No, not pleasures. Shorter – has to be shorter.'

'And all the sweet joys of life are gone...
For in her grave my beloved lies...
And my soul in despair cries...
Out and only the dark cold earth may ease...
My pain and give me peace...'

As Emily watched he ran his fingers through his hair and shook his head as if in pain, clearly dissatisfied with his work.

'No, no, it's not right ... no soul ... no soul...'

Mr Nicolas was a poet and obviously he was in some torment over his work. To Emily it was like a play or the pictures, but funnier. She was caught up by the drama of his torment and a sound that was part sympathy, part laughter escaped her.

He whirled round looking for the source of the sound but a bower of rose bushes hid Emily from his view. As he took a step towards her, she ran back the way she had come, not wanting him to know that she had witnessed his struggle to compose a poem he thought worthy. Emily thought the words beautiful – and he was beautiful, so fine and tortured and sensitive – but he thought his work was no good and he would not wish to be overheard. Besides, if she were caught spying on the family when she ought to be at work she might be dismissed. She saw the old green-painted water butt and made a beeline for it as she remembered what Miss Amy had told her.

This time she took the right turning and soon found herself in the familiar kitchen courtyard. An old wooden chair was outside the door and Billy the boot boy was cleaning a pair of gentleman's riding boots at a bench he'd set up, polishing them with a brush for all he was worth. A cat lay dozing in the sunshine and by the look of it she was expecting kittens soon. Billy grinned at her as she passed and Emily smiled, enjoying the sound of his cheerful whistling. Mrs Hattersley looked at her suspiciously as she entered the large room.

'And where have you been, miss?' she asked. 'You've taken your time.'

'I got lost again,' Emily apologised. 'I'll make a start on the vegetables as soon as I've washed the dishes.'

'You'll lose your head one of these days, my girl. Get on with you before I lose my patience.'

Emily was laughing as she went into the scullery. It was worth a little scold to have witnessed what she'd seen and heard.

Emily could hear an odd noise in the pantry, a scuffling sound that made her wonder. She opened the door and went in, giving a little cry of alarm as she saw the mouse scuttle away and disappear behind some jars and tins on the floor. It had come from the second shelf and on investigation Emily discovered it had been at a sack of dried fruit. There was either more than one or it had been going on for a while, because a hole had been nibbled through at one corner. She picked the little sack up and took it through to the kitchen to show Mrs Hattersley.

'Mice!' the cook shuddered. 'I hate those things. Filthy little beasts! This ought to have been put in a stone jar. Did you leave it out, Emily?'

'I've never seen it before this morning.'

'It was probably the last girl. Come to think of

it, it's months since I ordered these. Well, I'll have to throw this out.'

'Only one corner has been nibbled. Could you use just the top half if I put the fruit in a jar?'

'What are you talking about! Throw it out. I won't use contaminated stuff in my kitchen – and tell Tomas to set some traps.'

Emily took the sack through to the back room and placed it in a basket. Her mother wouldn't be so fussy. She'd use the top half and throw the stuff near where the mouse had been out for the birds.

Tomas came in as she was washing the shelf down and making certain nothing else was at risk from the mice. He shook his head when she told him that Mrs Hattersley wanted traps set.

'The damned creatures seem to know what you're after. They nibble the cheese and escape before the pin drops. I hardly ever manage to catch one.'

'You need to find where they get in and block it. That's what Pa did – and we had a cat that caught any that found their way in.'

'A cat?' Tomas nodded. 'There are plenty of strays in the stable. I'll shut one in here tonight. Cook will never know the difference.'

'Do you think you ought?' Emily looked at him doubtfully. 'Make sure there's nothing the cat can get at or we'll have trouble from Mrs Hattersley.'

Tomas glanced round. 'Nothing here to hurt I can see. Just make sure the meat and fish are on the top shelf and covered. I'm telling you, a cat is twice as good as a trap.'

'Emily!' Mrs Hattersley's cry of anguish brought her running from the scullery the next morning. The cook was staring at the kitchen table and quivering with temper. 'What's wrong?' Emily couldn't see anything on the table but the plate with Lord Barton's kippers. 'What's happened?'

'A cat – that's what,' Mrs Hattersley said. 'It sneaked in here and jumped on the table while my back was turned. I caught it sniffing at those kippers. I scared it off but the damage is done. How can I serve those to his lordship now?'

Emily looked closer. She could see one set of teeth marks where the cat had taken a quick bite before being driven away.

'We could cut that bit off the side and just run the rest under the tap. The heat of the frying pan will kill any germs – besides, it's only touched a little bit on the edge here.'

'I can't and won't serve those to his lordship.'

'I'll have them then,' Emily said. 'Kippers are a real treat – but what will you give his lordship?'

Mrs Hattersley looked thoughtful. 'He's fond of his kippers and he always has them on a Friday. What am I to do?'

'Why don't I just do this...?' Emily took a sharp knife and cut away a slice down one side, then did the other to match. 'There – he'll never know and the cat didn't touch the rest.'

Mrs Hattersley hesitated, then, 'You'd better trim the other to match or he'll wonder why only one has been done.'

Emily trimmed the second kipper to match. 'They look a proper treat. Don't be so anxious. What he doesn't know won't hurt him.'

'If he dies of food poisoning I shall blame you.'

Emily laughed. 'Believe me, there's a good many eat worse and never take sick. Honestly, the cat hardly touched it.'

'Well, against my better judgement...'

Emily smiled as she picked up the scraps and took them out to the yard. The pregnant cat was hiding under an upturned wheelbarrow. She laid the bits of kipper down for it and returned to the scullery. Three dead mice had been found when Tomas opened the pantry that morning. She reckoned the cat had earned her fish.

'You'd best get off then,' Mrs Hattersley said at the end of the week. 'Take the basket I've prepared. There's some calves foot jelly, which is good for weak chests. Your mother will know how to use it. I'm sending some of my special pickles and a joint of gammon for her to cook. It's my way of saying thank you to Mrs Carter for letting me have her daughter.'

Emily thanked her. Mrs Hattersley had been complimented on her new way of serving his lordship's kippers, and this was Emily's reward, 'Ma will be pleased with the things you've sent. It wasn't necessary but it's good of you.'

'Well, I'm allowed a few perks in my position and I like to share them. You're not the only one to take home a few bits when you visit.' She nodded and her three chins waggled with satisfaction. 'Has Mrs Marsh paid you?'

'Yes, she has. She told me she has decided to keep me on – and if I give good service my wage will go up to a pound a week soon.'

'Have a good day then.'

Emily shrugged on her coat and then picked up the basket. 'I shan't be late this evening. I'll tell you what my mother says when I get back.'

The sun was warm. Summer was really here now and it felt wonderful to have the day off and to be going home. She'd settled into the routine of the house and was enjoying her work, but it was still a good feeling to be free for once. She hummed a little tune as she walked across the fields, which were bright with wild flowers. On such a lovely day there was no need to waste money on bus fares; she could easily walk to her home.

There were people in the village as she walked through, women standing outside houses with cream-washed walls, in their aprons, often with a long broom or a duster in their hands, giving the windows a polish to make them shine in the sun. Some of the houses were very old, long and low with thatched roofs and small windows. Two men in working clothes were driving a farm wagon, the horse's coat gleaming with health, and its tail tied with red ribbons. She saw the milk cart ahead of her and waved, because she knew the man driving it. To her surprise, he halted his cart and beckoned to her.

'Going home, Em?'

'Yes, Bill. It's my day off.'

'Climb up then and I'll take you a part of the way.'

She thanked him and climbed on to the driving box beside him. It felt as if she were out with her father on his rounds again and she smiled at her benefactor. She wondered if he would ask lots of questions, but he merely nodded and kept his eyes on the road ahead, which was just as well because a motorcar was coming the other way and there was a loud pop as it passed them, causing the horse to shy. His milk churns rattled a little but he was in control and they were soon back to normal, plodding through the long High Street and out into the country lanes that would take Emily to her father's smallholding. He dropped her at the end of the lane leading to her house, tipping his hat but saying nothing as she thanked him.

As she approached the white-washed cottage that was her home, Emily began to think about her family. Was Derek still lurking about or had he stayed clear of the farm? She'd half expected her mother would write with news but no letters had come for her at the manor. A trickle of ice ran down her spine as she suddenly wondered if anything was wrong, and she ran the last few yards, bursting into the kitchen in sudden panic.

Ma looked up from her baking and frowned. 'Where's the fire? Nothing wrong is there? Have you been let go?'

'No. They are pleased with me.'

'What made you come rushing in as if your tail was on fire?'

'I wondered...' Emily felt foolish. 'You didn't write. How are Pa – and the child? I've missed him – and all of you.'

'Your brother has a name,' her mother said sourly. 'Why should I write and waste a stamp? I knew you would be home today. Your father was in the infirmary for a few days but he's all right now. His cough keeps getting worse but he says the doctor hasn't had the results of the test. I don't know if he's hiding something from me. He might tell you.'

Emily unloaded her basket on the sideboard. 'Mrs Hattersley sent these for you, Ma – and she was going to throw the fruit out, but the mice have only touched one corner.'

'Why did she send us food? We might not be rich but we're not a charity case.'

'She didn't mean it like that. It's just a few perks.'

'Well, I suppose I should thank her.' Ma glared at her across the room. 'Put the kettle on, girl. I don't have time to run after you.'

'Yes, Ma.' Emily filled the kettle and placed it on the range. 'Are you upset with me? What have I done?'

'You know very well what you did.' Ma's mouth twisted with dislike. 'Causing trouble between your father and Derek. Now my brother's gone off without a word to me.'

'Gone away?'

'I went over to see him to ask for the truth and found them clearing out his house. He'd sold his stuff and given up the tenancy. That farm had been in our family for years. What did you do to make him go off like that?'

'Pa must have told you what happened?'

'He said Derek was assaulting you but I don't believe it. My brother wouldn't do that to his own sister's girl. Your father must have misunderstood. Derek shouldn't have hit him like that but if your father went for him you can see why he did it.'

Emily clenched her hands. If she didn't hold on to her temper she would say or do something unforgivable.

'It wasn't the first time. He tried a few weeks earlier and then...' She gasped as her mother rushed at her, slapping her about the face and ears three times in quick succession. 'It's true, whatever you think. I didn't tell you because he apologised and said it was a joke – but the second time he had me on the ground and would have had his way if Pa and then Harry Standen hadn't arrived.'

'You are an unkind, sly girl,' Ma brushed tears from her cheeks. 'I shall never believe he did something like that without provocation.'

'I avoided him as much as I could but...' Emily stopped as she saw her mother was truly upset. 'I'm sorry. I know you're fond of him. Would you like me to leave?'

'Your father is looking forward to seeing you,' Ma said and her expression hardened. 'He's told me he won't have Derek here again.'

'I am truly sorry, Ma.' Emily took her wages from her pocket and placed the coins on the table. 'I didn't need to catch a bus so that's all of it. I don't need money at the house.'

Her mother barely glanced at the money. She picked up a tray of little cakes and put them in the oven, shutting the door with a bang.

'You will need some in future. Keep two shillings for yourself. The rest will help to pay the lad's wages. Your father told me he always paid Derek for his work so it won't make much difference.'

'It will help Pa.'

Ma cut a slice of her jam sponge and pushed it

across the table towards Emily. 'Sit down and I'll make the tea. I dare say you work hard enough.'

'The hours are long,' Emily said, biting into the cake, 'but I enjoy what I do.'

'Your father isn't happy about you being away from us all the time. He said to tell you that you could give in your notice if you're miserable. I said it would do you good to have a taste of life away from here.'

Emily caught the resentment in her mother's tone. 'I've always done my best, Ma. What is it that makes you take against me?'

'Do you want the truth?' Emily nodded and her mother turned away to pour boiling water into the large brown pot. 'It was always you with your father after you were born. He couldn't take his eyes off you, always saying how pretty you were, how much he loved you.'

'He loves you too – all of us.'

'You're the light of his life. He told me that if he lost you he wouldn't care if he lived or died.'

Emily sipped her tea in silence. She had an ache in her chest but her throat felt tight and she couldn't think of anything to say. Her mother's life had always been hard, because money was often tight, but this was something more – it struck deeper and made her realise how lonely and un-happy Ma must be. She realised that all the com-plaining over the years, all the finding fault with her father and the sullen looks might be down to the fact that Ma thought he loved his daughter more than her. It was sad and it hurt her, but no words of hers could ever heal the wounds her father had inflicted, whether he meant to or not.

For a moment the silence stretched between them, and then her mother lifted her head and looked at her. 'How is Miss Amy then? Everyone is talking about the way that man swindled all those investors and then threw her over.'

'Sir Arthur lost money too. I think she's all right but I don't see much of her.'

Ma looked up as the kitchen door opened. 'Here's your father come to see you. I'll leave you two alone for a minute while I see to Jack.'

Emily stood up and went to her father, who embraced her in a hug. She could smell the familiar scent of soap mixed with fresh sweat, his rough tweed jacket and a faint whiff of cow dung on his boots. It was a smell she remembered so well and it brought tears to her eyes as she realised how much she'd missed him. 'How are you, Pa? Is your cough better? Ma said you were in the infirmary for a few days.'

'I'm over it now, girl,' Pa said and moved back, as if embarrassed by his show of affection.

'Has the doctor told you the results of the tests?'

'Your mother told you to ask, did she?' He sighed and sat down at the table. 'It's not good, Em, but keep that to yourself. I've got signs of consumption. The doctor said I ought to go to the sea where the air is fresher, but I can't spare the time or the money.'

'My wages will help Pa. If there's anything more I can do...'

'I suppose we need the money – but I'd rather have you here, love. Christopher was asking after you yesterday.'

'Has he been busy?'

'The shop is ticking over. Without it there wouldn't be a hope of my going away for treatment, but your mother can't see that. She thinks I'm wasting my money on rubbish.'

'Some of it looks like rubbish, Pa.'

'I can't deny that, love, but Christopher is a marvel. He's polished a set of twelve mahogany dining chairs up a treat and mended a splat that was broken. I would have sold them for a pound each, but he managed to get eighteen pounds for them. At least, he's taken a deposit of five pounds and the rest should be paid this week.'

'That is a lot of money.' Emily was shocked. 'Did you know they were worth so much?'

'None of us did until Sir Arthur popped into the shop. I've got to deliver them. He's gone abroad but his bailiff will take them in for him and pay me the balance.'

'Gone abroad – I suppose he'll have gone to see what happened with his mine.'

'He'll be away for months then. He's our best customer.'

Emily's mother returned to the kitchen then with Jack. He'd been crying but was now smiling and held out his arms to Emily. She took him on her lap, cuddling him to her. He smelled of baby powder and gurgled as she bounced him on her knee. It felt good to hold him again, because whoever his father was, he was her brother and she loved him. She kissed his cheek and began to feed him tiny pieces of cake from her plate.

'How is my little love then?' she asked in a soft voice. 'I've missed you, Jack.' She kissed the top of his head, noticing with a frown that his hair needed washing. Was her mother not taking proper care of him? He'd been as spotless as a new pin when she'd been here to care for him.

'Jack needs a bath,' she said, looking at her mother in accusation.

'You do it then,' Ma snapped. 'I've got enough to do. Now you're having a good time up at the manor, I've all the work to do here. I can't be fussing over Jack all the time.'

At the sound of his mother's harsh voice, Jack whimpered. Emily stroked his face. 'Of course I'll give him a bath before I go,' she said. 'He's no trouble at all, are you, my darling?'

She shot a look at her mother but was ignored and felt a spurt of anger. If Ma was ignoring Jack because he was a little backward ... but she wouldn't. Emily was just imagining things because her pleasure in the visit had been spoiled by Ma's attitude and she would be glad to get back to the manor, where she was appreciated.

'Lady Prior is taking Miss Amy away to the sea for a few days,' Mrs Hattersley said when Emily returned that evening. 'I suppose she thinks she needs to get away for a while.'

'I expect it will do her good.'

Mrs Hattersley nodded, but didn't say anything, just got on with preparing a tray. 'Miss Amy wanted a light supper in her room. You can take it up for me.'

'What about Mary?'

'She's off on an errand so she won't know anything about it.'

Emily accepted the tray and carried it up the back stairs. Mary was jealous of her place with Miss Amy, and if she thought Emily was currying favour with her she wouldn't like it.

When she knocked at the door Miss Amy asked her to come in. She looked a little surprised, then half-smiled. 'Emily Carter. Are you settling in well?'

'Yes, thank you, miss.'

'Leave the tray there.'

Emily did as she was told, but as she walked to the door, Miss Amy spoke to her again. 'Would you take a note for me please?'

'Yes, miss, of course.'

Amy picked up the letter. 'It's for Sir Arthur. I don't want anyone to see it.'

Emily hesitated, then, 'I think he's gone abroad, miss – at least they were saying so in the village, Pa told me...'

Amy frowned, and then took the letter back. 'I'd hoped he might write to me. Very well, you may go.'

'I'm sorry, miss.'

'I don't need your pity.'

Emily heard the resentment in her voice and left. Miss Amy's temper hadn't improved. She was glad Mary was her maid and not her.

As she left the room and walked down the landing, she met Miss Lizzie. The girl smiled at her and stopped.

'Miss Carter. How are you getting on here?'

'Very well, miss. I like my job.'

'I'm so pleased,' Miss Lizzie said. 'Did you take a tray into Amy? Granny is taking us away because she is so unhappy but I don't think it will help.'

'No, miss. I don't suppose it will.'

'It was so unfair on her – him too. It wasn't Sir Arthur's fault that the government took those leases back. He believed they had been renewed in time – and it's my opinion he's been cheated out of his mine.'

'I'm very sorry to hear that, Miss Lizzie.'

'Yes, it has spoiled everything.'

Emily agreed and Miss Lizzie walked on. Emily was thoughtful as she returned to the kitchen. Miss Lizzie had been very upset, as much for Sir Arthur as anyone, which if he'd been cheated out of his mine was understandable. Emily thought she was a pleasant girl, more thoughtful and kinder than her sister.

Chapter 19

'Mrs Marsh says the family will be home tomorrow,' Mrs Hattersley said that morning in July. 'Miss Amy is feeling much better. She will be able to help with the fete as usual and that is at the end of the week, as you know.'

'Yes, I know,' Emily agreed. Since Lady Prior had informed them that this year the event would take place in early August, Mrs Hattersley had talked about the refreshments needed and the cakes she intended to bake for the stall that sold all manner of sweet treats. Emily had been honoured by being allowed to make some of the smaller fancies. She told Cook that she was looking forward to watching her make the rum truffles and butterscotch fudge.

'We'll make them together. You've been here long enough now and I know I can trust you.'

Emily felt pleased that her efforts had been appreciated, because she'd worked hard to please. She was allowed one evening off every two weeks and she'd written to Christopher, telling him to come over and see her, if he could manage it. He'd come on the appointed evening, and they'd gone for a walk to the village, where he'd bought her a lemonade in the Golden Hen.

Emily had seen how tired and ill Josh Bracknell looked and couldn't help thinking about the way he'd lost his daughter so tragically. Who could have murdered a young girl like that and left her lying in a field? It was a wicked, callous act and Emily dare not put a name to her suspicions. She didn't like Derek but he wouldn't do something like that, of course he wouldn't. Up at the manor, Mrs Hattersley still spoke about Carla often, because everyone wondered what had happened to the murderer. The police were no closer to finding him and all the maids had been warned not to speak to strangers if they went into the village.

Christopher had seemed very serious that evening when he came, and Emily asked what was wrong.

'Did you hear about that foreign archduke?' he'd asked her and she nodded. 'It was in all the papers when he was assassinated back in June. It's going to mean war Emily and this country will be dragged into it. I don't see how we can avoid it.'

'You wouldn't join up?' She looked at him in alarm. 'Christopher, you wouldn't?'

'I'll have to. It's my duty.'

'What will happen to the shop if you go? Pa couldn't manage it without you.'

'I know – but I'll have to go once it starts. I'm going to tell your father this week when he comes.'

'He will be disappointed.'

'I couldn't stay safe at home while others were fighting for king and country.'

'No, I don't suppose you could,' Emily said, shivering as the horror of it came home to her. 'I shall miss you, even if I don't often see you.'

'I'll miss seeing you too,' he said and hesitated. 'Will you come out with me next time you have an afternoon off?'

'It won't be for three weeks.'

'We'll make it a date then. I'll close the shop for an afternoon, leave a note in the window and work a bit later at night to make up for it.' He gave her an oddly shy look. 'Are you sure you want to come?'

Emily assured him she did and thanked him; she hugged his arm as he walked her home. Just before they got to the kitchen door, he aimed a kiss at her cheek, and then blushed. Emily thought of the intimate kisses she'd shared with Harry, but Christopher was different. He clearly intended to take things slowly. She kissed him back on the cheek.

'I'll see you soon,' she said and went into the kitchen.

'Wool gathering again? Got something on your mind, Emily?'

Mrs Hattersley's words broke into her thoughts and she jumped. She was supposed to be scrubbing the table, not staring into space. She rinsed her cloth and finished wiping the table down. 'Sorry, Cook. What did you say?'

'I asked you to fetch me some beans if Mr Saunders has any. If not bring the last of the asparagus or broccoli – or whatever is going.'

'I was thinking of something...' She looked Mrs Hattersley in the eye. 'Do you think there will be a war?'

Mrs Hattersley had been stirring a sauce on the range. She removed the pan and poured the sauce into a jug.

'Mr Payne thinks it will happen soon.'

'A friend of mine is going to join up when it does. He's taking me to the pictures on my next day off.'

'Let's hope it hasn't started before then,' Mrs Hattersley said. 'I don't know what will happen here. Mr Jonathan can't be spared but Mr Nicolas may feel it his duty – and some of the footmen and gardeners may go.'

Emily felt cold all over. 'I don't understand why our men have to go off and fight because some Austrian archduke was murdered.'

'It's all to do with treaties and quarrels between Serbia and Austria and France. We signed up to help if our allies were in trouble and we have to keep our word.' She looked at Emily oddly. 'I didn't know you had a young man?'

'Christopher is just a friend that's all. He works for my father in the shop.'

There was a gorgeous smell coming from the

oven. Cook bent down and took out a treacle tart. She poured her sauce over it and placed it to one side. A plate of small tarts went into the oven.

'I've seen your father's shop. Looks like a load of old rubbish to me, though I did see a nice silver vase in the window once.'

'Most of it looks like junk to me too,' Emily said with a laugh. 'I suppose Pa may have to close the shop until after the war.'

'There will be a lot of that going on,' Mrs Hattersley said and frowned. 'Think yourself lucky your father is too old to join up. A lot of wives and mothers are going to be weeping before long.'

Emily didn't answer her but tears burned behind her eyes. She was glad Pa wouldn't have to go but most of the young men would sign up. The thought of all those men being killed or maimed for life made her want to weep. War was horrible. She'd read about all the men who had died of fevers and dysentery in the Crimea and her heart ached for what was coming. Why did anyone want to go to war?

She blinked hard and pushed the thought from her mind. It would soon be the day of the fete and everyone at Priorsfield was looking forward to it, even though it would mean lots of hard work.

'It's a lovely day for it,' Mrs Hattersley said as Emily joined her in the kitchen that Saturday morning. They had both of them risen early so as to get a good start on the refreshments for the party. The family would still need to be fed, though it was tradition that they had a good breakfast and then a light buffet at lunch. 'I should think there will be a decent crowd with the weather like this – and especially because it may be a while before anything of the kind happens again.'

'Because of the war?'

'Things will be different once it starts. We might not get all the supplies we need and we're bound to lose staff. One of the Phillips brothers has already gone off to join up. He'll be leaving as soon as it starts.'

'Was it Tomas?'

'No. I dare say he knows he's on to a good thing here and will stick it out until the last. It was his brother.'

'He is brave to go off before he needs to, don't you think?'

'Brave or daft,' Mrs Hattersley said, beating eggs in a bowl. She'd already fried bacon, sausages, kidneys and triangles of bread, which were keeping hot under silver covers. 'Let's get these breakfasts out of the way and then we can start on the sandwiches and pastries. You baked most of the cakes yesterday and the jellies I made have set overnight in the pantry.'

Emily had been told all this before but didn't mind going over it again. 'What about the fudge and the coconut ice and all the rest of it?'

'They are better in the pantry where the footmen can't get at them. If they get the chance they'll disappear before they ever get to the stall.'

She laughed and got on with her work. They had to work hard in the kitchen but the fete was like a holiday and most of the staff would get a chance to visit the stalls or watch some of the games during the afternoon.

She worked solidly until ten as Mrs Hattersley had instructed and then began to load up her trays. They were using the older china, plain white and some Staffordshire blue and white dishes that were normally used in the kitchens. None of the expensive sets from Coalport or Derby or Minton were taken from the large cabinets where they were stored, because it was likely there would be breakages before the day was out.

Emily was sure of her way about the gardens now. Besides, it was easy to follow the stream of men and women walking back and forwards with various loads. The gardeners had baskets of fruit and vegetables, pot plants and cut flowers, which would either be raffled or used as a prize of some kind. Mary had been helping Miss Amy with clearing out the junk stored in a room kept for the purpose. She was carrying a pile of cushions, beaded purses, shoes and hats as they met and gave Emily a look of triumph.

'I'm going to buy some of these things for my-self,' she said. 'Miss Amy said I must take them all to the stall but then I can buy what I want when the fete starts.'

'That is a pretty hat,' Emily said looking at a green felt with a curling feather over the brim. Mary was gloating but Emily didn't mind; she was enjoying herself carrying trays of food through the gardens on such a lovely day. 'My mother would like that but you've got first choice, Mary.'

'I like the shoes. They were Lady Barton's and she's hardly worn them but they fit me lovely. I shall wear them to go out with Ken when he takes me to the dance next week.'

'Is it the one in Ely?'

'At the corn exchange. It's always good fun. Ken says he's got something to tell me.' She seemed pleased with herself and it was nice to see her in a good mood for once. Most of the staff were friendly once Emily got to know them but Mary was still a little sullen.

As the other girl trotted off with her treasures, Emily found her way to the cake stall. The vicar's daughter Janet was running it and she welcomed Emily's first contribution.

'Oh, what lovely cakes,' she said. 'Did you make them?'

'I made two of them and Mrs Hattersley made that one,' Emily said. 'I've got several more loads to bring so I shall have to make several journeys.'

'You've been busy already.'

'Cook said to stop the footmen pinching the sweets.'

Janet laughed. 'I know them of old. I shall make them pay like everyone else.'

Emily nodded and turned away. In her hurry to return to the kitchen, she was walking fast round a bend in the path when she collided with some-one. Looking up, she blushed as she saw it was Mr Nicolas who was carrying some more stuff for the white elephant stall.

'I'm so sorry, sir,' she apologised, her face on fire. 'I was in a hurry.' She bent down to pick up a silver vase and their heads touched again as he bent to retrieve something. 'Sorry. I'm so stupid.'

'Not at all,' Nicolas contradicted, his eyes laughing at her. 'I've seen you about since you started working here, but we haven't bumped into each other before.'

'No...' She saw he was laughing and couldn't help laughing too. 'I'll try to be more careful in future.'

'Don't worry. I rather enjoyed it.'

Emily's heart jerked. He was even better looking than she remembered; his pale, sensitive face smiling rather than pensive as it so often was. He had a soft mouth and eyes that challenged and provoked – and she had better get on with her work or she would catch it from Mrs Hattersley.

Just before she turned into the kitchen garden, she glanced back and saw that he was still watching her. Something made her smile and he saluted her, dropping one of his books again. Emily couldn't help laughing, though once she was out of sight she ran to make up for lost time. Whatever was she doing, dallying with the son of the house? Yet he was so charming that no one could blame her for responding to his teasing.

'You took your time,' Mrs Hattersley said when she entered the kitchen. 'I've baked some more almond tarts because we're bound to need them for the refreshment tent. They always run out before the end of the day.'

Emily loaded her tray and set off again. She couldn't help looking for Mr Nicolas but he was nowhere to be seen, though she met Miss Amy carrying an armful of clothes.

'Oh, Emily,' Amy said. 'You couldn't take these to the secondhand stall for me, could you?'

'Yes, of course I can, Miss Amy.'

Emily took the clothes, including some lovely dresses, which smelled of Amy's perfume –

251

something delicate and light and expensive. A trip to the second-hand stall would take her longer but she couldn't refuse a request from her employer's daughter. Leaving the clothes with the lady looking after the stall, she was about to start back to the kitchen when the lady asked, 'What am I to charge for these?'

Emily was surprised by her question. 'I don't know. Miss Amy just told me to bring them – but I should think they ought to be worth quite a bit. That blue dress is gorgeous.'

'Would you like me to put it aside for you?'

'Well ... yes, please,' Emily said. 'I'll come and look once the stalls are open. If I can afford it I'll buy it.'

She thanked her and walked away. A dress like that when new would cost more than she earned in a year, perhaps longer – but from a second-hand stall it might not be more than the six shillings Emily had to spend. If it was more she would just have to apologise and tell the obliging stall minder to put it out for general sale.

Chapter 20

'Well, I think that all went well,' Nicolas said to his sisters as they relaxed under the shade of a tree with a cup of tea. 'Father's speech was well received and everyone seems to be enjoying themselves.'

'Yes, I think they always do,' Amy smiled at him.

'We've all done our bit. I think the clothes I donated have all been sold – as has most of Mama's junk. The cake stall was cleared halfway through the afternoon and I saw Emily practically running backwards and forwards with plates for the refreshment tent.'

'It was all rather splendid,' Nicolas said. 'She's a pretty little thing, isn't she? I'd hardly noticed her about the place until we bumped into each other earlier this morning.'

'Emily is actually quite pretty,' Amy said. 'I thought she was just another farm girl at first, but she isn't. I like her – much more than Mary. I'm thinking of asking her to come with me as my maid when I go up to London next week.'

'Is it agreed that you're going?' Lizzie said. 'I asked Mama if I could come too and she said no.'

'It isn't a shopping trip and I shan't be visiting theatres or museums much,' Amy told her. 'I've heard about a voluntary scheme that the Queen has been involved in setting up. I'm going to an interview to see if I would be suitable.'

'Because you think there is going to be a war?' Lizzie looked at her sister. 'Why can't I join too?'

'Because Mama thinks you're too young. She didn't want me to go but I told her I couldn't sit at home doing nothing if there was something I could do to help. If Her Majesty thinks these voluntary things are worth while then it is our duty to do what we can. Father agreed with me. He thought it was better than me sitting around doing nothing...' Amy broke off as their father came striding towards them. 'Something is wrong...'

It was clear from her father's manner that he

was upset or anxious. All three rose to their feet as he approached.

'I'm afraid it's grave news,' he said. 'We have declared war on Germany. It's official now. There is no going back...'

'We expected it,' Nicolas said. 'Are you going to announce it? Everyone is enjoying themselves. It seems such a pity...'

'I think you'll find the news has already reached them...' Lord Barton said glancing towards the stalls. There was a buzz of excitement and everyone was talking and looking about them. 'People are starting to leave. No doubt some of the men will soon be off to join up.'

'It's just as well I've already done so,' Nicolas said. 'I signed up to the Royal Flying Corps some days ago. I was going to tell you this evening after dinner.'

Lord Barton stared at him for several seconds, and then inclined his head. 'Had I known this earlier I might have objected but there's no point in making a song and dance of it now.'

Nicolas looked relieved. 'Thank you, sir. I'm glad to have your blessing.'

'Well, we shall all have to do our bit now,' Lord Barton said. 'I dare say I may be called on to sit on a few committees. I heard that the government will be looking for houses to use as convalescent homes for the wounded. I do not think this house is quite large enough for their needs. Barton Abbey would have been ideal – but that belongs to your uncle...'

The look in his eyes told his children what he thought of that situation.

'Does this mean I can go to London with Amy?' Lizzie asked.

'No, I do not think so, my dear. Your mother is uneasy enough about Amy going without her – and she will be devastated when she hears Nicolas's news. Perhaps in a few months' time if the war continues, though they say it will be over quite soon.'

'You don't believe that?' Nicolas said softly and his father hesitated, and then shook his head.

'No, I don't believe it, but we should allow your mother and grandmother to do so, however. There is no purpose in upsetting them more than necessary.'

'I think we should mingle. People are looking to us for a lead. Perhaps you should say something, Father?'

'Yes, of course. I must do so at once.'

Lord Barton walked towards a little group of worried looking villagers and estate workers, his children following behind.

'Goodness knows what this means for the estate,' Nicolas said. 'I pity Jonathan. He will have a hell of a time finding decent employees. I dare say he will cope, but I don't envy him at all...'

Nicolas frowned as he saw the effect the news of war had on everyone at the fete. Of course most people had been expecting it for months, but it was a shock just the same. People looked at each other in fear, wondering what the future would mean, because a lot of men were going to die even if the war was over in a few months.

Nicolas didn't believe that for one moment.

The papers would be filled with jingoistic non-sense but the truth of it was that the Germans were far more prepared than they were. The government had been dragging its feet, as usual, hoping for peace rather than planning for war.

He was glad he'd volunteered before it happened rather than getting caught in the general rush. There would be queues at every recruiting station – hundreds of men eager and willing to sign up, but once they discovered the reality of war they would soon wish themselves back in their dull little lives at home.

Nicolas shuddered, and then glanced at Emily as she carted a pile of dirty dishes back to the kitchens. She worked like a trooper, because she'd been on her feet long before the family was up. He felt a pang of regret. Emily was lovely. He thought about the moment when their heads had clashed and he'd wanted to take her in his arms and kiss her. She'd taken all the blame herself, laughing and apologising for her stupidity, when it was just as much his.

Of course there could never be anything between them. Nicolas knew that the divide was too great. His father would disown him if he attempted to bring a girl of her class into the family, and Emily was too nice, too decent a girl for anything less than marriage. He'd always liked her, from the first time he'd seen her looking at him so proudly in the fields – and then at the dance when Amy had been so mean about her clothes. All Nicolas had noticed was that she was lovely, until his sister had pointed out the faults with her clothes and her boots. At least she had her white satin slippers now. He wondered if she'd been pleased with them; he hoped so. He would have liked to give her much more ... but of course that wasn't possible. It would never be possible and he should put her right out of his mind.

His entire family would be scandalised if he dared to think of courting a servant! Even if to him she was the most beautiful girl in the world.

Chapter 21

'Well, there it is then,' Mrs Hattersley said when Tomas brought the news to the kitchen. 'I sensed it was coming but that doesn't make things any easier.'

Lord Barton had made the announcement of war just as the fete was drawing to its close. Emily had been in the kitchen washing up, but she and Mrs Hattersley were enjoying a well-earned cup of tea when the footman entered, looking worried. As soon as he told them the news, she understood his anxiety.

'Are you going to join up, Tomas?' Emily asked.

'Not unless they force me,' the footman replied. 'I don't see why I should rush to volunteer.'

'I'm glad to hear it,' Mrs Hattersley said. 'Where would we be if all the men in the house rushed off to join the army?'

'My brother and two of my cousins are going. That's enough for any family,' Tomas said. 'I'm not a coward, Emily, so don't think it, but I can't see the point of rushing to throw my life away.'

'You can help Emily bring the plates back from the refreshment tent, and leftovers, if there are any,' Mrs Hattersley said. 'I don't know about dinner tonight. I'm all of a flutter. I think it will have to be something simple.'

'They shouldn't expect any more,' Tomas said. 'You've both been run off your feet all day.'

'I could do with a rest,' Emily said, 'but I suppose we'd better make a start. Bring those trays, Tomas. We might borrow one of the gardener's trolleys and bring back a load instead of carting one at a time.'

'You'll do no such thing,' Mrs Hattersley said. 'I don't want more of the china broken thank you. Mary dropped a tray when she was bringing back a pile of empty plates.'

Emily could understand Mary dropping a tray, because they'd all been on the go since five that morning. She was tired herself but Mrs Hattersley didn't seem to think she needed a rest.

Tomas looked at her a couple of times as they walked to the refreshment tent. Most of the stalls had been taken down but the trestle tables set up inside the marquee were still loaded with dirty crockery.

'Cat got your tongue, Emily?'

'I'm just tired...' She glanced at a man coming out of the tent. 'Oh no...'

'What's wrong?'

'I know that man. Don't leave me, Tomas. If he tries to come near me, don't let him. Please. It's very important that he shouldn't get me alone.'

Tomas's gaze narrowed. 'Who is he? Has he

harmed you? If he tries anything today, I'll knock his head off.'

'I thought he'd left the district.'

'He'll be leaving quick enough if he upsets you.'

'Thank you.' She shot him a grateful smile just as her uncle saw her and began to walk in their direction.

'Emily,' Derek said as he came up to them. 'Your mother told me I should find you here.'

'Please stand aside and let me get on with my work.'

'It's important, Emily. They've carted Joe off to the infirmary and your mother wants you to go to him as soon as you can.'

She stared at him, her heart thudding against her chest. 'How do I know you're telling me the truth?'

'I wouldn't lie to you about something like this.' Derek's eyes narrowed. 'I've got a truck I borrowed from your pa's neighbour, to take you, but if you don't want a lift find your own way there.'

'I'd rather go alone.'

'Suit yourself.'

Her heart caught as he turned and walked off. She turned to Tomas and fear was in her eyes. 'I need to get to the infirmary but I can't trust him. How can I get to Ely quickly?'

'I'll ask Mr Nicolas if I can take you in the Daimler. I drive it to the garage for repairs sometimes.' Tomas sprinted off while Emily watched her uncle's retreating back and agonised over whether she'd done the right thing. As she tried to fight down her panic, she saw Mr Nicolas turn his head and then start walking towards her. Instinctively, she went to meet him.

'Come with me, Emily. I'll take you in to Ely myself. Are you all right like that or do you need to change?'

'I should like to go at once, sir.'

'Tomas will explain to Mrs Hattersley so you will not be in trouble.'

She hurried to keep up with his long strides. In her distress for her father she had forgotten to be shy or to worry about keeping to her place.

'My father has not been well for a while. The doctor said he ought to be at the sea, because the air is better, but he wouldn't listen. He didn't want to take so much time off work.'

'Better a few months at a clinic than eternity in a box. Now he's had this setback he may listen to his doctor.'

Emily dug her nails into the palms of her hands. She could feel a scream building inside her head but she fought it down.

Her father couldn't die. He mustn't die, because she couldn't bear it if he did. The tears were close but she refused to let them fall. Her father was ill but he was strong. He would fight for his life and then he'd go to the sea and get better.

'I am sorry, Miss Carter. We sent your uncle for you immediately but that was some hours ago. Your father had an attack of coughing and his heart failed him. No one had realised that his heart was weak. His doctor told us he was in the first stages of consumption but any signs of heart trouble had been missed.'

'Damned incompetence,' Nicolas muttered.

'This is supposed to be a hospital. Surely you could have done something once you had him here?'

'I'm afraid it was too late by the time we realised he was in difficulty.'

'Is my mother here?' Emily asked. She was too stunned to think clearly or to blame anyone for her father's death, even though her companion obviously thought the infirmary was to blame. The smell of disinfectant and carbolic was stinging her nostrils and the dark cream and bottle green paint on the walls was depressing. It was a horrible place and she hated to think of her father lying here in one of the narrow beds with bars up the sides. He'd been too young – this place was for the old and the infirm, people who had nowhere else to go. 'Was she with him when he died?'

'Mrs Carter was waiting in the corridor. She had a small child with her and we couldn't allow her into the ward.'

'My father died alone?' Emily stared at the doctor in horror. Giving a cry of despair, she turned instinctively to her companion who responded to her need by putting his arms about her. Her father had been all alone in his last hours. The thought was unbearable, tearing her apart as she pictured him lying there in pain with no one to comfort him.

She should have been with him. She'd been having fun at the fete and her father was lying in a hospital bed dying. The pain intensified to such a degree that she thought she would die of it. Pa alone and frightened...

Nicolas stroked her hair as she wept against his

261

shoulder. 'He couldn't have known much about it, Emily. I should imagine he was unconscious – is that not so, doctor?'

'Yes ... of course, Mr Barton. He was already unconscious when he arrived. He couldn't have known or suffered after the first few minutes or so.'

'It's all right to cry, Emily,' Nicolas said and she felt the touch of his lips on the top of her head. He smelled of fresh, light cologne, leather and wood, and the clean scent of his linen. His arms felt strong as they supported her, his body warm and comforting. 'Would you like to see him? That would be all right, wouldn't it, doctor?'

'Yes, of course, sir.'

Emily looked up at the man holding her. His sensitive face was concerned for her, caring. The expression in his eyes made her dare to ask, 'Would you come with me please?'

'I should not dream of leaving you.'

She hesitated, then nodded and drew back. 'Yes, I would like to say goodbye. It was just the thought of him lying alone, thinking no one cared.'

'I'm sure he wouldn't have thought it even if he'd known what was happening. I imagine he knew you loved him.'

'He loved me. I'm not sure if he knew how much I loved him.' She looked at the doctor. 'Has my mother been to see him since it happened?'

'She left as soon as we told her the news. Apparently, the child needed changing and she wished to catch the bus to get home.'

Emily flinched, feeling as if she'd been struck. How could her mother just leave her husband lying there and go home without even saying goodbye? Ma had never truly loved him, but surely she cared enough to say goodbye? A wave of hopeless despair swept through Emily. If only she'd been at home with him, perhaps she might have seen how ill he was – she might have got him here in time?

But it was all useless now. He was dead.

'I should like to see him now please.'

Nicolas held out his hand to her and she took it. His strong fingers clasping hers tightly gave her courage.

'Death is only moving on to another place,' he said. 'If you believe in God you will believe in the resurrection.'

'Do you believe?'

'Most of the time,' he said and smiled wryly. 'It isn't always easy but I manage it most of the time.'

'Then I shall try,' she said. 'It's the least I can do for him.'

Nicolas nodded to her and her head lifted, pride giving her the strength to face the worst moment of her life.

Emily's eyes felt gritty from crying. She sat on the edge of her bed and looked round her room at the manor. She'd made it her own, bringing things from her bedroom at home, all the little pieces that her father had given her over the years – stuff that she'd thought of as junk. It wasn't junk to her any more, but precious, more valuable to her than the Sevres porcelain dishes that lived in the cabinets downstairs in the manor and only came out on special occasions.

Getting up, she walked over to the little chest of drawers on which her treasures were displayed. There was a cut-glass bowl with a silver top. Only one of a set and therefore not saleable, her father had told her. He'd given her the little Derby figurine too, because it had been repaired on one hand. There was an opaque glass vase with a tiny chip at the lip; it would have been valuable had it been perfect – and a set of silver brushes for her hair, slightly dented but nothing Christopher couldn't have sorted out. Pa had given her them as a birthday gift. At the time she wished he'd bought her a new pair of shoes, but the shoes would've been worn out by now and the silver brushes would last for ever.

'Oh, Pa...' she whispered, her throat catching. 'Why did you have to die? I loved you so much...'

Her life seemed to have gone so fast up to the point where she'd left home to live at the manor. She hadn't realised how lucky she was, often resenting those cold, wet days when she'd sat outside houses on the cart and waited for her father to return with an armful of treasures. Emily had longed for a different life and she was happy here – but just for a while she wished she could go back to the time when her Pa was well and always laughing at her.

She remembered the good days when he'd done well and bought her fish and chips in a newspaper. She'd sat beside him as he drove home at a leisurely pace, eating the delicious food and smiling and waving to the friends they met on the journey. They seemed sunlit, idyllic days and she forgot about the cold mists that crept over the Fen roads, soaking them both through and making her wish herself at home by the fire.

Pa wouldn't want her to feel miserable. Emily dashed the tears from her face and then washed it in cool water from her jug. She was daft sitting here moping. Mrs Hattersley would be rushed off her feet and the best thing Emily could do was to go down and help her.

A knock at her door made her stiffen and it was a moment before she said, 'Come in.'

The door opened and June entered. 'I'm so sorry, Emily,' she said. 'I heard about your father. If there is anything at all I can do please ask.'

'No, I don't think so. He's gone. No one can bring him back.'

'Death is so final,' June agreed. 'I was engaged to be married before I came here. My fiancé died two days before our wedding of a fever. I had no idea he was ill.'

'I'm so sorry. Did you love him very much?'

'Yes. I never had any desire to marry anyone else.' June smiled at her. 'So you see, I understand how it feels to lose someone – and I wanted you to know that we are all your friends here.'

'Thank you.'

Emily was close to tears again as the other woman went out, closing the door softly behind her. She'd never guessed that June had a secret, but the fact that she had been willing to share it to comfort Emily made her feel she was with friends and some of her loneliness eased.

'You will want time off for the funeral,' Mrs Hattersley said the next morning. She had bread baking in the oven and the smell was delicious. 'Shall I ask for the whole day for you, Emily?'

'No. I'll only need a few hours. I shall come back here as soon as the service is over.'

Emily had drawn her luxuriant dark hair back into a tight knot at the nape of her neck, fastening it with combs and pins. There were shadows beneath her eyes and her nose looked red, because of the tears she'd shed on waking.

'You won't go home afterwards?'

'I've nothing to say to anyone that can't keep for another day. I think my uncle is staying at the house with Ma. I shall never enter that house again while he is there.'

'Do you mind if I ask why?'

Emily hesitated, and then told her – including the part about her mother blaming her for her uncle's attack.

'It wasn't your fault.' Mrs Hattersley nodded to herself. 'That settles it then, Emily. I was wondering if I should come with you. After what you've told me I wouldn't think of letting you go alone.'

'Are you sure you can take time off?'

'We'll prepare dinner before we go and get a move on when we return. If they have to wait upstairs for once that's too bad. I'm coming with you, and there's an end of it.'

Mrs Hattersley's plump face reflected her distress and her voice wobbled; her eyes a little watery as if she was battling against tears. Emily's throat caught because she knew that the cook was her friend and was determined to look out for her.

'You've all been so kind. I don't know what I should have done if Mr Nicolas hadn't looked out for me. He handled everything.'

'Now that was good of him. It is very like Mr Nicolas. We shall miss him now he's gone off to join his unit. He's joined the Royal Flying Corps – that's the flyboys to you and me, Emily.'

Emily's heart caught at the news, because she didn't think she could bear it if anything happened to Mr Nicolas. He had comforted her when she was told of her father's death, holding her as she wept. She knew she could never see him as just her employer's son again; he was special to her, though of course she would never let him see it. He was a member of the family and she was just a kitchen girl – but that didn't stop her liking him more than any man she'd ever met.

'Everyone will be devastated if anything happens to him,' she said.

Mrs Hattersley looked grave. 'War is a bad business, Emily. I wish it hadn't happened. There will be a lot of young men going off to Belgium and some of them will never return.'

'I shall pray Mr Nicolas isn't one of them.'

'We must hope he comes through safe. You'll be wearing grey or black for the funeral I expect.'

'I don't have a black dress.'

'The upper parlour maids wear a black uniform. Mrs Marsh might allow you to have one so you could wear it to the funeral.'

'Thank you. That would be just right – if she would allow it.'

'I think she might. Now go and make a start on the vegetables. Sitting around moping never helped anyone.'

Emily got up and went through to the scullery, putting all thoughts of Mr Nicolas from her mind. She was happy to work. It helped to take her mind off the fact that her father had died alone and that she would never see him again.

'I'm sorry I wasn't there, Pa,' she said and a tear rolled down her cheek. She brushed a hand over her cheek, dislodging wisps of springy hair that hung about her face despite all her efforts to restrain it. 'I'm so sorry I wasn't with you when you needed me.'

Chapter 22

Emily felt frozen throughout the service. Clouds had obscured the sun as they arrived at the ancient church, but a thin ray filtered through the beautiful stained glass windows, sending spirals of colour on to the worn stone floor. She sat on the hard wooden pew behind her mother and uncle, with Mrs Hattersley by her side. The rest of the church was filled with friends and villagers. Joe Carter had been a popular man and a lot of voices swelled the choir when the hymns were sung.

Emily's mother was sniffing the whole time and her uncle was comforting her, for all the world as if he cared about what had happened. Bitterness swirled inside Emily as she remembered the day he'd tried to rape her and then punched her father in the stomach when he stopped him. If Harry

Standen hadn't arrived, he might have killed her father. She would always be grateful to Harry for being there at the right time and she would never forgive her uncle. Once during the service he turned his head to look at her but she stared through him and his gaze dropped.

Afterwards, when they followed the coffin outside, Emily was glad of Mrs Hattersley standing beside her. She could smell the sharp tang of freshly dug earth from the grave and the faint scent of decaying flowers from another grave nearby. The small graveyard was neat and these graves were set beneath the branches of a tree. Emily thought it was peaceful and hoped her father could see from wherever he was now, and would know she loved him.

Emily fought her tears as the vicar intoned the blessing and then Ma stepped forward to throw some dirt on the coffin. She was wearing black and weeping onto her brother's shoulder as he supported her. Emily threw a flower Tomas had picked from the gardens at Priorsfield Manor.

After everyone had melted away leaving just the family and Mrs Hattersley by the grave, Ma looked at her daughter.

'Are you coming back to the house?'

'I do not wish to come back while...' Emily looked at her uncle.

'Then you won't be coming home again. I thought to tell you in private but now you've made your attitude clear I might as well say it now. Your father's will leaves everything that matters to me. There's an envelope for you with his lawyer – and he's given that pile of junk in Ely to the person who works for him.'

'Pa left Christopher all his stock in the shop?' Emily frowned. 'What about the stuff in the barns? Pa told me it was mine.'

'It was worthless and I had someone clear it out, because I'm selling up and the next owner won't want that junk.'

'You've sold it already?' Emily was angry. 'It belonged to me.'

'Well it's gone now and most of it burned, as it should have been long ago. I got ten pounds for what was in the cabinet and I'm keeping five pounds of that.'

Emily felt the rage boiling inside her, but she wasn't going to argue over money when Pa was lying in his grave, even though she knew Pa's stock had been worth nearer a hundred pounds.

'Keep it,' she said and looked at Ma. She could see guilt in her eyes and knew that she'd lied about the amount she'd got for the stock, but somehow she didn't care. What did money matter when her father was dead?

Ma glared at her. 'I'm not paying rent for that shop a day longer than I need. Derek has given notice to the landlord and we'll be finished with it at the end of the week. I'm going to run a pub in Ely and I need all my money for the lease.'

'So you're just throwing Christopher out of work?'

'He can clear that rubbish out of the yard and sell it in the market. Besides, a man of his age should be joining up.'

'He has already done so,' Emily said, holding on to her temper because it was unseemly to

270

quarrel with her father lying in his open grave. She looked at Derek. 'Is *he* going to join up too?'

'Your uncle has flat feet. They wouldn't take him.'

'He's a bully and a coward,' Emily said, the bitterness so deep in her that she could taste it.

'You deserve a good hiding. Clear off before I slap you.'

Emily glanced back at her. The violence of her feelings was such that her mother's eyes dropped and for a moment she looked frightened, but then she stuck her head in the air and turned to take hold of Derek's arm.

'Take no notice, Emily.' Mrs Hattersley laid a gentle hand on her arm. 'Now isn't the right time and it won't bring him back.'

'Nothing can do that,' Emily said, but the gall was in her throat and she almost choked on the words. Her father had worked hard to build his stock, and he'd meant it for her. Her mother had stolen her inheritance yet again, but worse than that was the way she'd clung to Derek when she knew what he'd tried to do to her. Emily almost wished she'd gone to the police with her suspicions when Carla was murdered – but it was too late now. Besides, she'd never been sure.

Walking away with her friend, she could feel the sting of tears but she kept her head in the air. She was blinded by her grief and almost walked past the man standing just outside the lych-gate. Only when he spoke her name did she notice him.

'Emily. I had to come. I'm so very sorry. Joe was a good man.'

'Thank you.' She blinked very fast. 'It was good

271

of you to come, Harry. I know Pa would have appreciated it.'

'We were friends. I know I let you down...'

'It doesn't matter.' Emily managed a wan smile. 'I know you've married and I'm glad for you.'

'I wish things had been different.' He looked so wretched that Emily felt sorry for him. She thought that if she'd been at home and engaged to Harry, she could have stopped her mother stealing what was hers. It was just the same as when Grandfather had left her a silver watch. Ma had taken that and sold it; she'd also sold Uncle Albert's ring and now all Pa's stock from the barns. If he hadn't left the envelope at the lawyer's she would no doubt have taken that too.

Ma was walking away with Derek. Emily didn't look at her. She never wanted to see either of them again.

'Oh, look,' Mrs Hattersley said as they emerged on to the path outside the church. 'There's Mr Jonathan waiting to take us home. Now, isn't that kind of him?'

'Yes, very kind.'

Jonathan got out of the car as they approached and opened the back door for them to get in.

'Lizzie was adamant that you should not have to walk home,' he said and smiled. 'Since I had some business this way earlier I was happy to wait for you.'

'Thank you, sir,' Emily said as she slid into the back seat. 'You've all been more than kind.'

'Mrs Hattersley tells us we have a treasure in you, Emily,' he replied. 'Would you like to sit in the front with me, ma'am?'

'I'll sit in the back with Emily, sir.' Mrs Hattersley climbed in the back and nodded at her. 'Now this is a rare treat.'

Emily made an effort to be normal. 'Mr Nicolas took me to the infirmary in his tourer – but this is very special. What do you call this automobile, sir?'

'It's a Daimler,' he said and she could hear the smile in his voice. 'Or to give it its proper title, an Austro-Daimler. It's an Austrian car, though at first the factory originated in Germany. I'm not sure I would dare to drive it at the moment if they were still part of the German parent company.'

'But it's just a vehicle. It doesn't mean you like Germans.'

'I used to have some Austrian friends at college,' Jonathan said as he drew away from the church. 'They were very pleasant people. This war makes nonsense of friendships. If I should meet my friends in battle I should be expected to kill them. I think that is why Nicolas joined the RFC – at least in the air you don't see people as people, just as a target.'

'Have you heard from him, sir?' Mrs Hattersley asked.

'I believe Lizzie may have had a letter.'

'You spoke of meeting your friends in battle – may I ask if you intend to join up, sir?'

'If only I were free to do so, Mrs Hattersley. I feel it my duty but my father and grandmother insist my first duty is to the estate. We have to find a way of growing more food – which may mean ploughing up some of our lawns.'

'You never would, sir!'

'Only if it becomes necessary.' He glanced in the mirror at Emily. 'I hope everything went well for you today?'

'Yes, sir,' Emily said stiffly. Her tears had dried now but she was hurting inside and Mr Jonathan wasn't like Mr Nicolas. He was being polite but he didn't care in the way his brother had. She wished Mr Nicolas was with them now but it was stupid to let herself long for something that could never be. Emily had to remember her place, because otherwise it could lead to more heartbreak.

'I'm glad. If you need a little more time off I'm sure you could be spared for a day or so.'

'No, sir, thank you. I would prefer to work.'

'We'll look after her below stairs. No need to worry about our Emily – she's a part of our family now.'

Emily closed her eyes. Her head was aching almost as much as her heart. It seemed ridiculous that people could talk of life going on in the same old way. Glancing out of the window, she saw that the clouds had turned darker and it looked like rain. The heaviness in the air suited her mood. She felt as if a part of her life had been torn away from her, but the wound was inside where no one could see.

Mrs Hattersley continued to chat to their obliging driver and it was not long before he was stopping at the front of the house to let them get down.

She thought she would almost rather have walked home. The exercise would have done her good, though she knew Mrs Hattersley would have found it hard. She didn't glance back at Mr

Jonathan as she walked away, though she had the oddest feeling that he was staring at her back. Raising her head, she set her shoulders straight as pride carried her on. A part of her wanted to run to her room where she could lie on the bed and cry her heart out, but she refused to give in. To be miserable would let her mother and Derek win, and even her grief for her father wouldn't allow her to do that. Instead, she dwelled on her anger.

They thought themselves so clever, selling her father's land to buy a pub lease. Joe Carter had worked so hard to make a living for them, putting his heart and soul into his smallholding, but it hadn't been enough for his wife. She wondered how long it would be before the brother and sister ran through the money.

It didn't matter. Emily realised that the people she worked with and the people she worked for were her life now. Everyone that meant anything to her was here in this house – except for Christopher Johnson. She smiled as she remembered that they were to meet on her next day off – and then it struck her as strange that he hadn't been at the funeral. Harry had come, so why not Christopher?

Perhaps he had already gone to join his unit? If he had she would surely hear from him soon.

Mrs Hattersley had taken off her hat and coat and was rolling up her sleeves. 'You look pale, Emily. Mr Jonathan was concerned about you.'

'I'm all right now,' Emily said. 'I should like a cup of tea and a bit of your cake, but then I'll be ready to start again.'

'Good girl. We'll both have a cup of tea first. Mr Jonathan saved us time by fetching us home. I never expected that I can tell you.'

'It was Miss Lizzie's idea.'

'Yes, she's a real lady.' Mrs Hattersley looked at her oddly. 'Put the kettle on, Emily. Here's Mary and June too. I dare say they could do with a drink...'

Chapter 23

'Was Emily terribly upset?' Lizzie asked her brother when he entered the drawing room that evening. 'It must have been an ordeal for her. Nicolas said she was devastated by her father's death.'

'It was sheer incompetence that it happened if you ask me,' Jonathan said. 'If his doctor had examined him properly something might have been done sooner.'

'Emily told Nicolas that her father didn't want to take time off work for treatment for his chest.'

'It's the same with a lot of these small farmers. They work themselves into an early grave and for what? His widow has already put the land up for sale and sold all his equipment and stock. I told Grandmother about it. There were several good acres we might use for grazing to enlarge our beef herd. She wasn't interested.'

'Surely we have enough land?'

'Good land is always useful.'

'Granny may have other plans for her money.'

Jonathan frowned at her. 'She told me that she intends to leave all of us something, though she didn't say what. She offered me three thousand pounds in the meantime. I didn't feel able to take it.'

'If I'd been you I should have thanked her and taken it. You should have an independence of your own, Jonathan.'

'Mabel's father will settle ten thousand on us when we marry. I shan't have to worry about...' he broke off as the door opened and his mother and grandmother entered.

'Dinner is fifteen minutes late this evening,' Lady Barton said. 'Mrs Marsh apologised but Cook went to a funeral with that girl ... the kitchen help. I'm sorry everyone is waiting.'

'You should have vetoed it,' Lady Prior said harshly. 'If Mrs Marsh had come to me, as she ought, I should have told her that the girl could perfectly well go alone.'

'You were unwell so we didn't wish to bother you. It was such a little thing and a few minutes hardly matters. Besides, I couldn't bear to lose Mrs Hattersley; a good cook is worth her weight in gold.'

'Standards have to be maintained, Helen. Once you allow things to slide...'

'I fear things will not be quite the same in future,' Lord Barton said, following them into the room. 'We have only one footman. We shall need to take on more maids and they may not be fully trained. There is plenty of work for young women now; they will be taking the men's place on the land and in the factories – and the factory owners are paying them far more than we do. We may have to raise wages to keep them.'

'This tiresome war. It really is too bad.' Lady Prior accepted the glass of sherry her grandson offered. 'Has anyone heard from Nicolas?'

'I have, Granny,' Lizzie said. 'He says he is enjoying himself and it is all great fun. Had he known what good sport flying was he would have joined months ago.'

'Not if I had a say in it,' her father barked. 'If it were not for this damned war he would very shortly be at Oxford studying. What good will it do him after the war if he gets his pilot's licence?'

'It might be very useful. I think flying will become more popular in the future – it will become no different from catching a train or an omnibus,' Jonathan said.

'How ridiculous,' Lady Prior snapped. 'I have no wish to leave the ground in something that is so flimsy it might snap in the wind. I still prefer my carriage and horses to those noisy things you run around in, Jonathan…'

She was the autocratic matriarch, with nothing soft or forgiving in her manner. Diamonds flashed from her hands and the large pearls nestling against the wrinkled skin at her throat were worth a fortune. She was still living in an age when money was everything and the working class knew their place. All this talk of it being difficult to find servants was annoying her, upsetting the balance of her life. Lizzie knew that she clung to the old ways, just as she kept everything she'd inherited or been given or purchased, more or less regardless of its worth or suitability. She was a dinosaur, entrenched in her ways, dominating them all, refusing to give in and let the winds of change bring new life into the house. Her overstuffed, Victorian, buttoned-back chair was her throne and she a queen in her own domain.

Lizzie loved and admired her grandmother, even though she understood that her brother chafed at his bonds and both her mother and Amy resented being told what they should and shouldn't do. Sometimes, Lizzie felt trapped in this house with its air of decaying grandeur. She longed to spread her wings and escape into a wider world but at the moment there was no chance of her being let off the leash.

'Dinner is served.' The butler's voice from the doorway cut off Lady Prior's complaints.

'Thank goodness,' Lord Barton said. 'Lady Prior, please take my arm. Jonathan, take your mother in please. And please think of a more interesting topic than aeroplanes or the war if you can...'

Jonathan shot Amy a look that spoke volumes and she smiled. Lizzie giggled but then subsided as her father turned to glare at her.

'Cousin Maude is going to London soon,' she said. 'She told me she wants to join the ambulance service. Uncle Simon has taught her to drive and she's going to apply to be a driver and see what happens.'

'Good gracious! What can he be thinking of?' her grandmother said. 'Maude is scarcely older than you, Lizzie.'

'I know...' Lizzie paused for effect. She curled

her nails into her palms, because it was really so important to her but no one seemed to take her seriously. 'I should like to do something useful too.'

'Your mother is going to organise something here,' Lord Barton told her. 'You can roll bandages or knit socks, Lizzie. I am certain there will be something you can do. We might even offer a refuge for recovering officers in the dower house if your grandmother agrees. This house isn't big enough to be a hospital but the dower would accommodate officers who are on the mend but not yet ready to return to their units.'

'I suppose we may as well offer it,' Lady Prior said. 'Providing you are sure they won't try to take the manor.'

'Not big enough for us and them,' he said. 'I intend to speak to my brother about Barton Abbey. He has the room if he cares to make it available.'

'Well, he may do as he pleases. I shall certainly not offer this house. Sir William would turn in his grave.'

'It's a wonder the poor man can lie straight at any time,' Jonathan whispered to his mother, who shook her head at him but smiled just the same.

'Do you think Granny will let the dower house be used for convalescence?' Lizzie whispered to her sister. 'I should so like to do something – and I'm not a child.'

'Of course you're not,' Amy said. 'Perhaps if I try I might persuade Mama to let you come with us to London for a short visit.'

'Would you?' Lizzie hugged her sister's arm. Amy might be a snob but she could be lovely when she bothered. 'Who are you taking with you as your maid – Mary?'

'I thought I might ask Emily Carter,' Amy said. 'Granny won't let me have Mary. Anne is leaving us to get married next week – and June is no good at ironing my lace. Mrs Marsh told me Emily is better than Mary – and I dare say she can learn to do my hair properly.'

'Do you think she will want to go with you?'

Amy considered. 'I can't see why she wouldn't. It would mean more money and a chance to see something of the world.'

Lizzie was doubtful. 'I should think she's too upset at the moment – but ask her if you like.'

'I would take Mary if I could, but Granny absolutely refuses to let her come with me.'

Lizzie sighed. Granny was so stubborn. It was no wonder that there was always dissent in the house. Amy was lucky because she was going to London, whereas Lizzie would be stuck here for years. Sometimes she felt she was in prison and would never be released.

It was stifling in the house. Lizzie could hardly bear to be indoors, because the atmosphere was so oppressive. The papers had been filled with optimism during the first days of the war, but now since the first terrible news of the defeat at Mons everything had changed. People were anxious, worried about what would happen – and Lizzie was terrified something would happen to Nicolas. If he were badly injured or killed she thought she would want to die.

No one else understood her the way Nicolas did.

He knew how frustrated she felt in the dresses that were too young for her and the way everyone treated her as if she were still a child. If only she could escape to London, as Amy had.

Amy had been allowed to go and stay at the house in London, because Papa was going up on business. She'd taken Emily Carter with her as her maid, though Mrs Marsh had told Mama that Mary had made a terrible fuss because she'd been left behind and was now talking of leaving them to get married.

Lizzie understood why Mama had given her permission for Amy to stay with her cousin. These past few weeks had been a terrible strain for her sister. Amy had acted as if everything were normal, but Lizzie had heard her crying in her room and she'd seen the dark shadows beneath her eyes, which meant she wasn't sleeping. Mama had noticed them too, and because Amy had been dignified, not making a fuss or defying them, and accepting the end of her engagement, she'd allowed her to go to London.

Lizzie wouldn't have given in so tamely if she'd been engaged to Sir Arthur. She'd been at the bottom of the stairs the day he left Papa's study after telling Amy that he was withdrawing for her sake.

'Forgive me, Amy,' he'd told her, with Lizzie listening outside the door. 'If I allowed you to continue in this marriage, you would be tainted with the scandal. I care for you too much to allow – and until I clear my name I shall not marry.'

Lizzie thought Amy had accepted his withdrawal all too easily. She would have wept and begged him to run away with her, but Amy didn't love him. She'd accepted his proposal because of his money and the position she would have in society.

As far as Lizzie could make out, Arthur wasn't exactly broke, though he'd lost a lot of money. The worst of it was that he was being labelled a cheat and a scoundrel. The papers had written articles claiming that he'd known what he was doing when he floated the shares and until he could prove that he was as much a victim as the other shareholders, he would not be accepted in the circles Amy chose to move in.

Lizzie's heart ached for Arthur. She still thought he was wonderful, though he'd never done more than smile in her direction or ask her how she was. Now, left here at the manor while her sister was in London, with time on her hands and a feeling of heavy gloom hanging over everyone, she felt as if she would die of boredom.

It must be fresher out in the gardens surely? Lizzie decided to go for a walk. If she had to stay in the house another minute she would scream.

Leaving the parlour where she'd been sitting alone for the best part of the afternoon, she went out through the French windows and walked through the rose garden. As she disappeared into the shrubbery, she thought she heard her mother's voice calling her but ignored it. She was going to have a few hours of freedom even if she paid for it later.

It was much cooler in the fields, warm but with a pleasant breeze. Lizzie hadn't bothered with a hat or coat and the wind tugged at her long hair, blowing it about her face. The earth was dry and hard beneath her feet and she could feel stones pressing into the thin soles of her smart leather shoes. When she reached the freedom of the fields she ran and ran until she was out of breath, then flopped down on the grass and stretched her arms out behind her, lifting her face to the sun. Its warmth would probably give her freckles and Mama would complain that no lady allowed the sun to touch her face, but the feeling was wonderful and Lizzie had reached the point where she needed to rebel.

'Enjoying the sun then, Miss Barton?'

Lizzie opened her eyes and looked up at the man who had spoken. For a moment she didn't know him, because the last time she'd seen him he'd been dressed as a farmer with a tweed jacket and long boots. Now he was wearing what looked like a soldier's uniform, though only the trousers and the boots, with his shirt open at the neck. He must have taken off his cap and jacket somewhere, perhaps because it was so hot.

'Are you a soldier now?' she asked, trying to remember his name but unable to recall it.

He hesitated for a moment, and then inclined his head. 'That's right,' he said. 'I joined up to fight for King and Country same as all the other poor suckers.'

Lizzie looked at him doubtfully. 'I think all those men who joined the army are very brave.'

'I dare say you do, miss,' he said. 'It's the bloody stupid government I object to – sending half-trained men out there like lambs to the slaughter. Half of them don't know one end of a gun from the other.'

'Do you?' Lizzie asked innocently.

'I've been shooting game all my life,' he said and sat down next to her on the grass. 'You don't remember me – do you?'

'I think we spoke once but then my brother came along...'

'Name's Derek,' he told her and smiled in a way that made Lizzie's heart jump with excitement. 'Your name is Elizabeth, isn't it?'

'Everyone calls me Lizzie...' She looked at him shyly. It was exciting to be close to him. He was so different to her brothers ... more physical and sensual. The word popped into Lizzie's head, though it wasn't one she would normally have used. But his mouth fascinated her and as he leaned in closer, she knew he was going to kiss her and her heart stopped for one second before racing on. His lips brushed hers lightly but she was suddenly breathless, excited but also a little scared. 'I don't think you should have done that...'

'I probably shouldn't,' Derek said, 'but it was lovely.' He reached out and picked a blade of long grass, chewing the end. 'You didn't mind, did you?'

'No...' Lizzie admitted truthfully. 'But I'd better go now.'

'All right. I'll just sit here and admire the view – but you run off home like a good girl.'

His words stung her. She jumped to her feet and began to walk away. If Mama knew she'd let a soldier kiss her there would be trouble, and yet she would have liked to sit there with Derek and let him kiss her again. Glancing back, she saw that he was watching her and lifted her hand to wave. He grinned but didn't wave back.

Lizzie's heart pounded. What would have happened if she'd stayed?

Chapter 24

The London house was in a fashionable garden square and looked imposing, a brass knocker gleaming on the blue-painted door. Although it had a small frontage, there were three storeys plus the attics above and it extended out a long way at the back. The mews in the street at the back had once been used for keeping horses, but like others nearby it had recently been converted into living accommodation over a garage.

Emily followed the others round to the back and was invited into what she soon learned was the servants' hall. Mrs Jenkins, the housekeeper, was a small woman, thin and wiry and very different from Mrs Hattersley. Her husband seemed very conscious of himself and tried to impress on Emily that the situation at the house was not at all what he was used to.

'We need more staff here if his lordship and the family intend to stay long. Years ago we should have had at least three footmen and half a dozen maids, besides her ladyship's dresser, a cook and the various underlings.'

'Things are difficult,' Mr Payne pacified him. 'We're here to help, Jenkins – and both Tomas and Emily are very willing to do their bit. Emily has been a big help to Mrs Hattersley at the manor.'

'Well, I'm sure Mrs Jenkins will be happy to have her,' he said, slightly mollified. 'Rene will show you to your room, Emily, and also the situation of Miss Amy's rooms. You can unpack her things and then come down. There's a great deal to do if we are to be ready for the family's arrival tomorrow. The last tenants brought their own servants and I was not satisfied with their work. I hope you will do better.'

'I shall try, Mr Jenkins,' Emily glanced at the maid who was waiting to take her up. 'I can carry my own bag, Tomas. If Rene will show me the way I'll be ready to start work in a few minutes.'

Rene led the way up the back stairs. 'You don't want to take notice of old Grumbleboots,' she said with a cheeky look at Emily. 'He hates it when the house is left empty and thinks we should go back to the old days when it was kept just for the family.'

'Have you been here long?'

'Six months. I'm thinking I might leave soon. There's plenty of work going now – but my mother doesn't want me working in a factory. I might join one of those voluntary services, though. Ma says it would be much harder work but I'd be doing something worthwhile.'

'Yes, I suppose you would, but they would miss you here – and you might need a job after the war.'

'I'll be married before then,' Rene said and winked at her. 'My lad's off training to be a soldier at the moment, but when he comes back on leave we'll tie the knot.'

'Mary says the same thing.'

'Oh, Mary,' the girl said. 'I've heard about her. Sally says she's a mean bitch. I'm glad they didn't send her.'

'Is Sally the other maid here? How does she know Mary?'

'She worked at the manor for a few months last summer. They were short of staff and the house was let to some Americans. She was mad as fire because they give much bigger tips than the English families who hire the house.'

'I've never been tipped.'

'Maybe Mary doesn't share with you. Me and Sally always share – but it's the Americans that give the most.'

Emily let the other girl chatter on. She considered she was lucky to have her job and she'd just been given a rise but thought it might be best not to mention it.

'Here's your room; it's next to mine,' Rene said, throwing open a door for her. 'You'll find Miss Amy's room on the landing below this. She's the third one along on the right. I'll leave you to get yourself straight. Don't forget to come down as soon as you've unpacked.'

Emily assured her she wouldn't forget. Her room was smaller than she was used to at the manor and the furnishings very basic and plain. She'd made her room there nice by putting her own bits and pieces on the shelves, but here there was nothing but the bed, a single wardrobe, a chair and a chest by her bed.

Mrs Marsh certainly hadn't been joking when she'd told Emily that going to London wasn't to be a pleasure trip. Emily was expected to work and work hard. Yet she'd felt excited by her first glimpses of London and she couldn't wait until she got a chance to explore.

'It's your night off tonight, isn't it?' Tomas asked some days later, as he came into the kitchen bearing a tray loaded with dirty dishes. 'Rene said she was looking after Miss Amy because you were due a free period.'

'I've hardly stopped since we got here.' Emily eyed the loaded tray knowing that she would be expected to wash the dishes because both Sally and Rene were upstairs serving the guests the family had invited to lunch. 'I'm almost too tired to go out.'

'I've arranged to take my time off as well. I could take you to the pictures – or a music hall. It would be better than you going off alone. You might get lost.'

'I did have a couple of hours off last week and I took a tram to look at the shops, but Rene was free too so we went together.' She hesitated, and then smiled. 'Yes, I should like to visit the music hall with you, if that's all right.'

'It's your choice. It was a Keystone Cops picture but I like the music hall and where we live we don't get a chance to go most of the time.'

Emily poured hot water from the kettle into the sink and plunged the dishes in to soak. She rolled up her sleeves and started to wash them, putting them out on the wooden drainer. Tomas picked up a cloth and began to dry them. It wasn't his job and she was grateful to him.

'I've never been to a music hall. I know about Harry Lauder, Marie Lloyd, Vesta Tilley and Harry Champion of course, but there are lots of artists I've never heard of.'

'One of my favourites is George Robey. He's the Prime Minister of Comedy. When he tells everyone to stop laughing they just laugh all the harder. I've heard he's signing up to entertain the troops.'

'I love Harry Champion's songs – *I'm Henery the Eighth I am.* He is just so funny. We saw a clip of him on the Pathé news.' Emily put on a cockney accent and did a little dance, as she'd once seen the great performer do on the Pathé news at the cinema.

'It's the first time we've had a chance to go out together, Emily. You always seemed busy on your days off at the manor.'

'I went home or into Ely to see someone.'

Tomas nodded. 'Is Christopher Johnson your bloke?'

'He's a good friend. Ma closed the shop but I think Christopher had joined the army anyway. I'd thought I would have had a letter from him before this – but it may be waiting for me at the manor.'

Tomas didn't answer but went off whistling. Emily finished her work, feeling thoughtful. Christopher had seemed keen on her when they went out together once or twice, but then, Harry had kissed her and she'd believed he might ask her to marry him. She wasn't sure where she stood with Christopher and there was no harm in going for a

290

night out with the friendly footman.

She had no intention of getting married for ages, but it was better to go out with a friend than alone, especially in London. Emily didn't know her way about much yet and left to herself she would probably have gone to bed with a book.

'Did you enjoy yourself?' Tomas asked as they left the theatre later that evening. 'I think it was a good show. Everyone was very jingoistic of course, singing all the marching songs, but that's to be expected.'

People were streaming out on to the street. Everyone was laughing and talking, because they'd all enjoyed the show and some of them were singing the songs they'd heard on stage.

'Vesta Tilley singing *The Army of Today's all Right* was wonderful. You didn't sing many of them,' Emily said and looked up at him, suddenly sensing his mood and guessing what might be behind it. 'You shouldn't feel bad because a few silly people looked at you oddly this evening.'

'Do you know what these are?' Tomas thrust his hand into his pocket and then showed her two white feathers.

'White feathers?' Emily was puzzled. 'Is that someone's idea of a joke?'

'They were given to me by women whose husbands and sons were in the army. I was told I should be ashamed of myself.'

'Oh, Tomas, I'm so sorry,' Emily said. Her heart went out to him. Tomas was no coward and it was unfair for people who didn't know him to brand him as such just because he hadn't joined up immediately. Some people had objections to fighting and it wouldn't suit everyone to be a soldier. She didn't think less of him because he'd waited to put down his name. After all, he was needed at the manor.

'After the defeat at Mons the government is calling for more men to join up. It was a bloodbath, Emily. If things continue this way they will want every man who can stand up and hold a gun.'

'Does it mean you will have to join up?'

'Not yet. At the moment they're still asking for volunteers – but it's only a matter of time before they start conscription; that's what I've heard anyway.' He hesitated, then, 'I'll fight if I have to but I just didn't see the point of rushing off as soon as war was declared.'

Suddenly, the noise of the people leaving pubs and theatres seemed unnecessary and she felt uncomfortable for having enjoyed herself when men were fighting and dying in France. For all she knew Christopher was out there even now and might be in danger. Her eyes stung with tears and she sniffed hard. Tomas smiled down at her.

'Don't cry, Emily love. This was supposed to be a nice evening out.'

'It isn't your fault,' she said and took the handkerchief he offered, blowing her nose and wiping her cheeks. 'Thinking about those poor men who were wounded upsets me. I can't help thinking about Pa and wondering why he had to die like that; it was so sudden.'

'It's the way things happen sometimes.'

'Yes.' She tucked her arm through his. 'You

paid for the theatre so I'll buy us a pie and chips to eat on the way home – is that fair?'

'Very fair,' Tomas said and squeezed her arm. 'You'll be my girl yet, Emily Carter. You'll see. I'll get you in the end.'

Emily had to smile. She didn't think Tomas was in love with her, despite his flirting. He just enjoyed teasing her and she didn't mind that, providing he didn't become serious.

Chapter 25

'I'm so glad you were given leave and chose to spend it with me,' Amy said, looking fondly at her brother across the restaurant table. It was a busy, expensive place with crisp white linen, good china and excellent service. 'Lizzie will be so disappointed when she realises she has missed having lunch with you.'

'I adore Lizzie; she's a darling, but sometimes it's nice to talk to you alone, Amy. How are you enjoying your visit to town?' Nicolas asked.

'Very much. I've been to lots of meetings and visited some friends.'

'You'll be going home to the manor in a few days?'

'Yes, unless I'm asked to join a voluntary association in London. If I were stationed here it would be wonderful. There are so many things I should like to do – including some that Papa might not approve of.'

'Like what?' He raised his brows at her. 'I am your brother, Miss Barton. I hope you're not thinking of doing anything I wouldn't do – and some things I would?'

Amy's laughter rang out, because her brother was such a tease. If only she could find a man who amused her and made her laugh the way Nicolas did she would be happy to marry. For a moment she thought of Sir Arthur and the look in his eyes when he'd withdrawn his offer of marriage. Had he hoped she would refuse and declare that she would marry him whatever the scandal?

Amy had found the interview more painful than she could have imagined, because she truly liked him, but her father had been adamant that she must break it off and Arthur had done the decent thing by stepping back. Yet she'd regretted it so much, missing his company and the luxury of being adored and given expensive gifts. She'd missed being taken out and treated like a princess. Marriage to Arthur would have been very comfortable and yet there had been a part of her that had felt relief.

In answer to her brother's question, she said, 'I don't want to get stuck on the society treadmill. I was thinking of visiting museums, shops, parks and gardens, the theatre – and perhaps a Suffragette meeting. I know they've stopped making trouble for the duration of the war, but they still meet, though now, it's to discuss how they can help the war effort.'

Nicolas looked as if he agreed and changed the subject, telling her about his training for the RFC. Caught by his enthusiasm, it was a while before Amy realised that someone was staring at them hard from two tables away.

He was dressed with a sartorial elegance that made him stand out from every other man in the room, his clothes suitable for town but with a rakish air that made her think he would look his best dressed for riding. His hair was very dark, his complexion touched with olive tones and his eyes such a dark brown that they looked black with just a hint of silver in their depths. His mouth was wide and sensual – and she was staring too much.

Blushing, Amy turned her attention to her plate, feeling embarrassed. The man had been staring at her, but she had stared back with as much interest. Her heart quickened, because she had never seen a man she thought more attractive, though there was something in the arrogance of his manner as he summoned a waiter that made her think he might be dangerous to know.

'My beef fillet is very good; how is your salmon?'

Amy brought her attention back to her brother. 'Delicious. The sauce is even better than Mrs Hattersley makes, though you mustn't tell her I said so.'

'Excuse me sir...' The waiter hovered near their table. 'The Marquis of Belvane asked me to bring this to you, Captain Barton. He wishes to compliment you on the beauty of your sister and asks if you will introduce him.'

'Belvane?' Nicolas took the card from the salver the waiter was holding and looked at the expensive vintage Champagne with a frown. 'I'm not sure I know the fellow. Where is he sitting?'

The waiter indicated the table, and the man who

295

had attracted Amy's attention earlier. Nicolas stared at him for a few moments and then his frown cleared.

'Belvane,' he said and nodded as he read the card again. 'Yes, I believe we met at Eton when he was studying there – he was three years ahead of me. Would you like to be introduced, Amy? He's perfectly respectable, though only the second to hold the title. New money in the old queen's time, but the family did her a service in India and they were elevated to the peerage.'

'Please go and speak to your friend, Nicolas.'

Nicolas stood up, walked over to the marquis's table and the pair shook hands; then Belvane stood up and followed Nicolas back to their table. Amy made to rise, because he outranked them, but he begged her to remain seated.

'I have no wish to disturb your meal, Miss Barton,' he said in a voice as smooth as silk. 'I am pleased to meet you – Miles Belvane, at your service. If I may be of any assistance to you while you are in London, please do not hesitate to contact me.'

'You are very kind, sir.' Amy accepted the card he offered, her fingers brushing his for a second. The tingling sensation that shot through her was strange and left her feeling oddly breathless.

'Not at all. I've seldom seen such beauty in a woman.' His dark eyes seemed to convey all sorts of messages, most of which Amy suspected were not at all what her mother would think proper. 'Barton, would you care to bring your sister to a small evening party at my home? It is this evening and short notice but I'd no idea you were in town.'

'I have to report back to my unit tomorrow but I should like to visit you this evening. If it suits you, Amy?' Nicolas agreed with such enthusiasm that Amy imagined they had been good friends at Eton and assented.

However, after the marquis had taken his leave, which he did after exchanging more pleasantries with her and Nicolas, her brother sat down and gave her an odd look.

'Strange that,' he said. 'Belvane was years ahead of me when I was at school. He was an advanced student, way out of my league, brilliant on the rugby field and a first-class scholar. I'm surprised he even recognised me, let alone sent his card over.'

'Perhaps he wants something from you.'

'I cannot imagine how I could be of use to Belvane. As far as I know he is rolling in it – though of course there is a shadow over his birth. I've heard it said that the first marquis's wife couldn't give him an heir. There's a whisper that Miles's mother was an Indian girl, very beautiful but his mistress not his wife. His father's wife was an English lady of good birth, but not Belvane's mother so they say. When Belvane's father brought the boy home from India she accepted him as her child, but most people still think of him as a bastard of mixed blood, because of his looks.'

'There is something a little exotic about him,' Amy agreed. 'He is very attractive – but looks slightly dangerous, arrogant.'

'Arrogant, yes. I've never heard anything wrong of him. Wouldn't have introduced you if I had.'

'I doubt whether I shall see much of him. His

circles are too lofty for me.'

'Just as well. Father might not take to Belvane, because of the hint of scandal in his past. However, it might do you good to see something of the high life, Amy. Don't turn your nose up at him just yet.'

'No, I shan't,' she said and smiled. 'Are you going to have a pudding? I've seen some wonderful soft meringues floating in custard. I think I should like to try that – if you'll have something too?'

'Apple crumble if they have it or something else simple,' her brother said. 'Watch that sweet tooth, Amy, or you'll end up like Mama.'

'I shall not,' she replied indignantly. 'Besides, there's nothing wrong with Mama – she's had four children and two miscarriages, remember.'

'I was only teasing,' he told her. 'You'll age beautifully, darling. Just like Great Aunt Samantha Barton.'

'She was lovely,' Amy agreed. 'I was sorry when she went off abroad and died there.'

'She was far too scandalous to remain here. Three husbands and saw them all in the grave before she was forty. Her last husband's family banished her when she took that Italian count as her lover – but she told me they were doing her a favour.'

'I think it must be wonderful to have had such a life.'

'It would have suited you to marry Arthur,' Nicolas said. 'I suppose you haven't heard from him?'

'No. I did write to him about something but I

haven't had a reply. It wasn't important.'

'I'm sorry things didn't work out for you – but as you've just been made aware, there are plenty more fish in the sea.'

'Nicolas, don't be ridiculous,' she said and blushed. 'The marquis was simply being polite.'

Amy had noticed that Belvane had left his table. Their waiter was bringing the pudding she'd asked for. Belvane was looking their way. He smiled and inclined his head as he saw her glance at him. She was glad of the distraction the waiter provided as he put the tempting pudding in front of her.

Amy kept her eyes on her plate, though she knew Belvane was still staring at her even as he left the restaurant. She was beginning to get over her disappointment at last and being the object of a handsome man's admiration could only help her hurt pride. Arthur had given in so tamely to her father's demands that he should withdraw from their engagement that she'd wondered if he'd felt it was a mistake, even though he'd told her he still cared deeply.

Her heart wasn't broken, though she had cared for Arthur more than she'd realised. Her disappointment that she would not be the wife of a wealthy man, a man who could take her away from her dull, respectable life at the manor, had been overwhelming. She thought that if her mother hadn't agreed to this visit to London she might have done something foolish.

Her cousin Maude was already living in a rather large and expensive serviced apartment in London. Uncle Simon had bought it for her as a twenty-first birthday present and Maude had joined the ambulance service. She had her own maid to wait on her but the apartment was cleaned regularly by the management service of the apartment block and she either dined out or had meals brought in.

Amy envied her freedom. If she could just persuade her mother to let her join Maude in London she would be free at last. Until then she must make the most of her opportunities.

Belvane was exciting, even if she had sensed that he was dangerous. Yet the evening loomed enticingly before her and she found herself excited at the prospect of seeing him again.

'Why so pensive, Miss Barton?' A deep voice spoke at Amy's side, making her jump and look at the man who had approached her. 'I hope you're not bored?'

'Not at all, Lord Belvane,' Amy replied, catching the scent his skin exuded. It smelled rather exotic with tones of sandalwood and ambergris. 'You give wonderful parties. I particularly enjoyed the music earlier.'

'Your brother is playing cards. You do not find them amusing?'

'I don't mind a hand of whist occasionally, but I am not a gambler.'

'It would seem you are a paragon. Beautiful, good mannered and without vice.'

'I am certain that is not true, sir. I think you exaggerate on more than one count.'

'You were engaged to be married to Sir Arthur Jones I believe?'

'Yes.' Amy stiffened. 'He withdrew on the

300

grounds that his reputation was smeared and I accepted his wish.'

'Would you have married him if he hadn't done the decent thing?'

'Yes, of course. Why not? I may not approve of what happened regarding the shareholders, but I should have kept my word if he'd asked.'

'As I understand it, it was the company that lost money. Jones must have retained most of his fortune.'

'Yes. I had thought he would be morally responsible but his lawyers absolutely forbade him to admit any liability.'

'Naturally. Why should he sink with the company? One must protect oneself – do you not agree?'

'To a certain extent – but I feel for the people who could not afford to lose their investments.'

'Ah, a moralist. You were right; you do have a flaw, Miss Barton. One thing that annoys me is a woman who spouts morals at me. I would have seen you as adventurous – a lady after my own heart, ready to throw her hat over the moon.'

'I do not think of myself as a prude, but I believe that Sir Arthur was and is morally responsible for those who lost money. It was his company and he invited people to invest, endorsing it as being sound. I would have hoped he could do something to help those worst affected – had I money of my own I should have done so, no matter what the lawyers thought best.'

'I can see you have a mind of your own. I like that in a woman, even if you are a moralist. Perhaps I can lead you astray, teach you that life does not always have to be played by the rules?'

'I'm not sure I understand you, sir.'

'Oh, I think you might if you put your mind to it. You are quite lovely – and I adore beautiful women.'

'Yes, I imagine you might. However, I am not in the market for a relationship, sir. I was engaged to a man I liked very much and to become intimately involved so soon might seem uncaring.'

'I must have misread the signals, Miss Barton. I had hoped we might become good friends, intimate friends, but since you do not feel able to oblige me, I must stand back.'

'Friendship is always acceptable.'

'I had more than mere friendship in mind. I shall be plain, Miss Barton. I had thought you might become my mistress, but I see that I was mistaken in you. When I learned you had come to London and seemed to ignore the gossip concerning the termination of your engagement I thought ... but forgive me, I see that it affects you more than I thought. You are not ready for an affair of passion.'

Was he drunk? She had caught a faint whiff of alcohol on his breath but he seemed in control of himself. Yet to speak to her like that was outrageous. How could he imagine that she might consent to such an arrangement?

Amy watched him walk away to speak to his other guests. She felt an odd tightness in her breast and wondered why she felt torn between slapping him across the face and being caught up in his arms.

His mistress indeed! How dared he make such a suggestion to her? She was the daughter of a peer and respectable. Why should he imagine that she would wish for a clandestine affair?

She looked around the gathering, recognising only a few of the other guests. One or two were known to her, and had visited her home, but the men were among the more racy gentlemen, friends of her brothers. She would normally have little to do with them. The women in the room were mostly unknown to her and some of them seemed to be less than respectable, their gowns more revealing than her mother would think proper and their complexions heightened by rouge. Had she known what the gathering would be like she would have refused to attend it.

'Miss Barton, are you quite comfortable?'

Amy turned in relief to the man who had addressed her. He at least was perfectly respectable, a man she had seen in her father's company on several occasions. Older than she was by some years, and rather like Arthur in his ways.

'Mr Chester,' she said with relief. 'I had not seen you. I enjoyed the music earlier but have found myself at a loss since then. I do not wish to play cards and ... some of the company is not...' she stopped, lowering her gaze.

'I understand perfectly,' he replied with a slight smile. 'I must say that some of the gentlemen and *ladies* present this evening are not to my taste either. I was on the point of leaving when I saw you standing alone. Belvane seemed to distress you?'

'No, I am not distressed. I think he is a man who speaks for effect. I had not truly met him until this evening.'

Amy was conscious of a sense of disappointment. She couldn't help wishing that she'd been more receptive towards the marquis, because now he would just discount her as a prude – and she wasn't. His directness had taken her breath away, but it had also made her heart race. For a moment she wished she were brave enough to kick over the traces and do whatever he desired of her.

She felt a hot flush spread all over her body. Whatever was she thinking? She was a respectable young woman and she had no intention of throwing away her chance of marriage just for an affair with Miles Belvane – however exciting he was. Yet she couldn't help wondering what it would be like to be kissed by a man like that.

Chapter 26

Emily's heart caught as she saw the man walking down the landing towards her. He was dressed in a smart evening suit and looked so handsome that it took her breath away. She looked at him shyly as he stopped to speak to her.

'How are you, Emily?' he asked. 'I hope you're feeling a little better now?'

'I still feel sad for my father, dying alone the way he did – but I know he wouldn't want me to cry all the time. Besides, I don't have time for tears.'

'Work is a great healer,' he said. 'I'm taking Amy to a party this evening. I thought this would be a quiet leave but I've hardly had time to catch my breath.'

'If it isn't too rude of me, sir – are you enjoying your life in the RFC?'

'It isn't rude at all, Emily.' Mr Nicolas grinned at her. 'I love being up there in the clouds – most wonderful feeling in the world. Not sure how I'll feel when I have to start shooting at someone for real, but the training was fun.'

'I'm glad you're happy, sir. I'd best get on or I shall be shot at dawn for desertion.'

Mr Nicolas laughed, appreciating her joke. 'I'd better let you get on then. I hope they're not working you too hard?'

'Nothing I can't manage, sir.'

'If only the rest of the world were like you, Emily. We should have no wars ... just perfect peace.'

'You'd get bored then, sir. You need a little conflict to make it worthwhile – don't you?'

Emily laughed and walked on by, knowing that he was watching her. The look in his eyes told her he was far from indifferent. Her heart was still racing but she felt pleased that he'd taken the time to speak to her, instead of walking straight by as his father did. Neither Lord Barton nor his wife ever looked at her if she came within their orbit, and Lady Prior looked down her long nose at any servant who dared to step out of line, but the younger generation was different. Miss Amy seemed pleased with the service Emily gave and Miss Lizzie always had a nice smile when they met, and Mr Jonathan was very polite – but Mr Nicolas was the one she really liked. Not that she

305

could ever be anything to him or he to her – he was out of her class. Emily wanted to be better than she was, but she could never aspire to being the wife of a lord's son.

Now why had she even thought of that? Was she getting ideas above her station? Mrs Hattersley would certainly think so and Ma would say she was ridiculous – but Emily couldn't help noticing the way Mr Nicolas looked at her sometimes. She was sure in her own mind that he liked her a lot.

Of course it wouldn't be marriage he had on his mind, but he was too nice a gentleman to take advantage of a girl like her.

'Nicolas is taking me to a special party this evening,' Amy said when Emily went up to help her dress. 'I didn't bring many evening gowns with me as I did not expect to go out much.'

'It's a very pretty dress, miss,' Emily said, spreading the pale yellow silk gown on the bed. 'I know you wore it last week but your friends probably didn't see you.' It was a very simple dress but caught up at the back with a frill of cascading lace, and had been extremely expensive.

'No, they wouldn't have done,' Amy agreed. 'You've sponged it and pressed it very well, Emily. It will just have to do because I do not have anything else suitable.'

'You look lovely in this,' Emily assured her as she brought it across and held it over Amy's head so she could ease herself into the beautiful dress, which clung to her slender hips and was very stylish.

'Bring me the jewel box please.'

Emily fetched the leather case and Amy took out a pretty diamond pendant and some matching earrings. Emily fastened the clasp and then Amy slipped in the hooks of her earrings.

'I've locked this. You can put it away for me in my dressing case.'

'Yes, miss.' Emily carried the leather jewel case to the large dressing case and locked it inside, returning the key to her employer, who placed it in the drawer of her dressing table. 'Have a good time this evening, miss.'

'I shall be home before midnight. Until then you are free – unless you have work to do?'

'Tomas said he might take me to a volunteer meeting if I liked – just for a couple of hours.'

'I almost wish I was coming with you,' Amy said. 'I didn't know you were interested in the volunteer movements?'

'I was reading about the volunteer groups for women and what they were doing to help the war and Tomas saw the notice of the meeting so he asked if I'd like to go. I was going to ask you if that is all right?'

'Yes, of course.' Amy smiled at her. 'I probably haven't thanked you enough, Emily. I do know what good service you give me. We'll talk about it another time – but I must go now or I shall keep Nicolas waiting.'

'You mustn't do that, miss.' Emily laughed softly. 'He looks very smart in his uniform, doesn't he? I bet you were pleased to see him.'

'Yes. We are all very fond of Nicolas.' Amy picked up her purse and evening cloak and walked to the door.

Emily followed her from the room, and then went down the stairs to the kitchen, where Tomas was waiting for her. He looked at her and smiled.

'Are you ready to go to that meeting?'

'Yes, please,' she said. 'I've been looking forward to it.'

Emily didn't think she would ever be brave enough to join the band of women who tied themselves to the railings outside Buckingham Palace or Westminster, threw themselves in front of the king's horse or disrupted all kinds of meetings and social events. Sometimes they marched on rallies through the centre of London carrying banners and shouting, causing a disturbance, so the papers said. Many people considered they were just making a nuisance of themselves, but from what Emily read in the papers some men of distinction were now beginning to take their cause seriously.

She had often wanted to hear one of them speak and that evening they had a guest speaker from America. It should prove an interesting meeting.

'These arrived for you while you were out shopping, miss,' Emily said, carrying a huge basket of yellow roses into Amy's bedroom as she was brushing her hair the next day. 'They smell wonderful.'

'Is there a card?' Amy glanced at the flowers. 'They are rather lovely.'

Emily gave her the card. She opened it, glanced at the brief message and frowned. 'They are from the Marquis of Belvane – an apology.'

'The gentleman who invited you to that party the other night?'

'Yes.' Amy frowned. 'He said something that offended me and wishes to take me out to dinner this evening to apologise.'

'Shall you go?' Emily asked and then blushed. 'Sorry, it's not for me to ask, miss.'

'I think so,' Amy said and smiled in a way that puzzled Emily. 'We shall be going home tomorrow so I may as well make the most of my last evening in town ... unless Mama allows me to be a volunteer like my Cousin Maude.'

'I've seen the notices appealing for women to volunteer,' Emily said. 'What would you do, miss – become a nurse?'

'No, I hardly think so, though it's what Lizzie wants. I might join the ambulance service like my cousin.' She sighed, and looked speculatively at Emily. 'If I did come to London, would you come with me as my maid?'

Emily stared at her uncertainly. She'd accepted the invitation this time, because she'd wanted to get away from the manor and give herself a chance to get over her grief. She was feeling better now but wasn't sure what to do next.

'May I think about it please?'

Amy looked offended but inclined her head. She spoke only to give Emily orders after that and Emily knew she had annoyed her. Mary would have jumped at the chance and Emily wasn't sure why she hadn't. It was a chance for her to improve herself, but it had been so sudden and she needed time to think about the future. Miss Amy had been pleasant to her since she'd accompanied her to London, but she couldn't forget those cruel remarks at the village hall dance when they were younger. It might be wiser to stay in the kitchen with Mrs Hattersley and learn to be a cook, because she couldn't be sure she could trust Miss Amy.

'So we're on our way home tomorrow then.' Tomas said and looked at Emily oddly. 'Are you looking forward to it? You seem different today somehow – as if you've got something on your mind.'

'Do I?' Emily shook her head. She couldn't tell Tomas what Miss Amy had suggested to her, because she wasn't sure of her answer yet.

'You look beautiful,' Tomas said. 'I've been wanting to talk to you about something, Emily. I haven't quite made up my mind, but when I do you'll be the first to know.'

'Secrets?' Emily teased. 'You're a dark one, Tomas. Now what are you up to?'

'Maybe something, maybe nothing,' he said. 'I'll tell you in a couple of days, after we're back at the manor.'

Emily nodded. Mr Payne came into the kitchen then, enquiring about some of his lordship's shirts that had gone missing.

'I ironed them for you,' Emily said. 'You had so much to do and I had a few minutes going spare. They are hanging up in the butler's pantry. I promise I didn't spoil them, Mr Payne.'

'It was thoughtful of you, but please do not do it again. I like to look after his lordship's things myself.'

'I'm sorry,' Emily said as he hurried off to rescue the shirts, obviously fearful that she had ruined them. Some folk were never pleased.

She sighed, because sometimes she wished she was back at the farm, going out on the rounds with Pa and helping him to milk the cows in the evening. She missed her father and she missed her brother Jack. Sometimes she worried about him, because he hadn't been progressing as he ought and Emily was afraid he might be backward. She wished she could see him, but she didn't want to see her mother. Not while Derek was around. Her life was very different now. She enjoyed most of the work she did, but there were still times when her grief swamped her and she wished something nice would happen.

Emily told herself to stop dreaming. Her life was never going to be much better than it was now. She could either live in London as Miss Amy's maid or be an assistant cook at the manor. She would have to make up her mind soon or she might no longer have the choice.

'Can you stop for a minute, please, sir?' Emily begged. They had been travelling for more than an hour and she was feeling wretched. When Miss Amy had told her Lord Belvane would be driving them home instead of taking the train, as Tomas and Mr Payne had, she hadn't given it a second thought, but after the first half an hour she'd begun to feel very unwell. 'I think I'm going to be sick.'

'We shall stop in another twenty minutes or so for some lunch,' the marquis said without glancing back at her in his mirror. 'Surely you can wait until then?'

'I'm sorry but I think...' Emily clapped her handkerchief over her mouth as she felt the vomit rising. She was feeling so very ill and didn't think she could wait even a few minutes longer.

'Good God!' he muttered and pulled over to the side of the road. 'Get out quickly, girl. For goodness' sake don't vomit in my Daimler.'

Emily scrambled out of the vehicle and stumbled away to a patch of grass where she vomited violently, twice. She was wiping her mouth when Amy came over to her and touched her arm.

'I'm sorry you're ill. Was it something you ate?'

'It's the fumes in the back, miss.'

'You must be a bad traveller. I'm afraid the marquis isn't pleased with you.'

'I'm sorry, miss. If you could leave me at a railway station I could take the train back to the manor.'

'I would rather you stayed with us,' Amy said. 'Do you think you might do better in the front?'

'I couldn't do that, miss. Lord Belvane wouldn't like it – and you might feel ill in the back.'

'I doubt it. I'm never ill travelling. We'll change places when you feel able.'

There was a note in her voice that Emily hadn't heard for a while and she thought that her employer was annoyed with her. She felt irritated with herself. The last thing she'd wanted to do was to spoil the day for Miss Amy.

When she climbed into the front seat Lord Belvane looked at her angrily. He made no attempt to hide his displeasure and she felt nervous as he started the automobile off again. For the next half an hour they drove in silence. Emily still felt a little unwell but she was much better in the front.

Lord Belvane stopped eventually in the courtyard of an old coaching inn. Its walls were painted white and half-timbered with black beams, probably dating from the sixteenth century. Belvane got out and then took Amy's arm, leading her inside without a backward glance at Emily. Amy beckoned to her to follow but she shook her head.

'I think it's best if I don't eat anything, miss. I'm going to try riding in the back again when we leave here.'

'Poor you,' Amy said. 'It's odd, but it didn't affect me at all.'

While they went into the inn, Emily found a bench outside and sat down in the fresh air. After a while a young lad came out with a glass of lemonade on a tray. She accepted it gratefully, sipping the cool, fizzy drink a little at a time and beginning to enjoy the autumn sunshine. Her headache was easing and she was feeling better now. Perhaps she needn't ruin the whole of Miss Amy's day after all.

'Well, I'm glad to see you back,' Mrs Hattersley said when Emily walked into the kitchen later that afternoon. 'It hasn't been the same here without you. Did you enjoy your first visit to London?'

'Yes, it was all right,' Emily said. 'Tomas took me to the Music Hall and to a Suffragette meeting. Miss Amy gave me two pounds as a tip – and a dress she decided she didn't want to wear again.'

'She must have been pleased then,' Mrs Hattersley said and frowned. 'Has Miss Amy said what she wants you to do in future, Emily? She might want you to continue as her maid now you're back. Mrs Marsh has put some new uniforms in your room. Perhaps you should wait and see if you're sent for.'

'Well...' Emily glanced at Mary and saw her scowl. She'd hoped the other girl might have got over her sulks while she was away but it seemed she was still resentful and angry. When she knew that Emily might become Miss Amy's maid on a permanent basis she would be furious. 'I can still help you when I'm not looking after her, Cook.'

'They took advantage of her in the London house,' Tomas said. 'She was working all hours. If I had my way she'd tell them what to do with their job.' He looked about him defiantly. 'I'm giving in my notice – and if Emily has any sense she'll do the same.'

'Well, I shan't...' Emily began and then broke off as Mrs Marsh entered the kitchen and looked at her in a slightly disapproving way. She sensed what the housekeeper was going to say and her stomach clenched with nerves.

'So, Emily, Miss Amy is pleased with you – so pleased that you're to be her maid in future. She would like you to go up as soon as you're ready.'

'Yes, of course, Mrs Marsh.'

'You're to be her maid in future?' Mary was on her feet, eyes flashing with temper. 'You rotten little sneak!'

Mary flew at Emily, her nails going for her face. Emily grabbed her by the hair and pulled sharply, making her jerk back but Mary spat at her and then started kicking and punching until Tomas dragged her off. She struggled and yelled for a while but he was stronger and finally subdued her.

'That is a disgusting display,' Mrs Marsh said. 'I warned you what would happen if you did it again, Mary. If things were not so difficult I should turn you off at once. As it is, you may consider yourself under notice. I shall give you two months' wages and you'll go at the end of the month.'

'Please, don't do that on my account,' Emily said once she'd got her breath back. 'Mary is upset. I'm sure she won't do it again.'

'I don't want your rotten job much longer anyway,' Mary snarled. 'As soon as my lad comes back on leave I'm off. We're going to be married.' She rushed past Mrs Marsh and out of the room, clearly in tears.

'I know she thinks I tried to get the job away from her but I didn't – Miss Amy asked me and...' She lifted her head, because she'd decided she would do as Miss Amy wanted. 'Is it wrong of me to want to better myself?'

'Mary was entitled to the job, because she's been here the longest,' Mrs Marsh said looking grave. 'However, Miss Amy does what she wants and if she wanted Mary she'd say so.'

'I still think you'd do better with me,' Mrs Hattersley said. 'I'd have taught you a good trade.'

'I'd better go up to her,' Emily said. She felt the others still thought she'd done something to make Miss Amy prefer her to Mary and were faintly disapproving.

'I want to speak to you later,' Tomas said, giving her an odd look as she passed him.

They had got on well in London and Emily had enjoyed going out with him, but she hoped he wasn't going to ask her to be his girl, because she wasn't ready for a proper relationship with anyone just yet. Besides, although he spoke as if he thought something of her, she was sure he wasn't in love with her. Tomas had plans of his own and Emily suspected that it would suit him if she went along with him.

'There are some letters here for you,' Mrs Hattersley said. 'You may as well take them, Emily. I think one of them is from your father's lawyers.'

Emily accepted the two envelopes, one of which was bulky and felt as if it contained something more than just a letter. She slipped them into her pocket to read later and ran up the stairs to Miss Amy's room.

Emily opened the bulky letter first, which had come from her father's lawyer. Inside was fifty pounds in white five-pound notes and two letters – a brief note from the lawyer and a longer letter from her father. Emily stared at the money, tears stinging her eyes. How hard her father must have worked to save this much for her. She opened his letter with shaking hands.

Emily love, her father had written. *You'll know that I've given you three times as much as this, because a hundred pounds is what you'll get for the stock in the barns, if you sell it sensibly. If I'd had more time I should have given you more, but it has taken a lot of scheming to get this much put by. Your mother will have the land and house, as is her right, but I wanted my girl to have something. Jack isn't my son. I know your mother went with someone else, and she'll provide for her son.*

I wish I could give you more, love. You've always been the light of my life, but I know you'll make a good life. Christopher has the shop stock. Without his help I wouldn't have had this to give you. I owe him something and he'll know what to do with it.

When you read this I'll be gone. Have a good life, girl. I love you and I pray you'll find happiness. Don't marry until you find the right one. A lifetime is a long time to be regretting your mistakes.

Your loving father, Joe Carter

Emily felt her eyes sting with tears as she folded her father's letter. The money would sit in a bank until she needed it but it was the thought of how hard he'd worked to put so much aside for her that brought tears to her eyes and made her throat close with emotion. She wished he hadn't worked so hard. She would rather be able to go home and see his face than have all the money in the world. Sometimes he'd been harsh with her, but underneath he'd loved her deeply.

Dashing the tears from her eyes, Emily turned to her second letter. She didn't know the hand for certain but she thought it was from Christopher Johnson.

Dear Emily, Christopher had written in his flowing script. *I'm sorry I couldn't come to the funeral but I was in training camp. And what a shambles that is! Half of us don't have a rifle or the full uniform, but I dare say they'll sort it out before they send us to fight* the Hun.

I did call at the house to see you when I had a twenty-four-hour leave, but they said you'd gone to London. I hoped to see you before we're off over there, but I know we shan't get leave again before then. I hope you will write to me. I'll write first when we get settled and then you'll know where to write back.

You must be upset over your Pa and it's too soon to ask you to think of marriage. I wanted to tell you to your face how I feel. I would've taken my time if it hadn't been for the war but it all happened so quick. I've wanted to tell you for months but I've nothing much to offer you. Your father left me some stuff and it will fetch a few pounds one day when I can repair it. My father is going to store it for me until after the war. Maybe I'll have a little shop again then. Until then I don't have the right to ask you to be my wife, but I wanted you to know my heart just in case. I love you, Emily. I should like us to marry one day, but I know now isn't the right time.

If I come home safe and make a home for us – will you think about being my wife? You're the girl for me and always have been. If I hadn't been afraid to speak I'd have asked before, but I wanted to put a bit by first.

I love you, Emily. If you like me a little bit perhaps you'll write back when you have my next letter.

Take care, my love, and don't grieve for your Pa too much. He loved you and he would want you to be happy. Christopher. XXX

Emily could feel the tears running down her cheeks. She'd guessed that Christopher liked her but she hadn't dreamed he would write her a letter like this and it had come just when she needed a little cheering up.

She smiled as she folded it and put it into the old writing box her father had given her as a present once. It had a secret drawer and she slipped her money inside to keep it safe until she could get to the Post Office to deposit it in the savings account she'd started in London.

Christopher's letter had touched her and she had plenty of time to make up her mind before he came home.

Chapter 27

'It's such a beautiful night,' Amy turned to her companion with a smile. The air was warm, scented with jasmine and honeysuckle, both of which grew over the sheltering walls. 'I'm glad we came out for a little air, though I know Mama will quiz me about you later.'

Her senses were alert to him, because his nearness excited her. She had been amazed when he'd offered to drive her down and even more so when he accepted her invitation to stay for a few days. Despite his show of bad humour because Emily had been ill on the drive down, her fascination with this man had not abated. She wasn't sure what it was about him that made her spine tingle but she knew that no other man of her acquaintance had made her feel this way. All the young men her family had introduced to her seemed to pale into insignificance. Yet she knew that he was dangerous and doubted that her parents would approve even had he offered marriage, which she thought unlikely after his outrageous suggestions to her at that infamous party.

'I imagine you can handle your mama,' Belvane said, smiling at her. He took out his cigar case and extracted a cheroot, then offered the case to her and smiled when she declined. 'Still not ready to take the plunge?'

The mocking tone of his voice stung her, making her lift her head to meet the challenge. 'Just because I do not wish to smoke those doesn't mean I'm a prude.'

'Doesn't it?' Belvane threw the cheroot away unlit and reached her into his arms. He gazed down into her face for a moment, then bent his head and kissed her. His mouth was so demanding, his hold on her so firm, that Amy's head swirled. She had never felt this way in her life and her breath came faster as he finally released her. For a moment she felt as if she would faint, but something in his eyes brought her sharply back to herself. She knew she was trembling as she drew back.

'You shouldn't have done that...'

'Shouldn't I? It seemed wholly pleasurable to me, for us both.' He touched her cheek with his fingertips. 'Come to Russia with me, Amy. Run away with me tonight. I'll settle money on you. Even if I were an utter rotter you would still have your independence – but I promise you, I've no intention of leaving you in distress. I want you more than I've ever wanted any woman.'

'You want me for your mistress.' Amy raised her

320

head, gazing into his eyes. Her pride was stung that he should think her fit only for his mistress. 'Is that all you want – a brief affair? Why not marriage?'

'I might have asked you, had I been able,' Belvane replied, an odd twist to his mouth. 'Unfortunately for us both, my dear, I have a wife.'

Amy felt as if she'd been showered with ice. 'No one told me. Nicolas didn't warn me that you were married.'

'Very few people know,' Belvane replied. 'My wife is a minor member of the Russian royal family, a distant cousin of the tsar. She is seventeen and we were married by proxy a year ago, though as yet we haven't lived together as man and wife. Our parents made the match and neither of us was given a choice.'

'Good grief. I thought that sort of thing belonged to the dark ages – except for royal families...' Amy paused. 'Yes, I see. She is, of course, and you're wealthy. I suppose it was thought a good match for her.'

'My father and hers were great friends. It was my father's dearest wish. He was dying and I felt I had no option but to agree to the match. It hardly seemed to matter ... most of my family have married for money or land.'

'It isn't so very different in my family. I was given a choice but the expectations were there. I dare say my parents imagine I shall find someone suitable when I'm over the break up with Arthur.'

He looked at her in the darkness, his eyes glittering in the faint light of a shadowed moon. She watched his mouth curl in scorn, as if disappointed that she was so conventional, so tied by her family's morals.

'Shall you conform?'

'No, at least not for ages. I want to live in London, be independent for a while.'

'You won't throw your hat over the windmill and come with me?'

'You know I can't. It's too shocking.'

Yet how she longed to do as he asked. Every fibre of her being was alive with feeling, with a longing for the kind of life she might have with him – the excitement he could show her. For a moment she was tempted but the influence of her upbringing was too strong.

'Yes, I suppose it is for you. You know how tense things are in Europe at the moment?' Amy nodded. 'I shall return to Russia and I shall probably volunteer to fight for my country. I haven't decided yet. I might join the RFC in England instead.'

'You think of Russia as home?'

'My grandmother was Russian. Her father was a duke – Helena and I are cousins many times removed. I have divided loyalties. Should I fight here or there? It is a decision I must make.'

'I hate all this talk of war. I wish it was over.'

'Come to Russia with me while there is still time to have fun. We should make glorious love, Amy. My father is dead but Mama is alive. She would acknowledge you as her friend and my mistress. I will give you furs and jewels, beautiful homes to live in.'

'None of those things matter. If we loved each other ... but I do not know you, Belvane. I'm

322

sorry but what you ask is impossible.'

'I knew it would be,' he said and took out another of his thin cigars, lighting it this time. The smoke curled from his lips, disappearing on the slight breeze. 'Such a shame that you weren't ready. We might have been good together.'

'Perhaps.' Amy felt a pang of regret. Something deep inside her told her that she was throwing away a chance ... something precious that might never come her way again. She wished that she had the courage to run away with him, but she was afraid of losing her friends and her family. 'If you ever return to London...'

'The moment will be lost,' he said and smiled. 'I shall leave the day after tomorrow. You are still too much your mother's child, Amy. One day you will realise what you've lost. I hope you find fulfilment in other ways.'

'Do you have to go?' She felt a surge of fear, because she sensed she had lost him and she wanted to hold him, yet knew he wasn't the kind of man she could dangle on a string until she was ready. Her hand touched his arm, her look intent as she gazed up at him in the shadowed moonlight. 'Would you have married me if you hadn't been married already?'

'Perhaps. Who knows? I do not deal in what might have been.' He drew on his cheroot and then flicked it away into the shrubbery. 'We should go in, before your mama sends someone to see if I've abducted you.'

'I'm not a child.'

'No? Perhaps not but you aren't yet a woman, are you, Amy?'

Chapter 28

'Emily, I want to talk to you alone,' Tomas waylaid her at the foot of the back stairs. He'd taken his coat off and his shirtsleeves were rolled up to the elbows. She caught a whiff of strong drink and wondered if he'd been at the brandy Mrs Hattersley used for cooking. She always ordered a good one, because she said the family would know if she used cheap stuff. It was dark in the little well at the bottom of the stairs, because there were no windows and not much light managed to penetrate the gloom. 'Don't say you're busy, because they can finish up without you. You've hardly stopped since you got back from London.'

'I was just going to get myself a drink to take to bed. Mrs Hattersley told me earlier she didn't need me any more.'

'Then you can listen to me for a minute.' Tomas frowned at her. 'I know you like Miss Amy, and you're pleased with your new job – but you don't have to work all these long hours. I've got a chance to buy a little pub with living accommodation at the back. If you married me I could keep you in comfort.'

'Tomas...' Emily hesitated, because she didn't want to hurt him. 'You know I'm not ready to think about marriage. I like you as a friend but I'm not sure...'

'You think you'll better yourself looking after

Miss Amy, but she'll drop you as soon as it suits her.'

'I'm not ready to marry yet...'

'Listen to me, Emily. I shan't stop at one pub. I'll have two or three or maybe a shop as well. I'll be rich one day. I'll give you pretty clothes and holidays in London or at the sea. It would be a good life – and I really need you to help me. Between us, we could make it work, because you're clever and a good cook...'

'Tomas...' Emily touched his arm. 'Please don't be cross. I do like you very much – but I don't want to marry yet.'

'Whatever Miss Amy promised, you'll just be the skivvy, Emily.'

'I'm sorry, Tomas. I've given Miss Amy my word. If she goes to London I'm going to look after her.'

'You'll be working all hours for nothing,' Tomas said scornfully. 'You'll regret it, Emily.'

'I'm sorry. I like you and I wish you well – but I can't marry you. Besides, you don't love me, Tomas. You like me and you think I would be useful to you – but I want much more than that kind of marriage.'

'You'll wish you had one of these days.' Tomas stood back, a slightly resentful look on his face, because she'd caught him out. 'She's just using you, Emily.'

'I am a servant and it's all I want,' Emily said. She was a little annoyed, because she knew that *he* wanted to use her too. He wasn't madly in love with her, but he thought she would help him to make a successful business – and, if she'd loved him, it could have been a good life. 'And now I need a hot drink. My head aches.'

Tomas let her go and Emily entered the kitchen, but discovered that it was empty except for Mary. The girl looked at her resentfully.

'Mary, I'm sorry. I didn't try to take your job – it just happened.'

'Do you think I'd believe a word you say? You're a selfish bitch and I hope you get what's coming to you.'

Mary slammed out of the room, leaving Emily to stare after her in dismay. She'd upset two of her colleagues in one evening and her head was pounding. All she wanted was to make a nice hot drink and then lie down for a while. Being Miss Amy's maid was a step up for her but she'd been helping Cook too and she was exhausted.

'Have you seen the emerald pendant Arthur gave me?' Amy asked as Emily was helping her to dress for tea the next afternoon. She had settled on a pale green gown after discarding a dozen others, which lay on top of the satin coverlet waiting for Emily to put them away. 'When I looked in the box I couldn't see it.'

'I'm sure it was there before we left London.' Emily frowned. 'I'll look for it when you go down to tea, miss. It has probably just been placed in another box in your drawer.'

'I'm usually so particular about my jewels,' Amy replied and dabbed perfume behind her ears and on her wrists. 'Especially that pendant, because it is valuable and Arthur gave it to me.'

'Yes, I know you're fond of it. I'll make a

thorough search, miss. The catch was strong. I don't think you could have lost it.'

'No, that's what I thought. I expect it is here somewhere. Please look carefully, Emily. I should hate to lose it.'

'Of course you would, miss. You couldn't replace that if you tried.'

Amy nodded, picked up her handkerchief and dabbed some more perfume on it before leaving the room. She'd left the jewel case unlocked on the dressing table, as she sometimes did. Emily went through it carefully but the pendant was not there. She locked the case after her search, put it away in the drawer and tucked the key in its usual place in the silver vase on the dressing chest. Then she began to search the room. There were several small chests or tables with drawers, besides lots of pretty boxes, either enamel or wooden and she looked in all of them just in case.

Half an hour later, she'd been through every drawer in the bedroom, checked all Miss Amy's pockets and purses. She'd even taken all the clothes out of the wardrobe piece by piece in case it had caught on something, but there was no sign of the pendant. Surely it couldn't have come off when Miss Amy was wearing it? Emily vaguely recalled her wearing it last in London – and she thought it had been replaced in its box. If it wasn't here and Miss Amy hadn't lost it, what could have happened to the necklet? The only answer she could think of gave her a nasty taste in her mouth. No one in this house would take it. Had one of the London staff stolen it? No, impossible!

The idea was so shocking that Emily felt sick.

She put it out of her mind as she went down to the kitchen. Miss Amy was going to be so upset.

'Where have you been all this time?' Mrs Hattersley asked as she entered, then, 'What's wrong, Emily? Something upset you?'

Emily shook her head. She didn't want to talk about it because the idea that someone might steal from Miss Amy was too upsetting – and she didn't want to offend anyone by suggesting it. That suggestion would have to come from Miss Amy or her father.

'I've been busy, but I can help you with the...' She broke off as Mary burst into the room looking white and wild-eyed. 'Mary, what's happened?'

'What would you care?' Mary said rudely and then burst into tears. 'It's my lad. He's been wounded and they say he might not last long. He's in hospital in Portsmouth and I've been sent for ... but how can I get there?'

'I'm sure someone would take you to the station and you could get a train from there,' Emily said. 'If everyone is busy Mrs Marsh could telephone for a taxi to take you to the station.'

'I can't afford the fare let alone money to stay there...' Mary gulped, her cheeks wet with desperate tears. 'He'll die and I'll never see him again.'

'How much do you need?' Emily asked. 'I think I've got about four pounds you can have.'

'And I've another five in my tin,' Mrs Hattersley said. 'Dry your eyes and pack a few things, Mary. Mr Payne or Tomas will take you to the station.'

Mary stared at them, her cheeks flushing as she

met Emily's concerned look. 'You would do that for me?'

'Don't waste time wondering about it, Mary. Get packed and the money will be waiting for you when you come down.'

'Thank you. I shan't forget this,' Mary said. She gulped and then ran out of the kitchen.

'Poor girl,' Mrs Hattersley said and reached for the tin on the mantelpiece. 'I've got ten pounds here – are you sure you can spare what you offered, Emily?'

'Of course. Miss Amy gave me some extra money as a tip. Mary is welcome to it.'

'Let's hope she's there in time to see him alive,' Mrs Hattersley said. 'She must have had a telegram – there will be a good many getting them these days.'

'I'll go and get Mary's money,' Emily said.

She left the kitchen and ran up the stairs to her room, feeling a little surprised to see the door open, because she always left it shut. As she went in, she saw a man with his back towards her. He was bending over her bed and there was something in his hand.

'What are you doing, Tomas?'

He started and turned towards her, a guilty expression on his face. She saw a flash of green fire in his hand and knew instantly what it was.

'I've spent half an hour looking for that. Where did you get it? Don't tell me – you took it from Miss Amy's room.'

'Emily, I thought...' Tomas looked almost as green as the emerald in Miss Amy's pendant.

'You thought I was busy in the kitchen so it

329

would be safe to hide it in my room. You wanted Miss Amy to think I'd taken it, didn't you?'

'It isn't the way it looks. I don't want to hurt you – I just thought if she gave you the push you'd be glad to marry me.'

'Yes, I can see why you did it,' Emily said, her voice harsh. 'You say you care for me and yet you were ready to have me branded a thief to get what you wanted. It isn't me you love; you're in love with the idea of making a fortune, and you thought you could force me to go with you. Because you know I'm strong and willing to work long hours, you thought you would take advantage – well, it's not what I want. Give me the pendant, Tomas. I'll take it back to her.'

He hesitated, then stepped forward and held out the pendant. Emily put it in her pocket, then went to her purse on the dressing table and took out the money inside. She was trembling, upset and shocked that a man she'd liked, shared her thoughts with and imagined to be her friend could do such a thing. If she hadn't found him and her room had been searched, she would have been turned off without a reference, and branded a thief.

'I wouldn't take your money, Emily.'

'This is for Mary,' Emily said giving him a look of disdain. 'You're needed downstairs. Mary has to get to the station in a hurry.'

'Please Emily...'

'I should be obliged if you would leave my room. I have nothing more to say to you.'

'I love you ... really I do. It wasn't what you said ... not altogether anyway...'

330

Emily gave him a withering look that made him flinch. She walked from the room, leaving him to follow on as she ran back to the kitchen. Mary was already there carrying a small bag. She turned and looked at Emily, her face white.

'Thank you for this. I shan't forget.'

'Don't worry about paying me back,' Emily said. 'I'll pray he isn't hurt as bad as you think.'

Mary gave her a wan smile and accepted the money as Tomas entered the kitchen. He was pulling on his coat, his expression frustrated and angry.

'Mrs Marsh said I'm to take Mary to the station.'

'You'd better get going, Tomas. Mary can catch the next train to London and change there,' Mrs Hattersley said.

'Give me your bag,' he muttered and looked at Emily. She turned her head aside, not wanting to look at him. 'I'll get you there in time.'

Mary nodded and followed him from the room. Emily took a step towards the kitchen door.

'Where are you going? I thought you were going to help with dinner?'

'I'll be back in a moment,' Emily said. 'I need to speak to Miss Amy.'

She went out into the hall and then up the back stairs to Miss Amy's room. The door was open and her employer inside. As Emily entered she turned to look at her anxiously.

'Did you find the pendant?'

'Yes, I did. I've kept it safe in my pocket to give to you,' Emily said and took it out. 'It had fallen down behind the dressing table, miss. It must have got knocked off somehow.'

It was a lie but if she told the truth Tomas would be sacked without a reference and even though Emily was angry and disgusted she didn't wish him to be in trouble over the pendant now that they had it back. She wouldn't see him branded a thief even though he'd been prepared to do it to her.

Amy looked relieved. 'Oh, thank goodness. I was beginning to wonder if I had lost it, because it was the only explanation. Thank you so much for finding it, Emily.'

'I was glad to find it,' she said and placed it in Miss Amy's hands.

Amy hesitated, then, 'I hope you will not be offended, but I put out some dresses I no longer wear. I think that with a little alteration they would fit you – if you would like them?'

Emily glanced at the dresses lying on the bed. There were three afternoon dresses, two pale grey and of similar design with a high neck, long sleeves and a lace collar and the third a pretty pale lilac silk with short full sleeves.

'They are beautiful...' Emily drew her breath in sharply as she looked at them in surprise and pleasure. 'Are you certain you don't want them any more?'

'Quite certain.' Amy laughed. 'They are your own to wear or sell as you wish.'

'Thank you.' Emily smoothed her hand over the lilac silk. 'I've never had a dress half as good as these, Miss Amy. I hardly know how to thank you.'

'You already have,' Amy said. 'Now help me

332

change. I'm going to lie down for an hour and then I shall want you to help me dress for the evening.'

'Emily,' Tomas caught her arm as she started to mount the stairs later that evening, when most of the staff had gone up. He'd hung around on purpose to get her alone and gave her a pleading look. 'Please, you must let me explain. I never wanted to hurt you. You know I care for you.'

'I'm sorry, I can't believe that,' Emily looked him in the eyes. 'What you did was despicable, Tomas.'

'I only did it because I wanted to bring you to your senses. Miss Amy doesn't care about you or anyone but herself. I want you to marry me. I'll give you everything you ever wanted. We could go places together. I've got money saved and ideas ... I just need someone to help me make a suc- cess...

'You want an unpaid skivvy,' Emily said.

'That's not fair. I would see you got your share when the business picked up...'

'There's nothing I need or want except to do my job and be happy with my lot,' Emily said. She was carrying a pewter candlestick and the flame was flickering because there was a draught. 'My answer is final, Tomas. I'm not going to marry you – whatever you do.'

'Suit yourself,' he said and a look of anger came over his face. 'Got your eyes on better things I dare say.'

'I haven't got my eye on anyone or anything.'

'Don't think I haven't seen Mr Jonathan looking at you. Or was it Mr Nicolas you fancied? He turned your head when he took you to see your father in the hospital – and the other one fetched you back from the funeral. You think because Miss Amy favours you, you stand a chance with one of her brothers but you're far out. They might tumble you in the hay but...'

Emily lashed out with her free hand, catching him across the left cheek. For a moment his eyes sparked with fury and she thought he might hit her back but he just stared at her.

'I don't hit women – and I care for you even if you think I don't. It's all right, I've got the message. I shan't be bothering you again. After tomorrow you won't see me.'

She took a deep breath, her heart thudding as she looked into his furious face.

'Good luck with your pub – and I'm sorry I hit you.'

Tomas looked back at her, accusation in his eyes. 'I'm going to join the army. I've had enough of being given white feathers. I only kept out of it for you – and now I don't care. When I'm dead you'll be sorry.'

'Yes, I'll be sorry if you're killed,' Emily said, her eyes stinging with tears. 'I didn't want to hurt you – and I've never thought of Mr Jonathan or Mr Nicolas.'

'Haven't you? Maybe you don't realise it yet, but you will. Good luck, Emily. I hope you get what you want from life.'

Emily watched as he walked away from her and then went through into the back kitchen. The candle was throwing shadows over the walls and the stairs were dark and uninviting. Her lashes were wet as she dashed away her tears.

Why did things always have to be so horrible? Tomas was just being spiteful. He wasn't in love with her but he couldn't admit it, because he had just been trying to use her. He was wrong to accuse her of making eyes at her betters. It was true she had good memories of the way Mr Nicolas had held her when her pa died, and her heart did quicken every time she saw him, but that didn't mean anything.

Yet as she turned and walked upstairs there was a picture of Miss Amy's brother in her mind. He'd looked so handsome in his RFC uniform when he'd called at the house in London. Emily had only spoken to him for a moment but he'd made her smile. Even before he'd taken her to the hospital she'd seen him in the rose arbour composing a poem – and, if truth were told, she'd been fascinated. There was something special about Mr Nicolas – something that made her feel warm and comforted every time she thought of him.

She thought about Mary's distress when she'd learned of her lad's being shipped home badly wounded. If there was ever such news about Mr Nicolas, his family would not be the only ones to feel the pain.

Entering her room, Emily looked at the three dresses lying on her bed. She hadn't had a chance to try them yet but knew she could make them fit her, because she was clever with her needle. She'd never had anything remotely as good or beautiful as these clothes and she couldn't wait to try them on – especially the lilac silk gown. She wouldn't get much chance to wear something like that, but she would keep it for special days.

Chapter 29

'Don't slouch about, Lizzie. Sit up straight and try to look like a lady. It's time you put your childish ways behind you.'

Lizzie had been curled up on the deep stone sill in the library with her book when her mother entered. It was one of her favourites, *Sense and Sensibility* by Jane Austen, and she'd been carried away by the story. Now, feeling the sting and injustice of her mother's words, she got to her feet. Lifting her head, she looked at her mother defiantly. She was constantly being chided for not behaving like a young lady, but whenever she asked to be allowed to do something useful or visit with friends she was told it was impossible, because she was too young.

'Was there something you needed, Mama?'

'Your grandmother wants you. Please go to her now and stop wasting your time with those foolish novels.'

Lizzie felt the resentment stir inside her but kept the torrent of angry words to herself. She didn't want to quarrel with her mother, but she was so tired of being cooped up in this house. Amy was full of her plans to join the ambulance service, talking about the job she would do when she returned to London; Jonathan was always busy on the farm, and Nicolas was probably in Belgium by now.

A cold shiver went through Lizzie as she thought about the danger her brother might be in. She loved him more than anyone else and she couldn't bear it if anything should happen to him. Her letters from Nicolas were the bright spot in her life. She looked for them every day but none had come since he'd returned to his unit.

Please God let him be all right, Lizzie prayed as she walked towards her grandmother's rooms. She hoped Granny would have an errand for her in the village, because it would give her an excuse for a walk, and she might meet someone interesting, if she were lucky.

Nicolas glanced around the mess at the other young men lounging in old chairs or standing by the piano. A young French woman was playing some popular songs. She'd been employed as a waitress but on discovering she had a talent for playing the piano and singing, the men had soon persuaded her to entertain them with songs of home.

Louise had a pleasant singing voice, Nicolas reflected as he listened to her singing songs that were popular on stage in the English music halls. They sounded a little odd in her rather quaint accent, but that only made them all the more amusing. Besides, the men joined in the chorus, drowning her out; they stamped their feet and clapped as she declared enough was enough and rose from the piano stool. Despite their protests and entreaties, Louise shook her head and began to collect the dirty glasses, which was why she'd come into the mess in the first place.

Seeing that she was loaded with glasses and the door was shut, Nicolas sprang to his feet and opened it, letting her pass through. She smiled at him and thanked him, her dark eyes soft and appealing. She was a pretty girl, though not in his opinion as lovely as Emily.

The men were complaining about the loss of their pianist. Nicolas walked towards the seat Louise had vacated and sat down. It still felt warm, which was vaguely erotic. His fingers moved over the keys. He played a simple melody first, then a rousing piece by Rachmaninoff and then started pounding out some of the songs Louise had already played for them. His performance brought rousing cheers from his companions and a glass of beer was brought to the piano.

Nicolas was amused. All those years of practising for an exacting music master, who had urged him to become a concert pianist, might have paid off after all.

It was an hour later when Nicolas left the mess. He needed to be alone for a while and it was his habit to walk round their camp last thing at night, breathing in the scents of the night air. His thoughts were of home and ... of the young woman he knew he could never have.

Emily... Nicolas wasn't sure when she had worked her way beneath his skin. Had it been at that dance, when she wore that ridiculous home-made dress and he'd felt an urge to protect her from all the spiteful tongues? What had begun as an act of defiance had turned into something so pleasurable that at the end of the music he hadn't wanted to let her go. He'd known it was ridiculous, but he'd wanted to go on and on dancing with her.

Or had it been on the day war was declared? They'd bumped heads as they bent to pick up the same item while getting ready for the fete, and later he'd driven her to the infirmary and she'd cried in his arms.

Nicolas had been so angry with the doctors for not doing their job and saving Joe Carter's life. They were supposed to be doctors for goodness' sake! He knew even while he was angry that he was being unfair, but he couldn't bear to see Emily so devastated – and to know there was nothing he could do for her. He'd done his best to comfort her, but then he'd had to drive her back to the manor and leave her. He'd wanted to go on comforting her, to hold her, kiss away her tears ... but if he'd done that he wouldn't have been able to stop, and that was unthinkable. Emily was too fine and decent a girl to make her his mistress and even the thought of the alternative was so shocking that he hardly dared to contemplate it. Nicolas wasn't a snob; he wouldn't care what people thought but his family ... his parents and grandmother in particular would be horrified. He could just hear the tears, the scolding and the rage such a marriage would provoke.

No, it was impossible – so why couldn't he get Emily out of his mind? Why did she haunt his dreams?

She'd seemed a little better when he'd seen her

in the London house. She'd made a little joke, which had made him laugh – and she'd looked so adorable that he'd wanted to take her in his arms and love her. Of course he couldn't do that, because if he had it would have distressed her. Emily wasn't the kind of girl you could take advantage of in that way and he didn't want to. If his family hadn't employed her, if she'd still been a local farmer's daughter, might he have asked her ... to marry him?

A little shock went through him as he realised what he was thinking. He wanted to marry Emily Carter.

Impossible ... ridiculous! It couldn't happen, because his family would never accept such a marriage. He would run the risk of never seeing his parents, because his father would cut him off – and he might never be allowed to see his sisters again.

The thought of not being allowed to see Lizzie was painful too. She was special but he was fond of his sisters, his mother, grandmother, brother – and, in a way, his father, though they didn't often agree on things. He'd always respected his father's wishes as much as he could. His family meant a great deal to him – but did Emily mean more?

Nicolas frowned, hardly noticing the young woman until she came up to him and said good-night. He glanced at her, recognising Louise, and smiled.

'Are you off home now?'

'Yes, lieutenant,' Louise gave him a look that was clearly inviting. 'I live just a short distance from here ... alone since my husband died.'

Louise was a widow and her husband had been one of the first casualties of the war, which was why she now worked as a waitress. Nicolas knew what the look in her eyes meant; she was inviting him to walk home with her – and probably to take her to bed.

He hesitated for a moment. She was pretty and it would be easy enough to spend some time in her company, to shake off this mood of loneliness by making love to her – but she wasn't Emily. It was dark and he would see her safely home, but the rest of it wouldn't happen.

Now that he'd realised how he truly felt about Emily, there wasn't any point in trying to replace her. This feeling wasn't going to go away. He just had to make up his mind what he wanted to do about it...

Chapter 30

Emily looked at the pile of letters and cards that had arrived in the post and brought down to the kitchen for the staff. There was just a week to go until Christmas and Mrs Hattersley had been working hard to prepare all the puddings and cakes. Emily was still dividing her time between the kitchen and looking after Miss Amy. Sometimes when she tumbled into bed she was so tired that she was asleep almost as soon as her head touched the pillow. She sighed, sitting down at the kitchen table and easing her feet out of her shoes to rub them against the back of her legs.

'Is there anything for me?'

'I think there's a card come through the post for you, Emily, and … yes, I think there may be two cards.'

Emily looked through the pile. She found a card from Christopher and one with handwriting she did not recognise. Opening that first, she was surprised to see it was from Mr and Mrs Johnson, Christopher's parents, to wish her a Happy Christmas. She opened Christopher's next and saw there was a thin sheet of paper enclosed with a beautiful and very sentimental Christmas card. On the front of the card was a big heart with a panel of pink satin, which was entwined with Christmas roses.

My dearest Emily, Christopher had written in his letter, *I wish so much I could be with you this Christmas, but it seems impossible. We all thought this show would be over by now but it looks like… …* The next passage had been blue pencilled out. *I wanted to give you a special present but I don't trust the post from here. My father knows what I want and he will bring it to you before Christmas.*

I think of you all the time and I love you. Perhaps one day soon I'll get leave and we can be together. My fondest love, Christopher

'From your lad?' Mrs Hattersley asked and Emily nodded.

'One from his parents and one from him. He says he's sending me a special gift and his father will bring it before Christmas.'

'Well, that's nice. Now, if you've got a minute, I could do with a hand with the lunch. They've got

342

guests today and I'll be on my feet the whole time.'

'We need more help,' Emily said. 'If Mary doesn't come back soon they will have to replace her.'

'Mrs Marsh told me there's a new girl starting upstairs this week. And I'm to have help in the kitchen. She'll do the jobs you used to do, Emily. I only hope Esther will be as willing as you were when you started.'

'I'm willing now, but I can't be here and up-stairs with Miss Amy.'

'When you go to London I shall have to do without you altogether.' Mrs Hattersley sighed. 'I suppose I should be grateful that Lady Barton wouldn't hear of Miss Amy going off before the spring. She'll be twenty-one then and living with her cousin Miss Maude.'

'Miss Lizzie wants to go with them. She says she should be able to join a volunteer service too. She will be nineteen next year.'

Miss Lizzie had confided in Emily one day when she'd come into her sister's room as she was tidy-ing away some clothes. She'd sat on the bed watching and asking questions, chatting away just as if she were a friend rather than the daughter of the house. Emily had realised Miss Lizzie was lonely and felt sympathy for her.

It wasn't fair the way Miss Lizzie was kept from doing the things she wanted to do. She wasn't a child any more and Emily had noticed her walking alone in the gardens looking bored. Sometimes she went for long walks across the fields, even when it was cold. It puzzled Emily why she would want to do that, especially at this time of year when they had several visitors calling. She'd thought there was a secretive look about Miss Lizzie recently, a look that made Emily wonder if she was meeting a friend in secret.

There would be ructions if she were seeing a man. The thought of the uproar it would cause made Emily's blood run cold. She couldn't blame Miss Lizzie if she was courting on the sly, but he couldn't be suitable or he would come to the house. Lady Barton made no secret of the fact that she wanted Miss Amy married before Miss Lizzie was officially out, though she'd been going to some parties with her family.

Emily thought the family was playing with fire, trying to keep their youngest daughter on a leash. Any young woman would eventually tire of being cooped up in this house, hardly ever seeing friends. She needed something to keep her out of trouble – and the best thing her parents could do would be to let her go to London with her sister. She ought to be doing something useful.

Emily helped Mrs Hattersley prepare lunch, and then she went back up to Miss Amy's room to help her change for the afternoon. She wondered what Christopher had told his father to buy for her, and then forgot about it as Miss Amy started fussing over which dress she should wear.

'The family will be going to midnight mass. It is a tradition, in the same way as they give us a gift on Boxing Day. Their own presents are exchanged Christmas Eve, because they consider it wrong on the day itself.'

Emily nodded. Miss Amy had told her about some of it and she'd sneaked into the drawing room for a few minutes when the family were upstairs changing, wanting to catch a glimpse of the tree. It was a huge one, almost touching the ceiling and decorated with glass balls and bows of scarlet ribbon. Tiny parcels had been hung on the branches and the smell of fresh pine was delicious. Underneath the tree was a pile of brightly wrapped parcels waiting for the ceremony on Christmas Eve.

'I suppose it's more of a family party this evening. Just a few close friends and relatives?'

'Mr Jonathan's fiancée and her family will be here of course. Miss Maude is already here and her father and brother arrive today. Apart from that there will be just a few close friends.'

'Will Mr Nicolas be home?'

'Mrs Marsh said her ladyship wasn't sure. She was hoping he might come before the wedding, but he'd written to say he wasn't certain of getting leave.'

'Oh...' Emily was aware of disappointment, though it couldn't affect her one way or the other. She was hardly likely to see much of him, and she ought not to wish for it. Lord Barton's son wouldn't be allowed to court a servant, even if he wished to. 'It will be a shame if he misses his brother's wedding.'

'Well, you never know...' Mrs Hattersley stopped as someone entered. She looked at the man who stood respectfully in her kitchen, clutching his cap in his hands before him. 'Yes? Did you want something?'

'The housekeeper said I was to come. My name is Johnson and I've come to see my lad's girl – Miss Emily Carter.'

'This is Emily here,' Mrs Hattersley said her manner warming to him instantly. 'Come in, Mr Johnson, and sit down. Emily will make us a cup of tea. Would you like a piece of my Christmas cake? I make several and we've got one on the go.'

'That is very kind of you,' he replied and took the chair she indicated, his eyes never leaving Emily as she went about filling the kettle and fetching cups from the dresser. 'Well, this is a decent place you've got, Emily. I may call you that I hope?'

'Yes, Mr Johnson.' Emily smiled at him. 'I had a card from Christopher but he posted that ages ago and I thought I might get another letter before this, but I suppose they get delayed in the post.'

'That's why Christopher asked me to buy this for you, lass. He wanted to make certain you had it before Christmas.' He placed a small square box on the table in front of him. It was wrapped in brown paper but from the size and shape Emily suspected it was a ring box and her heart raced. Surely he hadn't sent her an engagement ring without even asking her? 'Christopher told me exactly what he wanted for you – and gave me the size, but if it doesn't fit I'll get it altered for you.'

Emily swallowed hard. She was certain the box contained a ring and it was meant to be an engagement ring.

'Well, Emily, what do you have to say to Mr Johnson?'

'Thank you...' She reached for the parcel with fingers that trembled slightly. 'I'll open it tomorrow.'

'I'd like to see if it fits. If you wouldn't mind looking at it now.'

'Go on, Emily,' Mrs Hattersley encouraged. 'Why wait when you can open it at once?'

Emily unfastened the wrappings. Inside was a black leather box embossed with gold. When she opened it she discovered the ring sitting in a bed of black velvet. It was yellow gold and had several small diamonds set in the shape of a daisy. Her breath caught, because something so beautiful must have cost a large sum of money.

'It is lovely,' she breathed. 'He shouldn't have spent so much on me. It is too expensive...'

Mr Johnson laughed, looking pleased at her reaction. 'It's a decent ring, Emily. My lad told me he wanted something good. He told me you were worth it – and having seen you, I can see he was right. We'll be looking forward to the wedding when he gets leave. I shall be giving you a good send off, lass – and you'll live with me until he gets back. Unless they want to keep you on here while he's away...'

Emily withdrew the ring and slipped it on to the third finger of her left hand. It fitted perfectly and she couldn't help feeling a thrill of pleasure, though she wished Christopher had asked his father to buy her something else. He ought to have waited and asked her to marry him when he came home on leave, because she wasn't sure how she felt about the idea. Christopher loved her, she was certain of that, and she liked him a lot, but marriage was for ever. If Emily agreed she would have to be faithful to her husband, and she didn't know if it was what she wanted. However, it was too difficult to explain her thoughts to his father. All she could do was smile and tell him how much she liked the ring.

'Let me look,' Mrs Hattersley said and Emily held out her hand. 'That is a lovely ring, Emily. What a lucky girl you are – and not a word to us about getting engaged.'

Emily felt too awkward to tell her that she'd never actually agreed to marry Christopher. She removed the ring from her hand and replaced it in its box, tucking it into her apron pocket.

'It's too good to wear while I'm working,' she explained as Mr Johnson frowned.

'No, you shouldn't wear it in the kitchen,' Mrs Hattersley said. 'Keep it safe, Emily. It isn't every girl gets a ring like yours.'

'I know. Thank you so much, Mr Johnson. I'll tell Christopher how lovely it is when I write to him next.'

'You do that,' he said. He took a bite of Mrs Hattersley's cake and rolled his eyes with pleasure. 'My missus makes good cakes but not a patch on this – I hope you'll teach Emily how to do it, ma'am?'

'She's a good little cook,' Mrs Hattersley said. 'Her cooking would keep any man happy, but she could have done well in the profession.'

'Then my Christopher is a lucky man,' he said and sipped his tea. 'I was a bit doubtful and Christopher's mother wanted to know more about her – but now I can tell her that Emily will do for our lad.'

'Emily is a good girl,' Mrs Hattersley said.

'Christopher is a kind, generous person,' Emily put in, because she needed to say something. 'My father thought a lot of him.'

'Aye, and my lad thought well of your father, Emily.' Mr Johnson finished his cake and drained the cup, then pushed back his chair and stood up, clutching his cap. 'I'll be on my way. I've got a few calls to make, but I wanted to come here first.'

Emily thanked him for coming and he invited her to visit him and his wife at his home, telling her that she was eager to meet his son's future wife. It seemed he thought it was all settled and she felt awkward, because she wasn't at all sure she wanted to marry Christopher – and she wasn't ready to get married at all yet. His words made her blush but she made no answer. She waited until he'd gone and then started to clear away some dirty dishes.

'Leave that for a moment and explain,' Mrs Hattersley ordered. 'You weren't expecting a ring, were you?'

'No. I thought he would wait and ask me when he came back.'

'Were you going to say yes?'

'I'm not sure. I like Christopher a lot. I may feel I want to be married when he comes home but I don't know yet.'

'And if you don't?'

'Then I'll tell him to his face and give him back

his ring.'

'You won't tell him you're not sure in a letter?'

Emily shook her head. She couldn't let her friend down while he was out there being shot at and suffering all the discomforts of the trenches. It would be too cruel and she liked Christopher too much to do that to him. Besides, she didn't know her own mind yet. Sometimes she thought there was someone else she liked much more but she knew she was being foolish. The person she liked most would never ask her to marry him.

What Emily had to decide was whether she wanted to get married at all – or just stay in service until she'd saved enough money to make something of her life.

Chapter 31

'Nicolas...' Lizzie cried as her brother entered the parlour where she was sitting reading. He looked so distinguished and handsome in his RFC uniform. 'I was thinking about you and hoping you would get home for Christmas.' She ran to his arms and was embraced. 'I'm so glad to see you.'

'I'm glad to see you, dear heart,' he said and kissed her cheek. 'You look well and pretty as always. Where are the others?'

'Amy and Maude are wrapping presents in the back parlour. Mama is lying on her bed with a headache; Jonathan is out somewhere and Papa was in the library the last time I saw him. Granny is in her favourite parlour with a book.'

'Everything as usual then.' Nicolas tipped his head to one side. 'Do you want your present now or wait until this evening?'

'Oh, I'll wait,' Lizzie said. 'It's enough for now that you're here. How long can you stay?'

'I've been given ten whole days, because I hadn't bothered to take leave for a while. It seemed best to save it up and have a worthwhile visit at Christmas.'

'Oh, that's wonderful. I've missed you so much. Your letters make me smile but it can't really be that much fun, Nicolas. I think you make up stories to amuse me.'

'Most of it happens as I write it,' he said. 'Some of the chaps are absolutely mad. I told you about Tuffy Broad, didn't I? He's the chap who takes his dog everywhere with him. Have him up in the kite – that's what the chaps call their planes – with him if the CO would let him; the damned thing sits all day at the edge of the field and waits. It knows the minute Tuffy and his crew are on their way home and starts chasing its tail and barking its head off. We always know that Tuffy is back home safe before we see his kite.'

Lizzie nodded. Her brother's letters were filled with such tales or descriptions of what he saw around him. He talked of drifting through the sky like a bird and the comradeship of his friends – what he never told her about was when they were killed or how awful it was in the air when the Hun was on their tail and his friends were being shot down. She knew about those things because she read the reports in the papers – and sometimes she

351

recognised the names of Nicolas's friends amongst those listed missing or dead.

'Jonathan will be pleased you're here. He was hoping you would be his best man and make the speech.'

'I'd rather not, but I suppose I can't refuse.' Nicolas grimaced. 'I ought to see how Mother is. I dare say she will be pleased to see me.'

'Yes, of course. You must go and tell her you're here. I'll see you at tea.'

Lizzie watched as her brother left the room. Instead of continuing to read her book, she glanced at the gilt clock on the mantelpiece. It was time to leave now if she was going to keep her appointment. Her pulse raced with excitement. Would he be there, waiting for her in their special place?

She never knew for certain whether he would come. That was part of the excitement, the uncertainty and the knowledge that her family would disapprove of her meeting Derek. They would disapprove of her meeting any man in secret, but she knew in her heart that her parents would never approve of Derek even if she brought him back to the house and introduced him.

In her heart she knew that nothing could come of these meetings. Derek wasn't the kind of man she could marry, even if he wanted to marry her. Lizzie wasn't sure she would want to marry him. When he wasn't wearing army breeches and boots, he dressed in cheap suits that looked as if they had come from the thirty-shilling store. Lizzie was sure he didn't have much money – and his manners were not those of a gentleman. He was rough and sometimes rude and often after she'd seen him she vowed she would not meet him again, but he was exciting and when he touched her she melted inside. His kisses made her want more and she allowed him to touch her in places that shocked and yet thrilled her.

Lizzie knew he wanted more. He kept telling her that he needed to make love to her properly and putting her hand on something hard in his trousers, telling her that it was painful for him to kiss and touch her and not go all the way.

Of course she knew vaguely what he was talking about. It was what lovers did – what you did when you got married. Lizzie had always called a halt when he tried to go too far. Once or twice the look in his eyes had frightened her when she pushed him away.

'One of these times you'll push me too far, Lizzie,' he'd said the last time they met. He was breathing hard and something warned her that she was playing with fire.

'I can't let you, Derek,' she'd said. 'You know I can't. If anything happened my father would kill me ... and you.'

That had seemed to sober him. His look was resentful as he said, 'It's best if I don't see you again. I'm a man and you're a girl. I need things you're too frightened to give me – so I shan't come next week.'

'It's Christmas soon,' she said. 'Come once more, please. I've got a present for you.'

'You know what I want.' He grabbed her and held her pressed so hard against him that she could feel his erection. 'If you come next time I'll know you're ready to be a woman...'

Lizzie had bought him a blue silk tie. It was expensive, much better than the ties he usually wore and she wanted him to have it and yet she was afraid of what might happen if she went to the meeting.

Three times she decided to go and three times she changed her mind. She had almost put on her coat when her mother came into the hall.

'Where are you going, Lizzie?'

'Just for a walk.'

'On a day like this? Don't be ridiculous. I want you to help me wrap my presents. I'm not sure that Maude will like what I've bought her and I need your advice.'

Lizzie sighed inwardly and yet in a way she was glad that her mother had called her. Derek was dangerous and she'd been a fool to let him touch her and kiss her the way he had. If she'd met him today he might not have stopped when she pushed him away.

Relief flooded through her as her decision was made. She wouldn't sneak away to meet him again.

'Of course I'll help, Mama,' she said. 'I was hoping you might let me go to London with Amy and Cousin Maude in the New Year – just for a while.'

'We'll see,' her mother said. 'I know you're growing up, Lizzie, but Amy ought to be married first. Your father has arranged for the dower house to be turned into a convalescent home as soon as it can be done after Christmas. If you are sensible I shall allow you to help me. You can visit the patients, read to them and write letters. Some of them have been terribly injured, blinded or maimed. I think you would find work like that worthwhile – do you not agree?'

'Oh yes,' Lizzie said and her face lit up. 'It's what I've longed to do – help those poor men who have been hurt in the fighting.'

'Well, they will be officers, of course,' Lady Barton said. 'If I let you join a volunteer unit you would have to look after all sorts. I do not wish you to be exposed to common soldiers, Lizzie. Officers are gentlemen and know how to treat a decent young girl.'

Lizzie felt hot all over. Derek was definitely not an officer. She wasn't even sure he was a soldier, though he claimed he was stationed nearby. Lizzie had been almost certain he was lying to her, but it had been just part of the game she played. Now it was over. She had something to look forward to and the future was brighter. She didn't even mind now if Amy went off to London without her.

For a moment she thought of Derek waiting in a rain-soaked field for her. He would be so angry, but he'd told her he wanted a woman not a girl so it was his own fault for threatening her.

Lizzie decided she would not think of him again.

Chapter 32

Emily saw Mr Nicolas walking towards her. She'd just come from Miss Amy's room and was carrying an evening dress of pale blue silk, which she was going to sponge and iron for his sister to wear that night. It had a heavily beaded panel at the front and it was difficult to get right. Her heart caught as Nicolas smiled at her and her throat tightened.

'Happy Christmas, Emily,' he said. 'I hope you are well and still enjoying your job?'

'Yes, sir... I'm Miss Amy's maid now and I am going to London with her next year.'

'Lizzie told me in one of her letters. I'm glad things are going so well for you.'

Emily's heart was beating so hard she could scarcely breathe. 'The family wasn't sure you would get home, sir.'

'I managed to swap leave with a friend so I could be at the wedding.'

'I'm glad you're here, sir,' she said and felt her cheeks getting warm. 'I know a lot of your friends have been hurt or injured.'

'Yes, they have,' he replied and the smile left his eyes. 'Don't tell Amy I said so but it isn't much fun out there. The boys on the ground are enduring the worst of it but if a kite gets hit ... there isn't much chance of getting out alive.'

Emily drew a sharp breath, because the look in

his eyes was revealing. He wrote cheerful letters to his sister, but he was telling her the truth. She felt touched, humbled because it was Emily he'd confided in, and she wanted to reach out and touch his face, to comfort him, but of course she couldn't. She mustn't show her feelings, because he would be embarrassed, but oh, how she longed to hold him as he'd held her at the infirmary that day.

'I think about you often, sir. We all do – and we all pray for you.'

'Thank you.' The twinkle was back in his eyes now. 'You know what they say – the devil looks after his own. So I'm guaranteed a safe landing every time.'

'Of course you are, sir,' Emily said and giggled, because it was good to share a joke with him. 'Well, I'd best get on or Mrs Hattersley will have my guts for garters.'

Nicolas gave a shout of laughter. 'You say the most amusing things, Emily Carter. No wonder I think of you when I'm up there in the blue sky...'

Emily felt the heat spread through her but she walked on and resisted the urge to look back and see if he was watching her. Mr Nicolas liked a joke – and she liked him a lot. She had since the day he took her to the infirmary and held her when she learned Pa had died. Of course she knew he was just being friendly. His smiles and jokes didn't mean anything. He was a gentleman and she was just a common farm girl – perhaps even worse, she was his sister's maid.

The divide between them was a huge gaping hole. He wouldn't ever think of marrying a girl like her – and she should put the idea right out of her mind or she would end up with a broken heart. Even if he liked her, it could never be more than a flirtation – without ruining Emily's reputation. Was he thinking she might allow him to seduce her? The thought made her hot all over and she thrust it from her mind. Mr Nicolas was too much the gentleman – surely?

Yet it made her feel good to know that he was back home safe and she liked his smile. Of course he didn't think of her when he was flying – why should he? She knew he was just being friendly, but it made her smile all the same.

Emily was still glowing when she entered the kitchen. She took the gown into the scullery and sponged a faint mark from the bodice, then returned to the kitchen and placed it over an elm spindle-back chair by the fire while she tested the iron. Various pots were simmering gently on the range and the kitchen was full of tantalising smells as dinner took shape. On the dresser an array of cold puddings and savouries had already been set out on large silver dishes with paper doilies.

'That iron will be a bit hot for that gown,' Mrs Hattersley warned. 'You'd best let it cool off a bit first.'

'Yes, I shall,' Emily replied. 'Did you know that Mr Nicolas is home?'

'Is he? Janet will need to set another place for dinner then. I'm told she's the new upstairs maid, until Mary comes back. I'm glad I made those macaroons. Mr Nicolas is partial to them.' Mrs Hattersley looked at her. 'I hope you're not in a dream over that ring?'

'No, of course not. I shan't wear it just yet. I need to think about it first.'

'It's a pity the lad didn't wait to ask you,' Mrs Hattersley said. 'He won't get all his money back for that ring.'

'I suppose not. It is a shame – but I might accept it. I'm just not sure.'

'Well, it's your decision, as long as you don't let him down while he's over there. They've got it hard enough in the trenches without getting a "Dear John" letter from home.'

Emily turned away to press the gown. She'd damped it a little, ironing it through a wet handkerchief, and the heat on water made little hissing sounds. When all the creases were gone, she hung it over the chair in front of the range to let it air.

She wished Christopher hadn't sent the ring because she didn't want to let him down. Her meeting with Mr Nicolas had made her very aware that she did not wish to marry Christopher, but she knew she was being foolish. There could never be anything between her and Mr Nicolas – and if she wanted to marry, Christopher was a lovely man. He'd always been her friend and yet she didn't know if marriage to Christopher would make her happy.

Did she wish to marry at all? Perhaps it might be better to stay unwed and seek a career, as Mrs Hattersley seemed to think was best.

Emily found the box on her bed when she went up to her room late that evening. She'd joined the others in drinking a nightcap and singing carols in the chapel and now she was tired – and there was the box lying on her bed.

Another present for her? Who could it be from? She'd given her small gifts to Mrs Hattersley, June and the others, sending Mary a pretty scarf through the post and telling her she hoped her fiancé would soon be better, and Emily had received a pair of silk stockings as a joint gift from them all.

'These are wonderful, so fine,' Emily exclaimed when she opened her parcel. 'I've never had such a lovely present. Thank you all so much.'

Miss Amy had already given Emily a pair of leather gloves, a warm scarf and two guineas, and Mrs Hattersley had told her that all the servants would receive an extra month's wages on Boxing Day as their gift from the family.

'We used to receive gifts but sometimes they were useless and Lord Barton decided that money would be more suitable.'

'I think he's right,' Amy said. 'Expensive soap and sweets are nice to have but money is more useful.'

So who had placed the velvet box on her bed? It hadn't been wrapped and was clearly a jeweller's box. Her hand shook slightly as she picked it up and lifted the lid. She gasped as she saw the daisy-shaped pendant of large white diamonds suspended on what looked like silver or perhaps a platinum chain. The diamonds in her ring were small compared to this and they had taken her breath away. She hardly dared to look at the card that had been tucked securely into the lid of the box and yet in her heart she knew.

Mr Nicolas! Emily read the card and then sat down on the bed as her knees threatened to give way. A present like this was so magnificent and so unexpected that her head was swimming from the shock. Why had he given her such an expensive gift?

'*To the most beautiful girl I know,*' he'd written in a bold hand. '*With love from your friend, Nicolas.*'

Mr Nicolas had given her the pendant... Emily was stunned, torn between feelings of excitement and pleasure, and doubts. Gentlemen did not give their sister's maid a gift like this unless...

She closed her eyes as the visions crowded into her mind. Mr Nicolas taking her into his arms, kissing her ... lying with him in a bed that smelled of fresh linen and ... there Emily's mind refused to follow.

It would be the worst mistake of her life. If she became Mr Nicolas's mistress she would lose her job and all her friends at the manor. She would also betray the man who trusted her and was hoping to make her his wife.

Emily would be a fool to exchange a promise of marriage for a brief fling, because that was all it could ever be. Mr Nicolas would never throw away his position, his family, everything he stood for in life – and that was what would happen if he stepped out of his class to marry Emily. It could never be and she mustn't let herself dream.

She couldn't let him do it, any more than she could contemplate the alternative. She would have to give the pendant back as soon as she could. Yet the temptation to try it on was overwhelming. She picked it up, holding it to her throat to fasten the catch, then went to the dressing table and picked up her small mirror. The diamonds sparkled in the light of her lamp.

It was just so beautiful, but Emily couldn't keep it. She would have to give it back, but just for a while she would wear it close to her skin. It would be hidden beneath her uniform during the day – and if she happened to meet Mr Nicolas she could take it off and give it to him. She could just keep the box and card, which would be enough to remind her of the exquisite gift.

Touching the pendant where it lay against her skin, Emily became aware of the cold and jumped into bed, pulling the covers up over her. It had been a day of surprises. Before she came to the manor she'd never even seen anything like this pendant except in the window of the jeweller in Ely – and even there she'd never seen anything as good. Many of Miss Amy's jewels were not as fine as these diamonds.

Her life had been a roller-coaster these past few months. The shock of her uncle's attack on her and the breach with her mother. Then coming here to work at the manor and learning to do things the way Mrs Hattersley liked them ... her father's death... She could never have faced that without Mr Nicolas's support.

Was that when she had given her heart, as she wept in his arms and felt his kiss on her hair? She hadn't known it until Tomas accused her of setting her cap at her betters. At the back of her mind she'd been ready to settle for Christopher. He was her friend and she'd thought it would be a safe,

362

secure marriage but now... Emily suddenly realised that she could never settle for less than love.

It was stupid and would cause her more grief
than pleasure, but she *was* in love with Mr Nicolas. She touched her pendant again, fingering it
with delight. She'd never, ever expected to have
such a lovely thing in her life. It must be returned, of course it must – but just for now she
would savour the pleasure of feeling it lie heavy
between her breasts.

She would never wear Christopher's ring. The
realisation made tears sting her eyes, because it
was such a lovely thing and must have cost her
friend more than he could afford. She wished with
all her heart that he hadn't been so extravagant.
He ought to have asked her first and waited for her
answer, but he'd wanted to show her how much he
cared – and that hurt Emily, because she would
have to refuse him.

To be the giver of so much pain was something
she would have wished to avoid. Christopher had
been a good friend to her father and he didn't
deserve to be treated so ill – and yet to marry him
when she was in love with someone else would be
cruel. He would be hurt but in time he would
recover and find someone else.

Tears trickled down Emily's cheeks in the darkness. Life was so unfair at times. She hadn't meant
to fall in love with a man she could never have but
it had happened and there was no going back.

Chapter 33

'Would you mind helping Mrs Jonathan change?' Amy asked as Emily put down the champagne she'd been dispensing into crystal flutes. 'Janet and June are both busy – so Mama thought of you.'

'I should be happy to help her,' Emily said. Mabel had been a lovely bride, her dress as pretty as a picture, so Emily thought. The gown must have been fabulously expensive and had been shipped all the way from New York. To Emily that seemed wildly extravagant, but Mabel's father was a rich man. When Emily thought of what the family at the manor had spent on Jonathan's wedding, she shuddered because it would feed several village families for a year.

'Her room is next to mine. She will be expecting you. Don't keep her waiting.'

'No, I shan't,' Emily said and left the room quickly.

As she did so she passed close to Mr Nicolas but much as she wanted to speak to him she did not dare to breathe a word. Someone would be sure to hear her or notice her. Instead she gave him a small, shy smile and then hurried from the room. Her pendant was still nestling beneath her uniform; she could feel it against her skin and could hardly resist touching it from time to time. Giving it back wouldn't be easy, but it was what she ought to do.

She ran upstairs and along the corridor to the room next to Miss Amy's. When she tapped at the door a whispery voice answered and she opened the door. The bride was standing in all her finery looking lost and alone and, as Emily looked at her, she dashed a tear from her cheek. Emily realised that for all the money spent on her she was feeling as much out of place as Emily had when she first came to the manor.

'You do look a proper treat, miss,' Emily said. 'I should call you Mrs Jonathan now, shouldn't I? What a lovely dress. We've all been admiring it.'

'Yes, it is beautiful. The silk was woven specially and has silver thread running through it,' Mabel said and threw her a grateful look. 'What is your name? I don't think I've seen you before.'

'I'm Miss Amy's maid. My name is Emily Carter.'

'Oh, yes. I've heard them speak of you.'

She had been unfastening the young woman's gown at the back while she talked and Mabel stepped out of it. Emily gathered it up and laid it reverently on the bed. Then she brought the smart travelling gown of green silk and slipped it over Mabel's head, fastening the hooks at the back. She stood back to admire the effect.

'You should have your hair up with this dress, miss. Would you like me to do it for you?'

'Please, if you would.'

Mabel sat down at the dressing table and watched as Emily swept her hair softly back from her face and gathered it into a large looped knot.

'Oh, that does look nice, much better than I

usually have it. I wish you could be my maid when we come home. Jonathan said the hotel would send a maid up for me while we're in Devon but...'

'I'll be in London when you return, miss – but you could ask for Mary, if she's back from leave. She's better than me at dressing hair.'

'Is she as friendly?' Mabel asked. 'Mother's maid always seems snooty, as if she is used to waiting on a better class rather than being grateful for the job...' Her cheeks flushed. 'I shouldn't have said that. I wasn't being rude...'

'Of course you weren't, miss. You take no notice of her. Mary's all right. I think she would enjoy being your maid.'

'Thank you for being so kind to me,' Mabel said as Emily offered her gloves and purse. 'I still wish you were going to be here, but I'll take your advice.' She hesitated, and then reached into her leather purse. 'Would you be offended if I gave you a tip? I never know what to do...'

'You give tips when you're a guest, miss. Most of the family give a scarf or a dress they've finished with now and then.'

Mabel took two gold sovereigns from her purse. 'Please don't be offended, Emily. I just want to say thank you – you've made me feel so much better.'

'There's no need, miss, but I'll take your money and say thank you. I shall save it for a rainy day.'

Mabel thanked her but then someone knocked at the door. Mabel called out that he might come in and Mr Jonathan entered. Emily excused herself instantly, but sent the bride an encouraging look as she left.

She had a nice warm feeling as she went back

downstairs to help with the clearing up. The wedding guests were departing, and June and Janet were both busy with coats and hats. Emily headed for the kitchen, because she knew there would be a pile of washing up.

Mrs Jonathan had reminded Emily of herself during her first few days at the manor. The young woman was shy and nervous, afraid of making silly mistakes. It was a pity that she didn't have more confidence, but no doubt that would come once she'd been married for a while.

'Emily...' Mrs Hattersley greeted her anxiously. 'Thank goodness you're back.'

'I know you're snowed under,' Emily said. The kitchen table was groaning under the weight of dirty dishes. 'I'll soon have this lot cleared up.'

'No, it isn't that,' Mrs Hattersley said and her expression sent a chill down Emily's spine. 'Mr Johnson is waiting to see you in my parlour. He's in such a state, poor man. Mrs Marsh took him through and gave him a glass of sherry – but he's got news for you, bad news I'm afraid, lass.'

'News...' it could only mean one of two things. 'Christopher is hurt or...'

'Go and speak to him, Emily. He will want to tell you himself...' Mrs Hattersley dashed a tear from the corner of her eye. 'This lot will wait ... and Mrs Marsh knows all about it so just do whatever you have to...'

Emily inclined her head. Her heart was thudding against her ribs and it was painful to breathe. She wanted to cry but her eyes felt dry and gritty, as if she was hurting too much for the relief of tears. Christopher was her friend. He'd wanted to marry her and he'd sent her that lovely ring.

Mr Johnson was standing with his back to her as she entered the small sitting room. His shoulders were bowed under the weight of his grief and when he turned to look at her she saw the pain in his eyes.

'Christopher...' she croaked because her throat was too tight to speak. 'Is he...'

'Badly wounded,' Mr Johnson said, turning his cap in his hands in an effort not to break down. 'He's been shipped back to England and they've taken him to a military hospital down south. I knew you would want to come with me. I've borrowed a van and if you can get away...'

'I'm sure Miss Amy will give me leave.'

'It's not going to be pretty, Emily. From what I hear he has burns to his face and the upper part of his body.'

'I shan't scream or run away in horror.'

'That's why I've come to you. His poor mother couldn't face it and ... I'd rather not go alone.'

'You don't have to, Mr Johnson.'

'Why don't you call me Bill?' he said, giving her a look of approval. 'Off you go now and pack a few things.'

'I shan't bother to change.'

She left Mrs Hattersley's parlour and ran hastily up the back stairs to her bedroom. Emerging with a small bag shortly after, she met Mary coming along the landing. Mary had returned to help with the wedding, but wouldn't be back at work full-time for a few more weeks.

'You're off then. Mrs Hattersley told me your lad had been hurt bad.' Mary looked at her with sympathy. 'I haven't forgotten what you did for me – do you need any money?'

'No, I'm all right, thanks,' Emily said. 'I know your lad is recovering and I'm glad, Mary. I just hope it will be the same for Christopher.'

'I'm going to be Mrs Jonathan's maid when she comes back from her honeymoon.'

'I'm so pleased for you, Mary. She's very nice and I think you will like her.'

'I'll still be getting married one day, but Ted will be in hospital for months. They're moving him to a military convalescent home nearer his family so I'll be able to visit – but it might be years before we can wed. Mrs Marsh said they would find him an easy job here when he's well enough.'

Emily nodded to her and ran past her along the hall and down the stairs. She hadn't had time to find Miss Amy and tell her, but she hoped she would understand that she didn't have a choice. Emily hadn't had time to think about the future, but she had a horrible feeling inside that her life might be about to change and not in a way she would like.

'The burns on Christopher's face will heal in time and we may be able to do something to help with the scarring,' the doctor told them before they were allowed on the ward to visit him. 'I'm afraid his hands are so badly damaged that he will have only a limited amount of use in the fingers. He may not be able to dress himself or ... what kind of work did he do before the war?'

'He was a cabinet maker, good at fixing things,' Mr Johnson said the tears running down his

369

cheeks. 'Ever since he was a lad he was always whittling away at a bit of wood or making something.'

'I'm afraid that is out of the question. As I said, he may need help dressing himself at first – and we're not sure about his eyes. When he was brought in he was totally blind, though there has been some improvement in that area. We think he may recover partial sight but the heat caused some damage to the eyes...'

Mr Johnson gasped and staggered. Emily caught his arm, steadying him.

'He's still alive,' she said. 'Cling on to that, Bill. We mustn't give way to grief. Christopher will not want us to feel sorry for him.' She lifted her head and looked at the doctor. 'I am Christopher's fiancée and I need to know the worst. Will he be able to walk and talk?'

'Yes, there was no damage sustained to the lower half of his body and he is able to understand what we say to him – and to answer if he feels like it, though he isn't inclined to say much. He is aware of what has happened to him and is finding his situation hard to accept at the moment.'

'Yes, I understand. It is a terrible thing to have to face,' Emily said. 'But we're here for him – aren't we, Bill?'

Mr Johnson looked at her gratefully. 'Thank you, lass. It's more than I could expect or ask of you. God bless you for being here. I'm not sure I could have taken this on my own.'

'Where else should I be?' Emily removed her gloves. She'd taken time to slip on her ring earlier. 'Christopher is my friend and I love him.

I couldn't desert him now.'

'Very well.' The doctor smiled at her. 'Not every young woman reacts to bad news like that, Miss Carter. Mr Johnson is fortunate – but, I'm warning you, he may not accept your decision. Some of our patients reject anything they think may be pity – and injuries like this can alter a man's personality.'

'I understand, but I want to be there for him when he's ready,' Emily said. 'May we see him now please?'

'Just don't expect too much at first.'

'He needs time to accept,' Emily said, outwardly calm.

Inside she was bleeding. Christopher was a special friend. She cared for him and she knew he loved her. He'd sent her his ring and he wanted her to marry him. She'd thought at the time that it would be hard to tell him she didn't want to marry him, but now it was impossible. She just couldn't turn her back on him now that he was so badly injured. She had no choice but to stand by him – and marry him when he was ready.

Disappointment and regret lurked at the back of her mind, but she thrust them away. She couldn't think of her own needs or desires when Christopher needed her so much. His life would never be the same again. The least she could do was to help him get through the pain and frustration as best he could.

As she'd followed the nurse past rows of beds with identical counterpanes, all of them neatly tucked under with proper hospital corners, Emily caught the familiar smell of antiseptic and carbolic soap plus an underlying odour of sickness. Somehow, the nurses created order out of chaos and pain, curtains discreetly closed about beds where patients were being violently sick or receiving treatment for ghastly wounds. Wheelchairs and commodes told their own tale, as did a pair of wooden crutches and a trolley with steel dishes and rolls of bandages.

Looking down at Christopher's bandaged hands and head, pity and grief tugged at Emily's heart. He'd been so young and bright and full of life. He was a clever man and she'd always believed that he would make a success of his life. Recalling his eagerness to join up and fight for his country, she felt her throat tighten with emotion. He did not deserve to be repaid like this – but then, none of them did. All the best and the brightest had been the first to volunteer and too many of them were dying or coming home badly wounded. It was such a waste.

'Emily ... it is you, isn't it? I can smell your scent,' Christopher's voice sent a tingle down her spine, because he sounded just like himself. 'You shouldn't have come, love. I'm no damned good to you now. Please go away and forget about me.'

Emily reached for him, her hand gentle as she touched his bare arm, which was showing above the sheet.

'I'm not going to leave you, Christopher. I'm wearing your ring and if you think you can get out of marrying me that easily you're mistaken. Breach of promise that is – I could sue you for a fortune.'

A strangled laugh broke from his lips. 'That's

just what I thought you'd say, Emily love, but it won't do. I love you too much to let you ruin your life looking after me. My father will do that...'

'I'm here, son,' Bill Johnson said, his voice gruff with emotion. 'Me and your mother would look after you, but Emily isn't going anywhere. She's stronger than any of us, lad. She won't let you down.'

'It isn't what I want...' Christopher moved his hands and moaned in pain. 'Look at these. What sort of a husband would I be?'

'We'll look after you,' his father said. 'You can live with us. In time you may be able to find some kind of work. Not what you're used to, son – but we'll manage.'

Christopher turned his head to one side. 'Please go away, Emily. I don't want pity.'

'I love you. I've always cared for you – and I'm not going anywhere. Get used to it, Christopher Johnson. I'm going to stick around no matter what you say.'

Christopher remained stubbornly silent. They stood in silence but he had closed off and refused to speak or look at them, and a few moments later a nurse came up to them.

'He's tired,' she said. 'Please leave now and visit another day.'

'Yes, I shall.' Emily bent down. She gently kissed his mouth, which was all she could see of his face and then each bandaged hand in turn. 'I'll be here tomorrow, Christopher – and every day. I'm going to be your wife one day, whether you like it or not.'

He moved his head negatively on the pillow but

didn't say anything. Emily walked away, her shoulders back and her head high. Outside the ward, she stopped and took out her handkerchief, wiping away the foolish tears.

'Don't cry, lass. You were wonderful in there,' Bill Johnson said. 'I shall have to go home and tell his mother the news. She may pluck up the courage to come and visit him now. Will you be all right here alone for a couple of days?'

'Yes, of course. You need to see your wife. I can find a room near the hospital so that I can visit often.'

'I'll help you get settled and then I'll be off,' he said. 'I'm proud of you for the way you've stood by my lad, Emily. I'll give you some money. I don't want you going short while you're here.'

Emily would have refused, but knew he wouldn't give in. He was a proud man like his son and wanted to do right by her.

'Could you send a message to the manor – let them know I'm staying here for a while. I'll need to report back to work in a few days, but I'm sure they will understand that I have to give notice. Christopher comes first now.'

'Aye, I'll do that for you. I meant what I said, Emily. Don't you worry about money or the future. You stand by him and you won't lose by it. I'll see you have a roof over your heads and enough to live on.'

'Thank you – but we have to wait for Christopher to accept what has happened. I shall be there if he needs me, but if he can't bear...' She shook her head. 'We won't think about that just yet. We have to think about him getting better...'

Chapter 34

'I can see a little now,' Christopher said as Emily sat by his bed that morning, a week after she'd first visited him at the hospital. 'They've been bathing my eyes and the sight is coming back little by little. The doctor says I'll see almost as well as before – but it's my hands that are the worst. I've lost three fingers on my left hand and the rest are badly burned. I shan't be able to work with wood the way I could, Emily.'

'When you're well again you'll find a job of some kind,' Emily assured him. 'I know you must be suffering a lot of pain but...'

'It's not the pain,' he said. 'You know I'll be scarred and ... it's not fair on you, Emily. You're so lovely. You could find someone else and have a much better life than I'll be able to give you.'

'You were there for Pa and me when we needed you. You're my friend and I love you,' Emily said. 'I'm not going to walk out on you, Christopher. I know you have a lot of frustration and pain to face but I'll do what I can to help – and if we love each other enough we'll get through it.'

'Can you really bear it?'

'You're the one who has to bear it,' Emily said. 'I can't take the pain away or the frustration. You'll be angry but you mustn't be bitter. You're alive and your injuries will heal in time.'

Christopher was silent for a moment, then, 'I

375

know you're right, Emily. We saw them in the trenches every day. They lost their arms, legs, some of them had their guts hanging out and others had no face left. Some were patched up and sent down the line, others we buried where we could.'

'It must have been hell for you. We can read what they say in the papers but we have no true idea of what it's like over there.'

'It's as well you don't, Emily love. One of the worst things was waiting for letters from home. Some of the men got letters that drove them to tears – wives, sweethearts, letting them down.'

'I would never let you down, Christopher. If I say I'll marry you I will.'

'Aye, I know and I'm lucky,' he said. 'I hope you won't regret it.'

'Well, I'm about to be given my marching orders,' Emily said. 'Sister is looking at me in a meaningful way. I'll come again this evening.'

'What will you do until then?'

'Oh, look round the shops – and there's a volunteer meeting in town this afternoon.'

'You make the best of everything, don't you?' Christopher turned his head towards her as she bent to kiss his mouth. 'I really love you, Emily. I promise I'll get right again for you.'

'I'm sure you will when you're well enough,' Emily said. 'Now I'd better go or Sister will have my guts for garters.'

A laugh broke from Christopher, followed by a moan of pain. She touched his arm and then left, stopping at the ward door to glance back at him and wave. He might not be able to see clearly but he would know.

Emily felt much better as she left the hospital. Out in the fresh air she could breathe more easily and take stock of what was happening. The streets were busy as people rushed from one place to another, their lives carrying on as usual. People got on buses and trams, did their shopping, went to the theatre and listened to the music as the Sally Army played hymns in the square. Life didn't stop just because a man was killed and another badly injured; it was only his loved ones that were left to pick up the pieces and carry on.

Christopher was so much more cheerful now that he could begin to see shapes again. He was hopeful for the future and that was all she could ask for. The struggle to get well would be long and difficult but at least he'd accepted that she wasn't going away. She would be with him, helping him where she could. It was true that for a long time she might be more of a nurse than a wife to him, but she wouldn't mind that, because she loved him in her fashion. It wasn't romantic love or the love she might have known with someone else – but that was impossible anyway. Emily was one for facing the reality of life and the reality was that she couldn't walk away from Christopher. If she'd done that she wouldn't have been able to forgive herself.

She was feeling hungry. She would find a little café, have something to eat and then go to that volunteer meeting. The shops were interesting but she didn't want to waste her money, because she might need it in future and there was nothing she particularly needed, so she would spend her afternoon listening to women talk about why they should have more rights.

It was nearly four in the afternoon when Emily left the meeting. It had been a little noisy, because some of the women had been angry about the way the government was running things, and shouted abuse from time to time. Emily suspected they might be members of the Suffragettes, who could not resist the opportunity to bring in politics, despite their leaders declaring a cessation of protests until the end of the war.

There had been murmurs of disagreement and some of the same opinion. The dissension continued throughout the meeting, ending in one woman who was screaming abuse being hustled out of the room. Emerging into a bitterly cold afternoon as the meeting ended, Emily turned up her coat collar and began to walk briskly towards the hospital. The lights were on, because it was dark and the shops would soon be closing for the night. Visiting time wasn't for another hour or so yet. She would have time to drink a cup of tea and eat a sandwich in the hospital canteen before visiting time began. She saw a man selling newspapers and glanced at the headlines, which were dour. It wasn't worth buying a paper with that sort of news, but she might buy a magazine to read when she went back to her lodgings after leaving Christopher. The nights were the worst, sitting in a small room by a tiny gas fire and thinking about things that she would rather not think about, because she was alone and there was nothing else to do. She was used to being busy and the time seemed endless.

It was as she reached the hospital that she heard someone shout her name and she turned, looking to see who it could be.

'Emily...' the voice came again and then she saw him standing under the light; he was striding towards her, making her heart beat wildly. He was so handsome in his uniform and her chest felt so tight that she could scarcely breathe. 'I'm so glad I found you. I asked Sister and she told me you came every evening so I thought I'd wait.'

'Mr Nicolas,' Emily gazed up at him, a smile of pleasure on her lips. 'It was kind of you to come down...'

'We're all concerned about you,' he said. 'Amy wanted to know if you were all right for money. Are you? Is there anything you need – anything I can do for you?'

'I'm going to have a cup of tea and a bun before I visit,' Emily said. 'Shall we go inside where it's warmer?'

'Yes, of course. It feels cold enough for snow.'

'I was thinking that on the way here. I'd been to a Suffragette meeting and I didn't know how cold it was until I came out afterwards.'

'This is a sorry business for you, Emily. I've seen Christopher and told him that if he needs work when he's on his feet again I might have a job for him. I'm thinking of buying more properties and letting them out and I'll need an agent to look after them for me.'

'That's good of you, sir. What did Christopher say?'

'He said he'd been thinking of looking for work

like that – apparently, Sir Arthur is back in the country and he's offered Christopher a similar position on his estate. Christopher's father was there when I visited earlier – Sister very kindly let me have five minutes with them.'

They had reached the canteen. Wooden tables were set in rows, many of them taken, people sitting and talking in hushed tones as they drank lukewarm tea and waited to see their loved ones. Most of them had shopping bags filled with fruit, magazines or sweets they'd somehow managed to scrounge to bring for the patients.

'There's an empty table near the window,' Nicolas said. 'You bag it for us, Emily, and I'll bring our tea.'

Emily did as she was bid, watching as he selected some sandwiches and cakes, which he loaded onto a tray and brought back to her.

'This feels odd,' she said, giving him a shy smile as he unloaded his tray. 'It's what *I* usually do.'

'You're not at the manor now,' Nicolas said. 'I doubt if you'll be back if you marry Christopher – and that makes us equals. You're not a servant and I can wait on you if I like.'

'I'm not grumbling,' Emily said and laughed. 'It was lovely of you to give me that pendant, Mr Nicolas – but you know I can't keep it, don't you?'

'I hope very much that you will accept the gift of a friend. I know that's all we can be to each other now – but I want you to know that I care about you, Emily. I wouldn't want you to make a terrible mistake by marrying for the wrong reasons.'

Emily looked into his eyes. She was sure that he

wanted to say more, but of course he couldn't. Even if he loved her, as she loved him, his family would never have allowed them to marry. Besides, she could not desert Christopher when he needed her so badly.

'Christopher needs me...' Emily shook her head and reached across the table to touch his hands. 'Thank you, sir. I ... appreciate you coming to see me.' Her voice caught on a sob. 'What I feel for Christopher isn't romantic love – but don't ask me to walk away. Nothing will make me desert him now.'

'You wouldn't be the girl I think you, if you said anything different. Amy doesn't truly understand – but I told her even before I came that you would stand by your friend.'

Emily swallowed hard. 'You mustn't think it's a sacrifice. If this hadn't happened, I might still have wed him, because he loves me ... but now he's so ill and I want to help him. I care for him in my way and I couldn't hurt him.' She lifted her gaze to meet his. 'Please understand why...' Emily wanted so much to tell him that she loved him, and only him, but it wouldn't be right. Nothing could ever come of her love, even if it was returned.

'Yes, I do understand,' Nicolas said and held her hands across the table. Something in his eyes made her heart ache, because they said so much he could never put into words. 'Please keep my gift, Emily. You could always sell it if you needed money in the future. If you ever need help, either Amy or I will be there for you.'

Her eyes stung with tears and she gave a little shake of her head. 'I shall stay here until they move Christopher nearer his home. The doctor said it would be a few weeks before he will be fit to be moved. It isn't just the external injuries – the smoke and gasses affected his lungs and he'll be a while before he recovers.'

'Yes, of course.' Nicolas let go of her hands and sipped his tea. 'Not quite like Amy's Earl Grey but better than we get at base. Can you manage for money? I'm quite happy to give you some if it helps.'

'I have enough for the moment, thank you.'

'You wouldn't ask me even if you hadn't.'

'Christopher wouldn't want me to take what he'd see as charity but I know you mean well, Mr Nicolas.'

'Can't we drop the Mr and be just Nicolas and Emily?'

'I suppose so – as long as no one can hear us.' Emily laughed. 'Mrs Hattersley would be shocked. She would tell me to remember my place.'

'You have your own place ... a very special place, Emily...' His knuckles had turned white as he gripped the teacup. For a moment she heard the pain in his voice and her heart caught. He did love her, but he couldn't tell her.

She shook her head. 'I'm nothing special.'

'That is a matter of opinion.' He laughed but his eyes seemed to hold hers, beseeching her. She felt the pain twist in her heart. 'You know you're special to me but my family ... they wouldn't...' He broke off and his eyes dropped away from her gaze.

A burst of laughter from the corner of the room made Emily look at the group of young men in uniform. They were probably waiting to visit one of their friends, but were managing to make light of the situation. She imagined they'd become used to seeing their friends either injured or dying over the past weeks. Christopher had been so proud to join up and fight for his country. She couldn't let him down now, even if she did have feelings for Nicolas.

'Yes, I know ... please don't say any more. It could never work between us.' Emily swallowed hard. 'I'm sorry, but I've made my decision.'

'I think of you when I'm in the thick of it. You're my talisman ... all the bright things of my life.'

'Please don't...' Emily's eyes stung with tears. His words were tearing at her heart. 'I ought to go. Christopher will be expecting me.'

'Can I see you again – take you home? We could go for a meal or to the theatre...' He looked desperate, as if fighting himself or his emotions.

Emily hesitated, tempted, and then shook her head. 'No, I don't think it would be wise, do you? I've given Christopher my promise and there's no going back.' She reached up and undid the clasp of the diamond pendant, then took his hand and deposited it on his palm. 'I think you should have this back, don't you?'

'I want you to have it to remember me by ... perhaps one day we might...' He offered it back to her.

She shook her head, refusing to let him return it to her.

'Please don't,' she begged, knowing that he must be suggesting clandestine meetings ... an affair.

'Don't tempt me, Nicolas. You must know that I care for you ... but I can't do this to Christopher. He needs me. I have to be with him now – for as long as he lives.'

'Emily ... don't go...' It was a cry torn from his heart.

Emily felt the tears burning behind her eyes. Her chest hurt and the pain was almost more than she could bear, but she forced herself to her feet, holding back the tears as she said, 'Forgive me. Christopher needs me.'

Turning, she walked to the door and then down the long corridor that led to the wards. She wouldn't look back, because if she did her resolution would crumble.

Nicolas could only offer her an affair and it wasn't enough even if she hadn't given her promise to Christopher. She loved Nicolas, but she wouldn't be his mistress.

Part Three

1915–1917

Chapter 35

'Emily isn't coming back – ever?' Lizzie stared at her brother in shock. 'Does Amy know?'

'She was furious – said Emily had to give notice and she wasn't going to pay her any wages unless she worked out her notice. Of course I shall see that she does receive them. I imagine the poor devils will need every penny they can get.'

'Amy is just being mean. I'm sure she will relent when she's over her temper.'

'I wouldn't be sure of that,' Nicolas frowned. 'She's off to London at the end of the week and she doesn't have a maid.'

'She will have to find one in London or share Maude's.'

'I doubt that would work. She'll have to take Janet. Mary will be coming back full-time in a few weeks so Mama has told her she can have the new maid.'

Lizzie nodded, understanding her sister's reluctance to be fobbed off with a maid who was nowhere near as obliging as Emily had been, but her sister's troubles were not her most pressing problem at the moment. The letter was burning in her pocket. She hadn't destroyed it yet and she was terrified her mother might see it. Derek had written an apologetic letter, begging her to meet him. She wouldn't go of course, but she felt apprehensive, uncertain of what to do. Ought she to write to him or just ignore it?

She noticed that Nicolas looked serious, almost as if he were angry – or distressed about something. His gorgeous smile was missing and she wondered if he was concerned about returning to his unit. She touched his hand.

'Is something the matter?'

He shook his head, but there were shadows under his eyes and she guessed that something had made him deeply unhappy.

'I shall miss you when you leave tomorrow.'

'I'll miss you too, princess,' he said but she felt the reply was automatic.

Lizzie was convinced something was wrong but he obviously wasn't going to tell her.

'Papa is going to start organising the convalescent home tomorrow. They are moving the extra beds in and the nursing staff will arrive next week.'

'You're looking forward to helping out there, aren't you?'

'Yes, very much. If Mama would let me I should join the VADs but she won't. So I'm just going to help out where I can.'

Lizzie knew that her brother wasn't listening to her. Something had happened when he went down to that military hospital to see Emily. A thought occurred to her but she dismissed it almost at once. Nicolas couldn't be in love with Emily Carter – could he?

Emily was going to marry the soldier who had been so badly wounded. She wouldn't do that if she had the chance to marry Nicolas. No one could resist Nicolas; he was so gorgeous and so lovely. Lizzie studied her brother. No, he wasn't suffering from a broken heart, or at least she didn't think he was – so perhaps he was just worried about going back to the war.

He would never tell her if that was the case, lest she thought him a coward. Lizzie would never do that, because she loved him more than anyone else in the world.

Remembering the letter in her pocket, she decided to burn it. If she became involved with Derek again she might end up by being banished from the family and then she might not be able to see Nicolas.

That silly affair was over and she wouldn't think about Derek again.

Lizzie sat on the edge of Amy's bed and watched as she sorted out her clothes. She had packed a few things but then taken them out again, because they wouldn't fit into the case. Some of them had crumpled and would need ironing.

'You will miss Emily looking after your things,' she said.

'Mother says I can have Janet, but I don't much like her,' Amy said. 'She is so staid and boring. Emily used to make me laugh.'

'You didn't like her at first. You called her a common farm girl.'

'Well, she was a farm girl – but she certainly isn't common. I'd got used to her and she'd learned to do my hair properly, and now I have to start all over again.'

'Poor you. What about Emily's feelings? She's getting married to that soldier and he is scarred and still very ill. He probably won't be able to work for years and he might never be normal again.'

'Then she shouldn't have chosen him,' Amy said, showing her annoyance. 'I would have let her do some volunteer work in London if she wanted to nurse the sick.'

'As long as she looked after you first.'

'Don't be so rude, Lizzie.'

Lizzie arched her brows, jumped off the bed and left her sister to pack. Amy didn't like to be told the truth, which was that she was selfish and spoiled. Lizzie supposed that she was too in a way, though Amy had had so many more chances than Lizzie.

Lizzie thought about Sir Arthur as she went downstairs. Jonathan had told her that he was back in England and she'd wondered if he would come to visit them. So far he hadn't, so perhaps he was still in disgrace?

Wandering downstairs, she saw her father entering the hall. He looked at her and nodded.

'Just the person I need,' he said. 'They've asked me to make an inventory of everything at the dower house. I know you want to be involved – and someone is going to keep a record of what is needed and what is spent. The War Office will reimburse us but we'll need accounts. How do you feel about helping me to oversee setting up the place?'

'I should love to,' she replied. 'I have nothing else to do.'

'It hasn't been fair on you these past months,' her father said. 'Your mother ought to have brought you out last year, but somehow she didn't get round to it.'

'I think I'd rather be helping at the convalescent home now that there is a war on. It's so awful out there, especially for the men in the trenches. Nicolas doesn't say much but I know it is terrible for him too.'

'It was his choice to join up,' her father said, a look of annoyance in his eyes. 'But I suppose he couldn't have stayed out of it once it started.'

Lizzie decided to change the subject. 'I shall need a journal to write everything down in.'

'Come to the study now and I'll give you what you need.'

Lizzie followed him into his room. He'd brought his own things with him when they moved to the manor, and it had always seemed dark and oppressive in here because of all the brown furniture and leather chairs. Now she saw that he had silver photograph frames on his desk, a bronze figure in the corner and a brass inkwell – and with the sun peeking in at the window it didn't seem so bad – or perhaps she was growing up and no longer so intimidated.

Armed with her book and pencils, she left the manor and set off for the dower house. At last she had something to do with herself!

Approaching the house, she saw a man looking at the outside. He was wearing the uniform of an army officer and was staring up at the landing window, which had been left slightly open, but turned as she walked up to the door and produced the key. Relief broke out over his face.

'I was just wondering how the hell I got into the

damned place,' he said. 'These old houses are all very well, and the War Office is glad of somewhere to put the injured – but give me a decent hospital any time.'

'I expect they've got all the things the men will need to recover. After all, they are supposed to be getting better when they come here – aren't they?'

'The poor devils that end up here will probably never be better,' he said with a tinge of bitterness in his voice. 'I'm Captain Manning – are you one of the people running this place, trying to make it halfway decent?'

'I'm Lizzie Barton. My grandmother owns it – and my father asked me to do the inventory for him.'

For a moment he looked embarrassed, but then he held out his hand to her. 'Pleased to meet you, Miss Barton. I'm sorry if I was rude but I've had one hell of a day. I have more than a hundred permanently disabled men to find beds for and I need to know how many I can rely on here. Some of the places we've been offered are wrecks and we can't afford the repairs.'

'Granny has always kept the dower house in good repair. Please come in and have a look,' Lizzie said. 'I think they finished moving things around this morning. Some of the furniture is ours, of course, but the beds are new and were sent down by someone in London.'

'That's my department,' he said. 'The beds arrived then? Thank God something went right. The idiots in my office are continually losing vital pieces of paper and things seem to go astray.'

'It's just as well I'm here to make an inventory then, isn't it?' Lizzie laughed. He removed his cap and ran his fingers through dark brown hair that seemed to have a will of its own, sticking out at all angles. Now that she looked at him, she noticed that he was attractive and had nice eyes and an interesting mouth. He was wearing his army uniform and she saw now that it was different to the one Derek had worn. She'd always thought that somehow his wasn't right – a relic of an earlier era perhaps.

Inside the house they could smell polish and lavender. Some girls from the village had been employed to come in and give it a good clean right through, because it had been shut up for years. You wouldn't have known that now. Some of the walls had been painted and everywhere was as clean as it could be. There was a large sitting room for those men who were able to get up, and it was supplied with a bookcase, desk and lots of chairs rather than sofas. In the next room someone had taken the pictures down and put up a dartboard; there was also a billiard table and a card table.

'Yes, not bad,' Captain Manning said. 'It seems I was a bit hasty; this will do very nicely. Now how many beds do we have altogether?'

They made a tour of the house, Lizzie noting down everything she found in each room. Captain Manning frowned, because most of the rooms had only one bed and even in the larger chambers there were only two singles. He made a note on his own pad, and turned to Lizzie.

'We only have fifteen beds here and I'm sure we could squeeze in another fifteen. Most of these

393

rooms will take two singles and the blue room might take four at a pinch.'

'So many?' Lizzie arched her brows. 'Papa thought this arrangement would be more private and comfortable.'

'We have thousands of injured men being sent back from the Front Line. Young women like you wouldn't understand but privacy and comfort has to go out of the window when we're desperate. I'll send another fifteen beds – tomorrow, if you could be here to see them in?'

'Yes, of course, if you wish it.'

He looked pleased and went into details about what was needed, where things ought to be put differently and the possibility of some extra toilets, showers and washbasins being fitted in the annexe at the back of the house. When Lizzie looked doubtful he promised that the expense would fall on his department and that everything would be put back as it was at the end of the war.

Lizzie nodded, knowing that her grandmother might not be too pleased at more building work being done on the dower house, but she would explain it as best she could. Captain Manning spent two hours making more notes and planning, told Lizzie that the builders would be there in the morning and said he hoped to move the first of the recovering patients in within ten days.

Lizzie thought that was optimistic from what she'd seen of the local builders when they made repairs to the manor but he explained that the builders would be soldiers. Apparently, they were used to putting up temporary sanitation, which was rather different to a permanent fixture.

When Lizzie finally locked the door of the house, he shook her hand and walked away to his car, which was a rather battered-looking tourer. Until then she hadn't noticed that he had a pronounced limp. She'd been too busy writing her notes and listening to his plans to notice anything else. He must have been injured in the first months of the war himself, she thought. Perhaps that was why he was so concerned for his men's comfort, because he knew what they were suffering.

Walking back to the manor, Lizzie felt happier and more at peace with herself than she had in a long time. At last she was of use to someone and she rather liked Captain Manning. She hoped this wouldn't be his last visit to the dower house.

Chapter 36

'I never thought this day would come,' Mr Johnson said, looking at Emily with undisguised tears. 'When they moved my boy to the Tower Hospital in Ely I thought he might just give up, but you kept him going. It's you that's brought him through, Emily lass. I can't tell you how grateful I am.'

Nearly seven months had passed since Emily had first gone to Christopher in the hospital and there had been times when everyone had thought he might die, but now he was coming home.

'I'm not sure how much of it was me and how much his own will,' she replied. 'But it's such wonderful news that he can come home at last, isn't it?'

Sir Arthur had let them have an empty cottage – and he'd paid for all the alterations that would enable Christopher to manage, with a downstairs toilet and washing facilities too. As soon as Christopher was well enough they would get married and she would move in with him.

She could not help being moved by Mr Johnson's emotion. She'd been living with him and his wife in their own cottage on the estate. His wife wasn't as friendly as he was, and Emily thought she didn't particularly like her, although she didn't say much; it was more a look in her eyes, as if she didn't think Emily was good enough for her son.

Miss Lizzie had sent over her things when Christopher was moved nearer to his home. She'd visited too, giving her the wages she was due. When Emily had tried to thank her, she'd shaken her head.

'I think what you've done is wonderful, Emily. Standing by your fiancé like that – a lot of girls haven't done that, you know. Quite a few of the men at the convalescent home get horrible letters telling them that their wives or sweethearts have found someone else. Captain Manning says it's because they can't bear to look at their scarred faces or empty sleeves.'

Emily shook her head. She hadn't had much of a choice. Mr Johnson had considered her engaged to his son, and she would have felt wretched if she'd tried to explain that Christopher had never actually asked her to marry him. Besides, Christopher loved her so much and she couldn't let him down, even though her heart often ached for the man she loved but could never have. When she'd looked through the things that Miss Lizzie brought over, she'd found Nicolas's pendant. She'd returned it to him at the hospital but he must have put it in her room with her things, refusing to let her give it back. She locked it away in the secret drawer of Pa's writing box, because she could never wear it now that she was to marry Christopher, and yet she was glad to have it back. One day, when she could bear it, she would take it out and admire it, but not yet.

She didn't want to talk about her problems.

'Who is Captain Manning?' she asked, to change the subject, and saw a faint colour in Miss Lizzie's cheeks.

'He's in charge of the convalescent homes in the area. He came to make sure we had all we needed for the patients at the start, and he visits once a month to see how things are going.'

'So what do you do there?'

Emily had been surprised at the change in Miss Lizzie in the last few months. She seemed to have matured a lot, had more confidence, and she was wearing a dress without frills, her hair swept up into a bunch of curls at her nape. Emily thought the change suited her, but wondered that her mother had allowed her to work at the home.

'I'm in charge of supplies, the inventories and the expenses. Also, I talk to the men and try to help them if they have problems. I can read letters, write for them if they are unable to hold a pen and I read books for those that have lost their sight sometimes.'

There was a new dignity about her. She'd seen the kind of suffering Emily had witnessed in Christopher and other patients at the military hospital. It made a kind of bond between them, breaking down the barriers of class in a way Emily had not thought possible. Lizzie had always been kinder than her sister, but now she was a compassionate young woman and Emily really liked her.

'Perhaps I can come and visit one day,' she said, and then, uncertainly, 'Would you like to come to my wedding? It will be just a very small affair. Christopher will be in a bath chair and it will be held in Sir Arthur's house. He's arranged for a small private ceremony and a reception. Christopher's family and a few friends will be there – but I have no family. I was going to ask Mrs Hattersley but there isn't anyone else.'

'Who will be your witness?'

'Sir Arthur says he'll give me away, and Mr Johnson is Christopher's witness.' A lump lodged in Emily's throat, but she hadn't let herself cry. Miss Lizzie had nodded sympathetically and promised she would be there.

Time had moved on since then, Christopher gradually learning to walk a few steps with the help of the nurses and of Emily, who spent as much of every day with him as the doctors would allow. His hands were still very painful and he could only move a few fingers of one hand. The left hand, which had been so cruelly injured, was curled up like a bird's claw and he'd been told it might never straighten out. However, he said that there was some feeling returning to his right, which meant he would be able to feed himself in time, and perhaps manage to dress.

The miracle for which they were all thankful was that his sight had returned, though he now needed spectacles to help him read. In a few months he might actually be able to do the job Sir Arthur had created for him. In the meantime, Mr Johnson had insisted on paying for their cottage to be furnished. Emily had asked him to allow her to choose the furniture. From Pa's stock that Christopher had stored in one of Sir Arthur's barns, she'd found a set of four yew stretcher chairs for the kitchen and a good pine table. She'd also rescued a pine dresser, two rocking chairs and a mahogany wine table with a piecrust edge. The table was worth a bit if she'd wanted to sell it, but it would look wonderful in their tiny sitting room. She'd purchased two shabby but comfortable leather armchairs from the market in Ely and a Persian rug, which had a stain in one corner. Emily had given it a good scrub and it looked almost new. She'd also managed to get hold of a Georgian sideboard, which someone had cast out because it was old-fashioned, but which Emily knew was quality.

What she lacked was bits and pieces, and regretted the things her mother had sold from Pa's barns, but she couldn't do much about it. The parlour downstairs would hold a single bed for Christopher until he could manage the stairs, which she hoped might happen in a few months. She had a brass and iron bedstead and a big ugly chest of drawers in her room, also one of the wardrobes Pa had been going to chop up for firewood. It was as much as she needed for the time being, though she would collect small pieces of china and glass for her dresser whenever she had money to spare, which wasn't going to be often.

Mr Johnson had been all that was kind and thoughtful and treated Emily as if she were his own daughter. His wife still wasn't as friendly. She gave Emily some strange looks, as if she were suspicious of her for some reason, but so far they had managed to get along. After all, it was Christopher who mattered and Emily spent most of her time with him.

Christopher had a job waiting for him with Sir Arthur when he was properly on his feet again, but that was a few months off. Emily would have gone out to work if she could, but Mr Johnson wouldn't hear of it.

'No, lass. I want you to look after my lad. There's no need for you to work while I've a few bob in my pocket. Christopher wouldn't want his wife to work – and he'll need looking after.'

Emily couldn't deny the truth of his words. Christopher needed assistance with just about everything. He could use his right hand a little now and struggled to put on his clothes, but he couldn't do his tie up or his bootlaces, and someone had to cut his meat into small pieces so that he could fork them into his mouth. He was able to walk to the bathroom with the aid of a stick and refused help getting there, but when he returned his trouser buttons were always undone.

At the hospital the nurses had done them for him but once they were married, Emily would have to take over such tasks he could not manage alone. What made things worse was that his mother fussed over him and he resented it. He would accept help from Emily, but if his mother offered to help he pushed her away.

Emily soon discovered that the best way to get through was to make everything a joke and they laughed a lot, but she knew that underneath Christopher was humiliated. His mother showed her pity too plainly and that made him angry. Once the bandages came off his face Emily had seen the terrible scars he would bear for the rest of his life. Mrs Johnson turned away in tears but Emily just met his questing gaze and nodded.

Emily had felt a wave of sympathy the first time she saw the ugly scars, but he didn't want pity so she'd kept her feelings to herself. She took him magazines, sweets she'd made herself and flowers from the garden they would share once he was home.

Now he was coming home and her heart was beating so fast that she felt she couldn't breathe. Christopher was waiting with his small suitcase packed and ready when she and Mr Johnson entered the ward. His father picked up the valise and Christopher limped down the ward, responding to a chorus of good wishes from the other patients with a nod of his head. He didn't respond to Emily's smile and she guessed he was feeling nervous about leaving the hospital, even though he didn't want to admit it.

Miss Lizzie had told her that quite a few of the long-term patients who convalesced at the dower house were nervous of going home.

'Captain Manning says they feel cut off and

protected in hospital but once they leave, they have to face the reality of life.'

Emily knew that Christopher was concerned about the future. He was fiercely independent and wanted to do everything for himself, but it was probably never going to be possible for him to perform certain tasks alone.

'I think you will like the cottage,' Emily said as they went out to the taxicab that Mr Johnson had arranged to take them home. 'It's a little bare of bits and pieces now but we'll soon make it more homely.'

'Don't try to please me all the time,' Christopher said roughly. 'I know I need help with things – but you have a life too, Emily. You mustn't think that you have to wait on me hand and foot.'

'Of course not,' she said, feeling a little hurt, but understanding how much worse it was for him. 'I've made it nice for both of us, not just you.'

'As long as it's what you want,' Christopher replied but he still didn't smile.

Emily could see the tension in him. He answered when his father spoke during the journey to Sir Arthur's estate, but he didn't look at Emily and he didn't initiate conversation of any kind.

Clearly, he was feeling depressed and uncertain, dreading the life that would now be his. Emily's throat tightened with pity but there was nothing she could do, no words she could say that would take away the terrible injuries that had ruined his life. Somehow he had to come to terms with what had happened.

When Christopher was established in one of the rocking chairs by the kitchen range, cushions at his back and the newspaper waiting there for him to read, Emily put the kettle on. His father stayed to drink a cup of tea and then left them.

Emily walked him to the door. 'He's just feeling a bit strange,' Mr Johnson said, looking at her awkwardly. 'It must be difficult after all those months in hospital.'

'Yes, of course,' Emily said, forcing a smile. 'Facing up to the future can't be easy for him. All I can do is to care for him and hope it is enough.'

'I'll be back this evening, Em.'

Emily nodded. Mrs Johnson had insisted that Christopher's father should look after him at night. 'It wouldn't be right or decent you staying there alone with him at night, Emily. Just until you're married you can come and stay with me and his father will see to him.'

She'd tried to help her son but Christopher couldn't bear her to touch him and asked Emily to do whatever was needed instead. Emily knew his mother was hurt by his attitude and she'd seen a flash of anger in Mrs Johnson's eyes when she looked at Emily, because he was always ready to accept her help, but she hadn't said much. Yet Emily could sense the resentment building in her and knew that her feeling of dislike was growing. Mrs Johnson didn't like the girl her son had chosen and, had the circumstances been other-wise, she might have tried to dissuade him, but Christopher needed someone to care for him and he wanted Emily. So she contented herself with disapproving looks.

Returning to the kitchen after seeing Mr Johnson off, she found that Christopher had struggled to his feet and gone through to the parlour. When she entered, he was sitting on the single bed, which was where he would sleep for the moment. He looked up at her as she hesitated on the threshold.

'I think I'll lie down for a while, Emily. You get on and do whatever you want.'

'I thought I would make a shepherd's pie for this evening's meal,' she said. 'Perhaps apple pie for afters?'

'Sounds fine. It will be better than the hospital food. Do whatever you want, Emily. I'll need help with some things, but I shan't ask for help if I don't need it – so you can go out in the garden or off to market when you like.'

'I've done enough shopping to last us for a few days, and your mother will get anything I need from the local shops. I thought you might like me to read to you – or we could play cards?'

'Perhaps another day. For now I should just like to rest – and I can read with the spectacles they gave me so bring me the newspaper through, then get off and do whatever you want. Don't you want to visit your family?'

'I wouldn't mind seeing my brother. I do miss him and think about him often. I wonder how he is, because he is a little slow – but I don't get on with my mother or her brother so I can't visit. Perhaps one day I'll visit my friends at the manor – but not until we've settled in here.'

She had already cleaned the cottage from top to bottom. There wasn't much furniture to polish and Christopher's mother had already filled a tin with her own cakes and pastries. Obviously, Emily was going to have a lot of time on her hands.

'Just give me a call if you need anything,' she said and Christopher nodded.

Emily wanted to cry but she held the tears back. Perhaps after a few days things would be better. After all, she couldn't expect Christopher to be happy about his situation.

He would need a few days to get over the change of environment. Their wedding was planned for the end of August and it was now mid-July. Perhaps by then Christopher would have become used to the idea of being home...

Chapter 37

Emily finished shopping for all the essentials she needed on the market, and then made her way to the library. It was her weekly treat and she looked forward to choosing the books that were her only real pleasure.

Over the past few weeks, she'd managed to buy a few items from the sale at the cattle market, little things like a blue and white set of plates, cups and saucers to set out on the dresser in the kitchen. A careful rummage through a box of junk left for sale with the auctioneer had turned up such treasures as a small silver rose vase, a single brass candle-stick and some pewter mugs. Once they were cleaned and set out on the dresser, the kitchen began to take on a more homely look.

'You've made this look comfortable, though I

would have given you a few bits if you'd asked,' Mrs Johnson told her when she visited the previous day. 'Christopher looks better ... don't you think?'

Seeing his mother's anxiety, Emily had reassured her that she thought he was improving all the time. He spent an hour or two every afternoon lying on his bed, but he had begun to venture out into the garden. As yet he couldn't undertake any heavy work, but he'd fetched a hoe from the shed and she'd seen him struggling to chop up the weeds. It had taken him a long time to clear a small patch, but when he came in from their small garden he'd looked more cheerful than she'd seen him in months.

'I've done a bit for you, Em,' he said, copying his father's manner of addressing her. 'I'll do some more another day.'

'Thank you.' She moved away to the sink, filling the big copper kettle with water. Her instincts had been to tell him not to tire himself, but she knew that was the worst thing she could do. He enjoyed doing what he could and perhaps that was for the best. Besides, the doctors had told her not to fuss over him, but to let him do things in his own time. She'd tried to tell Mrs Johnson but her remarks had been met with a look of accusation and so she kept quiet when she saw his mother trying to help and being brusquely refused.

As she returned from the library, Emily saw that her father's old shop was empty again. She crossed the road to look at it and read the notice in the window – the rent was just ten shillings a week. For a moment her heart beat rapidly. Pa had had such high hopes for the shop once – and she still had most of the fifty pounds he'd left her, because Mr Johnson had insisted on paying for the furniture for their cottage.

Could she – dare she take it on? It was true that Christopher couldn't mend things the way he had once, but he could look after a shop. At least, she thought he might be able to manage it, because he was trying to do what he could in the garden now. But would he want to? Would he be angry if she suggested it?

She made a note of the telephone number and slipped the paper in her pocket. She could phone from the newsagent on the corner in Witchford for a small payment, if she dare. If Christopher was agreeable she thought she had enough money to start them off, and they could deal in small pretty things – decent stuff that didn't need mending. Emily wouldn't mind buying in the market or even going out on the rounds with a cart as Pa had done. Of course she couldn't lift anything heavy and Christopher couldn't either – but small pretty things had always sold the best. If they made a success of it she could employ a young lad to help her...

The excitement surged through her and she was smiling as she turned and almost bumped into someone.

'Thinking of going into business, Emily?'

Her heart caught as she saw Nicolas and then it started to race. She couldn't breathe and for a moment she thought she might faint.

'Pa's old shop is empty,' she said. 'I should like to open it again – if Christopher agrees.'

'How is your husband?'

'We're not married yet. Christopher insisted we should wait until he could walk down the aisle with me ... but it's booked for the end of the month, because he is a little better.'

'Congratulations,' he said, his eyes serious as they swept over her. 'What about you, Emily? Are you happy?'

'I'm trying to be,' she answered him truthfully. 'It isn't easy for either of us – but you look well. Are you home on leave?'

'I'm here on a training course. I'm one of the senior pilots now, Emily. They asked me to do six months over here training the youngsters. Too many of them think it's all a lark and they do stupid things, like flying under bridges and looping the loop when they should be looking for the Hun. We've lost quite a few promising young men through stupid pranks.'

'I'm sorry about that...' Emily's breathing was returning to normal, though his nearness made her weak at the knees. 'I shall be glad to think that you're safe.'

'Sometimes I wonder whether any of it is worth the bother...' His voice throbbed with emotion. 'I miss seeing you, Emily...'

Tears stung her eyes and threatened to well over. He mustn't think or speak that way, because it made their situation worse. She could bear her life the way it was – but only if she didn't think of Nicolas.

'I ought to go...'

'There isn't a bus for another hour. Let me take you to lunch at the Temperance – please Emily. Is it so much to ask?'

'No, it isn't – but people would talk if we were seen together. Someone would be bound to tell Christopher's father or mother. I can't hurt him like that ... it wouldn't be fair.'

'What about me?' Nicolas said and then gave her a wry smile. 'I'm wasting my breath, aren't I? Christopher is a very lucky man...'

He turned and walked away, leaving Emily staring after him. The pain swathed through her. She wanted to call him back, to say that she would lunch with him at the small hotel, but the words stuck in her throat. If she did that her resolve would crumble – and she couldn't let Christopher down now. Besides, she didn't want a dirty little affair.

She mustn't even think of Nicolas. The church was booked and Sir Arthur had told them they could have a reception in his annexe. Not that there would be many guests, because Christopher had invited only his family and she had asked just Mrs Hattersley and Miss Lizzie. She hadn't even considered asking her mother, though she couldn't help thinking that she would have liked Jack to be at her wedding.

Every time she visited Ely she thought about her brother and wondered if he was well. It was nearly a year since she'd seen him and he must be walking by now – and talking properly ... unless he was still very backward? The thought of her young brother made her throat catch, but she couldn't go to see him ... she couldn't risk seeing her uncle.

For a moment she felt so alone. If only her father hadn't died ... if he'd been alive she could have gone home sometimes. She couldn't afford to feel sorry for herself or regret the things she couldn't have. She must just make the most of her life.

Holding on to her tears as best she could, Emily walked round to the cattle market. The sale would be starting soon and she'd seen a box with an assortment of glass. If it went cheap she would buy it, because wrapped in tissue right at the bottom was a Georgian glass with a spiral stem. The rest of the things were moulded glass, which she could use in the cottage, but the glass was worth something – and if she persuaded Christopher to open the shop again, it would become a part of their stock.

'Did you have a good morning?' Christopher asked as she struggled in with all her parcels and the box of glass. 'I was beginning to wonder if you'd run off.' He smiled as he spoke and she laughed, liking it that he could tease her sometimes. Theirs was a difficult situation, but just now and then she felt the old friendship, the warmth that had been theirs when he worked for her father.

'I wanted this box from the auction, but they were ages getting to it,' Emily said. 'Most of it is just bits and pieces for the house, but there's a lovely air twist glass.'

'Is it perfect?'

'Yes. I wouldn't have bought it otherwise.'

'You've got more business sense than Joe,' Christopher said. He looked at her for a moment, then, 'I've been told your pa's old shop is for rent – ten bob a week. I was wondering...'

'Were you thinking we could run it together?' Emily asked, her face lighting up. 'I've got the landlord's telephone number here in my pocket. The Post Office let people use their phone for a small fee. If we dealt in small pretty things that didn't need repairs you could manage it ... couldn't you?'

'I thought we might have a go,' Christopher said and looked more animated than she'd seen him since before the war. 'We could put out some leaflets, Em – and borrow a cart once a week. You've got a good eye for stuff and I think I should still be able to sell things – even if this is useless.' He held up his clawlike hand with a rueful smile.

Emily felt the relief sweep over her. She'd thought he might never smile again. Moving towards him, she put her arms about his waist, lifted her head and kissed him, softly, on the lips until he put his right arm about her and pulled her in close. Their kiss deepened and when he let her go, she nestled her head against him, just standing there, feeling happy that at last he'd thrown off the mood of depression that had come with him from the hospital.

'You're feeling better,' she said. 'I'm so glad.'

He looked down at her, an enquiring smile in his eyes. 'You are happy, aren't you? No regrets – only if you have, tell me now. My mother was here this morning, on about the wedding and how lucky I am to have you, Emily. If it isn't what you want say something, because...'

She reached up to kiss him again. He sighed and touched her face.

'You're so lovely and I know what I look like.

I'll always need help, even though I managed the stairs while you were gone. It isn't much of a life for you, Emily.'

'I think I should find it hard living here with nothing else to do, because I've always been busy – but if we have the shop to plan for it will give us both something to keep us occupied.'

If they could have their own small business they could make some sort of a life for themselves. Christopher needed something to occupy his mind, and she would feel better if he were more like his old self.

'Show me that glass...' Christopher looked eager as she went to take it from the box, unwrapping it carefully to show him. The tall slender glass had a tiny fluted bowl at the top and a stem with a white spiral running all through. Christopher turned it over and looked at the rough pontil mark on the bottom. 'That's where they break it off when they've finished blowing it ... it's old, Emily, and perfect, just as you said.' He set it down on the table carefully and she carried it to the dresser, putting it at the back of the shelf so that it would be safe. 'I've got a box of bits in the attic at home. Nothing as good as this, but pretty things I was saving for you. I reckon we could have the shop open by September, don't you?'

'After the wedding,' Emily agreed. 'It will be fun, Christopher. We'll share the workload and in time – when we have a family – you'll be strong enough to look after it yourself.'

His smile dimmed. 'I'm not sure we'll have a family, Emily...'

Emily felt the disappointment hit her, though

412

she struggled not to show it. She'd always hoped to have at least three children of her own, but she couldn't let Christopher see her distress.

'Well, we'll make a go of the shop then,' she said. 'I'm sure I can find enough to keep me busy...'

As she unpacked the rest of her shopping she was fighting the selfish tears. Christopher had lost so much. She mustn't weep just because another of her dreams had crashed in flames.

'I'll be out in the garden if you need me, love.'

Emily nodded but couldn't bring herself to look at him. The empty years seemed to stretch ahead of her. She'd hoped children would provide a direction and purpose to her life, but if Christopher couldn't give her children ... just what kind of a marriage would it be?

Yet she had to make the best of it. She wasn't going to give in to regret or disappointment. Somehow she would make a good life for them both.

'I hope you will be very happy, Emily,' Miss Lizzie said and kissed her cheek. 'I hope you didn't mind my bringing Nicolas? He wanted to come and you said you hadn't got many guests of your own.'

'No, of course not,' Emily said, putting on a smile despite the way her heart lurched at the sight of Nicolas in his uniform. His eyes seemed to dwell on her and he wasn't smiling. She felt he was angry with her – angry because she'd chosen duty above love. Yet he must know that she couldn't have married him even if she hadn't felt Christopher needed her. 'It is just a buffet and Mrs

Johnson has provided far more than we shall need.'

'We hope you will like our present,' Miss Lizzie said. 'It's a set of Coalport china – tea and coffee service. I wasn't sure but Nicolas thought you would like it.'

'It is perfect but far too expensive. I shall keep it for best,' Emily said. 'You look well – and happy?'

'I'm enjoying my job at the convalescent home.'

Miss Lizzie's eyes were full of secrets. Emily wondered what else was making her smile but didn't ask.

'How is Miss Amy?'

'Oh, she's working with the fire service in London. She hasn't written for weeks. Mama is cross with her, but she's probably too busy to think about us.'

'Would you rather be in London with her?'

'Not now.' Miss Lizzie's smile was confident and content.

Emily turned away to greet someone else. She was aware of Nicolas watching her all the time they were making speeches, toasting the bride and groom and cutting the cake. Emily saw the smouldering anger in his eyes and fought her tears. He probably hated her for choosing Christopher and perhaps that was best. She was Mrs Christopher Johnson now. The die was cast and there was no going back.

'Alone at last,' Christopher said as he closed the door behind him. 'You won't have to leave me tonight, Emily.' He reached out to pick some confetti from her hair. 'Have I told you how beautiful you are?'

'Not for ten minutes,' she said. 'I'm feeling quite deprived...' She gave a gurgle of laughter as he reached out to draw her close, his mouth eager as he kissed her deeply. Emily opened to him and leaned into his body, wanting it to be right. If they were going to make a success of their marriage she must never draw back, never allow Christopher to know that she longed for another man's arms.

'I love you, Mrs Johnson.'

'Me too,' she said because it was too hard to say 'I love you'.

'Sir Arthur sent this over for us.' Christopher showed her the bottle of wine on the table. He'd set it on a tray with two pretty glasses that had been a part of the gift. The corkscrew was lying there waiting. He picked it up, then frowned and handed it to Emily. She accepted it from him, drove the metal spiral into the cork and then pulled. It came out with a little pop, making them both laugh. Emily poured the wine and gave Christopher his glass. He drank all the wine and then poured himself another. 'Why don't you go up now, Emily?' he suggested. 'I'll come in a while.'

'Yes, it won't take me long to get ready.'

Emily felt warmed by his consideration. He was giving her time to get undressed and into bed.

She walked up the stairs and took off her pretty dress, hanging it up before standing in front of the chest and her dressing mirror. She slipped off her petticoat and pulled on a nightgown, then started to brush her hair. Dabbing a little rose perfume behind her ears, she got into bed and sat up against the pillows waiting.

Time passed and Christopher did not come. Emily started to feel sleepy but was determined to keep awake. At last she heard the sound of Christopher's halting steps on the stairs and took a deep breath. She looked towards the door with a smile, which was wiped away as she saw the way he lurched across to the bed. He must have been drinking all this time.

Christopher turned the oil lamp down low, and then pulled his shirt up over his head. It was a way he'd developed of getting out of it without asking for help, though he still couldn't do the buttons up himself. When he turned back the covers and got in beside Emily, she braced herself. Christopher had clearly needed the wine to give him courage, and she was feeling in need of some herself, but when he turned to her, reaching out for her, she moved closer, pushing herself against him as he started to kiss her.

'You're so lovely, Emily,' he said, his voice a little slurred. His right hand moved to caress first one breast and then the other. He kissed the little hollow at her throat and then down to her navel. Lifting her nightgown, his hand moved between her legs. He stroked and touched her for a few minutes, his breathing heavy. 'I love you so much...'

Emily responded when he kissed her. She lay still and let Christopher stroke her as he would, feeling the moisture between her thighs. She wasn't quite sure what ought to happen next, though being a farm girl she had a good idea of how mating in animals took place and her intelligence told her what to expect. Yet although she

416

felt pleasure from her husband's kisses and the touch of his hand, after a while he gave a little moan and moved away.

'It isn't going to happen,' he said. 'I thought ... hoped it might because I want it to so much. I'm sorry, Emily. I can't make love to you.'

'You have made me feel nice...'

'You know what I mean. I can't do it... I can't have sex. I can't make babies with you.'

'Perhaps it's just too soon.'

'I was told it might be like this ... that I might never be able to make love. I'm sorry, Em. I shouldn't have married you.'

'It's all right,' she said softly. 'Perhaps you had too much wine.'

Christopher didn't answer. She thought he might have fallen asleep. Pity and sadness for his disappointment swelled through her, but she wouldn't let it overwhelm her. She wouldn't give way to self-pity. Even if they never became lovers and never had children, she was determined to make something of this marriage. She would give her husband all the love she had inside her and pray it was enough...

Chapter 38

Amy hurried through the gloom of a wet afternoon. The London streets were greasy and dirty beneath her feet and the noise of the traffic seemed worse than usual, a tram clanging its bell

417

in the next street. She'd been given time off that afternoon and she wanted to purchase some new underwear, because some of her things had been ruined by the service wash. They charged the earth for their special service and returned expensive silk petticoats looking like pieces of rag. Emily had always kept them perfectly, and Amy had thrown most of what she considered to be ruined away.

Amy supposed she was spoiled. She'd always been used to luxury and these past few months in London working as a volunteer for the fire service had been a revelation. Janet had left her in the lurch three weeks after they arrived, saying she didn't like being in London. Amy had had to engage another maid and she expected twice what Emily had earned, and wasn't worth half. If only Emily hadn't been so ridiculous and gone off to marry that soldier!

Of course Amy could return home and marry Arthur. He'd written to her, telling her that he had cleared his name of all blame in the scandal over the mine. It was something to do with government leases and a misunderstanding. Amy wasn't bothered. Arthur had suggested coming up to London to see her and she suspected that he wanted to ask her to marry him once more.

She hadn't replied to his letter yet, because she didn't know if she still wanted to be his wife. He'd made her angry when he'd walked away. For a while she'd been distressed, crying into her pillows at night, but then she'd put him out of her mind and made herself a new life here in London. Her job was interesting and well within her capabilities, but she'd begun to find it a little boring. In time she would want to marry but as yet she hadn't found a man who made her pulse race.

Lost in her thoughts, Amy didn't see the man in a dark overcoat emerge from a doorway just ahead of her and they collided. She dropped one of her parcels and the man picked it up, giving it back to her with a smile as their eyes met.

'How odd,' Belvane said in that soft, seductive voice of his. 'I was thinking of calling on you this evening. Your sister gave me your address when I enquired for you at the manor some days ago.'

'Belvane ... I thought you were in Russia or Paris? Didn't you tell me that's where you were going last year?' Amy felt the shock run through her, her breathing quickening. After they'd parted the previous year, she'd thought about him a few times, but hadn't expected they would meet again.

'I was in both places for a time – but I decided my services would be of more use here. I've joined the RFC. Your brother is one of our ace pilots. He was rather odd about something when we spoke. Did you tell him I was married – what I said to you?'

'Yes. Nicolas threatened to thrash you for what you said – but I doubt if he could. Please do not allow him to quarrel with you. It was foolish of me to tell him.'

'Did I insult you, Amy? I assure you my intention was never to harm you. I simply find you fascinating.'

'I did feel angry at first, but then I stopped.'

'Ah...' He smiled. 'It is very wet out here for

conversation. Shall we have tea somewhere – or would you allow me to take you to dinner this evening?'

'Dinner would be nice. I have something to do this afternoon. Will you call for me at seven?'

'I should be delighted, my dear.' He took her gloved hand and held it, air kissing the back. 'I will delay you no longer – and look forward to what I am sure will be a charming evening.'

'Take me somewhere expensive,' Amy said, arching her fine brows. 'I shall dress for it. Until this evening...'

She walked on, knowing that he had turned to watch her. She was smiling, feeling that she'd held her own, and yet her heart was racing. Amy hadn't expected him to return. He'd spoken of fighting in Russia the last time she'd heard from him. His letter some weeks after her return from London had seemed to put an end to any relationship between them, but now he was back – and she found him as fascinating as ever.

Amy knew that she was playing with fire by accepting his invitation. He would naturally take it as a sign that she was willing to consider his proposal to become his mistress – and the terrible thing was that he would be right.

Arthur would probably ask her to marry him if she agreed to see him, and he would give her all the things she'd hoped to have – the money, social standing and solid marriage she was entitled to expect as Lord Barton's daughter. Yet it felt like a prison sentence. Amy wanted excitement and danger ... she wanted to taste love, the kind of love she would find in the arms of a man like Belvane.

He wouldn't marry her because he was already married, but she could become his mistress. If she gave him what he wanted, she would make certain of the settlement he'd promised and costly jewels. What would happen when their affair ended she had no idea, though perhaps she could go abroad and live, as Great Aunt Samantha Barton had. If she were fortunate, that would be several years down the line. It would be better to live her life to the full as the mistress of the marquis than to marry a man she no longer cared for.

Amy had enjoyed the freedom living and working in London had given her but she would also enjoy the luxuries of the high life that being Belvane's mistress could bring. In England she would be seen as fast and a fallen woman, but in America and the European resorts patronised by the rich and famous she would be one of many who had chosen to dispense with formality.

She approached the shop she'd been looking for. She would choose her lingerie carefully. If she wanted to be Belvane's mistress she would require something enticing and very expensive. It was just as well that she still had some of the money her grandmother had given her for her trousseau...

Amy's spine tingled as she thought about the evening ahead. She was almost certain Belvane would make love to her and she was ready to give herself to him – eager for the excitement he would bring to her life.

'You are certain you are ready for this?' Belvane's hand caressed the back of her neck, causing a shiver of delight to run down her spine. 'You are so very beautiful, Amy. I meant to put you out of my mind when I left England – but I couldn't. You haunted me and I had to come back to England. It's the reason I chose the RFC over the Imperial Army.'

'I'm glad you did,' Amy admitted. 'I wished I hadn't let you go. I wasted too much time...'

They were alone in his luxurious apartment. It was twice the size of her cousin Maude's and furnished with every luxury imaginable, the floors marble with white scatter rugs, beautiful leather sofas, gleaming glass tables with bronzed legs and French cabinets from the Napoleonic period, far grander than anything Amy had ever seen. There were huge gilt mirrors with ebony and silver stringing, pier tables to match and the most exquisite porcelain and bronze figures of naked men and women. The large vases were early Sèvres and fragile, as was the Venetian glass from a much earlier century. The whole place had a feeling of decadence and almost obscene wealth.

It was the kind of place a man like Belvane would take his mistress when he wished to seduce her. She'd known the outcome as soon as he'd asked her if she wanted to go home or to his apartment. She'd chosen with her eyes wide open and she was ready, her body tingling and ready to be loved. She lifted her face for his kiss, her lips parting beneath his. He tasted slightly of good wine and cigars and she felt a spasm of desire curl through her stomach.

'I want you so much,' he murmured huskily. 'I think I'm in love with you, Amy. I didn't want to be but I couldn't help myself. You know that I

422

cannot divorce my wife? We are both Catholic and it would be impossible – but I want you. You'll be my mistress and I'll look after you. I'll give you houses and money, jewels. You'll be independent if anything happens to me. I've already spoken to my lawyer and he'll draw up a settlement...'

'Please don't,' she said. 'We'll talk of business another time. I want you to make love to me, Belvane. I've never felt this way about any other man. You make me want to melt into you, to be a part of you...'

'My beautiful darling Amy.' Belvane caught her up in his arms once more, his kiss so passionate and hungry that she was trembling when he allowed her to breathe. He turned her round and expertly unhooked her gown, slipping it down over one shoulder and then over the other, kissing her skin. As it slid to the ground, he cupped her breasts with his hands, caressing the nipples through the fine materials. Then, turning her, he slipped first one strap and then the other off her satin shoulders, letting it slither to the ground. 'So lovely...' He lowered his head, his tongue licking delicately at her nipples and then taking them one by one into his mouth and sucking.

Amy arched her neck, her head going back as she gasped and moaned with pleasure. Belvane knelt before her, easing her silk knickers down over her hips and kissing the patch of moist hair between her thighs.

'I want you now,' he muttered and stood up, sweeping her off her feet to carry her to the bed. He lay her down and sat beside her, his eyes burning into her. 'You're mine now and I'll never let you go.'

Amy responded by clinging to his neck and kissing him on the mouth. She was trembling with need and urgency, her back arching to meet the touch of his skilful fingers as he stroked and touched, finding her moist warm centre.

'Yes...' Amy breathed and gave a scream of pleasure as his hand brought her to a little climax of pleasure, making her writhe beneath him. 'Oh ... that's so lovely ... thank you...'

'I knew you would love it,' Belvane whispered and stripped away his own clothes before joining her on the bed. It was too long for Amy and she was reaching for him instantly, her body arching and moving in exquisite agony as she waited for him to begin the delicious assault on her senses once more. 'You're hot for me, aren't you? You're ready for me, my darling?'

Amy was so lost in sensual pleasure that she hardly knew what she said, but when his hand parted her legs and he slipped up inside them she cried out with need. His first thrust was shocking and she felt pain, but his mouth was on hers and then he was moving slowly, sensuously, each movement making her arch and writhe beneath him as she reached for something she did not understand.

When the explosion of pleasure rocked them both, she screamed his name aloud, her nails raking his shoulders. The exquisite agony rippled through her, making her cry out again as the spasm shook her body. Then she was crying, clinging to him as he held her and stroked her hair.

'Did I hurt you?' he whispered. 'It was your

first time...'

'A little – but I liked it,' she said and her eyes gleamed as she looked up at him. 'I liked it all – when can we do it again?'

'My greedy little cat,' Belvane said and laughed. 'I think you're insatiable – just as I expected. I knew from the first that we belonged together. There's so much I can show you, darling, so much we can learn together. Believe me – that was only the beginning. There are ways to heighten the pleasure ... prolong it in a way that will drive you mad with desire.'

'Teach me,' she demanded, her hand stroking his neck and down the smoothness of his back. 'Show me how to please you more.'

'You please me very well as it is,' he said and rolled over to the side of the bed. He took his gold cigar case, which had his initials embedded in diamonds, and extracted a thin cheroot, then offered it to Amy. She took it without hesitation, sitting up against the pillows. Belvane laughed as he lit it for her from his own. 'Don't draw too deeply at first. Some of these vices need to be taken slowly.'

Amy experimented and then smiled. 'It's not as bad as I feared. What else are you going to teach me?'

'You want it all at once, don't you?' he said and laughed. 'I shall have to teach you moderation, Amy. It can be dangerous to dabble in things without learning how to handle them.'

'You won't harm me,' she said. 'I know you're dangerous and some people would think you bad – but you're what I want, what I've always wanted.'

'No regrets?' he asked, tossing his cigar into a large onyx ashtray and taking hers from her. He began to kiss her shoulder. 'You know you can never go back?'

'I don't want to,' she whispered. 'I want to be with you always. I don't want to go home...'

'You couldn't move in with me here in London, Amy. We have to keep this a secret or people will talk and your family will order you home in disgrace. It would mean living abroad, somewhere you aren't known.'

'Then that is what I want to do,' she said and laughed, gazing up at him with adoration in her eyes.

He stroked her throat delicately. 'I shall keep you for myself in a palace by the sea. When the war is over we'll travel. You'll love the side of Paris I can show you,' he murmured huskily. 'We have to be careful for a while, Amy, keep our secret. I can't just walk away from the RFC. I'll need a few weeks to get out of it – and you'll need to give them notice at your job. You'll want papers so that you can travel. I'll see to it all.' He leaned over her, powerful and dominating, his dark eyes holding hers prisoner. 'You won't miss your home and family?'

'I don't have a home. The manor belongs to my grandmother. My family won't matter to me if I have you.'

'They may one day but perhaps you can mend fences when they've got over the shock.' He laughed softly, kissing her lips. 'Life will be so full of excitement and decadence that you won't even think of your boring life here. Believe me, Amy. I shall make you forget all you ever knew...'

Going to him as he reached for her again, Amy laughed recklessly. Soon he would take her away from all she had known. She was free at last and nothing mattered but this glorious feeling inside... For this moment in time she did not care if the whole world knew her shame. She was gloriously in love and it was all she had ever wanted.

'I'm being sent to France next week,' Belvane said and sipped from his glass of vodka mixed with champagne. 'Come with me, Amy. We're almost living together most of the time. You're going to have to make the break one day – do it now.'

She'd been lying back against the black satin pillows, her eyes shut, a look of satisfaction on her face. Her thick dark lashes flickered, and then she opened her eyes and smiled, pushing herself up against the pillows.

'Of course...' She reached for her glass and sipped. 'You know I wouldn't want to stay here if you go. I couldn't stand being away from you – you're like that drug you indulge in at times. I have you in my blood and I can't do without you.'

'My sweet adorable Amy,' he murmured bending down to kiss her lips. 'You know that once we go – once we're openly living together the whole time – your family will disown you?'

'Some of them perhaps.' Amy traced the rim of her glass with her forefinger. 'If they want to be stuffy let them. Lizzie would speak to me – and Nicolas. Nicolas won't condemn me. I know his secret...'

'Does he have one?'

Amy nodded. 'He's in love with Emily. She used to be my maid but she married a soldier. He's been miserable ever since.'

'Well, well, how amusing,' Belvane said. 'He should have made her his mistress.'

For a moment Amy felt coldness at her nape. Had she been a fool to throw away so much for his sake? Would she regret it one day? It was too late now – and she lived for the time they spent together.

She ran the tip of her tongue over moist lips. 'When shall we leave?'

'The day after tomorrow. You'd better pack your stuff and I'll have it shipped over for you. I have a chateau in France. We'll spend time there when we can, though I'll be based in Belgium. We can pop back and forth in my kite.'

'Are you allowed to do that?'

'Rules are made for others.' Belvane smiled. 'Come here, my delicious one. I want to feast on those lips and that soft flesh of yours.'

'I think you're a vampire,' Amy said and laughed, holding her arms up to him as he bent over her. 'Just how wicked are you going to be today?'

Chapter 39

'I'm going to be in the area for a few days,' Jack Manning said to Lizzie that afternoon. It was the week before Christmas and she'd been helping the nursing staff to put the decorations up when he arrived. He'd brought presents for the nurses and small gifts of whisky or chocolates for the patients. 'I wonder if you'd like to come to a dance with me one evening? There is a rather nice affair going on at a hotel in Cambridge...'

'I should love to,' Lizzie said, her heart racing at the thought. She was so busy these days that she hardly had time to think about her life, though most of the officers in the home had asked her to marry them at one time or another. She knew they weren't serious, but it was a running joke amongst them. Lizzie was popular because she always had a smile for everyone and was always willing to help in any way she could. 'When is it on?'

'This Friday,' he said. 'I'll pick you up at the house, shall I?'

'Yes please,' Lizzie said. 'Why don't you come and have tea with us? Mama thought you were so nice when she met you. I know you'll be welcome.'

Her honesty brought a faint flush to his cheeks, but he offered his arm and they walked up to the house together. Taking him through to the drawing room, she said, 'Look everyone, Captain Manning has come back for tea.'

Her words fell into a heavy silence. Lizzie looked from her mother to her father and then her grandmother. They were all looking shocked. Jonathan had a grim expression and Mabel sat like a frightened mouse, giving the appearance of wanting to disappear through the floor. Had there been a terrible defeat for the Allies? Lizzie knew that the war wounded had been coming back in ever increasing numbers – but what had happened to make her family look like this?

'What's happened?' she asked. 'Granny – is someone ill? Please won't you tell me?'

'Captain Manning,' Jonathan spoke at last, his manner stiff. 'Will you forgive me if I ask you to return another time? As a friend of Lizzie's you are of course welcome in this house, but I fear the family has had bad news.'

'Of course. Forgive me, I should not have intruded.' He glanced at Lizzie, his brows arched. 'Friday at seven?'

'Yes, please. I'm so sorry.' Lizzie watched as he walked away. The clock ticking on the mantelpiece sounded so loud in her ears. The expressions on the faces of her parents and grandmother shocked her, making her feel very frightened. 'What has happened?' she asked again when the sound of his footsteps had died away. 'Please ... is it Amy? Is she ill...?'

'Your sister is dead,' Lady Barton said. 'Dead to you and me and her family. She has disgraced us. You will not speak her name again in this house.'

'Steady on, Mama,' Jonathan said. 'Amy's behaviour is very shocking but she isn't dead.'

'She is dead to me and to her sister. I shall never permit her to enter this house again.'

'What has she done?' Lizzie looked at her brother, pleading with him to tell her the truth. 'Please, Jon – why is everyone so upset?'

'She's run off with that fellow Belvane,' Lord Barton said. 'Met him in London apparently. Seems Nicolas took her to one of his parties. Shady fellow so I've heard – and your sister has gone off with him to Paris or Russia or some such place.'

'Are they married?' Lizzie asked, her throat tight. 'Surely Amy wouldn't...?'

'He's already married,' Jonathan told her. 'Nicolas wouldn't have introduced her if he'd known.'

'Thank God I did not allow you to go to London with her...' Lady Barton said and sat down in her chair. 'I feel quite unwell.'

'Take a grip on yourself, Helen,' Lady Prior said. 'There is not the least necessity for you to have the vapours. What are we to do about the gel, Barton? Shall you fetch her back – or simply cut her off as this daughter of mine is suggesting?'

'There must be some mistake,' Lizzie said, her throat tight with tears.

Her sister couldn't, wouldn't shame them all this way. Surely it couldn't be true. Once the scandal broke it would reflect on the whole family, but most especially on her. People would whisper behind her back and her chance of a good marriage was lessened by Amy's selfishness.

'In this case I believe Helen is right,' Lord Barton said. 'The scandal is going to be most unpleasant, but if we break with her we may protect Lizzie from too much damage.'

'You will have to be very careful in future,' Lady Barton said, looking at Lizzie. 'We've given you too much freedom recently. I never approved of you working at the convalescent home and now I think you should stop.'

Lizzie stared at her in horror. She couldn't mean it – she couldn't go back to spending every day in the same dull routine, sitting in a frilly dress reading or playing the pianoforte. She would be so bored. It would be unbearable after her taste of freedom.

'I'm useful there. Please, Papa, tell her that I'm doing a good job at the home. Don't make me give it up – please.'

Her father looked at her unhappily. 'I know you wouldn't let us down, my dear, but perhaps your mother is right ... just for a while. When the news of what Amy has done gets out ... unless you are seen to be above reproach, your chance of a good marriage would be gone.'

'Captain Manning asked me to a dance at a hotel in Cambridge on Friday. You said you liked him, Mama. Please don't say I can't go...'

'You must know I would never approve,' her mother said. 'If you were engaged it would be acceptable – has he spoken to you yet?'

'We hardly know one another...'

'Then that speaks for itself. He must come to the house if he wishes to see you. Your father will explain and invite him to dinner. That is the proper way to proceed, Lizzie. Had you had your season, you would have met suitable young men at private houses. A private dance would be perfectly acceptable if we knew the hostess – but I shall not give you permission to go out with Captain Manning alone at night.'

Lizzie looked at her in dismay, her eyes pricking with tears. Her mother was trying to keep her on a rein and she would be nineteen next spring. Many girls of her age were working as nurses or drivers in the voluntary services. They were marrying their soldier sweethearts – and she was stuck here in this mausoleum of a house with her

432

parents and grandmother. Didn't they know that it was the twentieth century? The war had changed so much. Young women had so much more freedom these days.

A surge of rebellion went through Lizzie. She was not going to spend the rest of her life as a prisoner in this house. She would sneak out to meet Jack Manning on Friday night whether her mother allowed it or not.

Lizzie went up to dress for dinner as usual on Friday night, but when Alice came to dress her hair, Lizzie told her that she had a terrible headache. Alice was the new maid and had only been at the house a few days. Alice responded to instructions to tell Mrs Marsh she was ill and would not be down to dinner and went off leaving Lizzie alone. She locked her door and waited until her mother came to ask why she wasn't coming down.

'I have a terrible headache,' she whispered. 'Please, Mama, just let me sleep.'

'Open this door at once.'

'I've taken a tisane for my head. Please go away, Mama.'

'Very well. I shall speak to you in the morning. This sulking is not becoming, Lizzie.'

Lizzie didn't answer. She counted to fifty after her mother had gone, then slipped a velvet evening coat over her dress, picked up her purse and peeped out of the door. The coast was clear and she breathed a sigh of relief. Her family would be in the drawing room having a pre-dinner sherry. If she slipped down the back stairs, after locking the door to her room, she might make her escape without being seen.

Her heart was racing as she ran along the landing and down the stairs to the servants' hall. They were all busy in the kitchen and she could hear the sound of pans clattering and voices raised in laughter as they went about their work. A delicious smell of dinner permeated the air, making her feel hungry. Tight with tension, she slipped past the kitchen and out into the back courtyard. It was dark outside apart from the light spilling out of the house. Lifting her skirts high, and taking off her satin dancing shoes, Lizzie ran past the old water butt, through the rose gardens to the front of the house.

She had brought a handkerchief, which she used to dry her feet before slipping on her shoes and disposing of the dirty handkerchief behind a rose bush, then walked sedately to the end of the drive just as Jack Manning's automobile turned in at the gates. He halted, opened the door for her to get in and then turned to look at her. Lizzie knew he was surprised to see her waiting for him here rather than at the house. She could hardly look at him as she made her excuse.

'Mama had a headache and the house was too warm,' she said. 'I thought I would take a little air.'

He accepted her explanation without question as she slid into the passenger seat. Lizzie breathed a sigh of relief. She'd made her escape, though if her parents discovered what she'd done she would be in trouble. Yet they already kept her almost a prisoner so what more could they do to her?

'You look beautiful,' Jack said. 'I'm really looking forward to this evening, Lizzie. Unfortunately, it will be the last time that I shall see you for a while. I've been passed as fit and they're sending me back to the Front after Christmas.'

'Oh... I'm sorry,' she said. 'I shall miss you.'

'Yes, I shall miss seeing you at the home,' he said. 'But I'm glad to be going out there again with the lads.'

Lizzie nodded, hoping he might ask her to write to him, but he didn't and she wondered exactly what she meant to him – was this just a pleasant way to spend an evening? She'd hoped he might be starting to care for her.

'Thank you for a lovely evening. We must do it again sometime – when I'm home on leave.'

Jack leaned forward to kiss her cheek, and then got out of the car and opened the door. Lizzie slid from the seat. She thanked him again for her lovely evening, waiting, hoping, he might say something more. When he didn't she turned away and walked up to the house, entering by the front door.

The dancing had been wonderful and Lizzie had enjoyed every moment, but if she'd expected it to be a romantic interlude she'd been disappointed. Jack had met some of his friends at the hotel, a group of three couples; the men were army officers and the ladies were friends. Lizzie was the outsider, but they'd made her welcome and she'd danced most of the evening, either with Jack or one or other of his friends. They had all enjoyed a delicious dinner, which was served between dances and Lizzie had felt very grown up. These people treated her as if she were a woman with a responsible job, laughing and talking about the war and life in general.

They spoke about women working in factories for a wage of thirty shillings a week, as if it were the most natural thing in the world. Jack and his friends discussed Mr Churchill's resignation, and they spoke of the terrible reverses inflicted on the Allies at Gallipoli – and of the certainty that conscription would come in very shortly.

The women seemed as knowledgeable as the men and Lizzie felt very gauche and ignorant, because there was so much she didn't know – wasn't allowed to know. Somehow she'd managed not to show her innocence too openly, discussing the convalescent home with first-hand knowledge of the men's suffering. Because of that they accepted her and she was feeling content when Jack said it was time to leave – but she'd hoped that he would say something, show that he wanted a relationship and it hurt that he hadn't. He hadn't even said he would write or asked her to write to him.

Perhaps it was because of that vague disappointment that she forgot she had sneaked out and went in at the front door. She was halfway up the stairs when her mother's voice called to her from the landing above. Lizzie looked up, catching her breath as she saw the expression in Lady Barton's eyes.

'And where have you been, miss – as if I didn't know?'

Lizzie felt the ice at her nape, but she stood her ground and looked her mother in the eyes. 'I kept my appointment, Mama. I'm almost nineteen, old enough to go out with a gentleman alone if I wish.

This isn't the Victorian age. Young women are doing all kinds of work these days – and doing a better job than the men are in the factories, according to the newspapers. You cannot keep me a prisoner just because of what Amy has done. It isn't fair...'

'How dare you defy me? You wicked, wanton girl!'

Lady Barton's hand snaked out, slapping her hard across the cheek. Lizzie recoiled as she felt the sting but she refused to cry. Instead, she stuck her head in the air and walked on past her mother.

'How dare you walk away from me? I haven't finished with you yet.'

Lizzie ignored her and continued to walk to her door. She found it open and realised that her mother had suspected something and found another key. Lady Barton caught hold of her arm, swinging her round roughly.

'If you dare to ignore me you will be sorry.'

'I refuse to be treated like a child. If you stop me working at the home I shall run away – go to London and join the VADs...'

'Give me the key to your room. I shall lock you in and you will not come out until you beg my pardon.'

'Never!'

Lady Barton's hand shot out, slapping Lizzie again even harder.

'Stop it, Helen,' Lady Prior said, coming down the landing towards them. She walked haltingly with her stick, but her voice carried the ring of authority. 'Lizzie has been foolish, but she has a point. You do try to keep her a prisoner and she isn't to blame for what her sister did. It is hardly any wonder if she disobeys you.'

'You will please allow me to chastise my daughter in my own way. I may have to live in your house but Lizzie is still my daughter and...'

Lady Barton would have said more but at that moment the older lady's face turned purple and she gasped for air. She tugged at the high neck of her nightgown, seeming to choke and then, with a little sigh, she collapsed onto the floor.

'Granny...' Lizzie flung herself down on the floor, untying the strings of her grandmother's nightgown. 'She's ill... Please, Mama. Granny needs help. She needs the doctor...'

'Now see what you've done,' Lady Barton said and looked angry. 'You are a wicked girl, Lizzie Barton – and if your grandmother dies it will be your fault...'

Chapter 40

'I had to come and tell you,' Mr Johnson said as he entered the kitchen that morning, two weeks after Christmas. 'Lady Prior has been taken ill and they aren't sure whether she will live.'

'Miss Lizzie will be very distressed, I must find the time to visit soon,' Emily said and got up to set another cup and saucer on the tray. 'You will have a cup of tea?'

'Thanks, lass,' he said and sat down at the table. 'What's this I hear about the two of you opening a shop in Ely? I thought Christopher was going to work for Sir Arthur?'

'Well, he was but the shop came vacant and we're renting it on a month by month basis. Christopher seems interested in setting it up, though I'm not sure he knows what he wants.'

Emily frowned. Things had improved in the bedroom, because instead of trying to make love to her, Christopher merely held her and kissed her before saying goodnight. He had been silent and thoughtful for a few days after their wedding night, but then he'd started to work in the garden again, and he'd fetched down the box of bits and pieces he'd told her about. There were candlesticks, a pair of Worcester vases with pretty rural scenes, a tray set with mother of pearl, an inlaid wooden trinket box, a brass pen tray and inkwell and several other vases and jugs, also a cut-glass dressing table set. All of them had some age to them, though nothing was as special as the air twist glass Emily had discovered at the bottom of the box of junk she'd brought home.

Christopher told her he'd bought the things from the auction in the market and saved them for her. She could keep what she wanted and the rest would go into the shop as stock. Emily kept the dressing table set, because there was a tiny chip on one of the trays. She liked all the bits and pieces, but they needed stock to open their shop, which they were planning to do very soon. Emily had given it all a good clean but nothing else much needed to be done other than transport a cabinet and some bits and pieces from the barn to furnish it. The last tenant had put up several shelves, which would be useful for displaying their bits and pieces. They were both excited about the shop and if only things had been better in bed, she was sure they could have been truly happy.

'Nothing wrong between you two, is there?' Mr Johnson asked. 'Christopher seems a bit quiet and you don't smile as much as you used to, Em. If I can do anything to help – if it's money...'

'No, thank you. We both had some savings and you've been more than generous as it is,' Emily said. 'I dare say we've both had a lot on our minds.'

'Christopher isn't worse, is he? You would tell me?'

'Sir Arthur took him into Ely this morning to see a doctor. He should get his final discharge from the Army on grounds of medical unfitness to serve, but as far as I know he is improving all the time.'

'They ought to look after the lads better,' Mr Johnson grumbled. 'Give them compensation or a pension...'

'Christopher has been receiving part of his pay until now. I'm not sure what will happen when he's discharged completely.'

'Sir Arthur would have paid Christopher a decent wage. This business of yours is a bit dicey.'

'Sir Arthur says Christopher can change his mind if he wishes. He has been so good to us, Dad. They send us vegetables and eggs from the estate – and we had a lovely chicken last Sunday.'

'Sir Arthur is a decent man. I thought he was going to marry the elder of the two Barton girls, but from what I hear of her behaviour it may be

440

just as well he didn't.'

'What do you mean?'

'I'm not one for gossip, but I heard that she'd run off with some man – a foreigner by the sound of it. Bell Vane or something of the sort.'

'Belvane,' Emily was shocked. Surely it couldn't be true. She knew Amy had liked him. She'd gone out with him a couple of times when they were in London just before the war started – but to run off with him? 'Why would she do that? Surely the tale is just a wicked rumour?'

'It came from someone connected with the manor – can't repeat the tale word for word, but the way I understand it is that he was married and she went off to live with him abroad somewhere.'

'If that is true – poor Miss Lizzie.' Emily felt a wave of sympathy for the girl she'd come to think of as a friend. 'Her mother has always kept her at home, giving her very little freedom. What will happen now, I don't know.'

'You can never be sure if these tales are true, but it sounds bad. Reflects on the whole family. As I said, Sir Arthur is well out of it as it turns out.'

Emily made no reply. Had Sir Arthur not been involved in scandal himself, Amy would have married him. She might never have met Belvane and she certainly would not have run off with him.

If the tale were true, Amy had ruined herself. She would be an outcast from society and her family would probably cut her off. Miss Lizzie was going to suffer and it would make things uncomfortable for the whole family.

For a moment Emily let her thoughts dwell on

441

what might have been. If she'd listened to Nicolas that night, and turned her back on Christopher and walked away with the man she loved ... what would have happened then? There was no point in dwelling on it. She'd had her chance and she'd turned it down. Having made her bed she must lie in it.

Just as Mr Johnson was preparing to leave, the door opened and Christopher walked in. His expression was serious but as he saw his father he nodded to him, making an effort to appear cheerful as he did whenever one of his parents came to visit.

'How are you, Dad?' he asked. 'And Mum?'

'We're pretty fair. How did you get on with the doctor, lad?'

Christopher frowned at Emily, then he said, 'He says I'm probably as fit as I shall be – which isn't fit enough to return to service. I've been classed as disabled and I'll be getting a discharge, and perhaps a few shillings a month as a pension.'

'I was saying to Emily, they ought to do more for our lads. You gave everything for the country and you deserve a better life.'

'I'm fit enough to work according to the doctor so I shan't get much. He'll put his report in and we'll see – but I don't want their money. If the shop doesn't work out I'll be working for Sir Arthur. I might not be able to work with wood the way I used to but I can keep accounts and collect rent – and, if I decide to take his offer, I'll be getting a bike. There's nothing wrong with my legs.'

Mr Johnson nodded and took his leave. After the door closed behind him there was silence in the kitchen. Christopher had bought a paper and he sat down with it, not speaking to Emily.

'He asked where you were. I didn't think you would mind me telling him you were visiting the doctor to get your discharge.'

'I didn't...' Christopher put the paper down and stood up. 'I asked the doctor about down there – my wedding tackle. He says there's nothing wrong physically and it's just in my mind.'

'Really?' Emily felt a sense of relief. 'Then it will be all right ... when you're ready?'

'If it's a mental thing I should get over it, Em – if you can put up with me a bit longer? I know I'm not easy but... I feel I'm letting you down. It wasn't meant to be this way. I'd a bright future ahead of me and I wanted to give you so much. I do love you...' He grinned at her in his old way and her heart swelled with love, because he was trying so hard to overcome his disability and he was her dearest friend.

'I know – and I love you,' she said, her eyes wet with tears, because she so wanted to make things better for him. She knelt at his side, looking up at him. 'Is it me – am I doing something wrong?'

'No, of course you're not, Emily. Perhaps I've been in too much of a hurry.'

'There's no hurry. I do love you, Christopher, and I want to make you happy.'

'You have, of course you have.' He was silent for a moment. 'I think we're together too much, Em. I was talking to Sir Arthur – and I think I'll go for that job. We'll take the shop for six months. You can look after it yourself. You don't need me for that, Em. You know as much about these things as I do. Try it and see how you get on – and if it doesn't work I'll still have my job and you can just give a month's notice on the shop.'

Emily got to her feet, turning away as she tried to sort out her feelings, which were mixed. She'd planned on working with him in the shop, making it a joint venture. Christopher was good at selling and she wasn't sure how she would manage it alone. Besides, there was the house – and she was his wife; she was supposed to look after him.

'I thought... What about the housework and cooking?'

'You can open the shop four days a week. There's not much to do here – and I can manage to put the kettle on to make myself a cup of tea. If you prepare supper before you leave, I can put the pot on the stove ready for when you get back. It would give you an interest – and I'll still be here to help in any way I can.'

'You wouldn't mind?'

Christopher was offering her a life she would enjoy, but it wasn't one most men would accept. His parents would be horrified; they would say her place was at home and perhaps it was – but without a proper marriage and children... Yet perhaps if the doctor was right and it was all in his mind they could try again.

'If things sort out as I want and we do have a child, you can employ someone to take over in the shop,' Christopher said as he rustled his newspaper. There was a story on the back about some trouble in Russia and a rumour that the czar might abdicate soon. 'Besides, it might lose money and then you'll know it wasn't a good idea.'

Emily's throat felt tight. She'd tried to hide her disappointment that they might not have a family but he'd known, he'd known and it had hurt him. She'd never wanted to hurt him. He was her friend and she cared for him. She moved towards him, putting out a hand to touch his cheek.

'You're so good to me, Christopher. I want it to be right for us – I truly do.'

'I know, Em. None of it is your fault. I have to find my own way. There's not much I can't manage now – except for this damned thing.' He looked at his injured hand with disgust. 'The doctor thinks they might be able to do something for me in time. I'll never be as good as new, but maybe I'll be able to use my hand a bit if they can separate the thumb from the fingers.'

'It would mean another operation I suppose?'

'Yes, but I'd do anything to be right ... for you.' He smiled and reached out, touching her cheek. 'We'll try again ... tonight, if you're willing?'

'Yes, of course I am.' She gave him a loving look and reached up to kiss him. 'You know I love you, Christopher. All I want is for us both to be happy.'

Emily lay with her eyes closed. Christopher lay beside her sleeping. It still hadn't quite happened for him but he'd seemed less intense and his lovemaking had made her cry out with pleasure. Tears had trickled down her cheeks as she jerked and held on to him, her mewing cries of pleasure seeming to give him pleasure even though he hadn't penetrated her. But he had felt something,

445

and afterwards he'd told her that he was sure it would happen soon.

'I thought it was hopeless,' he said as he held her close, 'but there was something ... enough to tell me the doc was right. It will happen, Em – if you can put up with me.'

'If failing is as nice as that, I shall look forward to the day it happens,' she said and kissed him on the lips. 'You are a lovely man, Christopher Johnson, and I'm lucky to have you.'

'I wouldn't say that,' he said, but laughed softly as he kissed her. 'It will happen for me, Em – I know it will. The doctor told me just to relax and enjoy giving my wife pleasure. He says that the rest will happen in time if I'm patient.'

'It was beautiful for me,' she told him, snuggling up to his body. 'You don't regret marrying me now – do you?'

'I could never do that,' he said. 'I'm happy enough, Em. If they can put my hand right I'll be able to help with the shop as well as my job with Sir Arthur. We'll have a future, Em – and perhaps in time we might even have a child.'

'I'm so glad you're not bitter. I can be happy, Chris, if you can.'

'I am,' he assured her and held her close. 'I will be a proper husband to you soon. I promise.'

'You've made me happy tonight,' she said and kissed him. 'Just keep getting stronger, dearest – that is all I want...'

'Go to sleep now, Em,' he said. 'I'm going to dig over the garden this next week or two, then plant some fruit bushes – and I'll talk to Sir Arthur about starting work soon...'

'And I think I'll visit Miss Lizzie,' Emily said. 'I expect she's feeling very upset over Lady Prior...'

'Fine,' Christopher said. 'I might clean those brass candlesticks for you if I get time.'

'That's lovely,' she said. 'Whatever you want...'

'You know I love you?'

'Yes, of course. I love you too.'

'Goodnight then, Em...'

'Goodnight...'

Christopher had soon drifted into sleep but Emily lay awake thinking. If things continued to get better for them they might manage to have a good life together after all.

'Granny *has* been very ill,' Miss Lizzie told her when she came down to the kitchen to join Emily for a cup of tea and a piece of Mrs Hattersley's cake. 'I'm sorry I didn't let you know, but I've been sitting with her most of the time.'

'I was very sorry to hear about your grandmother,' Emily said. 'I wanted to come last week but couldn't get away, though I don't suppose there's anything I can do...'

'I'm sure you have enough to do and we can manage,' Miss Lizzie said and then sighed. 'I do wish you still worked here, Emily. I feel so lonely sometimes and there is no one to talk to – no one I can ask for advice.'

'I'm not sure that I'm qualified to give advice – but if ever you need to talk you are welcome to come to the cottage or I could meet you somewhere.'

'Thank you.' Miss Lizzie smiled gratefully. 'I shall write to you in advance, because I know you are busy.'

'To be honest, at the moment I sometimes have time on my hands.' She wondered what Miss Lizzie would think if she knew that Emily wished she'd never left service at the manor. 'However, I may be busier soon, because we're going to open a shop in Ely. We have collected some nice things and we plan to try it for six months to see if they will sell.'

'How exciting! Is your husband looking forward to returning to the job he had before he joined up?'

'Actually, I shall be running the shop. Christopher is going to work for Sir Arthur.'

Miss Lizzie looked surprised, as well she might, for although more women worked these days, they were mostly in factories or unpaid voluntary positions. It was almost unheard of for a woman of Emily's class to be running her own business. Emily felt a spasm of nerves in her stomach. Was she stepping too far out of line? Would people boycott the shop, because they considered her to be too forward or behaving in a way that was unbecoming?

'Well, I think that is terrific. You are so brave, Emily. I wish I had your courage – but even if I wanted to leave home I couldn't while Granny is so ill. It's my fault, you see.'

'I'm sure it isn't...' Emily began but Mrs Hattersley came back in from the scullery, where she had been instructing her latest help how to shape vegetables to look elegant on the plate.

'Well, then, isn't it good to have Emily back?' she said, beaming at them. 'It's always nice when you come down for a visit, Miss Lizzie.'

'I like to visit sometimes, especially when there are cakes straight from the oven – but I ought to get back now. I need a fresh jug of barley water for Granny, Mrs Hattersley, if you wouldn't mind getting it for me?'

'I'll send June up with it later, miss.'

Miss Lizzie glanced at Emily as she stood up. 'It has been nice seeing you.'

Emily guessed that she'd wanted to say more but Mrs Hattersley had not taken the hint to make herself absent for a few minutes longer. Whatever Miss Lizzie wanted to say was obviously private but must keep for another day.

'Now we can have a cosy chat,' Mrs Hattersley said. 'Put the kettle on, Emily, and we'll have another cup of tea.'

Emily did as she was bid, though glancing at the wall clock she thought she would soon have to be going home. She'd left Christopher for three hours as it was but the next bus wasn't due for half an hour so she might as well spend it talking to her friends.

Just as the kettle was boiling, June came down to join them and then Mary. Mary was married now but her husband had been sent back to Belgium because he'd been passed fit, even though in his wife's opinion he wasn't ready. She held forth about the army sending men back to fight too soon and somehow the time slipped away and Emily knew it was too late to catch her bus now.

She finally left the manor to walk to the village forty minutes later. Emily had enjoyed herself talking to her friends, but she'd left her old life behind and was eager to get back to her husband and her home. When she thought about it, she had a lot to look forward to, especially now that Christopher seemed so much more like his old self. Emily wasn't going to look back – or think of what might have been.

She was still lost in her thoughts as she got off the later bus and walked the short distance to her cottage on Sir Arthur's estate. It took about ten minutes after leaving the bus and it was just beginning to get dark as she went into the kitchen and then stopped short as she saw that both Mr and Mrs Johnson were there and also Sir Arthur – and another man she didn't recognise.

'Where have you been?' Mrs Johnson demanded the moment she got in. The look she threw at Lizzie was murderous. 'We've all been trying to think where to find you but no one knew where you'd gone.'

'Christopher knew I was going to see Miss Lizzie,' Emily said and frowned as she looked round the kitchen. 'Where is he – and why are you all here?' A sliver of ice slid down her back as she saw their expressions. Sir Arthur looked sympathetic but Christopher's parents were upset, angry with her, especially his mother. 'Where is he – what has happened?'

'If you'd been here, as you ought it might not have been too late,' Mrs Johnson said bitterly. 'By the time Father found him he was unconscious. Sir Arthur sent for an ambulance but they said he was dead...'

'Dead?' Emily's heart caught. How could he be dead when last night he'd seemed so much better?

He'd told her he loved her, made love to her so tenderly, and she'd thought it was all going to be all right – and now he'd gone. She was swamped with guilt because she'd been sitting laughing with her friends when Christopher was dying. 'I don't understand. He was feeling so much better last night, talking of taking Sir Arthur's job and helping me get the shop started. He told me to go visiting because he didn't need me.'

'Well, he would, wouldn't he?' Mrs Johnson said bitterly. 'My boy didn't like to be a burden to anyone – and especially you. He loved you, though it was obvious you didn't feel the same...'

'Now then, Mother,' Mr Johnson said. 'There's no call to say such things to Emily. It isn't her fault it happened while she was out.' He looked at Emily and she saw the pain in his eyes. 'Perhaps he didn't tell you – but it could've happened at any time. There was a piece of shrapnel lodged in his chest and the doctors told him it might move. He knew what to expect if it did but he made me promise not to tell his mother, because he didn't want people fussing over him.'

'Why didn't he tell me?' Emily said. 'When he came back from the doctor's the other day he said everything was fine ... that he could do whatever he liked...'

He'd come to her bed, made love to her so sweetly ... giving her pleasure, and he'd told her it was going to come right for him ... but he'd known it was a lie ... and that he might not have long to live.

Oh, Christopher, why didn't you tell me?

'He didn't tell you the truth, Emily,' Sir Arthur

451

said. 'Christopher was a very proud man. He asked me what would happen if he died, whether you could stay on here. Naturally, I told him the cottage was yours for as long as you wish...'

'I was always against him marrying a serving girl...' Mrs Johnson said bitterly. 'Have you no sense of loyalty? It was your duty to be with your husband...'

'That's not fair, Mother...'

Emily felt the tears burning. She felt so ashamed. She deserved Mrs Johnson's anger, because she ought to have sensed that Christopher wasn't telling her everything. She should have been here with him and she couldn't bear to think of him dying alone. She might not have been in love with him, but he was her dear friend and she was going to miss him.

'He felt guilty for marrying you knowing it might be for just a short time,' Sir Arthur went on, 'but I know you made him very happy...'

Yes, just for a little time the previous night ... Christopher had been happy then before he went to sleep.

Emily couldn't bear to look at anyone as she asked, 'Where is he?'

'They took him to the hospital. I tried to explain that the death wasn't unexpected but they insisted there would need to be an investigation into the cause. You might be able to see him if I took you now...'

'No, I don't think so,' Emily raised her head. 'I would prefer to think of him as he was when I left him.' *As he'd been in her arms the previous night.*

She saw the accusation in his parents' eyes but turned her face aside. Inside she was weeping.

Oh Christopher ... why didn't you tell me?

'If you wouldn't mind, I think I should like to be alone for a while.'

'There's the funeral to think of, lass...'

'Time for that another day,' Sir Arthur said. 'I think we should leave Emily to grieve in her own way. I shall be happy to arrange things for you if you wish, Mrs Johnson?'

She realised he was looking at her. Emily nodded, grateful for his support. 'If you could ask the vicar to call tomorrow, I shall feel more like discussing things then – thank you for all your help, sir.'

She stood up and walked upstairs. As she reached the landing she heard the kitchen door open and then close again, and then silence descended. Emily sat on the edge of the bed as the tears cascaded down her cheeks. Why hadn't Christopher told her he might die at any moment? Had he refused to admit it even to himself, hoping that he would make a full recovery?

Remorse and grief tore at Emily. *He'd died alone and she should have been with him.*

Her guilt hurt too much for her to find relief in tears. For a long time she sat on the edge of the bed, hugging herself. She felt so cold and numb. *If she'd been here he might still be alive...*

After a while she lay down on the bed and pulled the coverlet over her, but she didn't sleep. Her tortured thoughts wouldn't let her. It was too soon to know what she wanted to do.

One thing was certain. She couldn't go back. Emily had enjoyed visiting the manor but she knew she wouldn't want to work there again.

Whatever she did in future, she wanted to make something of herself. Being a servant for the rest of her life would be a waste of that life. Christopher had wanted more for them both. She wasn't sure that she wanted to open the shop alone but she didn't know what else she could do.

She could almost hear him telling her to be happy...

Chapter 41

Lizzie thought that Emily looked very pale. Her widow's weeds didn't suit her, taking the colour from her face, and there were dark shadows beneath her eyes. She walked alone behind the coffin. Mr Johnson had been one of the coffin bearers and his wife was with a woman Emily had never seen before, perhaps a sympathetic relative, because she made a show of supporting the stricken mother – but neither of them looked at Christopher's widow.

The service was quite brief and when they followed the coffin from the church to the open grave, Lizzie went to stand by Emily, touching her arm in sympathy.

'I'm so very sorry,' she whispered. 'If I can help at all...'

'Thank you, but I'm not certain what I wish to do yet,' Emily said. 'Will you come back for tea afterwards?'

Lizzie hesitated, and then nodded as the vicar

began the burial service. She watched as Emily went forward to throw a single flower into the grave. It was an early snowdrop and looked as if it had been plucked from a garden that morning. Emily looked tired and almost ill but she didn't cry. When she heard the whisper behind her, Lizzie could hardly believe her ears.

'She hasn't shed one tear, the little hussy,' a woman said spitefully. 'She made my poor boy miserable and now she has everything he owned – I dare say it amounts to more than a hundred pounds. And all she gives him is a snowdrop from the garden. She should be ashamed of herself.'

'Be quiet, Mother,' Mr Johnson said sternly. 'Now isn't the time – and you're being unfair to the girl. She did her best. It's not her fault that the boy died.'

Emily came back to stand beside Lizzie. Feeling angry and protective of her, Lizzie reached for her hand and took it. She held on tightly as the older Mrs Johnson stepped up to the grave and threw in a bunch of shop-bought flowers.

Lizzie wanted to defend Emily but she couldn't cause a scene at a funeral. Emily would never forgive her.

As they went out of the churchyard, she saw her brother Jonathan waiting for her. He asked her if she wanted him to take her home and she shook her head.

'I'm going back to Emily's for a while.'

Jonathan nodded. 'Ask her if she would like a lift – but I suppose they have cars to take them.'

'No, I don't think so,' Lizzie said. 'Look, they are beginning to walk. I must go, Jon. I promised

Emily I would go back.'

'I'll come and pick you up in an hour, all right?'

'Yes, thank you...'

Glancing round, she saw someone she hadn't imagined would be here. Her heart jolted as he looked at her and frowned. He was wearing a cheap dark suit and had been staring at Emily. Seeing Lizzie he looked angry, then turned and walked away.

What was he doing here, Lizzie wondered and then forgot about him as she ran to catch up with Emily and the small group of people walking just behind her. She took Emily's hand again, giving her a shy smile.

'I wanted to come before but Granny was still very unwell. She seemed a little better today and told me I should go to the funeral if I thought it right.'

'I'm glad you're here,' Emily said and held on tightly. 'It has been an ordeal and I need someone to talk to.'

'I'm glad I came,' Lizzie said. 'I haven't been anywhere much for ages, because of Granny. Mama blames me for what happened, though Granny says it could have happened at any time. Her heart is a bit weak and this attack was a warning to be careful. It was my fault that she was upset, though.'

Emily asked why and Lizzie explained. Emily frowned but made no comment, because they had reached the cottage. The door opened as they arrived and a young woman looked at Emily.

'I hope everything is as you would wish, Mrs Johnson.'

456

'I'm sure it will be. Sir Arthur was very good to send you down, Clarissa.'

'He thought it best if someone was here to look after things for you.'

A tea of sandwiches, cakes and biscuits had been laid on the big scrubbed pine table. A pile of plates, cups and saucers were set ready for people to help themselves and a kettle was just about to boil. Only three people had followed them back to the house other than Christopher's parents. Sir Arthur was one and the other two were a couple, the woman being the person who had comforted Mrs Johnson in church.

'Please help yourself to the food,' Emily said and made a pot of tea. She brought the pot to the table and Clarissa asked people whether they took milk and sugar, handing them the cups and then taking plates to each of the guests. The older Mrs Johnson accepted a cup of tea but refused the food, though Mr Johnson ate some sandwiches and a couple of buns. Lizzie guessed that Emily had made them herself, which was perhaps why her mother-in-law had refused them.

'I was surprised but pleased to see you here, Miss Barton,' Sir Arthur said as Lizzie stood by the window looking out at the aconites and snowdrops, which were blooming well. 'How is your grandmother now?'

'Better I think,' Lizzie said, and lifted her head to look at him. 'I'm sorry about what Amy did, running off like that. I know it must have hurt you.'

'A little but I always knew she didn't love me. It was the money and the freedom she would have had as my wife that appealed. I assure you that I am over it now.'

'She was a fool.' Lizzie's tone was fierce. Her heart beat very fast and she realised that he was still the man she liked best of all those she'd met, including her brother's friends and the patients at the home. Captain Manning had not been worth the quarrel with her mother. She'd never stopped loving Sir Arthur, even though she'd tried to forget him. '*I* would never have let you walk away...' She flushed suddenly as he smiled and she realised that she'd revealed more than intended. 'Oh, I shouldn't have said that...'

'Please do not give it a second thought. I am flattered that you still find me a proper person to be seen talking to.'

'Of course you are. Papa understands now that you were cheated of those leases. You lost as much as everyone else when the shares became worthless – and he regrets that Amy didn't marry you. I heard him say that he wished he hadn't made her give you up.'

'I am sorry it turned out so badly for your family...' Sir Arthur was thoughtful for a moment. 'Do you imagine your father might see me if I called on him? I am interested in buying a piece of land that Lady Prior owns and I wasn't sure if I should approach your father or Jonathan.'

'Jonathan runs the estate but perhaps you should consult Father first. He would receive you I'm sure.'

'Then I may call next week perhaps.' He put down his cup and turned to Emily as she offered him cakes. 'No thank you, Mrs Johnson. May I call in the morning to speak with you privately?'

'Yes, of course, Sir Arthur.' Emily looked a little anxious. 'Is something wrong? The cottage...'

'Nothing like that. I shall call at about ten tomorrow.'

After Emily had seen him to the door she returned to the kitchen. She looked at her mother-in-law. 'You may say what you have to say now. I have no secrets from Miss Lizzie. She is my friend.'

'What about Christopher's things?' Mrs Johnson said. 'He had some gold cufflinks my father left him and a silver watch chain. I don't see why you should have them. You've only been married a few months and you didn't care about him.'

'Now then, Mother,' Mr Johnson said. 'I've warned you over this. Emily is entitled to all Christopher had – she's his wife and...'

'If I find those items I shall give them to you,' Emily cut across his words. 'Christopher gave me some things he bought for me but everything Mr Johnson bought is yours once I leave the cottage.'

'No need for that, they were a wedding gift and are now yours.'

'I shan't need them once I leave here, thank you, sir.'

'Where will you go, lass?' Mr Johnson asked. 'Take no notice of Mother – she's just upset and she doesn't mean it.'

'I think she does and she's right,' Emily said. 'Christopher was my friend but I should never have married him. I thought I was doing the right thing but perhaps I didn't make him happy, though I tried. I will return the family things to you, if I can find them.'

'I doubt you will find them,' Mr Johnson said. 'I believe he sold them to buy something he wanted more.'

'He wouldn't do that – they were his grandfather's things,' Mrs Johnson snapped, annoyed with her husband.

'Christopher wanted to buy a good ring for Emily. I think that's where the money may have come from, though he didn't want me to tell you.'

Mrs Johnson glared at Emily but said no more. She tapped her friend on the arm. She and the other woman left the house, the woman's husband following them out. Mr Johnson lingered for a moment, looking uncomfortable.

'Forgive her, Emily. Christopher loved you, and you did make him happy – as happy as he could be in the circumstances.'

Emily blinked back her tears but didn't answer him.

Clarissa cleared away the used cups and plates, putting them into the sink. Lizzie moved closer to Emily, putting an arm about her shoulders.

'I'd better go,' said Mr Johnson. 'I'll come to see you another day, lass – but don't go blaming yourself. Christopher died because the shrapnel moved, not because you weren't here. You couldn't have saved him had you been with him.'

'No but I could have been with him. I wish I had been.'

Mr Johnson nodded, turned and went out, followed a moment or so later by an embarrassed Clarissa. Emily sat down, her head bowed.

'She shouldn't have said those wicked things to

460

you, Emily,' Lizzie said.

'She loved her son and she hates me because she thinks I let him down – and perhaps I did. I should have been here when he needed me.'

'You couldn't have known. He didn't want you to fuss over him – and you heard what his father said, you couldn't have saved him.'

'No, but I should have been with him. I sat talking too long ... enjoying myself.'

'Don't feel guilty, Emily.'

'No, it won't help.' She got up and began to put the things back on the dresser.

'What will you do now?'

'I'm not certain...'

'I know Mrs Marsh would take you back. You've been missed.'

Emily gave a little shake of her head but didn't comment. Lizzie sighed. Life was so difficult. She was in disgrace with her mother for sneaking off to meet a man and, if Lady Barton had her way, she would have been more of a prisoner than ever, but her grandmother had supported her and somehow she'd made Mama see that she must allow Lizzie some freedom. She was going to be allowed to return to her work at the convalescent home, though on a strict promise that she would never again slip out to meet a man without her mother's permission.

Lizzie had given it freely. It had shocked her when Granny had that heart attack. She'd blamed herself, though both Jonathan and Papa told her it was not her fault. Lady Prior had been unwell for a while, but no one had told Lizzie how serious it might be if she were upset.

Lizzie had since realised that she didn't particularly wish to see Captain Manning again. After meeting Sir Arthur at the funeral, she knew that the feelings she'd had for him were more than just infatuation. She liked him very much. She liked the way he'd behaved to Emily and his kindness spoke for itself. He was the man she would marry if he wanted her – but would he even look at her after the way Amy had treated him?

'You should go home before it gets too dark,' Emily said. 'Thank you for being here this afternoon. I don't think I could have stood it alone.'

'I wasn't much use.'

'Just you being here meant a lot.' Emily smiled and touched her hand. 'I'll come to the manor before I leave the district.'

Lizzie was shocked. 'Where will you go? I thought you were going to open a shop in Ely?'

'That was when Christopher was alive; I'm not sure I could manage it on my own. I think I might join one of the volunteer units – if they will take me. I want to do something useful. I might even train as a nurse.'

Lizzie sighed. She'd wanted to join one of the volunteer associations but her mother had refused her permission and there was no chance of it happening now. She glanced out of the window and saw how dark it was.

'I'd better start walking back. Jonathan said he would call for me but he must have forgotten.'

'Would you like me to walk a part of the way with you?'

'No, I'll be all right,' Lizzie said and kissed her cheek. 'Please come and see me when you can.'

'Yes, I shall, and thank you for being my friend today.'

'We are friends. If you need me let me know.'

Emily hugged her and Lizzie left the cottage. It was chilly out and she wished that her brother had come to fetch her as he'd said he would. Perhaps if she walked to the village she could catch a bus to Witchford. Otherwise she was going to have a long walk home.

She had taken a few steps when she became conscious that someone was following her and she stopped, looking back in case Emily had decided to come with her after all. As the shadow loomed out of the darkness towards her, she gasped. It was Derek. He'd seen her at the funeral and he'd come here, followed her. She dug her fingernails into her hands, feeling a rush of apprehension as she remembered that she'd never answered his letter.

'I've been waiting for this opportunity,' Derek said. 'I hung around a lot at the old place, hoping to see you, but you never came.'

'I couldn't. I was working...' Lizzie's heart thumped as he came closer. She could see the anger glittering in his eyes and was suddenly afraid. She had all but forgotten him but he hadn't forgotten her and he was determined to pay her back for what he saw as her humiliation of him. Her mouth was dry and she took a step backwards, feeling sick as he moved in closer. 'Go away, Derek. If you try to touch me I shall scream.'

'Go ahead and scream. I can't see anyone around, can you? You're an arrogant little bitch, leading a man on and then dropping him because he wasn't good enough. I saw you with that army officer, laughing up at him the way you did with me – I bet you gave him plenty of what you denied me.'

'No...' Lizzie's throat tightened with fear. 'No. I'm not like that ... really. I liked you but you went too far. I didn't understand at first and then... I shouldn't have met you or let you kiss me.'

'Don't pretend to be innocent. I know you for the sly bitch you are ... just like the other one, but I showed her who was boss.'

Lizzie let out a desperate scream as he came closer. She tried to run but her feet seemed glued to the ground. As he grabbed her, she screamed again and again, trying to fight him off, her nails scraping his cheek, but he grabbed her by the throat, his eyes staring at her oddly as he said something she did not understand.

'I taught the other one a lesson she couldn't forget. I'm going to have what you promised me, you bitch, and then I'll do the same to you as I did to...'

'What do you mean?' Lizzie couldn't think what he meant but she sensed the evil in him and gasped, struggling and screaming again. 'No...'

'Let her go, you brute.'

Lizzie knew Emily's voice even though she hadn't seen her coming. She hardly understood what happened next, except that Emily must have attacked him from the rear. She had something in her hand and then Lizzie saw it was a garden hoe. They were only a few yards from the back of Emily's house. She must have heard or seen something, come out and grabbed whatever was to hand. She was shouting at the top of her voice and wielding her hoe like a weapon, hitting out at

Derek over and over again. He staggered back, looking bewildered, the blood running down his face. Emily's first blow had taken him by surprise and the blade had cut him above his right eye.

'I'll kill you,' he muttered and lunged at Emily, seeming to forget Lizzie in his desire to wreak revenge on his attacker. 'If your pa hadn't come that day in the field I would have shown you then...'

'He means it,' Lizzie said. 'He's evil...'

'Bitches! I'll teach you both a lesson.'

'I know what you are,' Emily said, keeping him at bay with her hoe. 'You've always been a bully – and I think you had something to do with Carla's murder. I saw you hanging about after her... What happened, did she turn you down? Is that why you killed her?' She saw the guilt and shock in his eyes and knew she was right. 'I'm right, aren't I? Good grief ... you did kill her...'

'I'll shut your mouth for good...' He moved towards her menacingly.

'You leave her alone, you wicked man,' Lizzie said and rushed to help Emily.

Derek swore and lunged at her with his fist. It connected with her chin and she went down like a stone, lying unconscious as the battle raged about her. She was unaware when the newcomer arrived on the scene. Nor did she hear what was said as someone picked her up and carried her back to Emily's house and laid her on the bed in the parlour.

Lizzie woke to see a stranger looking down at her. She gave a little cry of fear and then someone came into her view, placing a hand on her arm as she started up.

'It's all right, Lizzie,' Sir Arthur said. 'You are with friends now. This is the doctor and Emily is in the kitchen making us tea.'

'She saved me...' Lizzie shuddered. 'That man ... he was ... attacking me...'

'We know,' Sir Arthur said. 'We think he must have mistaken you for Emily. He is her uncle and he already tried to rape her once before she came to work at the manor. Derek Black thought he was attacking Emily – and that was his mistake, because she had come after you. She discovered that you'd left your purse on her table and she was going to return it to you.'

Lizzie swallowed cautiously. She hadn't left her purse behind. Emily knew the truth. Had she made up this story to protect Lizzie from the scandal that must result if the attack on her was made public?

'She attacked him and then...' She touched her chin. 'He hit me and I don't know what happened next...'

'I happened to return to the cottage. There was something I wanted to tell Emily. I heard the screams and ran to help. It was just too late to stop you being hurt but in time to stop either of you being murdered. I heard his threats to you – and Emily suspects that he's killed before.'

'Do you mean Carla Bracknell? She was murdered in the spring of 1914. I remember it was just about the time Emily came to the manor and Granny was most upset that it should happen in our village. Do you think – could he really have done it? It seems so wicked...'

'Emily has told us about her suspicions, which are only that – and also about the day he tried to rape her. She didn't go to the police then, but she is willing to do so now. I saw him attacking you both and heard him say he would kill you both. I think her testimony and mine should be enough to convince the police to investigate further without them bothering you too much, Lizzie.'

Lizzie knew that they had got together to protect her. Emily would use her part of the story to have him arrested, but it was sure to come out that she'd been involved, though if Emily swore that he'd been trying to attack her, Emily, she might not get dragged into a scandal. After all, it had taken place near Emily's cottage.

'What happened after you arrived?'

'He saw me and ran off. I considered you needed me and let him go. The police have been alerted and he will be arrested. We shall keep your name out of it as much as possible, Lizzie. Your brother arrived ten minutes ago. He was delayed and blames himself for not being here when he promised.'

Lizzie felt the tears slip down her cheeks. She wanted to tell them about meeting Derek and that it was her fault he'd attacked her, but she couldn't find the words. Sir Arthur would think she was cheap and she wanted him to like her.

Emily came through then, bringing a cup of tea. 'Your brother thinks you should stay here tonight, Lizzie. He will tell your mother that you fell and hurt yourself ... it is all arranged.'

'He won't come back ... Derek?'

467

'He won't get near the cottage,' Sir Arthur said. 'I shall have a man outside all night – and, believe me, Black knows what is waiting for him if he shows his face here. The penalty for murder in this country is still hanging. If they can prove he killed that poor girl, he will undoubtedly hang. And he would be arrested for assault if nothing more.'

'It's only our word...' Lizzie faltered. The thought that Derek might hang was horrible despite what he'd done.

'Oh, I think Emily's testimony will be enough.' Sir Arthur frowned. 'Besides, the police have been watching him for some time. They believe he attacked two girls in Ely. The girls had been to the public house he owns and runs with Mrs Carter and were attacked on the way home. They didn't report it for some days but when they did the police decided to keep an eye on him. Also, they know he's been buying beer that was stolen from the brewery. Mr Black is going to be in a lot of trouble when the police catch up with him.'

Lizzie's head was aching. She closed her eyes, shutting out the pictures that crammed into her mind. Derek had made her feel so dirty and she couldn't help feeling that she was in part to blame – but if he'd killed one girl and attacked others perhaps he deserved to be punished.

'I think Miss Lizzie would like to rest now,' Emily said.

'I shall leave something to help her sleep,' the doctor said.

'I'll be back tomorrow,' Sir Arthur said and smiled at her. 'I'll take you home then. Lizzie –

don't worry, your mama won't blame you. You were quite innocent in all this...'

Lizzie didn't answer as he went out, but she opened her eyes once she and Emily were alone.

'I feel so awful ... so dirty.'

'I know. It makes you feel like that,' Emily said and squeezed her hand. 'He isn't worth feeling pity for, Miss Lizzie. Believe me, he deserves to be punished. I should have gone to the police years ago, when Carla was murdered. I knew what he was – and I'd seen them together – but I didn't dream he would do something like that, though I should've known what he was capable of. I can't know for sure but when I accused him of it, the look in his eyes told me I was right. He tried to rape me and he hurt my father. I was lucky that a farmer I knew came to the rescue.'

'It was lucky for me that you came out when you did...'

'I thought I heard a cry.' Emily frowned. 'He must have thought you were me. If he'd come into the house when I was alone...' She shuddered. 'He has always wanted to get his own back on me for what happened that day.'

'He was at the funeral,' Lizzie said thoughtfully. Perhaps Emily was right. He couldn't have expected to see her or to know she would go home with Emily. He'd probably hoped to get Emily alone when everyone had gone. 'I did know him a little. We spoke a few times and – and he kissed me...'

'Derek was always a charmer if he wanted to be. Don't tell anyone about that kiss, Miss Lizzie. We don't want you to lose your good name over him.'

'Mama would be furious with me. I don't think she would ever let me out of her sight again.' She clung to Emily's hand. 'If you hadn't followed me...'

'I'm glad I was there.' Emily smiled at her. 'We're friends and we'll see this out together. Just rest and try to forget what happened. He isn't worth it.'

Tears slid down Lizzie's cheeks. She felt weak and sick and shamed and all she wanted to do was to hide her head under the bedcovers, but she knew she was going to have to face it all some time, because this wasn't just going to go away.

Chapter 42

Lizzie was conscious of the bruise on her cheek when Sir Arthur called to collect her the next morning. She waited a little self-consciously as he told Emily that the cottage was hers for as long as she wanted it – and that she could store her things in his barn just as Christopher had, if she didn't want to stay there.

'There is a Dutch charger among the things in store,' he'd told Emily. 'It is slipware and I think very amusing, though to those who don't understand it might look crude and rather ugly. I think it is quite valuable and I would be prepared to offer you fifty pounds for it. You might perhaps get more if you placed it with a London auction house.'

'That is very fair of you to tell me, sir,' Emily

said. 'I recall seeing the charger but I thought it rather naïve and a little ugly. I should probably have sold it in the market for a few shillings. Fifty pounds will be very acceptable – if you are certain you wish to buy it?'

'I should be pleased to do so,' he said, 'though, as I told you, it may make more in auction.'

'I would rather you had it. And I should like to store some things in the barn until I can find somewhere else to live.'

Lizzie waited as they talked of Emily's plans for the future. Then Lizzie kissed her cheek, thanked her for looking after her and went out to Sir Arthur's automobile. He was driving a Daimler Phaeton with the fold-down roof up in place, because a cold wind was blowing. She shivered and he glanced at her, his expression reassuring.

'No need to be nervous, Lizzie. Jonathan would have explained to your mama – and he blames himself for not being on time.'

'Mama will not be pleased. I was already in trouble with her.'

'Jonathan told me, but your crime was really not so very bad.' Sir Arthur's gentle smile made her feel better. 'You ought to have been out before this, with friends of your own age, and it was unfair of your family to treat you as a child. You are a young woman, Lizzie, and it is only right that you want to try your wings ... go dancing with a young man who was returning to the Front.'

'Captain Manning was just a friend. We were not alone at the hotel – his friends joined us and we all danced with each other. It was harmless but I shouldn't have sneaked out like that, because it led to another quarrel and Granny was upset.'

'You mustn't blame yourself for that,' he said. 'Lady Prior has a weak heart and it could have happened at any time. Besides, I think Lady Barton is more to blame. She quarrels ceaselessly with her mother.'

Lizzie acknowledged the truth of his words. Lady Barton had blamed Lizzie, but she had been the one making a fuss, which had upset Granny. Even so, Lizzie knew that she should not have gone to the dance. It had been pleasant but not worth risking Granny's life.

Sir Arthur looked sideways at her once or twice as they drove to the manor. He told her about his plans for the future. His investment in the ill-fated mine had failed but he had made other sound investments and he expected to recoup his losses in time. He had set up a fund to help the smaller investors, who might have lost money they could not afford, because, he told her, he felt guilty for having sold them the shares in the mine, even though he'd believed it a wonderful opportunity at the time. It wasn't his fault that the leases had been withdrawn, making the mine worthless. His agents told him that a corrupt minister had pocketed money to redirect the leases to another consortium, but he was unable to prove it. He ought, he confided to her, have stayed with the tried and trusted industries his grandfather had started up years ago.

'It was an unpleasant lesson,' he said, 'but I am the wiser for it and I've done what I can to make reparation.'

'You believed the leases were in place when you

floated the shares.'

'Yes, but I should have made certain,' he said. 'I shall not be as careless again, believe me.'

Lizzie felt calmer as she listened to his business ideas. He was giving one of his properties to be used as a convalescent home and talked knowledgeably about the war and the likelihood that it would drag on for some time. Despite conscription obliging many young single men to go to war, the country had suffered terrible defeats over the past months and he could see no end to the conflict.

'I volunteered but they gave me a job in logistics, which means I shall have to do some extensive travelling in the next few months. I should have liked to serve in the forces, but it was thought I would be of more use arranging the transportation of food and munitions.'

'I read in the paper that they're still having trouble with getting supplies to the troops on time. Perhaps you could make a difference.'

'I'm certainly going to try,' he said, hesitated, then drew into a lay-by and stopped the car. 'My job means I shan't always be around, Lizzie – but if I don't come to see you, I want you to know that I shall be thinking of you. I'm much older, perhaps too old for a young girl like you – but I've come to admire you and ... if you wouldn't object I should like to take you out to a party myself. I would arrange for it to be the kind of party of which your mama would approve...'

Lizzie's cheeks were warm as she shot a shy look at him. 'I should like that very much, Sir Arthur.'

'I think we can drop the sir, don't you?' His smile warmed her. 'I was a fool, Lizzie. I noticed you when I first came to the house but you seemed very young – and Amy bewitched me. I know now that I chose the wrong girl.'

Lizzie's heart slammed against the wall of her chest. She knew she was blushing but she couldn't keep the happiness out of her eyes as she said, 'I've always liked you very much, Arthur. I was very angry when Amy behaved so badly.'

'It no longer bothers me.'

'As long as she didn't break your heart,' Lizzie said and looked at him shyly.

'If she did it is mended,' he said. 'I think I should like to get to know you better ... if you would like that, Lizzie?'

'Yes, I should,' she said her heart hammering against her ribs. 'Very much.'

'We'll take it slowly,' he said and leaned forward to kiss her cheek. 'I'm too old for you, my dear – but perhaps in time we might be more than friends?'

Lizzie wanted to tell him she'd always loved him, but he hadn't used the words yet so she wasn't able to confess her own feelings, but she was growing more confident as he drove the rest of the way to the manor.

Her father was waiting for them as they went into the house.

'Go up to your mama, Lizzie. I'm not angry with you, but there is something you should know...' His expression sent icy trickles down her spine. 'The police telephoned me a moment ago...' The chill increased as her father explained that the

474

police had suspected Derek Black of being involved in the Bracknell girl's murder but had no proof. Sir Arthur's testimony prompted them to arrest him. However, he escaped and was chased down Bull Lane in Ely as far as the Cresswells, which was a part of the riverside. He'd then scrambled up the embankment to the iron railway bridge and tried to flee across it in front of a train. Tragically for him, his foot got caught in the rails and the train driver was unable to stop...

Lizzie turned faint and would have fallen but Sir Arthur supported her, holding her close to him. She turned her face to his chest and wept as she asked in a muffled tone, 'Is he dead?'

'I imagine instantaneously,' her father said to her back. 'The good thing is that this means your name can be kept out of it, Lizzie. The police wanted him for questioning about Miss Bracknell's murder and he ran so they are presuming he was guilty – so her father will be told the case is closed.'

Lizzie was sobbing. It was all so horrible. Cold shudders ran up and down her spine, as she realised that what had happened to Carla could so easily have happened to her. She wondered why Derek hadn't strangled her when she wouldn't give him what he wanted, but she would never know now because he was dead. She was shaking so much that Arthur drew her close and kissed the top of her head.

'It's all right, my darling,' he told her. 'None of this is your fault. Black brought it on himself and, if he killed that girl, as well as attacking other young women, he deserves his punishment.

Had they caught him he would almost certainly have hanged.'

Lizzie drew away, accepting his handkerchief. She half expected her father to rebuke her for weeping in Arthur's arms, but she saw he was looking on indulgently.

'I was hoping for a few minutes of your time, Lord Barton,' Arthur said.

'Certainly, Sir Arthur,' Papa smiled. 'Run along and see your grandmother, Lizzie. I must speak with Sir Arthur – and then I'll talk to your mother.'

'Thank you,' Lizzie said, swallowing hard before giving Arthur a grateful look. She ran on into the house and up the stairs, along the landing to Lady Prior's room. Her grandmother was propped up against the pillows, her eyes closed. She opened them and looked at Lizzie, relief flooding into her face as she held out her hand. Lizzie went to take the blue-veined hand in her own. 'I'm so sorry to have worried you again, Granny.'

'You were not to blame for what that wicked man did,' Lady Prior said and she sighed. 'Poor Lizzie. I should have given you a season myself while I was still able.'

'It doesn't matter. I think... Sir Arthur ... he hasn't asked me to marry him yet but I think... I'm sure he will. He will probably speak to Father about me and in time... I still love him...' she finished with a laugh of delight.

Her grandmother stared at her for several moments in silence, and then nodded her head. 'He's too old for you, of course. However, I know you love him and so I am pleased for you, dearest Lizzie. You will not leave us too soon?'

476

'Oh, no, we're taking things slowly, getting to know one another. Arthur will be travelling a lot for his job so I shan't see him as much as I would like. It may be a few months ... perhaps a year before we think of getting married.'

'Why wait if you love him? There is a war on, my love. If he were younger I dare say he would have been called up before this...'

'He volunteered but they asked him to take a desk job, overseeing the transportation of food and munitions to the troops. They still haven't got it right, Granny. Supplies are delayed too often.'

'Incompetence, as always. We must hope that Sir Arthur will make a difference.' Lady Prior smiled. 'Well, your mother will have the big wedding to plan that she missed with Amy. Perhaps that will put an end to her complaints for a while.'

Lizzie nodded, taking her grandmother's hand. She told her that she hoped she would be well enough to attend and the old lady declared that nothing would keep her from such an occasion. She would, she said, give Lizzie a large sum of money for her trousseau, which would be ordered in London.

'If Mama will take me.'

'If she is foolish enough to refuse, I'll manage it myself somehow.'

Lizzie laughed, because her grandmother's determination had brought a sparkle to her eyes and she seemed stronger than she had since her attack. Despite Lizzie reminding her that nothing was actually settled, she was full of her plans for the future, Lizzie's wedding gift and the list of people that must be invited and the shadow that had hovered at the back of Lizzie's mind began to fade.

When Lady Barton came in an hour later, it was obvious that Lizzie's father had told her Sir Arthur intended to court her daughter, and she made no mention of the attack on Lizzie. Their talk was of the trousseau that must be bought and the reception that would be held at the manor, because no expense was to be spared for Lizzie. Sir Arthur would not be permitted to hold the reception at his home. Lady Prior was adamant it must be at the manor. She herself would oversee the arrangements and it would be a large, lavish affair.

Lizzie gave up reminding them that she wasn't engaged yet. As far as she was concerned the wedding could not come soon enough. Though she half wished that they would let her have a smaller wedding, but the two ladies were intent on outdoing each other with their plans and Lizzie slipped away at last to change for luncheon, happy in the knowledge that for once they were in perfect agreement.

'Lizzie my dear,' her father's voice called to her as she walked along the landing, 'a moment of your time.'

Heart racing, she waited for him to come to her, but he was smiling. 'I know nothing is settled yet – but Sir Arthur told me he hopes you *will* marry him – perhaps in a few months or so. I think this business over that rogue Black has made him realise that life is short, and he wants to make up for lost time.'

'He hasn't proposed yet, Father. We want to get to know each other better first ... but I love him.

'I always have. When he asks me I shall say yes.'

'Good. I wanted to make certain you were happy. I think it an excellent match for you, my dear. Sir Arthur was involved in a small scandal but that has been resolved to most people's satisfaction. He has done all he can to put things right and that is enough for me. Your sister was not right for him, but I think you truly care for him.'

'I love Arthur, Papa. I always have – but he wanted Amy and then he went away and I was lonely and unhappy.'

'I should have insisted that your mother gave you a season, but everything is settled now, Lizzie.'

'Granny and Mama are planning a huge wedding, which Granny is determined to pay for – even though I've told her we aren't actually engaged yet.'

'You will be soon I dare say. I shall give you what I can, of course, but Sir Arthur has assured me that he will make you a generous settlement.'

'Papa...' Lizzie sighed. Why was money so important to them all? She wouldn't have cared if Arthur had nothing but a tiny cottage and his army wage. All she wanted was to be with him.

'We must thank Mrs Johnson for her kindness to you,' Papa said. 'If she wished to return to her job here we might promote her to cook's assistant.'

'I think she intends to join a voluntary service,' Lizzie said. 'She is quite independent, Papa. I shall invite her to call and have tea with me. Perhaps we could help her in some other way?'

'I don't have a great deal of cash to spare – but I understand she likes antiques. Perhaps I might make her a gift of a pear-wood tea caddy or some such thing?'

'I should think a piece of treen or something silver would be acceptable,' Lizzie said. 'She likes to collect things like that, Papa.'

'Does she indeed?' He frowned. 'It sounds as if she has hidden depths. Very well, I shall find something that you may give her as a gift for saving you from further harm – though in a way it was her fault that that devil was there, lying in wait for you.'

'No, Papa,' Lizzie said quietly. 'Please don't blame Emily. I assure you that she has done nothing to encourage him. She hated him. He attacked her before she came to work here.'

'Perhaps if she'd gone to the police then you would have been spared such a fright?'

'Emily was concerned for her mother's feelings at the time.'

Her father nodded and walked on, leaving her free to go up to her room. As she changed into a pretty yellow silk afternoon frock, Lizzie wondered how the news of her uncle's death would affect Emily. She'd hated her uncle but the tragic way in which he'd died would surely upset her terribly.

Chapter 43

When Sir Arthur told Emily the tragic news, she knew that she ought to speak to Ma. At their last meeting she'd sworn she would never speak to her mother again, and she still felt angry with Ma, but her conscience nagged at her. Emily had hated and feared her uncle, but Derek had meant everything to Ma. His death must have hurt her terribly. She would be alone now apart from Emily's brother Jack and it would not be easy for her to carry on running the pub in Ely alone.

A part of Emily asked why she should bother with a woman who had made it plain she did not love her as a mother should. She'd stolen from Emily and taken Derek's side against her. She did not truly deserve that Emily should visit her – she hadn't even written when Emily married or when her husband died.

Three times she decided to visit and changed her mind, but her conscience was uneasy and after a couple of months she decided that she must at least call and see how her mother and Jack were faring.

Emily dressed in a simple grey dress and slipped on the coat she'd worn to Christopher's funeral. She decided not to bother with a hat, but put a headscarf in her pocket in case it started to rain while she was out. She must visit her mother first but after that she would have to seek out the landlord of Pa's old shop and tell him that her plans had changed. The pleasure she'd anticipated from running it with Christopher's help had completely disappeared. She'd been disappointed when Christopher had decided to take Sir Arthur's job although she could still have managed the shop with a little help, but now there seemed no point. Christopher's mother's evident dislike had made her feel she would like to go away somewhere and all she could think of was to join one of the volunteer services. She thought that after she'd visited her mother she would make the final arrangements for her departure.

Emily caught the bus into Ely. She decided that she would speak to the landlord Mr Hadden first. He was entitled to ask for rent for the whole six months of the lease they had agreed if he chose, which would leave Emily's slender funds much depleted. She hoped he might be able to let it again quickly and would charge her less, but when she spoke to him he looked annoyed.

'I've been keeping that shop for you, Mrs Johnson. This is most inconvenient.'

'I could pay you for six weeks now – and perhaps you could let it again.'

'Well...' he sounded a bit odd. 'Supposing you give me two months now and we'll call that quits, but when Mr Johnson signed the lease he did promise he would pay for the whole six months even if he closed the shop. It was the reason I let him take it on.'

'Yes, I know,' Emily said and then something struck her. Christopher had signed the lease not Emily – so perhaps she wasn't liable at all? 'My husband is dead as you know – so I think if I pay six weeks, which is what we owe you from the time of his death, my obligation is over. *I* didn't sign anything, Mr Hadden.'

He looked at her as if he could cheerfully strangle her but grunted his assent and Emily knew she was right. She'd paid the money owed, as was correct, but there was no reason why she should pay more as she had not signed the lease. The three pounds she'd paid him was more than she could truly afford, but Emily would make certain all their debts were paid before she left for London.

Mr Hadden owned several shops in Ely, besides being one of several butchers in the small city. He was a wealthy man and she was certain that he would re-let the shop within a short time. Her business done, she walked the length of the High Street, passing the Cathedral Mews, to the hill, where Woolworth was situated and on to the pub halfway down.

She saw that the pub had a closed notice on the door and hesitated before lifting the knocker. She rapped three times, her heart racing as she wondered whether Ma would answer. Hearing a lock being turned, her breath caught and she was taut with tension as the door opened. For a moment Ma stared at her, the hatred in her eyes so strong that Emily wondered if she would slam the door in her face.

'You'd better come in,' Ma said and stood back.

Emily followed her inside. The place smelled of spilt beer and something less pleasant, which turned her stomach. She was shocked that her once house-proud mother could have allowed the pub to become so dirty. She'd expected it to be scrubbed and clean, as their kitchen at home had always been. Looking at her mother's back, she saw that her dress looked creased and dirty, as if that too needed a good wash.

Ma led the way upstairs, away from the strong odours of beer and cigarette smoke and what Emily strongly suspected was the stench from the lavatories at the back of the pub. The parlour upstairs was better in that it did not smell so much, but it was untidy and the furniture was dingy, as though it hadn't been polished in ages.

Feeling shocked, Emily's gaze went to the child lying on the floor. His eyes looked dull and he was crying and his nose needed wiping. She hardly recognised her little brother and suddenly she was angry. He had clearly been neglected and looked dirty, as if he hadn't been washed in days. Bending down, she picked Jack up and cradled him in her arms. He stopped crying, put his thumb in his mouth and looked at her, as if wondering who she was. Emily took out her handkerchief and wiped his nose. She looked at her mother, accusation in her eyes.

'He needs to be changed. He's wet himself.' She shook her head in disgust. 'Surely he should have been out of nappies by now. Is he walking yet?'

Her brother was three years old but, although he'd grown, he seemed still a baby, unable to do much for himself. His manner was listless and he just lay on a mat, whimpering to himself.

'The brat always needs something,' Ma said and glared at her. 'If he isn't hungry he's messed himself. I never knew a child to take so long to be potty trained, but he's slow in the head that's what he is! I should've drowned him at birth – all men should be drowned at birth.' The bitterness poured out of her, as if a flood tide had been turned on. 'Bloody men – none of them are worth a piss...' Sitting down hard in a sagging chair, Ma burst into tears, her head bent. 'I loved him, gave him everything – and what did he do? He took every penny I had, hit me when I dared to challenge him and then...' Ma looked up at her. 'Now he's dead – dead because he ran from the bloody police. They say he murdered that girl in Witchford...' She shook her head. 'Derek wouldn't ... not that...'

'He was seeing Carla. I'm nearly sure it *was* Derek that killed her. When he attacked Miss Lizzie I accused him of it and he went mad,' Emily said. 'He would have raped me if Pa hadn't stopped him, remember.'

She left her mother to cry it out and went through to what looked like Jack's bedroom, because his dirty clothes were strewn everywhere. After stripping away his soiled underclothes, she washed his poor sore little bottom in the washbasin, then dried his skin, found a pot of cream in the cupboard on the wall and soothed it over him. Then she hunted through the chest of drawers to find some clothes, which looked as if they might be clean, before dressing her brother. He smiled at her, holding out his arms and said what might have been her name. Jack ought to be talking properly now and running around, but it was obvious that no one had bothered to teach him anything. Emily was swamped with guilt. She'd thought about her brother from time to time, but she'd assumed that her mother would look after him. She hadn't dreamed that the child was being mistreated this way. If she'd known ... but what could she have done?

'You're thinking I've neglected him,' Ma's voice said from behind her. 'I've had to work all hours to try and keep this place going – and for what?

No one will come here now. I shall have to let it go ... go away somewhere no one knows me.'

'And what will you do then? I never thought you were a coward, Ma.' Stella looked at her, cheeks flaming. 'What good will it do to run away? You should stay here. You paid good money for the lease – what will happen if you leave Ely? How will you live then?'

'You tell me, clever boots.' Ma sagged against the wall, all the fight drained out of her. 'You're all right. They will take you back at the manor. You could get a job anywhere. I can't run this place alone and care for Jack. It was hard enough when Derek was alive; it would be impossible without him.'

Emily stared at her in silence for a long moment. She knew what her mother was asking her – she was trying to make Emily help her. All her instincts rebelled against it. She would be a fool to throw her life away ... she had her own plans. Yet as she looked from her mother's defeated eyes to her little brother she knew that she didn't have a choice. If she walked out and left them, Jack's condition would just get worse and worse. In the end he might suffer a miserable death from neglect. It was her duty to care for him, however much she might dislike and distrust her mother.

At last, reluctantly, she said, 'You don't have to. I can help you. With a good scrub from top to bottom we could make this place the sort people want to drink at.'

In the silence that fell after her words, Emily cursed herself. What on earth had made her say such a thing? She was going to London to join a voluntary service ... but how could she leave Jack to a life of misery? He was her half-brother and Stella was her mother, even though she'd sworn she would never forgive her for stealing her inheritance and taking Derek's side against her.

'Why?' Ma asked in a hard tone. 'Why would you do that for me?' Her eyes narrowed. 'No, not for me – it would be for Jack, wouldn't it? You think I can't be trusted to look after him, don't you?'

Now was the time to walk away and leave Ma to go to Hell in her own way. Emily wanted to do it. She hated the stench of this place, which she knew would take days of scrubbing to remove. She didn't want to live with Ma or to devote her time to caring for a public house – but she couldn't abandon the child to a mother who had forgotten how to care for him.

'Well, can you? I can help you turn this place around – but not if you don't want me here. I had other plans, but for Jack's sake I'll move into the spare room, bring my stuff from the cottage here – and I'll clean this place up while you take care of Jack. Once it's clean we'll open for business again, and we'll serve bar food. If it sells we might start doing a proper lunch – but we'll see how it goes.'

'And if no one comes?'

'We'll have to sell the lease – but there will be more chance of getting your money back if it's clean.'

Ma gave her a shame-faced look. 'I couldn't do it all alone – you don't know what it was like. What he was like...'

'I think I do,' Emily said and looked her in the

487

eyes. Her mother stared at her for a moment and then her eyes dropped. 'I'm willing to give it a try – if you are?'

Ma was silent for a long moment then inclined her head. 'Don't have much choice, do I?'

'Neither of us does,' Emily said. 'I'll make a start on the living accommodation today. Tomorrow I'll arrange for my things to be brought here and I'll move in – and then I'll scrub the downstairs until that stink has gone.'

'It comes back,' Ma said looking sullen. 'I tried at the start, Emily. It got on top of me.'

'Once we can encourage a different class of client to drink here it should be better. All we can do is try – and you'll have to do your share. For a start you could put a clean dress on and take Jack out for a walk in the park while I sort this mess out.'

Ma's eyes narrowed and Emily thought she would refuse, but instead she went through into the hall. Emily heard water splashing as her mother began to tidy herself up in the tiny bathroom. She started picking up the old newspapers, bits of stale food and ashtrays that were overflowing with stubs. She discovered a paper sack in one of the rooms and stuffed all the rubbish she found into it. There must be a dustbin in the yard at the back, where she could get rid of anything she thought ought to be dumped.

She'd already tidied the sitting room when Ma reappeared. She'd put on a long dark skirt and a cream blouse, brushed her hair back and fastened it with combs, and was carrying a warm red wool jacket. Now Ma looked like the woman

Emily had known and she nodded approvingly. Ma took Jack's hand and, telling Emily she'd be about an hour, she went out.

Emily opened some windows to let in fresh air; glancing out she saw her mother and brother walk to the bottom of the hill and turn left. The entrance to the park was halfway along Broadstreet and all the locals went there, even though the land actually belonged to the cathedral. She turned away to look about her, seeing the dirty clothes strewn over chairs and lying on the floor.

She would need some polish to brighten the furniture. Her mother's room was the first bedroom. Next to that was the tiny room where Jack slept; there were two more. One was empty of furniture and looked out over the back yard, and the second had obviously been Derek's and had the best view of next door's garden. She closed the door on that, because she didn't feel like clearing her uncle's things out just yet. Emily would put her own furniture in the empty room, even though it was smaller than the one that had been her uncle's. For the moment that door would simply remain closed.

After tidying both bedrooms, Emily took all the dirty clothes she could find downstairs. Once again the stench of the pub hit her, making her gag, but she tried to ignore it as she went through to the kitchen at the back. It was a large room with two oak dressers and several cupboards. There was a huge pine table in the middle and an assortment of chairs, most of them from Pa's cottage. Ma's collection of china was set out on one of the dressers and a hotchpotch of china on the other.

Besides the large black range there was a modern gas cooker. Emily eyed it doubtfully. Mrs Hattersley had denounced them as tools of the Devil and vowed she'd never have one in her kitchen, but Emily thought a gas cooker might be better in the summer because the kitchen often became too hot unless lots of windows were opened.

The range was still going, though it needed to be banked up. Emily did this and put two kettles on to boil. Behind the large kitchen was a small scullery. She found a copper in the corner and fetched three buckets of water. Having filled the copper, she lit some paper and wood underneath it to heat the water and then added soda she found lying on a table nearby. She dumped all the clothes in to let them have a good soak. Tomorrow she would wash the clothes and put them outside to dry in the small yard at the rear of the pub.

One of the kettles had heated sufficiently. Emily carried it upstairs with a bucket, scrubbing brush, a cloth and some strong soap. Ma had everything she needed in her cupboards for cleaning; she just hadn't bothered recently.

Emily scrubbed the wooden boards in the three bedrooms they would use and took the dirty water into the toilet, tipping it down the washbasin and rinsing. Then she took the bowls back to the kitchen and returned with the polish and rags. The polish would brighten dull wood and the scent of lavender would make the rooms sweeter. Almost two hours later, she had just about finished to her satisfaction when the door opened and Ma entered with Jack. She'd bought him a lollipop, probably from the sweet shop in Broadstreet, and he was sucking contentedly.

Ma glanced about her, a look of shame on her face. 'You've made a difference here, Emily. It hasn't looked or smelled like this for months.'

'I'm going home now,' Emily said and reached for her coat. 'I shall make arrangements to move into the spare room. My stuff will come tomorrow if I can arrange it or as soon as I can. I'll start downstairs in the morning.'

'What do you want me to do?'

'Look after Jack for now and have a rest. Once we open again you'll have enough to do – though I'll be getting us some help. A strong lad to help with the barrels and a girl to help in the bar and with serving the meals.'

'Do you have enough money to employ staff?'

'I think I can manage, at least for long enough to get us started. I have some things I can sell if I need to – and I still have money I saved.'

Emily decided not to mention what her father had given her. Ma might resent the fifty pounds, though she'd stolen the rest of what Pa had left Emily.

'Thank you. I don't deserve this...'

Emily dropped to her knees and kissed Jack's cheek. 'You might not,' she said, 'but he deserves better. He's my brother and you're my mother. I'll do what I can for you both – but if it doesn't work out we'll have to think again.'

Leaving the pub, Emily made a mental note of all she had to do when she got back to the cottage. She would need to pack as much as she could carry to bring with her in the morning, and the rest of her stuff would go into boxes and bags. Sir Arthur had told her that one of his men would help her move her stuff to the barn. What she needed to decide was what she wanted to store and what to take with her. She would need her bed, wardrobe and chest of drawers. She also wanted her rocking chair from the kitchen, and the kitchen table and chairs would go well in the large bar, which she planned to turn into an area for dining. Her wine table would go in her room, and she would want all her personal bits and pieces, especially the things Pa had given her. The furniture Mr Johnson had bought could go into the barn, together with Emily's dresser – which was too good to put in the pub, at least until she was certain it was a success.

Her head filled with plans, she was home before she knew it. She made herself a cup of tea, some toast and scrambled egg with bacon. All that hard work had brought back her appetite and she was feeling better than she had since Christopher died. Even the feeling of guilt had faded into a dull ache. It wasn't really her fault that her husband had died alone. Emily hadn't realised it could happen and Christopher had told her to go and visit her friends.

At least he'd been happy the night before he died. He'd held her and loved her, and she would hold that memory and forget the pain of his sudden death. She had to move on and make her new life work – for her brother's sake and for her own.

Her plans for working in London had had to be shelved, but perhaps it wasn't important. She would have been late volunteering and perhaps they wouldn't have wanted her – and then she would have ended up back at the manor.

Now at least she had the chance to run her own business. Emily hadn't been confident enough to run the second-hand shop alone, but one thing both she and Ma could do was cook and serve drinks. If they had someone to help in the bar it should be manageable. Once Emily had finished scrubbing and cleaning, she would whitewash the walls and get someone to paint the old beams with a topcoat of black.

She was smiling as she started to pack her clothes, linen and china into boxes. Christopher had given her several lovely things. If she'd opened the shop she would have had to sell them to keep it going, but now she could keep them. They would brighten up her room, and in time she might use some of the pewter and copper down-stairs. In her mind, Emily could see an oak dresser in the large bar set with tankards for special cus-tomers and jugs of flowers. She had plenty of pretty jugs with little cracks that wouldn't matter if someone accidentally broke one. Yes, she could just picture the pub – how it could look if she had her way.

Of course, she had to hope that people would come in and order drinks and food, because if they didn't Ma would need to sell the lease. At least if the pub looked special, someone would want to buy the lease – wouldn't they?

Emily had to believe they would, because she had nothing else. Ma couldn't manage alone, and Jack needed a loving sister to take care of and love him. He had to be encouraged to walk and to speak, and he must learn to use his potty. Her heart broke for the way he'd been left dirty, hungry and wet since she'd gone to work at the manor. Emily had always had Pa's love even if her mother hadn't been kind to her. Jack hadn't had anyone to love him until now – but now he had Emily and she had no intention of deserting him.

Somehow she would make a good life for them all, with or without her mother's help.

Chapter 44

'If Jack isn't any better by the morning I shall take him to the doctor,' Emily said, listening anxiously to her brother's dry cough. 'He's had this too long and I'm worried about him.'

'You fuss over him too much,' Ma said. 'He will be perfectly all right.'

'I think you should stay up here and watch him this evening,' Emily said. 'We can manage downstairs.'

'It's Thursday and we're always busy in the evenings,' Ma objected. 'If you're that worried about him you can pop up and look at him every now and then. I shall be serving behind the bar, as usual.'

Emily stared at her mother hard. Ma was looking much better these past few months. She'd had her hair cut and colour-rinsed so that the sprinkling of grey was covered and the difference had made her seem much younger. Men had started giving her more than a passing glance and Emily knew that was why she had refused to stay upstairs and look after Jack. Every Thursday night, a certain travelling salesman came in to the pub for a few drinks. His name was Ian Smith and he sold lingerie to various department stores in the area. He often had free samples, which he gave to Ma, and Emily couldn't help wondering what her mother had given him in return. Ma sometimes disappeared for nearly an hour on a Friday morning. Emily wondered if she met Ian Smith, but she couldn't accuse her mother of seeing a man.

They had managed for some months with a kind of armed truce between them. Emily's hard work had paid off and the customers had started to come in gradually, perhaps not the ones Derek had favoured, but farmers called for a pint and a meat pie or a roll with cheese and pickles on Thursdays. Men like Ian Smith, who visited the area often, made it a regular call and Emily had been asked several times if they had considered taking in a lodger.

She'd thought about clearing Derek's room but a lodger would mean more work and at the moment both Emily and Ma needed to work in the bar. If they could afford to take on more bar staff then a lodger might be the next step, but Emily was taking things slowly. Every morning she was up early to scrub the bar and the kitchen, opening windows to let out the smell of stale beer, which still crept back whatever she did. Once she'd got Jack up and given him his breakfast, she started preparing the food they would serve in the bar. Each week she tried something different, but so far she'd stuck to things like pasties, pies, tarts and soups with fresh bread, and a range of sandwiches, which were made to order. Her dream of providing proper meals had not come to anything, because although their trade had steadily picked up she could not yet afford to employ more than one girl and one lad for the heavy work in the yard.

During closing hours, she washed pots and pans and cleaned the rest of the house. Ma took Jack for walks in the park or to the river to feed ducks on fine days and on wet days she reluctantly gave Emily a hand with the chores upstairs. Emily was doing three-quarters of the work, but she'd expected that and it had seemed worthwhile, because Jack was so much better. He said Emily's name now and talked in sentences of two or three words, mostly 'Jack want...' or 'Emily kiss...'. He'd learned to tell them when he wanted the toilet and had suddenly started to walk, clinging on to things at first but gradually getting stronger.

Because she loved her little brother, who, she sadly acknowledged, wasn't quite all he should be, Emily had found a kind of contentment in her work. She'd written to her friends at the manor. Miss Lizzie had replied, telling her she would be getting married in the summer and inviting her to visit her at the manor when she had time. Mrs Hattersley had come to visit once and stayed to drink a lemonade shandy and eat one of Emily's pasties.

'It might be better for a dab more pepper,' she said, 'but your pastry was always good, Emily. Didn't I tell you, you should be a cook?'

They'd talked for a while and she'd told Emily to visit her in the kitchen at the manor whenever she had the time. Emily thanked her, but of course there never was time. She was on her feet from early in the morning until the door was locked behind the last of the customers at night, and some of them lingered over their drinks for as long as they possibly could. The man she employed sometimes had to persuade a rowdy drunk to leave. Thankfully, they didn't have many of that kind of customer, but there were always going to be a few, and sometimes they were not noisy louts at all, but unhappy men escaping from a nagging wife or a miserable home life.

Emily listened to their stories and their complaints; sometimes they made her smile, and other times they brought tears to her eyes. If she'd had time to think about it she would have said that she was lonely, but she seldom had time to dwell on her own feelings. At night when she finally fell into bed she was exhausted – more tired than she'd ever been at the manor.

Emily sometimes thought regretfully of the time she'd spent there and whenever she remembered a certain Christmas a lump came to her throat. She still had Nicolas's necklace, which she wore beneath her dress all the time. Emily wasn't sure why she did that, except that she felt it was the safest place. A public house was just that – and there was little to stop anyone going up the back stairs to their private rooms when she and Ma were busy in the bar. She'd put up a notice saying Private, but she'd seen Ian Smith coming down the stairs once when she'd been going to check on Jack. He'd told her that Ma had said he could use their private toilet, because the one in the yard was blocked. That had been true so Emily couldn't complain, but she kept all her best things locked in a private cupboard upstairs. As yet she hadn't had to sell any of her treasures, because they'd done reasonably well almost from the start – and she didn't want to lose her precious things to light-fingered strangers.

They were very busy that Thursday evening and the bar was crowded, people asking for drinks and food. Emily soon ran out of pasties and meat pies and had to go into the kitchen to make sandwiches and toast with bacon rashers for her customers. When she returned she discovered that her staff was rushed off its feet and there was no sign of Ma. She served the customers who had ordered food and a few that were waiting for drinks, then told Vera behind the bar that she was popping upstairs to check on her brother.

'You don't know where Ma went?'

'She was talking with that travelling salesman,' Vera said and went off to serve another pint of beer.

Emily frowned as she ran upstairs. It was too bad of Ma to sneak off with her fancy man, if that's what she'd done – but perhaps she'd gone to check on Jack? Emily passed her mother's room on her way to her brother's. She heard something but took little notice as Jack cried out. Going quickly into his room, she picked him up and discovered that he'd wet himself.

'Jack bad,' he said and started whimpering.

'Jack is not bad, we'll soon make him dry

again,' Emily said and took him into her arms to kiss him. She heard a shriek from next door but was too intent on making her brother comfortable to take much notice. She changed the bed, dried Jack and put him into a clean nightshirt, then settled him back in his bed, stroking his forehead. 'Go to sleep now, dearest.'

Jack sucked his thumb and closed his eyes. Emily smiled. He wasn't coughing so much, so perhaps it had been just a little chill after all.

As she turned to leave him, she heard another cry and stiffened as it was followed by a man's laugh. Of course! She might have known. Ma had taken the travelling salesman to her room and Emily could guess what was going on inside. She felt a rush of anger and was tempted to go storming in, but common sense told her there was no point in having a row at this hour. Rather than confront Ma in an embarrassing situation, she would speak to her privately in the morning.

She went down the stairs to the pub, deliberately letting the door marked Private bang behind her in the hope of giving them a fright. Emily was disgusted with her mother's behaviour. How could she value herself so little that she was willing to give herself to a man for a pair of silk stockings or a pretty petticoat?

Returning to the busy bar, Emily controlled her disgust and her anger. She hadn't come here for Ma's sake but for the child. She wasn't the keeper of her mother's morals, but if Ma wanted to sleep with her salesman, she could do so in her own time – not when there was a pub full of thirsty customers!

'I'm taking Jack to the doctor,' Emily said the next morning. 'I thought his fever had gone, but he's burning up and crying so he needs to see the doctor.'

'What about the bar food and the washing up?'

'You can do the clearing up for once,' Emily shot over her shoulder as she picked Jack up, wrapping him in a blanket. 'I'll do the food when I get back. If you'd been around more last night I would have done the clearing up then but I was on my feet the whole night.'

'I had a headache,' Ma said sourly. 'You fuss over that brat all the time but you never spare a thought for me.'

'Ian Smith rubbed your neck for you, did he?' Emily gave her a look that made Ma's cheeks go bright red. 'Oh yes, I know he was in your room last night. I heard you when I went to check on Jack. Do what you want in your own time, Ma – but just remember our arrangement. I don't mind doing most of the work but unless you do your share I'll walk out and take Jack with me. I could get a job with fewer hours anywhere...'

With that parting shot, Emily left. She was too anxious for her brother to worry much about what Ma thought of her threat to leave and take Jack with her. It wasn't really an option, because she didn't have anywhere to go – except back to her cottage. Sir Arthur had told her there would always be a home for her on his estate if she needed it, but Emily would rather not have to go back. It was true that she could find work easily, but she would need to find someone to look after her brother, and that might be expensive. Yet if need be she would do it, though she hoped the threat would be sufficient to bring Ma to her senses. All Emily asked was that she did her share of the work, especially when they were rushed off their feet.

Jack was coughing again and his skin felt hot to the touch. Emily forgot about Ma as she walked quickly towards the doctor's surgery. She wasn't certain but she thought that Jack might have a rash coming on his legs. He did get a little rash sometimes when he was wet, but Emily had kept him mostly dry recently and she was really worried this time.

There had been a queue at the doctor's surgery. Emily had taken her seat, moving up one each time someone was called in. She had to wait well over an hour and a half before her time came and by then Jack was whimpering and crying, his skin very hot.

'I think he's really ill ... there's this rash on his legs...'

The doctor uncovered Jack's legs and frowned. He looked at his arms and then the rest of his body and shook his head. 'I'm not sure it's anything to worry about, Mrs Johnson. Children have a lot of these rashes and fevers. I'll give you a cooling lotion and a mixture to ease the fever. Take him home, put him to bed and keep an eye on him. If he gets much worse have someone fetch me – or get someone to telephone me. I shall be here for most of the day at the surgery unless I'm called out on an emergency. If I'm not available and you're worried call an ambulance and go to the hospital with him.'

Emily thanked him, paid for the medicines the doctor gave her and left. Jack seemed better again out in the open air and she kissed his forehead, which was a little damp. She would put some of the balm on his legs when she got home and give him a measure of the doctor's medicine.

She was home before the pub opened. Glancing in the kitchen, she saw that the washing up had not been touched. Ma hadn't even wiped a single one of the tables down. Feeling her anger rise, Emily carried her little brother upstairs and put him on the bed. She took his clothes off, smoothed ointment over his body and dressed him in a clean shirt, leaving his legs free to the air. Then she poured a spoonful of the mixture and got him to swallow it. She sat stroking his head for a moment and he seemed calmer, as if he would sleep.

Emily left him and turned towards the stairs, then changed her mind and returned to Ma's room. It was time they sorted things out. Opening the door, she went inside and then stopped in dismay. Every drawer of the chest was open and Ma's things were hanging out. Her wardrobe door was open and empty apart from a couple of very old dresses. All the bits and pieces from her dressing table were gone.

A chilling thought entered Emily's mind. Ma had gone off and left them ... but she only had a few pounds in her purse. A nerve jangled at the back of Emily's neck. She wrenched open the door to her own room and looked inside. Ma had been here too. She'd been through Emily's drawers and her wardrobe – and she'd broken into the locked cupboard where Emily stored her treasures. Feeling sick, Emily went to investigate. Every one of the silver items Christopher had given her was gone. The ring box containing his engagement ring was also missing and so was the beautiful enamelled compact Pa had given Emily.

It was that last that made the tears well up in Emily's eyes. Ma had stolen everything she knew to be of value, leaving anything damaged or chipped behind but taking the rest. Even Emily's purse was empty of all but a few coppers. Yet it was the compact that left a hollow feeling inside her.

Thank God she didn't know about the money Pa had left her. Emily scrambled to the bed and slid her hand under the mattress. Her Post Office book wasn't there ... she searched both sides of the bed and then sat down on the edge. Ma had taken that too. Emily had thought that at least must be safe, but Ma would forge her signature and in a town where Emily wasn't known she would be able to steal her money.

Emily had nothing left but the damaged things Pa had given her, whatever was in the till downstairs ... but Ma would have taken that too. How could she do this to Emily and Jack? Yet she should have known. Ma had taken Uncle Albert's ring and the silver watch and chain left to her by her grandfather, also the stock from the barns, which Pa had left to Emily. Now she'd taken everything else of value ... except for the pendant Nicolas Barton had given her, which, since Christopher had died, and could not be offended, had always hung around Emily's neck.

She'd been such a fool to trust her! Why hadn't she just taken Jack and left her mother to sink into her own misery?

Emily fought back the senseless tears. Now she knew where she stood. Somehow she would manage. She would get back on her feet and make a success of her life, even if it meant that to keep going she had to sell the pendant Nicolas had given her.

No, she wouldn't sell it; she would pawn it for enough money to run the pub until she was in profit again, and then she would buy it back.

Her decision made, Emily went back to her brother. He seemed to be sleeping peacefully and she smiled. She still had Jack. She had a reason to fight and go on with her life.

The mess up here could wait until later. She had a pile of washing up to do downstairs and then she must make pastries and pies, plus a load of sandwiches. Perhaps her mother hadn't taken her float too. Emily had hidden it in a jar in the kitchen. Only five pounds but if it was there she had something to replenish her stocks of food for the bar.

She went down to the bar and checked the till. The coins were still there. Obviously, Ma had been in too much hurry to bother with the change. She hadn't taken any of the pewter or copper from the bar either, which meant she either didn't know it was worth something or she wasn't certain it belonged to Emily rather than the brewery from whom she'd leased the pub.

Emily frowned. She'd asked her mother how

long the lease lasted but Ma had been vague. She remembered signing a contract but couldn't remember how long it was for. Emily would have to find out – and to discover how much the brewery would ask for an extension. However, that might be years away yet, perhaps another two or three years before she needed to raise a lump sum.

Emily was glad she'd paid her staff the previous night. At least they'd had their wages, and if Saturday was a good day she would be able to manage until she recovered from the damage her mother's betrayal had inflicted. She'd lost a lot of pretty things, but apart from the compact nothing had any sentimental value to her. Her engagement ring had always made her feel slightly guilty and, had Ma not stolen it would probably have been the first thing she sold. Glancing at her left hand she remembered her wedding ring. It would fetch a pound or so perhaps.

Emily felt a return of optimism. Ma had done her worst but she couldn't harm her any more. She would work hard to make the pub pay and she would give her brother a good life.

It was nearly two-thirty before Emily was able to lock up and go upstairs for her break. She'd managed to pop upstairs a couple of times during the morning and Jack had seemed to be resting. His skin was no longer as damp as it had been and she thought he must be getting over the fever. She decided she would wake him now, give him milk and a sandwich and some more of the doctor's medicine.

She went into his bedroom, half-expecting him

to be sitting up waiting for her but he was lying just as she'd left him, his eyes closed. Her heart caught with fear and she rushed to the bed. Please don't let him be dead! He was cool to the touch but he wasn't dead. Emily felt her eyes wet with tears as she gathered him up in her arms and held him tight. He gave a whimper of protest, opened his eyes and looked at her, smiling.

'Jack hungry,' he said. 'Emily give Jack bun?'

'Yes, darling, you can have a bun,' Emily said. 'We'll go to the baker and buy some.'

She dressed him in clean things, put his coat on and fetched her own. Then, going back down to the bar, she took a pound from the till. She couldn't really afford to buy cakes from the baker's shop at the moment, but she hadn't made any that morning and her darling brother deserved a treat, even if she couldn't afford it.

And while she was out, she would call in at the pawnbroker's shop and discover what he would give her for the pendant. She wouldn't sell it just yet, but if she became desperate she would sell anything of value she had left, though Ma hadn't left her very much.

Chapter 45

'You look beautiful, Lizzie,' Nicolas said and kissed his sister's cheek. He handed her a small parcel wrapped in silver tissue. 'This is just for you on your special day, dearest. So my little princess

506

is all grown up and about to marry her prince?' His eyes went over her, noticing the sparkle in her eyes. 'I've no need to ask if you're happy.'

'Very happy,' Lizzie replied and hugged him. 'I'm so glad you could get back for the wedding, Nicolas darling. You've been away such a long time. I've missed you.'

'You don't need me now,' he teased. 'You have your Sir Arthur and soon you'll be Lady Jones.'

Lizzie had opened her parcel, exclaiming over the beautiful silver bangle. 'This is wonderful,' she said and clasped it on her arm. 'Arthur has given me so much but I love this... I truly do.'

'Well, I'll leave you to finish getting ready,' Nicolas said. Then he said, 'I suppose you don't know where Emily went, do you?'

'Emily Johnson?' Lizzie looked at him, a little surprised. 'Didn't I tell you about her husband?'

'Yes, you told me he'd died. You thought she would be running the shop in Ely, but it is a hairdressing salon now.'

'Oh yes, I suppose I did think that at the time – she changed her mind so much. First it was the shop and then she wanted to join a voluntary service in London – in the end she went off to live with her mother in a pub in Ely. I think it does quite well. Arthur says he had a lunch there one Thursday and it was good – but of course I haven't been there...'

Nicolas raised his eyes and Lizzie flushed. 'I thought you were friends?'

'Yes, we are. I invited her to my wedding. She sent me a piece of beautiful old lace as a gift, but told me she couldn't spare the time to come. I was a bit hurt actually but... I suppose she thought I'd been avoiding her. You know what Mama would say if I visited her at a pub, Nicolas. She didn't approve when Emily lived on Arthur's estate, but Granny supported me – and she certainly doesn't approve of Emily working in a public house. She might have had her old job back here if she'd asked...'

'Perhaps she had good reason for doing what she does?'

'Perhaps...' Lizzie pulled a face at him. 'Don't be cross with me, Nicolas. I'm very fond of Emily, you know I am – but well, I don't think I should like to visit a public house. It probably smells awful.'

Nicolas nodded his understanding. Lizzie could not help her upbringing. She'd been a bit of a rebel for a while, but now she was to marry a respectable man and she'd reverted to her class. A girl like her wouldn't normally visit a public house and, if Emily had turned down the invitation to her wedding, perhaps it was for the best. For a time their worlds had come together, but now they'd drifted apart and perhaps both were content in their own way.

And in a way he'd been just as bad, because he hadn't spoken out that day when he'd met Emily at the hospital. He'd hinted at his feelings, but he hadn't told Emily he loved her – and he hadn't asked her to marry him, something he'd regretted a thousand times. If he'd asked she might have said yes.

Leaving his sister to dress for her wedding, Nicolas went down to the hall. He had time to go riding, because the ceremony was not until two-thirty that afternoon. Feeling restless, he walked down to the stable. He wasn't sure what he'd hoped for when he'd been given leave for Lizzie's wedding.

Knowing that Emily had married out of duty had lain on his conscience all this time. He shouldn't have let her throw her life away. Nicolas had felt hurt and angry in turns; knowing that he wanted her, his jealousy had ground away at his insides. Only when his stint as a flying instructor was over and he was back in Belgium, flying his kite, had the image of her white face left him. Then he could recall her as she'd been when he'd held her in his arms after her father died; the funny things she said that made him smile, the scent of her hair and the desire that had swept through him – but she had chosen someone else.

He hadn't actually asked her to be his wife, because he feared a quarrel with his family.

Nicolas cursed himself. He was, he knew, one of the fortunate ones. The young pilots he'd trained were now becoming old hands, those that survived – and other young recruits had been sent to take their place, some of them dying on their first sortie. He was considered to have a charmed life and perhaps he had – but it often felt empty to him.

He'd tried dating other girls, even taking one or two of them to bed – but still the memory of Emily's eyes had stayed in his head.

Nicolas had hoped that he would see her again, just walk into the shop to buy something ... he'd also hoped that she would no longer have that strange hold on his heart that he could not shake off. Lizzie might not be able to go to a public house, but Nicolas could – and he would, after the wedding.

Lizzie was a beautiful bride, just as he'd known she would be – as Amy would have been had she not chosen to run away with her lover the previous year. Nicolas felt a little sad that Amy had disgraced herself and her family ... but today was not the time for regrets!

Nicolas watched as his sister took her vows and then walked back down the aisle on her husband's arm. Outside, he threw confetti over them and joined with his family as the photographer had them all lined up for the official pictures. It took a long time for the photographs to be finished, because they had to wait for each pose to be perfect and then for the exposure, but in the end Lord Barton said they should leave for the reception. Some of the guests had modern automobiles; some were still using a horse and carriage. Nicolas took two of the bridesmaids in his open tourer.

Because the weather was so pleasant, he had the top down and the pretty girls giggled and laughed, enjoying the ride. One of them had blonde hair and large blue eyes. Nicolas was amused by the way she fluttered her lashes at him, hanging on his every word. She told him her name was Celine and she was eighteen. She had just left her finishing school and was preparing to join the ambulance service in London.

'A lot of people think the war is almost over,' she told Nicolas, 'but Papa says there is a long way to go yet and he wants me to do something useful with the education he gave me – before I get married.'

Her eyelashes fluttered flirtatiously and Nicolas knew that she was telling him she was available for romance, if not marriage just yet. She amused him, because her chatter was so innocent and open that it reminded him of Emily when she'd first come to the manor.

Nicolas supposed Emily would have changed a great deal over the years. She'd been a widow for several months now and was running a successful business. If she'd wanted to see Nicolas, she could have written to him via Lizzie – but perhaps she had forgotten that night when just for one moment she'd been tempted to go away with him.

'How long is your leave?' Celine was asking. 'I don't have to join my unit for another week...'

Nicolas looked at the pretty young woman and smiled. The invitation in her eyes was clear now. 'I have ten days,' he said. 'I was due leave, because I'd deferred it for Lizzie's wedding – and now I have some time to myself.'

'So do I,' Celine said, her mouth soft and inviting. 'Isn't that a coincidence?'

Nicolas laughed. She was a very bold young woman and he liked her. She attached herself to his side when they reached the house and, when the dancing started, Nicolas felt obliged to ask her to dance. After that he had to dance with the other bridesmaid and some of Lizzie's other friends, then with the bride herself and his mother and, finally, a very slow dance with Granny.

'You look very well, Granny dear,' he said, leading her to her seat afterwards. 'I think you will miss Lizzie?'

'Dreadfully, but don't tell her so,' Lady Prior said. 'Jonathan's wife is dull – and Helen and I don't see eye to eye.' She raised an eyebrow. 'Tell me, Nicolas – when shall you oblige us and bring a bride to this house?'

'I don't think it would be fair until this show is over – do you?'

'Surely it can't go on much longer?'

'Who knows?' Nicolas squeezed her arm. 'I shall wait until I'm no longer being shot at, dearest. I don't want to make my bride a widow too soon...'

He frowned as he recalled that he'd meant to visit Emily after the wedding, but somehow he'd got caught up in the celebrations and it was too late now. She would be tired after working long hours in that pub. He would drive to Ely in the morning and see if she would speak to him...

Chapter 46

Emily could scarcely recall a busier night at the pub. She'd made several lots of fresh sandwiches and the pastries she'd cooked earlier had run out ages ago. She'd tried out some relishes to go with the rolls, cheese and cold meats she put into her sandwiches and they had been selling well too. It would take her a while to feel certain but she thought she was going to make enough money to see her through the winter, when the pub was not as busy as this every night. In summer they had several tourists visiting; people came to see the cathedral and quite a few men came down for the fishing. Emily knew that if she wanted the extra money she could let out two rooms – at least during the summer, but she was reluctant to do it, because she was alone here with her brother. Occasionally, one of the customers would try to flirt with her but she never responded. She knew that other widows did take in lodgers, but some of them didn't mind providing extras. Emily certainly wasn't prepared to sleep with her lodgers.

She'd noticed a man looking round the pub. He seemed very interested in her and what she was doing. He'd asked about the food she provided, and whether she would consider giving her customers a cooked meal – and if she took lodgers. Was he trying it on? Somehow she felt there was something more behind his interest, and, just as the customers were leaving, he suddenly asked if he could speak to her about a private matter.

Emily hesitated, and picked up a tray of dirty glasses. 'If you would come into the kitchen I can spare a few minutes...'

He nodded and followed her. Again, she noticed his eyes moving about the room, taking in its appearance.

'You've made some changes here and in the bar. I think I may say that you have picked up the trade and improved it considerably. Is Mrs Carter here this evening?'

'No, not this evening,' Emily said, feeling uneasy though uncertain why. 'You can speak to me in her place, Mr...?'

'Steven Richards and you are Mrs Johnson, Mrs

Carter's daughter I understand. They tell me you are a widow?'

'Yes.' Her sense of unease increased. 'What makes you ask, Mr Richards?'

'As you know your lease is due to run out next month. The brewery was not intending to renew because we were not satisfied that the pub was being run properly on our last visit – but you have certainly improved it. I think I shall recommend that a new lease be offered after what I've seen this evening.'

Emily caught her breath. 'You say the lease runs out next month – so I have three weeks before then?'

'Yes.' He frowned. 'Do you not wish to be considered for a new lease?'

Emily looked at him. 'That depends on how much it is, Mr Richards.'

'Well, in view of the work you've done here and considering how much trade you're doing... I would think we might consider a two-year lease on payment of a hundred pounds.'

'A hundred...' Emily's heart sank. She had no chance of raising even a fraction of that money. Had Ma not taken everything when she ran off, Emily might have managed to sell enough to raise most of it – and there was her diamond pendant – but she couldn't be sure how much she would get for that. Nor did she know if her trade would continue through the winter. Even if she sold all the things Pa had given her she might not manage to cover the lease – and then she would have nothing left. 'I would need a little time. I'm not sure I can find that much.'

514

'Ah, I see. I did hear that there had been a tragedy in your family. Mrs Carter isn't around now, is she?' He took her silence for confirmation. 'I'm not sure the brewery could let a young woman of your age take on the lease ... even if you had the money. Had Mrs Carter been here ... the brewery does require the proprietor to be over twenty-five but perhaps...'

She knew that her case was hopeless. Just for a moment he'd seemed to offer a chance but Emily wasn't old enough to run the pub even if she could somehow manage to get the hundred pounds.

'It will take me a little time to clear my things...'

'Yes, I dare say – well, you have the three weeks, Mrs Johnson. I shall not tell the brewery your secret in the circumstances. It is a pity Mrs Carter isn't here. This place hasn't been as well run in an age.'

'If I could find the money ... need you tell them at all?'

'Mrs Carter would need to sign the lease.' He looked regretful. 'I'm sorry to be the bearer of bad news, especially after seeing what you've done here. Good evening, Mrs Johnson. If you should want to apply to the brewery in a few years I would recommend that you be given a try.'

Emily didn't answer. She stared at him as he went out, feeling as if she'd been run over by a steam engine. Ma had taken so much more than the treasures Emily had loved; she'd taken her means of making her living.

So now what did she do? Once she'd paid her debts and arranged for her things to be moved, she would be out of a job once more. Tears stung her eyes. She dashed them away angrily. It wasn't fair. Why did everything go wrong for her?

All she'd wanted was to take care of Jack and give him a future and now even that had been snatched away from her. Lifting her head, she went back into the bar, which was now almost empty. Remembering the filthy ruin she'd come to a few months earlier, she was angry that all her hard work had gone for nothing. It was just so unfair. She wanted to hit out at someone, scream or shout – but what was the point?

There was nothing more she could do for now. Even if she could raise enough money for the lease by selling her pendant, the brewery would refuse her the lease because she was too young.

Emily had no choice. She was going to have to move back to the cottage or store her things and move on...

Emily had hoped that in the morning things would look better, but in the cold light of daybreak, her future seemed bleak. She knew that she could find a job somewhere. They might give Emily her job back at the manor if she asked, but what would happen to Jack? She wouldn't be allowed to keep her brother with her if she returned to service so that meant she had to look for a job elsewhere.

Alone, Emily could find work anywhere but with a young child in tow... It was going to be difficult. The last thing she wanted was to put Jack into the care of a stranger, but she couldn't see an alternative. Here at the pub she'd been able to look after him herself, taking him out for some fresh air during the hours the pub was closed. Could she find work of a similar nature? Perhaps – but she would also need a place to live.

It hardly seemed worthwhile cleaning the pub, but Emily hated the smell first thing in the morning so she scrubbed the floors, cleaned the toilets and washed the tables down before starting to make food for the bar. As soon as her staff arrived, she went upstairs to feed her brother and tidy herself.

She was just preparing to go back downstairs when she heard a heavy tread on the stairs. Her spine became icy. Who would come up here without an invitation? Had Ma returned? Yet surely they were a man's footsteps? Emily looked round for some kind of a weapon and picked up a heavy candlestick just as a knock sounded at her parlour door; the door opened and someone looked round.

'Vera told me to come up – is it all right, Emily?'

Emily stared in disbelief. Tears started to her eyes but she struggled to hold them back as she saw him.

'Nicolas...?' she whispered and the pain and grief welled over. She'd thought she might never see him again, and the relief made her weak. She dashed the tears from her cheeks. 'I'm so foolish. It's just that everything has been so awful – and now you're here...'

'Emily, my darling...' Nicolas strode towards her, taking her into his arms to hold her as she wept against his chest. The tears flowed, because Emily couldn't stop them. 'What is wrong? Won't you tell me – please?'

Somehow, Emily managed to control her emotions. She accepted his handkerchief and wiped her face. Sitting down in one of the old armchairs, she found the words flowing out of her. She told him about how she'd planned to open the shop but been too nervous to do it alone after Christopher died; she told him about coming here and finding her brother in a terrible state – and of all that had happened afterwards. She concluded with the brewery's agent telling her the previous night that she had three weeks to leave the pub.

Raising her head, she found the strength to smile. 'I'm sorry for being such a wet week, Nicolas. How are you? It's a while since I heard from Lizzie, apart from the invitation to her wedding. I wondered if you would come home for it.'

'She was a beautiful bride, but I have another nine days' leave,' he said. 'Why didn't you let me know things were difficult for you? You must have known I would help you.'

'I was managing...' Emily shook her head. 'I know I could have my job back but it means I have to find someone to look after Jack.'

'Jack is your brother?'

'Yes...' Emily hesitated, then, 'He's my mother's child but we have different fathers. Ma had an affair with someone; it broke Pa's heart. I should never have trusted her, but I had to do something for Jack.'

'Yes, of course you did.' Nicolas looked thoughtful. 'Would you carry on with the pub if you could?'

'Yes, I think so. I've built up the business and I can manage here. It would be much harder if I had to find lodgings that would take us both – and someone to look after him if I was at work.'

Nicolas took a deep breath, hesitated, then, 'You could marry me and let me take care of you, Emily.'

She was too shocked to speak for a moment, her heart slamming against her chest like a bird trying to escape the bars of its cage. She allowed her eyes to look into his. Nicolas had been angry because she married Christopher. She'd thought she must have killed his love, but it seemed he still wanted her. Yet surely he wasn't offering to marry her? It was impossible – he must know that?

'Marry you...?' she said on a breathless note. 'You don't ... you can't mean it. Nicolas, have you thought what it would mean?'

'I've thought of it a thousand times and I know what I'm saying. I didn't ask you when you married Johnson, Emily. It seemed too difficult, and I knew you felt you owed him something – but I've regretted it so many times. I want you to be my wife. I love you so much ... without you, life just isn't worth living. To hell with all the rest, I want you...'

'Nicolas, I do love you so...' Emily blinked hard, still unable to believe it. 'Are you sure? Would you be willing to take on my brother? He isn't just like other children and will always need to be looked after...'

'He's your brother, Emily,' Nicolas said. 'Besides, I like children...'

'I wouldn't want you to feel obliged...'

Nicolas moved towards her, taking her into his arms. His mouth sought hers and he kissed her, long and sweetly. When he let her go at last, she was trembling. Her throat caught as she gazed up at him.

'I want you so much. I know it won't be easy. My family will not like it – but I can't give you up again, Emily.' There was a little sob in his voice. 'I couldn't bear to lose you a second time.'

'I've loved you all the time, Nicolas. I was wrong to marry Christopher. It wasn't a proper marriage – and that hurt him. I did what I thought right but perhaps I was wrong...'

'Don't be sorry,' Nicolas said. 'You did what you thought was best and that is one of the reasons I love you, Emily. You've always done the right thing and you've put others first. Now it's time to let me help you. Marry me, be my wife, and I'll take care of you and Jack. I love you and I'll love him.'

'Oh Nicolas, are you sure?' It seemed like an impossible dream. Could it really be happening?

'Yes, if you are.' He took her hands, gazing down at her with love. 'If you wanted this place I would take on the lease for it and let you run it for yourself – but I would rather we married, if you could bear it?'

'I don't think I could bear not to now,' Emily said, her throat working with emotion. 'But what of your family? Will they accept our marriage?'

'If they love me they will, but if not...' Nicolas held her strongly, refusing to let her go as she pulled back. 'It's you I want, Emily darling. I want you to pack a few things for you and Jack. I'm going to take you away with me now. We'll go to the seaside for a few days. Afterwards, I'll take you to the manor to meet my parents as my wife. If they refuse to accept you, I'll find a house for us. I have some property, which I've let for the duration of the war, but I can find a house for us to let until I'm home for good and then we'll have a place of our own.'

'What if they won't...?'

'No doubts, Emily,' Nicolas said and kissed her again. 'I'm not a rich man, my darling. I have some money my grandfather left me, but most of it is in property. I've always expected to work for my living and I may make a career of flying – perhaps in commercial aviation, which I believe will be the thing of the future. I'll provide for you and Jack, and any children we have.' He kissed her hands, which were red from scrubbing the floors, but when she tried to pull them away in shame, Nicolas wouldn't let her. 'Go on, pack a few things and we'll go – I don't want to waste a moment of the time I shall have with you.'

Emily went through to the bedroom to collect a few of her decent things. When she went to collect Jack's clothes, she found that Nicolas already had the boy in his arms. He handed Jack to her and took the cases she'd packed.

Emily stopped in the bar downstairs, telling Vera that she was going away for a few days. It would be time enough when she returned to give the girl her notice and arrange for her personal things to be cleared. She gave Vera the keys, knowing that she could trust the girl to look after the bar while she was gone; it might not be run as she'd run it, but it hardly mattered now.

Leaving the pub, she settled Jack in the tiny back seat of Nicolas's automobile and slid into the front beside him. He smiled at her and she felt her heart soar. It was so wonderful that she could scarcely believe what had happened.

Nicolas was here with her and he wanted to marry her. Nothing else mattered.

'It's so beautiful here,' Emily said as they stood together on the cliffs late one evening and looked out at the sea as the sun began to set. 'I've never been to such a lovely spot, Nicolas. Look at the way the sea seems to boil and thrash about those rocks and send white spray into the air – and the colour of the sky as it touches the sea. It's almost as if someone has set a torch to it ... orange and red and gold with dark blue streaks...'

'That's poetry,' Nicolas said, looking at her lovingly. 'I didn't know you had the soul of a poet, my darling.'

They had driven down to Cornwall in Nicolas's motorcar, stopping now and then to eat or drink, and they'd spent one night in a hotel. He'd made love to her that evening and if either of them had entertained doubts, by morning they'd fled, because it was perfect. Their loving was so sweet and tender, so right that Emily knew they were meant to be lovers, meant to be together always.

The next day Nicolas had gone to the registrar's office and obtained a special licence so that they could marry without delay. The following day they continued their journey to the sea, where Nicolas had secured a beautiful suite for them. As a part of the hotel service, they were able to leave Jack in the evenings because the resident baby-sitter was paid to look after him. She was a pretty young woman and had formed an immediate bond with the child, making it easier for Emily to leave him sometimes. During the day, they mostly took him with them, buying him ice creams, sweets and showing him how to build sandcastles on a small secluded beach that was still open to the public, because it would be impossible for German ships to pass the rock barrier, around which the sea boiled and foamed. Jack was having a wonderful time and had started to call Nicolas *Dada,* which made him smile and throw the child into the air, catching him securely in loving arms.

'If I sound poetic it must be because of all the wonderful things you write in your poems,' Emily said and held his hand tightly. 'I'm not sure that I noticed all the little things until you showed me your poems. A butterfly's wings moving as if in slow motion as it sips nectar from a flower, the gossamer silk of a spider's web glistening with dew in the white of morning...'

'I shall have a rival,' Nicolas said. 'Don't you know that you're all my bright things wrapped in one, Emily? My poetry was often dark and painful until I found you – and now I see the joy in everything about me. Even a scurrying ant is beautiful now. When I'm up there floating above the clouds and it's peaceful, my head is filled with you and what you mean to me.'

'You should be thinking of getting back safe,' she scolded and then leaned in to kiss his lips. Earlier they'd eaten shrimp from little tubs and he tasted of salt. 'We're so lucky, Nicolas. Do you think love is always like this ... so fine and delicate that it makes you ache?'

'Perhaps. I've never loved anyone else like this. I avoided all the young ladies my mother paraded for my benefit. I don't know why you touched something inside me – but it was like a light going on, as if I'd never seen the world before. Always before there was a shadow, a darkness that gathered in my mind. You've banished the darkness and brought me into the light.'

He took something from his pocket that looked like a silver watch, but then he pulled the winder off, held it to his eye and pressed a little knob on the side.

'What is that?'

'It's a Ticker – what they call a spy camera. Jonathan bought it for me, because it slips into a pocket and I never have my box camera with me when I want it.' He took a step back. 'Pose for me, darling, put your head back so that your hair blows in the wind. I want some pictures to take with me.'

Emily did as he asked, laughing at him and twirling, gazing back at him over her shoulder. Then she held out her hand for the camera so that she could take a photo of him. Afterwards, Nicolas took pictures of Jack and Emily playing together. It was as if they were a real family and for the first time in years, she was aware of intense happiness. Love for this man curled inside her, making her ache with longing for the night when he would take her in his arms and love her once more.

Nicolas's face was so pale and intense, so sensitive that her throat tightened as she reached out to run her fingers through his hair. He'd washed it that morning and without the oil it was springy and curled beneath her fingers.

'You make me want to cry. I'm not sure I'm worthy of such love.'

'You're worth far more. I'm not clever enough to tell you how much I adore you – or how much I need you.'

'I love you, Nicolas. I only know that I never expected to love like this or to be loved in return. I still can't believe it's real.'

'It's as real as we are,' he said and stroked her cheek. 'Whether we exist or we're all part of some god's dream I'm not sure. Humans are such puny creatures we must be here for the amusement of some higher being don't you think? They watch from on high and laugh as we struggle with the adversities they throw at us.'

'That's too deep for me,' Emily said. 'I just know that I want to love you and have your babies. Nothing else matters very much.'

'Is that so? In that case I think we should return to the hotel and see what can be done to give you what you want, my darling Emily.'

'You tease me and I love it,' she said. 'But it's true. You are my life. Loving someone is all that really matters.'

'Yes, I know. I used to be tortured by the meaning of life, searching for the key – that elusive piece that would make it all worthwhile, but I've found it in you.' He kissed her hand. 'I think I've died and gone to heaven.'

Emily clung to him, savouring each precious moment they spent together here by the sea. Nicolas was filled with confidence, but she could not quite banish her fears. How long would their perfect happiness last?

Nicolas intended to stay here another three days and then they would go to the manor. Emily dreaded the moment when he told his family that they were married, because she knew in her heart that they would never accept her.

Chapter 47

'Are you nervous, darling?'

Nicolas looked at Emily as they turned into the manor drive. It was the first time she'd really seen the grand frontage to advantage and she realised just how beautiful it was, its mellow yellow stone walls dreaming in the evening sunshine. Three storeys high with the attics above, its windows were long and elegant, reflecting the flame of the sky. This part of the house must be much newer, perhaps eighteenth century, while the buildings that housed the kitchens and servants' halls were older, probably medieval with lower ceilings and overhanging roofs that made it dark inside except on very sunny days. The house looked even bigger from this vista and the realisation of just what she'd done hit home like a hammer blow. How could she ever belong in a house like this?

'Your family will be so angry...'

'They can't really hurt us. If they refuse to acknowledge you I shall simply drive on to London. London would be convenient for me when I'm on leave – unless you would prefer to live locally?'

'I don't mind where we live – but I would prefer you were not estranged from your family, Nicolas.' Emily breathed in deeply. 'I shall understand if they don't like me – but they mustn't cut you off completely.'

'If I have you I have all I need.'

Emily smiled but didn't answer. Her stomach was tying itself in knots and the palms of her hands were sweating. She knew Nicolas was more apprehensive about their reception than he would say, because a little nerve was flicking at the corner of his temple, but she had accepted that they might be turned from the door. However, as they got out of the car, the front door opened and Lizzie came flying out to meet them.

'Nicolas dearest. I'm so glad to see you. We just got back from our honeymoon and walked into a horrid row. Father got your letter telling him you were married. He is sulking in his study and says he shan't come out but Granny and Mama are in the small front parlour waiting for you. They've agreed a truce for the moment because they both say they are determined to see you whatever Papa says.'

'They must see Emily as well or I shan't stop,' Nicolas said. 'Say hello to Emily. She's my wife, Lizzie – and she makes me very happy. And this is her brother Jack. They are both a part of my family now.'

'Yes, of course.' Lizzie turned to Emily with a smile. 'I hope we shall always be friends because Nicolas is my very best friend in the world.'

'I should be honoured to be your friend,' Emily said and held out her hands, her throat catching.

527

'We both love Nicolas so we should be able to love each other.'

'You're my sister now,' Lizzie told her. 'I don't care what anyone else thinks or says. I'm glad you've married Nicolas, because it makes him happy.'

'Thank you, dear heart,' Nicolas said. 'I shall bring Emily in to meet Mama and Granny – but then I need to speak to Father.'

'He might not see you.'

He reached for Emily's hand. 'Bear up, my love. It isn't the end of the world if they disapprove of us.'

'Of me,' Emily said and laughed. 'I'll bear it as best I can, my love. Just stay with me for a while please.'

'Of course.' He held her hand, drawing her towards the small front parlour. 'We might as well face the lions straight away and get it over with...'

Emily held his hand tightly. Lizzie had offered to take Jack to the kitchen and give him a glass of milk and some biscuits, and Emily had agreed. Miss Lizzie probably wanted to avoid the confrontation with her mother and grandmother and was no doubt glad that she no longer had to live at the manor.

Her head high, Emily controlled her nerves as they entered the parlour. Lady Barton was standing by the window, while Lady Prior sat straight and stiff in her chair. Seeing the disapproval in their eyes, Emily's worst fears were realised. They resented her being brought into their family and would never welcome her to their home, but because they cared for Nicolas they were willing to tolerate her.

She remained standing by his side as he made the introductions. Both ladies inclined their heads to acknowledge her but neither uttered a word of welcome.

'You might have told us of your plans, Nicolas,' Lady Barton said coldly. 'Your father is very angry. He instructed me to refuse you, but you are my son ... whatever you choose to do.'

'And Emily is my wife, Mama. If you wish to see me you must accept her, because I love her and I will not have her insulted.'

'What is done is done,' Lady Prior said. 'Since you chose to marry the gel we must accept it – but your father is not pleased. However, while I live you will be received here, and of course your wife.' She looked down her long nose at Emily, clearly displeased with what she saw.

'Thank you, Granny,' Nicolas said. 'Emily, I suggest you go upstairs. Mrs Marsh will show you where. You will want to rest and look after Jack...' He squeezed her hand and she smiled at him gratefully, glad to escape.

The interview with Lord Barton was bound to be stormy and she would prefer not to be involved.

Going out into the hall, she saw Mrs Marsh lingering, as if awaiting the call. Emily asked to be taken up to their room and the housekeeper inclined her head.

'Very well, madam,' she said. 'Please come this way.'

'I'm still Emily...'

Mrs Marsh looked at her. 'No, madam, you are Mrs Nicolas – and the staff will address you correctly. I know what is due to the family.'

Feeling rebuked, Emily followed her up the main stairs. She knew her way via the servants' stairs but she had never actually been to the bedrooms by this route. Since Mrs Marsh had made her feelings clear, she made no further attempt to make conversation.

Alone in the room she would share with Nicolas while they stayed here – if they stayed here – Emily sat on the edge of the bed and hugged herself. She was shivering with cold, because somehow this felt wrong. While she was alone with Nicolas she could forget the wide divide between their worlds, but here at the manor she realised just what she'd done by marrying him. He could lose his whole family because of her – and even if his mother and grandmother received her there would always be a barrier between them.

She had been sitting there for some minutes when someone knocked at the door and then Lizzie entered.

'Jack is with Mrs Hattersley. She is making a fuss of him so you need not worry about him. How did it go downstairs?'

'Your mother and grandmother were polite, Miss Lizzie,' Emily said. 'They were not warm or welcoming but they were polite. I can accept that. It isn't easy to accept a servant as one of the family.'

'You mustn't call me Miss Lizzie now. We are sisters now. Just because you worked for us it doesn't mean you're worth less than we are. If Nicolas is right, you're worth more than the lot of us put together.'

'Nicolas loves me. You mustn't think I'm more than I am. I shall try not to let Nicolas or his family down, but I know I'm not what you expected or wanted for him.'

'I didn't think he would marry. He used to disappear when young ladies came to tea. I'm glad he found you, Emily. It must be awful doing what he does every day, especially for someone of his nature. Having you at home waiting for him will make him more careful.'

'Thank you.' Emily smiled. 'I'm never going to be the wife your family would have preferred – but we are truly happy.'

'I think Nicolas is lucky...' Lizzie broke off as she heard the sound of running feet and then Mary rushed into the room. 'Mary, we were talking privately. You should have knocked...'

'Yes, Lady Jones, I know – but Lady Barton is faint and Lady Prior is ill and Lord Barton has had a fit...'

'My father...' Lizzie stared at her in shock. 'Mama and Granny ... what shall we do?'

'Has the doctor been sent for, Mary?'

'Yes ... Mrs Nicolas,' Mary said looking at Emily awkwardly. 'Lady Barton is in her room. Mrs Marsh is trying to revive Lady Prior in the parlour. Mr Jonathan and Mr Nicolas have carried their father up to his room.'

'I'm still Emily to you. Lizzie, you'd better go to your mother. I'll see if I can help Mrs Marsh with your grandmother. Your father needs the doctor and we can't do much for him until he comes.'

'I'll go to Mother,' Lizzie said, looking white and shocked. 'What happened to Granny, Mary?'

'It seems she stood up quickly and then just crumpled into a heap. Your mama had the hysterics and your father ... he shouted at her and then he slumped down in a chair and passed out.'

'Poor Granny,' Lizzie said, tears in her eyes. 'She's been ill for a long time but she never complains. It must have been the shock...'

'Lizzie, please don't say any more,' Emily warned. 'Go to your mama now. I'll help Mrs Marsh if I can...'

'How is she?' Emily asked when Nicolas entered the parlour where she was sitting alone later that evening. 'The doctor said your father's apoplectic fit is a warning to slow down but he thinks he will recover this time. I think it is Lady Prior who has suffered the worst.'

'Granny is still unconscious,' Nicolas said. 'Apparently, it could have happened at any moment these past six months or more.'

'I'm so sorry, Nicolas. Was it the shock of your marriage?'

'I think it was seeing my father in a temper. She was trying to calm him down and it just happened. Jonathan knew that Father's heart was not all it should be – but I had no idea...'

'I'm so sorry.'

'Don't be, it isn't your fault.'

'Your grandmother too... I feel terrible. We shouldn't have come here.'

'Granny is a proud lady, but she was willing to accept my marriage. Father upset her by ranting at her – and me.'

'She stood up for you even though he wanted to

forbid you to the manor.'

'She's so stubborn,' Nicolas said, 'but despite her pride and the fact that she is undoubtedly a snob where her family is concerned – I loved her.'

'Of course you did.' Emily stood up and went to him. 'I'm so sorry. I know you must be hurting. To have both your father and grandmother ill at the same time...'

'Father will recover. He has been told not to get angry and advised to cut down on his drinking, but he carries on as always. Granny is another matter. She's old and frail, Emily – and I'm sorry I hurt her.'

'Because you married me?'

'No, because I insisted on having it out with my father. I didn't think he would go barging into the parlour and start shouting at Mama and Granny.'

'It might have been better to wait.'

'Perhaps – yet I wanted him to accept you. Besides, the doctor said that Granny could have had the stroke even if nothing had happened, but I shall always feel partially to blame.'

'No, it isn't your fault,' Emily said. 'You told your father in private. He should have been more considerate.'

'Perhaps...' Nicolas sighed. 'I have to leave for my unit the day after tomorrow. I suppose I could ask for compassionate leave, but they are unlikely to grant it unless someone is dead.'

'I could stay on for a while,' Emily said. 'If I can be of help...'

'Jonathan has arranged for a private nurse to come in and look after the invalids. Mabel is here and Lizzie may stay for a day or two – and my mother will cope when she's calmed down. I want to see you settled in a house of our own, Emily.'

'You think I should not be welcome in your grandmother's sick room?'

'I'm not saying that – but best to leave them to get on with it. They've accepted we're married, but I don't want to throw you to the lions if I'm not around to defend you.'

'I'm not that fragile, Nicolas.'

'I know – but it's too soon. Give them time. We'll come down again when I'm next on leave. Lizzie is fond of her grandmother. Once she comes round, Lizzie will sit with her and read to her. I'm sure that's what she'd prefer.'

'I see…' Emily turned away. 'Well, I have to have my things put in store and give my staff notice. If it will be easier, I could find a house to let somewhere locally – and when you come home next time you could look for something in London.'

Nicolas hesitated, and then nodded, 'Yes, perhaps. I'll give you some money and you'll receive a part of my wage while I'm serving overseas. You can write to me, let me know where you are – that way we could have one last day here…'

Emily nodded her agreement. She walked over to the window and looked out. The roses were in full bloom, a beautiful white one cascading down a south-facing wall. As the breeze ruffled it some petals detached themselves and fell, looking like a shower of white raindrops. It was so beautiful but everything else was ugly. She fought her desire to cry. Her offer to help had been instinctive and it hurt that Nicolas had turned it down.

'Don't be hurt, my love.' Nicolas put his arms

about her from behind, kissing the back of her neck. 'I love you. You are my world. My mother and grandmother will accept you in time – Father too. We just have to let them come round in their own way.'

'Yes, I know.' Emily turned in his arms, reaching up to kiss him. His familiar smell calmed and comforted her, easing the tiny pinpricks of hurt. 'We shan't quarrel, Nicolas. Our time is too precious. If there's nothing more we can do let's go to bed – and then I'll be alone and you'll be back in Belgium.'

'The days will pass and I'll be home again,' he said and bent his head to kiss her lips. 'You can't help Granny if you stay. The doctor says she has a fifty-fifty chance of recovery. She doesn't have much time left to her I'm afraid.'

'That's sad,' Emily said and took his hand. 'Shall we go up? I want to lie in your arms. Everything was so perfect and now...'

'It's the way life is,' Nicolas said and smiled. 'But whatever happens here we're strong. Nothing but death will ever part us for long...'

Chapter 48

Nicolas drove Emily into Ely that morning. He looked regretful as he gave her a long, lingering kiss on the mouth.

'I wish I didn't have to leave. I should have liked to see you settled, Emily – to know you were safe in a decent house.'

'I have the money you put into an account at your bank for me. I have to tidy things up at the pub, so I might as well stay there with Jack until I find a little house of my own. I don't need a big place until you come home, then we'll find something together. Surely this war can't go on for much longer?'

'According to the paper British deaths were more than 127,000 in August alone. We're just standing still, Emily. Somehow we have to make a push or this conflict could drag on for years.'

So many dead. The number had lingered in Emily's mind after her husband had driven away. Compared to that, what was the illness of one old lady who had outlived the world she knew? Yet Emily knew that Nicolas was feeling guilty because he'd inadvertently caused her to have the stroke and because he'd had to leave before he knew whether or not she would recover. Emily wished that the family had accepted her because she would have liked to help nurse the old lady, whom she admired despite knowing that she was despised.

Emily walked down the hill to her pub – not hers for much longer now. She must give the staff a week's notice and arrange for her things to be moved, though she wasn't sure where she wanted to live. There must be some houses available in Ely, unless she went further afield...

Emily disliked the idea of giving Vera and the youth who'd been so handy in the yard the sack. Of course they would find work easily enough; young Fred would probably have to join up soon if this wretched war dragged on. Emily didn't want to think about that, because the longer the war went on the more likely it became that Nicolas's fabled luck would run out.

No, she wouldn't let herself think about that, because she loved him too much and she couldn't bear to lose him.

Emily found the perfect little cottage for her the following day. It was in Waterside, not far from the river, an end of terrace, which had once been an alms house but was now let to tenants. The rent was modest and would not stretch her budget too far, because Nicolas had given her fifty pounds, telling her that she would receive another fifteen each month from his salary. He'd also promised to send some more funds to her bank as soon as he was able to arrange the transfer.

Nicolas had told Emily that she had no need to work, but the idea of being a lady of leisure did not attract her. For the next several days she would be busy with packing, moving and scrubbing out the pub so that it was clean for the next owner. The thought of leaving her little haven wrenched at her heart, but she knew Nicolas would have hated her to continue to run a public house. It was bad enough that she had done so but to continue after their marriage would cause his family outrage.

Emily moved into her cottage ten days after taking it on. She spent three days polishing and cleaning and was pleased with the result, feeling that she deserved a treat. As it was a fine September day, she put on a light jacket, and dressed

Jack decently in the new clothes Nicolas had bought for him while on holiday, before taking him to the park. When she left the park she saw the newsvendor selling papers and stopped to buy one. She scanned the headlines for news of the war, which seemed as dire as ever, but didn't read much of the local news until that evening. About to turn over the page giving details of the latest births, deaths and marriages, a name caught her eye and a little shock went through her.

Lady Prior had passed peacefully away at home. The funeral was to be the following day at St Mary's Church in Ely.

Emily's throat caught with pain. No one had let her know. She'd been left to discover it in the paper – and she hadn't been invited to the funeral. She was Nicolas's wife and yet she'd been ignored. For a moment the hurt swathed through her and then she became angry.

Nicolas would be devastated when he heard of his grandmother's death, but he would want Emily to attend in his place, of that much she was certain. She would probably not go back to the house, but there was no reason why she should not slip into the back of the church unnoticed.

Emily's head went up. She would go whether the family liked it or not.

Emily's plan of slipping into the church unnoticed went sadly awry when she arrived to discover Lizzie and Sir Arthur standing outside the church waiting for the funeral cortege to arrive. Lizzie came to her at once, her eyes dark shadowed by grief as they embraced.

'I'm so glad you came, Emily,' she said. 'You got my letter? I sent it to the pub because I wasn't sure where you were.'

Emily told her that she'd moved and that she'd seen the notice in the local paper, but she felt warmed because at least one of the family was pleased to see her. When Lizzie insisted that she join with the rest of the family to follow the coffin into the church and sit with her and Sir Arthur, she could not refuse, though she saw Lord Barton give her a furious glance before he turned his head away. His cold look made her feel uncomfortable but Lizzie was crying softly and she reached for Emily's hand as the vicar began the eulogy.

After the interment, Lizzie asked her to drive back to the manor with them, assuring her that Sir Arthur would take her home later. Emily was hesitant but they were both so friendly and so insistent that she was family and must come to the reception that she felt compelled to agree. Lady Barton looked at her once, inclining her head and then averting her eyes. Jonathan smiled at her encouragingly, but Lord Barton steadfastly ignored her. Emily lifted her head proudly. She was Nicolas's wife whether his father liked it or not and she would have to get used to being treated as an outsider by Lord Barton – but she must do her best to be on good terms with the others, because otherwise she would be letting Nicolas down.

The manor was a sombre place, draped in black in the drawing room to mark the occasion, and Lady Prior's chair noticeably empty. People looked at it but preferred to stand rather than take the throne that had belonged to the proud lady who had outlived her era.

Emily watched the servants serving guests with wine, some of them known to her and some extra helpers brought in especially for the sad occasion. She felt a wistful longing to be one of them, because at least when she'd worked at the manor she'd known her place and she'd felt useful. Now the servants were respectful to her, even if some of them looked at her oddly. Lady Prior's friends and relations stared at her from a distance, only one or two giving her a nod of recognition. Had it not been for Lizzie and Sir Arthur she might have turned tail and run, but pride kept her head high and her face expressionless. She wasn't going to beg these people to like her. When Nicolas came home he would decide what to do about the attitude of his family towards her, but for the moment she must just carry on and accept it.

'Mrs Nicolas,' Mrs Marsh came up to her quietly. 'Lord Barton has asked to see you in his study before you leave.'

'Thank you. Please tell him I shall be leaving in a few moments – if that would be convenient.'

Mrs Marsh went over to her father-in-law. He listened, glanced at Emily and then nodded. Seeing him leave the reception, Emily went to follow. Lizzie caught her arm, asking her where she was going. She frowned as Emily told her, and then warned her not to let him intimidate her.

'Jon, Arthur and I will support you. I'll come over soon and see you – if you leave me your address.'

'I'll write it down for you before I go,' Emily promised, her heart racing as she walked to the study, knocked at the door and waited to be invited. Inside, she saw her former employer standing by the fireplace. It was an intimidating room, with lots of dark leather and sombre hues. Pictures and bookshelves lined the walls and a huge mahogany desk hogged the centre of the floor. He stared at her for a moment, before inclining his head.

'I suppose I must thank you for your attendance today,' Lord Barton said. 'My son insists that it would have looked odd had you not come – but I must tell you that your presence in my house is not acceptable to me.'

'I'm sorry if I've upset you.'

'I am not interested in anything you could do. I've asked you to come here to tell you that I wish you to leave my house at once. I shall have you driven to Ely or to the station, or wherever suits you. It is my intention to do everything in my power to force my son to remember his duty to his family and seek a divorce.'

Emily gasped, feeling as if he'd thrown cold water over her. 'Nicolas will never agree to that. If you say such a thing to him he will simply stop coming here.'

'Unless he agrees to my terms I shall disown him and he will not be permitted to visit his mother or sister. I was forced to accept this while Lady Prior lived but I am the master here now and my word is final.'

His expression was cold, his mouth hard, eyes looking straight through her. She could feel the anger and hatred emanating from him.

'You would really hurt your wife, Lizzie and Nicolas just because I was not born of your class?'

Emily looked him in the eyes. 'I did not marry Nicolas because of anything he could give me. The manor means nothing to me – though I had friends here. I love him and he loves me. I think you are harsh to ban him from his home but that is your choice. For me it means nothing but I am sorry that you will hurt others for the sake of your pride.'

'I am not interested in your thoughts or feelings on the matter. Please leave now. I have nothing more to say to you. You will speak to no one but the maid waiting for you; she will escort you from the house. I trust you have enough money for the taxi fare?'

'If I hadn't I should not ask you to loan it to me,' Emily said. 'I am sorry for you, sir. I hope you will not live to regret what you've done.'

His eyes bulged, his neck turning red. He looked as if he might have another apoplectic fit.

'Damn your impertinence. You're nothing but the kitchen skivvy. Get out now!'

Emily lifted her head proudly, then turned and walked away without another word. Outside in the hall, Mary was waiting for her.

'I'm sorry, Emily. I was told to see you left without speaking to anyone – but if you want to pop into the kitchen...'

'No, I shan't do that,' Emily said. 'I'll write to my friends, Mary. All I want is to leave now.' Her eyes were pricking with tears but her pride wouldn't allow her to cry. 'Tell Mrs Hattersley what happened.'

'I've been told I'm not to say.' Mary bit her lip. 'I'll tell Cook, Emily, but I will have to make her promise not to tell anyone else.'

'Thank you.'

Emily glanced around the hall. She had come to love this house but now that Lord Barton was the master here it was unlikely that she would return to the manor again while he lived.

Distressed by the unpleasant scene with Lord Barton, Emily forgot her promise to leave Lizzie her address. All she wanted to do was to get home, fetch Jack from Vera's house and hide away from the world – at least the people who lived here in this house.

Emily only remembered her promise to let Lizzie know where she was living three weeks later. She'd posted her latest letter to Nicolas, giving him her love and telling him what she'd been doing. Not once had she mentioned how cruel his father had been to her, because there was no point in distressing him. Emily had mentioned the funeral but not gone into details. Instead, she wrote of a voluntary group she'd joined. It was just a friendly little group of women who knitted scarves and socks for the troops and collected scrap. She'd entered Jack into a kindergarten group and thought he was better for having someone of his own age to play with. Her life was busy if not entirely happy, but how could it be while her husband was away?

The fear that someone would knock on her door with a telegram never quite left her. She knew that Nicolas had sent some money to her bank. He'd promised fifteen pounds every month, which was more than enough for Emily's needs. So she had no need to work, though the manager of the Temperance Hotel in the High Street had approached her, asking if she would care to work for him. The wage he'd offered her would be sufficient to pay Vera to look after Jack for the hours he wasn't at his playgroup, and had she not thought it would offend her husband's relatives she would have taken the job. However, despite Lord Barton's rudeness, she considered herself bound to take the family into consideration and turned down the manager's kind offer.

Sending her letter giving her change of address to Lizzie at Sir Arthur's estate, Emily thought no more of it. If Lord Barton had made his feelings known Lizzie might think it diplomatic to cut ties with Emily – at least until Nicolas returned home.

It was perhaps two weeks after sending her letter to Lizzie that Emily opened her door to see Jonathan Barton standing there. He looked so serious that her heart caught with fright. Her mouth was dry and something told her that his visit boded no good.

'May I come in please, Emily?'

'Yes, of course.'

She stepped back, inviting him in. He looked about, frowning as he took in the small rooms, which Emily had decorated with fresh paper on the walls. They were comfortable, a fire burning in the sitting room and the smell of lavender polish everywhere.

'You've made this pleasant, but I thought Nicolas would have found you something better.'

'He didn't have time. I'm renting this until he comes home – and then he wants to live in London. I think he has some...' Her words faded as she saw the look in his eyes and she went cold all over. 'Nicolas...'

'I'm so sorry, Lizzie. The War Office sent the telegram to us. Nicolas couldn't have told them that he had changed his next of kin ... he was shot down two weeks ago and is missing...'

Emily felt the room spin around her. She clutched at a chair to steady herself, then sat down with a bump on the wooden seat. He must be wrong. This couldn't happen to her. She loved Nicolas so much and they'd been so happy ... for such a short time.

'No,' she whispered. 'He promised to come back to me. He put some money into the bank for me just this week...'

'The bank does that every month, Emily, from Nicolas's pay on his instructions. If need be – if he *is* dead, I shall tell the bank to continue it. I'm Nicolas's executor and everything he had is for you. He wrote out his will and Mr Hattersley and I witnessed it ... so if the War Office stop paying his money, I'll make certain you still have what you need from Nicolas's personal account.'

'Don't!' Emily felt sick. How could he speak of money at a time like this? 'I don't want anything. I loved him. It wasn't for the money...' A sob rose in her throat. 'I can't bear it...'

Jonathan reached out, drawing her close to his chest to comfort her as she was taken by a storm of weeping. She felt his lips touch her hair. He was trying to be kind, but he wasn't Nicolas and she didn't want him to touch her – she didn't want anyone but Nicolas to touch her. For a moment she was too weak to move, but then she pushed him away.

'Emily, I'm so sorry. I had to tell you – but missing doesn't mean dead. We may hear better news...'

Emily wasn't listening. Her throat was tight and her eyes were burning with the tears that still gathered. 'Please, leave me. I know I'm not welcome at the manor – but if there is a funeral... Your father told me I wasn't welcome but...'

'Father had no right to be rude. I had it out with him, Emily. He was angry that day because he'd learned that Lady Prior had left the manor to me. However, Lizzie and Nicolas are to have some money. My mother has a trust fund and so does my father – but most of it came to me. When we're certain how things stand, I'll come to see you again.'

She shook her head, turning away as the numbness started to creep over her. She didn't want to know about wills or money or anything of the sort. All she wanted was for Nicolas to come home and take her in his arms, to hold her and love her – to tell her it was all a lie. He wasn't dead; he couldn't be, because without him the world seemed an empty place.

'Please,' she said. 'I should like to be alone now.'

'Are you sure? Do you want me to fetch someone for you?'

Emily shook her head. There was no one – no one would, no one could fill the empty place her life had suddenly become.

All she wanted now was to cry this terrible hurt out of her, but she knew it would never go away.

Chapter 49

Emily wasn't sure when she finally realised she couldn't face living in Ely any longer. She'd waited for news of Nicolas, perhaps for the funeral if his body had been found. She bought the local paper each week, scouring it for any mention of his death or his funeral but there was never anything reported. Several times she was tempted to go to the manor and ask if anyone in the kitchens knew more, but somehow she couldn't bring herself to go near the house.

She'd settled in her little house, but now she found the sight of familiar things almost unbearable, and she felt she needed to go away somewhere she wasn't known. Emily didn't want Jonathan to tell her about Nicolas's property or his will. The payments into her bank had stopped, which seemed to confirm what Jonathan had told her. Nicolas had been reported missing but because the War Office had stopped her payments, this had to mean he'd been confirmed dead.

Once again, no one had let her know, despite Jonathan's promise to visit her as soon as he had definite news – and to continue paying money into her account if Nicolas's money from the War Office was stopped. She should have known, Emily thought bitterly. Even when Nicolas had been alive she hadn't been welcome at the manor and now they didn't want to know her.

She'd seen Lord Barton in the High Street in Ely on one occasion and he'd looked through her, clearly refusing to acknowledge that she existed – which she never had for him. It seemed to Emily that she would do better to leave, go away somewhere and try to make a new life for herself and Jack. Before long her money would dwindle and she would need to find work, because she would never ask for a penny for herself from Nicolas's estate.

Feeling numb, Emily went through the ritual of her days until the morning she woke up and was sick three times before breakfast. When it happened again the next day and the next, she visited the doctor. His news shocked her and she left the surgery with her head in a whirl.

She was carrying Nicolas's child! Emily's emotions were a mixture of wonder and delight that she was having her husband's baby and the despair she felt because Nicolas would never know. Tears trickled down her cheeks as she walked away from the doctor's surgery.

What ought she to do now? She could not afford to carry on renting her cottage for long, because Nicolas's money from the air force had stopped when he died and what she'd saved would not last long – and she had to think about when she had the baby and couldn't work.

Still lost in thought she almost walked past Vera until she touched her arm. Her former employee looked at her curiously.

'Is something the matter, Emily?'

Emily hesitated, and then told her of her discovery. She explained that she couldn't afford to stay at her cottage for long and would need to find work.

'Why don't you move in with us?' Vera asked. 'I know we're a bit out of Ely, but you could catch a bus in – and Ma wouldn't charge you much rent. What kind of work were you thinking of?'

'I thought I might ask for a job cooking or serving at the Temperance,' Emily said. 'They did offer me work before but I didn't need it then.'

'Lucky you. I tried but they wouldn't take me...' Vera looked thoughtful. 'I could look after Jack, bring him in to his kindergarten school and fetch him home. He'll be starting school properly in a year or so, won't he?'

'Yes, perhaps.' Emily sighed, because she never mentioned it to anyone but she wondered whether Jack would be able to go to school. At the moment he was still a little slow, though he'd improved vastly from when Emily had found him dirty and wet. People told her he would grow out of it, but Emily wasn't sure he would; she would face that when the time came. 'That might be a good idea, Vera. Are you sure your mother would want us all there? I mean there's Jack and there will be a baby in a few months.'

'I'll ask her and then come and tell you this evening,' Vera said. 'If you get the job you can pay me a bit for looking after Jack – and the baby too. I like children and it isn't easy finding a job that Pa will let me do. He doesn't want me to go to a factory, because he needs me sometimes on the farm.'

Vera was a sensible girl and a good worker. Emily had trusted her when she worked at the pub and she realised it was probably the best solution. She hadn't wanted to stay so close to the manor, but if she was working all day in the kitchens and living out near Stuntney, which was in the opposite direction to Witchford and the manor, she was unlikely to see anyone from the family. The last thing Emily wanted was for them to know that she was having a child.

She didn't want Jonathan's pity or his money, and she knew the idea that she was carrying his son's child would anger Lord Barton. It would be better to just disappear and let them forget her.

Vera came to Emily's cottage that evening. Her mother was delighted with the idea of having her as a lodger. She could do with a little extra money coming in and would be happy to have Emily stay until she was ready to move on again.

Emily thanked Vera and told her she would come the next day. She decided that this time she would sell her furniture rather than putting it into store. The money she raised from selling her things would help her through the first months after the baby was born and she couldn't work. She hoped to have her own home again one day, but for the moment she was content to stay with the kind people who had offered her somewhere to live.

She found an advert in the local paper and made a telephone call from the new red box on the corner. The man came the next day and agreed to clear the house. He offered her twenty-five pounds for everything, which Emily knew was too cheap, but it would make her that little bit more secure – and she would start again when she was ready. When she packed her things to move into Mrs Green's house, she had only her and Jack's clothes and a few of Pa's trinkets, all of them chipped and valueless according to the second-hand dealer. Of course she had Nicolas's ring and the diamond pendant he'd given her, but she would have to be desperate to sell those.

The manager of the Temperance Hotel had been eager to give her the job. He'd tasted her food at the pub and said she was the best cook he'd come across in a long time. Emily smiled and thanked him. Ted Jackson was a pleasant man, not good looking but generous and easy to get on with – and the wage he offered her was very acceptable. She was to start at three pounds a week, which was twice what the women earned in the munitions factories, doing dangerous work.

Emily had been honest and told him that she was expecting her late husband's child, but instead of turning her away, as she'd feared, he was sympathetic and concerned. He would he said be glad to give her leave when the time came and to take her back when the child was born.

'If you want to bring the baby in with you, I dare say we could find a space for him or her during the day. Your brother needs to be at school, but a baby is no bother to me.'

Emily smiled to herself, reflecting that babies cried a lot and needed changing at inconvenient moments, but she would not return to work until the baby was old enough to be left with her friends.

The Green family lived in a large old-fashioned

farmhouse along the lonely country road to Stunt-ney. They had three sons who had grown up and moved out when they married, which made plenty of room for Emily and her family. Vera's mother was a plump, bustling woman, who always had time for a chat and a cup of tea. She reminded Emily of Mrs Hattersley. She'd made it clear from the start that she was looking forward to a bit of company and the rent she charged was so small that Emily tried to make up for it by helping with chores when she could and baking sometimes.

Emily had known as soon as she moved in that she'd done the right thing. Her bedroom was large and airy and Jack had the small one leading through from hers – what they called a Jack and Jill room. It was just right because he couldn't go run-ning off without her seeing him and she was close enough to comfort him if he cried in the night, but he settled in instantly, enjoying being taken for a ride on the great lumbering farm horses by Mr Green. Seeing him toddling round the yard by the side of the large but gentle man, Emily's mind had been set at rest. Mr Green was very like her father had been when he was young and strong, and she soon felt at home with the family.

Once the period of Emily's morning sickness had passed, she began to feel very well. The work in the kitchens at the Temperance Hotel suited her, because it was a nice, respectable place with a good class of customer. The menu was left to her, though Mr Jackson had set her a budget for the cost of the raw materials, which Emily found generous. The regulars at the Temperance liked good, substantial meals, such as steak and kidney pudding, chicken and ham pie, sausages and mash, a roast or some ham and salad. Emily cooked the ham she bought from the butchers in the High Street, and it was so much liked that the bar customers started asking for ham sandwiches in the evenings.

'You've picked up trade already,' Ted said to her a few weeks before Christmas. It was the third Christmas of the war and as yet there seemed no possibility of the hostilities coming to an end, despite a sprinkling of victories to the Allies. The Russians had suffered terrible casualties, but far too many men of other nations were dying, British, German and French. Emily knew that things were hard at home, but in the trenches the men were enduring unspeakable hardships; their feet rotted from the damp that constantly seeped through their boots; dysentery, fevers, boredom and cold were just some of the discomforts that they lived through – and every day they were bombarded with shells.

Emily enjoyed her work. She was on her feet for long hours, but for the first few months she was able to manage without feeling too uncomfortable. She even did extra shifts over Christmas, because Ted Jackson told her to bring her brother in with her. He took the boy in with his family, even putting a present under the tree for him and giving him a proper Christmas dinner. Jack had started walking properly since Mr Green had taken him under his wing and though he was still slow, he had improved his mobility and his speech a little. Emily had joined the family when the dining room was shut. She'd eaten her meal in between serving others but she had a slice of the flaming pudding, which had been kept to the last so that she could join Jack and Mr Jackson's family.

Ted had been a widower for some years; he was a man in his early forties with an attractive personality. He had a good sense of humour and, though he had no children of his own, he had two brothers, both of whom had brought their wives and children with them. They took Emily and her brother to their hearts, making a fuss of the child and giving him extra presents of money to spend on sweets.

Emily thought later that night that it was one of the best Christmases she'd ever had, because when she finally got back home there had been another little party at the Greens' house. Everyone had been so kind that she shed a few tears in her bed that night. Why couldn't Nicolas have come home for Christmas? Why had he been shot down – and why had she never heard any more of him?

Jonathan had promised to tell her for certain when he knew, but he hadn't come near her while she was at the cottage. Emily hadn't told anyone at the manor that she'd moved, though she had sent Christmas cards to Lizzie and to her friends in the kitchen. None had come for her, of course, but that was her choice. She didn't want pity and that was all she would get from Nicolas's family. His brother had said he would see that money was placed in her account each month, but although Emily had checked twice at the start she hadn't looked since she moved and started work. She didn't need more than she could earn in her present situation.

Despite all that had happened to her, Emily knew she was lucky. Her mother had gone from her life and she doubted she would see her again, but she'd made new friends. Ted was very easy to work for and he made it clear that he liked Emily. In fact he'd hinted a few times that he would be happy if she saw him as a friend rather than an employer. Emily tried hard to be friendly, without giving him cause to think her ready for a relationship. Of course he knew she was recently widowed for the second time and he hadn't made any unpleasant suggestions. Had he done so she would have had to leave, but she knew it was likely that one day he would ask and then she might have to move on.

Perhaps it was because she was now so heavily pregnant that Ted was being so circumspect. By the end of April it was no longer possible for Emily to work. Ted was reluctant to see her go, because he said she was impossible to replace.

'I'll get someone as a stand in until you feel able to come back,' he said as he gave her her wage packet for the last time. 'You'll find a bit extra in there, Emily. Let me know as soon as you're ready and I'll have you back like a shot.'

'You've been so kind to me...'

'Nonsense,' he said gruffly. 'I know I'm a bit old for you, Em – but I think we might suit, if you wanted to think about it once you're over the baby.'

Emily felt the colour seep into her cheeks. She smiled but didn't answer, because she knew he wouldn't expect her to now – but, as she'd suspected, he was thinking of a relationship, though whether he meant marriage she wasn't sure. Ted liked her, but what he really wanted was a permanent cook for the hotel.

It would have been rude to say no instantly, but of course she could never think of marrying again. In her heart Nicolas was her husband. Her marriage to Christopher had never been a proper marriage and she would never want another man in her life.

Somehow she would manage when the baby was born. Emily wasn't certain what she had in the bank, and the day following her enforced retirement from the hotel, she caught a bus into Ely and visited the bank in the High Street. She asked for a balance and when it was given to her she asked again, but the same answer was given.

She had one hundred and fifty five pounds. When she enquired further she was told that her monthly payments had been inadvertently stopped, because of a mistake by the bank itself, for two months, and then restarted. It was nothing to do with the War Office!

'You were sent a letter of apology, Mrs Barton.'

'I had moved,' Emily said. 'I had no idea that the payments were still being made.'

Emily's heart was racing as she left the bank. Why hadn't she checked her account before this? Possibly because she'd been working so hard that she really hadn't had the time – and because she'd managed on her wage.

What did the reinstatement of her payments mean? Was the government still paying her part of Nicolas's wage as a pilot – or had Jonathan arranged it? He'd promised to do so, but she'd thought he'd forgotten or neglected to keep his word.

Her throat caught with tears. It was ridiculous to hope that Nicolas was still alive and yet, illogically, she could not stop the little seed of hope from growing inside her. Could Nicolas still be alive? Should she write to Jonathan and ask him – or visit the manor herself?

A part of her wanted to rush there at once, but she forced herself to be sensible. It was ridiculous to hope for too much. Besides, she didn't particularly want his family to know she was carrying Nicolas's child. Lord Barton would deny it and if by chance he believed her, he might try to take the child from her once it was born. He was a powerful man and he hated her. Emily had a small but ridiculous fear that somehow he could force her to give her baby up to him.

Perhaps she would write to Jonathan and explain that she'd moved. He might have written to her at the cottage in Waterside or even visited.

Even though she told herself over and over again, Emily couldn't help hoping that a miracle had happened. After all, she'd never seen a notice of Nicolas's death – and yet if he were still alive he would have found her. Even though she hadn't told her family where she was living, people knew. Anyone who really wanted to know could have discovered where she worked – couldn't they?

It was stupid to hope, just because some money had been paid into her account, but at least it meant that she didn't have to worry how she would live until she could work again.

Emily wrote her letter that evening and gave it to Vera to post when she took Jack into Ely. However, three days later the girl confessed that she'd forgotten it so it was not posted until the next day. Emily couldn't scold her, because she'd had months to write and it was foolish to be impatient for a reply.

Ten days passed and no letters came for Emily. It was midway through that morning that she felt the first pains. The child was coming several days early and Emily felt a rush of panic. Had she harmed her baby by working too long – or had the shock and anxiety she'd felt after that visit to the bank brought the birth on too soon?

'You mustn't fret, lass,' Mrs Green told her when her waters broke. 'Mr Green's gone for the doctor but he likely won't get here until it's over. That baby seems in a hurry to be born.'

'Will it be all right? It's too early...'

'I was a month early with my first son,' the kindly woman said. 'He was as strong as a horse from the moment he popped out – still is come to that. Don't you worry, me and you will manage just fine on our own. Vera is putting the kettles on and I've had four of my own, besides helping others.'

Emily nodded, but cried out as the pain ripped through her. She felt as if she were being torn apart as she bit down on her lip and tasted blood. It was sheer agony and for a while she thought she might die, but then, pushing when she was instructed, she felt a pain worse than all the others and in another moment the child came rushing out of her in a mess of blood and slime.

'There, what did I tell you?' Mrs Green said as

she dealt efficiently with the cord then wrapped the child in a towel before placing it in Emily's arms. 'You've got a lovely boy – beautiful child he is, though not as big as my Sam was when he was born.'

Emily looked at the child in her arms and saw Nicolas's features. His eyes were open, blue and wide, staring in wonder at the strange place he'd come to in such a hurry. Tears stung Emily's eyes and trickled down her cheeks as she looked at him. He was so very beautiful and her love swelled, pouring out to surround him as she drew him closer. He was her little Nicky, a part of her husband come back to her.

'That's it, see if he wants a bit of a feed,' Mrs Green encouraged. 'My Sam was a greedy bugger, sucked me dry he did – and it can hurt. Hold your nipple between your fingers, lass, and put him to you. He'll know what he wants once you show him.'

Emily laughed. Happiness flooded through her. She was no longer alone. She had Nicolas's son ... she had Nicolas's son...

Chapter 50

Emily was sitting in the parlour, Nicky in a cot beside her when Mrs Green came in to tell her she had a visitor. For a moment her heart raced but she nodded her head, feeling almost sick with apprehension when Jonathan entered. He looked at her and then at the cot.

'Mrs Green told me you have a son?'

'Yes. Nicolas's son,' Emily said. 'He was a little early but he's quite healthy.'

Jonathan looked down at the child and smiled.

'He looks like his father. Was he born here in this house – before the doctor arrived?'

'Mrs Green was very good and he was in a hurry to be born.'

'Had you told me, you would have had a doctor in attendance.' Jonathan frowned. 'Why did you just go off like that, Emily? You knew I intended to keep in touch.'

'You didn't come and I – I couldn't afford to keep the cottage on when the money stopped coming. I know it has been reinstated – why?'

'Because Nicolas wanted to make sure you were all right...'

Emily knew her face must have gone white with the shock, because he looked alarmed. She closed her eyes, tears trickling down her cheeks as she said, 'He's alive? Where is he?'

'Alive, yes – and living with us at the manor,' Jonathan said hesitating, then, 'it is not good news, Emily. Nicolas was badly burned in the crash. He was picked up by a foreign ship and taken to a hospital in Jersey. We didn't know anything until about four months ago. He'd been ill and for a long time no one knew who he was – other than that he was a British pilot. When he finally felt like talking his survival was reported and he was moved to a hospital in England.'

Emily felt a wave of sadness wash over her. Her throat was tight with grief and it was a while before she could speak again.

'Where are the burns?'

'One side of his face – and he can't see well, Emily. The doctors think he may recover partial sight in the future, but they can't be sure. At the moment he can only make out shapes and sometimes colours.'

His injuries were so like Christopher's that it struck Emily to the heart. She knew that it wasn't unusual; too many men bore the same terrible injuries. Fire was such a wicked thing and men caught in an explosion suffered terrible burns; the hospitals were filled with them.

'My poor darling Nicolas...' Emily whispered. 'How can he write his pocms when he can't see? How can he bear it?'

'Not well,' Jonathan said. 'He asked about you but when I said I would have someone trace you he forbade me to tell you what had happened. I am breaking a promise, but I thought you had the right to know. You're not a widow, Emily – though Nicolas doesn't want you to sacrifice your life for him.'

'You mean he regrets our marriage?'

'That's bloody rubbish,' Jonathan said. 'He loves you and it's breaking his heart because he is refusing to see you – had I been able to find you before I should have told you as soon as we knew.'

'The letter I sent...'

'I'd been away. I haven't told him. I didn't want to raise hopes if you would rather not see him.'

'Of course I want to see him.'

Emily was aware that she was crying. She didn't

know whether they were tears of happiness because Nicolas was alive or tears of despair because he was in such pain. She knew what had happened when she insisted on marrying Christopher. Emily had wanted to make him happy, but instead she'd made his life a living nightmare. Supposing Nicolas couldn't bear her being near him ... and felt desperately unhappy because he couldn't be the man he had been when they married.

She could see that Jonathan was angry with her, angry because she was silent and because he thought she was hesitating for her own sake. If she tried to explain he wouldn't understand. No one could know what it felt like to be in hers and Christopher's shoes unless they had suffered the same fate. She longed for Nicolas with all her heart – but he might not want her.

'I love him,' she said at last. 'I'll come as soon as I feel able. Please don't say anything until I do. If you do he might refuse to see me.'

'The burns aren't a pretty sight, Emily.' Jonathan looked at her doubtfully. 'I've heard of cases where women just run out of the room when they first see their husbands or lovers ... you wouldn't do that?' Emily's head went up and he smiled oddly. 'No, of course you wouldn't. You've had experience of something very similar I know. I just don't want him to be hurt more than he has been.'

'Will your father accept me in his house?'

'He has no choice,' Jonathan said. 'I told you, the manor belongs to me – and it is Nicolas's home for as long as he needs or wants it – and you will always be welcome as Nicolas's wife. I've always admired you, Emily. Believe me, you need have no fear about coming to us.'

'Thank you.'

Emily sat back in her chair and closed her eyes. She was lost in her own thoughts and the pain that came over her in waves as she thought of all the lost days and weeks when Nicolas had been alone, believing she'd deserted him, wanting her and yet denying her because he did not want to ruin her life. He had such terrible injuries, but so many men had come home from the war with burns and, in severe cases, blindness. Yet Nicolas had escaped lightly compared to Christopher; for if Jonathan spoke the truth, his injuries were less extensive, despite the burns and the blindness. Christopher had practically lost the use of his hands, and his internal injuries had been much worse than she'd known when she wed him. It was doubtful Nicolas would see it that way, but it was true.

For a moment she felt bitterness and anger that it should have happened again. She'd been through this with Christopher. Could Fate be so cruel a second time? Yet in another moment she'd dismissed the unworthy feelings. Nicolas was alive and she had another chance.

Could she convince him that she loved him and wanted to be with him – and that his terrible injuries meant nothing to her other than for the pain they gave him? Or would she just make him unhappy if she tried to force him to accept her?

'You're tired and this has been a shock,' Jonathan said. 'I'll go – but let me know when and I'll come to fetch you, Emily. Nicolas needs you. He might not admit it but he does...'

Emily was paying for her taxi when Lizzie came flying out of the house towards her.

'Where have you been all this time?' she demanded. 'Jon nearly went mad when he couldn't find you...'

'I wasn't far away if anyone had looked,' Emily said but her cheeks flamed. She ought to have told Nicolas's family where she was living – and that she was having his child.

'Jon told me he'd seen you but Nicolas doesn't know. If he did he would probably refuse to see you. Don't let him know Jon told you or he would be so angry with him.'

'Of course. He thinks I would sacrifice myself for him and he can't bear it ... the foolish darling. Where is he? May I see him please?'

'Yes, of course. He might shout at you and tell you to go away. He makes Mama cry every time she tries to visit him. He won't speak to anyone but Jonathan or me.'

'He will speak to me whether he likes it or not,' Emily said. 'Would you take the baby for me please, Lizzie? I would rather not shock him too much at first.'

'Can I really?' Lizzie took the warm bundle into her arms. 'He smells delicious – of talcum I think. Do you mind if I take him to visit Mabel? She lost her baby and it might cheer her up to see him.'

'Oh no, how awful for her,' Emily said. 'Yes, of course you can take him to see his aunt if you're sure it won't upset her. Is Nicolas in his old room?' Lizzie nodded. 'I'll see myself up.'

'Yes. Good luck,' Lizzie said. 'I'll take Baby Nicolas to visit his grandmother as well.'

Emily nodded. She walked up the main staircase, after handing Hattersley her gloves, bag and short coat. He stared at her in shock but she smiled and walked on, turning to the right at the top and walking along the landing to Nicolas's room. She took a deep breath and knocked.

'Go away, Lizzie. I don't feel like talking.'

Emily opened the door and went in. Nicolas was sitting in an elbow chair by the window, the sun on his face. She saw the extent of his burns immediately and felt a rush of tears but held them back. His beautiful pale face was red and angry on one side, though the other was just the same as it always had been. She must not cry. Nicolas would not want pity. It would make him angry, hurt – even destroy him. She must never ever show pity, only love.

'It isn't Lizzie, it's Emily,' she said. 'I'm sorry I haven't been before but I didn't know. I thought you'd died in the accident.'

'Who told you?' he demanded harshly.

'Lizzie, just now,' Emily crossed her fingers as she told the small lie. He wouldn't be cross with his sister and Jonathan had only done what he considered right.

'You didn't know before you came? I forbade Jonathan to tell you but I know he's been trying to find you in case you need money.'

'Jonathan didn't find me. I decided it was time to see my friends.'

'They will be pleased to see you in the kitchen. Go away, Emily. Lizzie shouldn't have told you.'

'Lizzie did just as she ought. You are my husband. If I'd known I would have come much sooner.'

'I don't need pity. I have a nurse in Lizzie if I want her and the doctor visits once a week. You're wasting your time here.'

'I have no wish to be your nurse. I'm your wife. If you're angry with me for running away I must apologise – but I just couldn't bear it when Jonathan told me you were dead. I felt I wasn't wanted here and I couldn't face anyone. I wanted to be alone.'

'Then you'll know how I feel.'

'You are not the only man to come home with injuries like this, Nicolas. There must be hundreds of men with scars on their faces and blindness too. Lizzie said there was nothing else wrong – nothing to stop you living your life and making it a good one.'

'Nothing else? Isn't this face enough?' he asked, a note of bitterness in his voice.

'It isn't that bad. I've seen worse. At the hospital ... some of the men were much worse off than you. You have all your limbs and your senses.'

'Should I think myself lucky?'

'I feel lucky to have you back.'

'Go away, Emily. I don't want you here.'

She took a deep breath, her eyes smarting. 'I'm sorry, because Jonathan told me this is my home. I can bring Jack if I want, and I shall, of course, though Mr Green loves him, and when he's older he might go to live with them. I've decided I shall live here.'

'Why?' Nicolas's voice was harsh. 'I don't need

pity and I don't want you to stay with me out of duty.'

Emily's laughter rang out. 'Is that what you think – that I would stay with you out of duty?'

'It's what you were prepared to do for Christopher Johnson.'

'I cared for him as a friend. I love you, Nicolas. You are the only man I've ever loved. I want to be with you, and to spend my life with you, loving you – if you will let me?'

'What's left of me. I can't see you. I'm scarred. I can feel the ridges on my face even if I can't see them and I know I must be a monster. I don't want that for you, Emily. Jonathan will give you money. You can divorce me and find a new lover.'

'I wouldn't even think of it.' Emily hesitated, then, 'So you don't love me? What have I done to be sent away as if I was less than nothing? Do you hate me for ruining your life? Have you decided that your father was right – that I'm not good enough for this family?'

'Hate you?' Nicolas stood up, took a step towards her, hands outstretched. She could see tears running down his cheeks. 'How can you think I could hate you or think you not good enough? I love you too much to let you ruin your life looking after a wreck like me. You didn't have a choice before – and I want you to know that you can choose to walk away now. I shan't blame you.'

'I don't want to walk away.'

'Think of what you'll be giving up ... tied to a man who can't see...'

'I love you, Nicolas. I've never stopped.'

'It isn't fair to you, Emily. I can't see... If I can't

see I can't write about what I see. Without my poetry I'm only half a man...'

Emily's voice was a whisper, charged with emotion. 'I can see. I can be your eyes, Nicolas. I can tell you when the leaves are out and what colour the grass is and when there's dew on the spider's web...'

'You would be tied to me. You should have a life of your own, Emily.'

'Do you recall standing looking across the Fens on a clear day when the skies seemed to go on forever ... endlessly?'

'Yes, of course.'

'And then the dark clouds gathered and the mist rolled in across the flat land making it all become one and the loneliness closed in around you so that you could hardly breathe?' Nicolas nodded. 'That is how your life is now, lived under lowering skies.' She moved closer to him. 'You do not have to stay in this room. We can start by walking in the garden. You can learn to count your steps and use a stick. You don't have to be a prisoner. With me as your guide it will be easy. We can reach for the endless skies and if we try we shall find them.'

'And what can I give you? A few clothes...'

'Hush, my darling.' She placed her fingers to his lips. 'You can give me love and that is all I ask. Besides, don't you think it fair that your son should know his father?'

'My son...' Nicolas's face reflected shock, pain, and then wonder. 'I have a son? Emily ... is it true?'

'Yes, my dearest one. We have a beautiful son. He was born three weeks ago, a little early. I think perhaps I worked too long. It was only after he was born that I had the courage to come here. Someone persuaded me that your family had a right to know there was a child and I realised they were speaking the truth. I wanted a family for my son. I wanted him to have the things his father would have given him; love and stability and honour and so I came. It has taken me a long time to find the courage to come. Please don't send me away, Nicolas.'

'I didn't know... I didn't know...' the tears were streaming down his face as she went into his arms. 'Where is he? Can I hold him, touch him?'

'He is meeting his family,' Emily said. 'Why don't you take my arm and we'll join them downstairs for tea?'

Nicolas hesitated, and then smiled. 'I don't have much choice. You have all the cards, Emily. You'll have to be patient. I haven't bothered to leave this room. There wasn't a reason to do so.'

'Now there is,' she said. 'First you must meet little Nicky – and then I feel like a stroll in the garden. I noticed the roses were just beginning to bud. You remember the white climber – it rains roses all down the south wall. They are in tight buds now but when the petals fall they look like white rain falling.'

'Raining roses?' Nicolas laughed. 'What odd things you say, Emily. Yes, I remember what that looks like. The petals fall like rain when the wind ripples through the branches ... and it is usually a glorious sight.'

'It smells glorious too,' Emily said, 'clear and fresh. There is so much to see, Nicolas, so much to smell and touch – and I can make it come alive for you. Remember what it was like in Devon? You said that I made you see all the bright things? The world is filled with them and we'll find them together...'

Afterword

Jonathan looked out of the window. He could see Emily and Nicolas walking near the rose arbour. It was still only spring but the sun was already warm. Emily was talking and laughing, and Nicolas was responding. Behind him, he heard his wife's laughter as she played with young Nicky. Emily had also brought her young brother Jack to the manor when she moved in, but he'd cried for his friends and after a plea from them was allowed to return to the Greens at their farm in Stuntney, though he would visit now and then.

Since Emily arrived a few days previously, Mabel hadn't cried once. When Lizzie first offered her the baby she'd held back for a moment, unsure or resentful because she'd lost her own baby, but then she'd taken Nicky in her arms and a look of wonder had come over her face. She'd fallen in love with him instantly, as had most of the family. Perhaps Emily's child would fill the empty space in her heart; he hoped it might be so.

He turned to look at Mabel. She looked almost pretty as she nursed the child. It was a pity she would have none of her own – if the doctor was right. Jonathan hadn't told her yet. He didn't love her but he didn't want to destroy her. He'd been a fool to rush into a marriage that meant nothing to him. He should have waited and followed his heart, as Nicolas had. His grandmother had meant to leave him the manor all along.

He could divorce Mabel if she failed to produce a child; they could arrange something, but she didn't deserve that. Jonathan realised that he didn't want to change anything. Emily had given him all he needed. She'd provided an heir for Priorsfield and in the years to come she would probably produce half a dozen healthy brats, because there was nothing wrong with Nicolas but a few scars and the blurring of his eyesight. Women of her class so often did have a string of healthy brats. He hoped she would. It would fill the house with noise and laughter and that was what the manor needed – it had seemed empty since Lizzie married and moved away, but now they had Emily, her brother and Nicolas's son. Already, it seemed more alive than it had been since his grandmother died.

No, Jonathan wouldn't divorce his wife. No doubt Mabel would have objected strongly, even though he didn't think she was happy with things as they stood. Perhaps she would find a way to fill her empty days; he hoped so. He thought that he would take a mistress when the right opportunity presented itself.

Hearing laughter through the open window he turned to watch Emily as she picked a spray of some scented shrub and held it to Nicolas's nose. Jonathan hadn't told his brother yet but he'd sent some of his poetry to a publisher – the dark stuff he'd done in the war. It was the best verse he'd ever written and deserved to be seen by the world at large. Nicolas had started to write a few lines again – at least, he dictated and Emily wrote it down. She was constantly at his side, helping him, persuading him, making him laugh. Often, she and Nicolas sat in the gardens, talking and laughing, little Nicky in his pram nearby. Jonathan joined them whenever he had the time. Watching them together, he felt a pang of envy.

Nicolas was damned lucky despite his injuries.

Amy was still abroad with her lover. She'd written once but said it would be years before she returned to England. Perhaps by then the scandal would have blown over.

The parlour door opened and Lady Barton entered. She came to stand by Jonathan's side as he watched the couple in the garden.

'She's good for him, isn't she?'

'Yes, Mother. She's good for us all.'

'I suppose she is,' Helen said. 'Your father is still sulking but I think he's beginning to realise that she has worked a little miracle with at least two of our household.' She glanced at Mabel. 'Your wife is much happier looking after the baby – and Emily is so good about sharing.'

'Emily is good at everything,' Jonathan said and smiled. He called across to his wife, 'Mabel – why don't you ring for tea, my dear? Nurse will take Baby if you're tired.'

'I feel much better, not at all tired,' Mabel said. 'You ring for tea, Mama. I'll take Nicky up to the nursery and then I'll join you.'

'As you wish, my love.'

Mabel smiled and walked out of the room. Jonathan glanced back at the couple in the garden. They were kissing, their bodies pressed together in an embrace of passion and desire. He envied them because they had so much, but he also loved them because of all they gave.

'Yes,' he murmured. 'Emily is good for us all. Ring for tea, Mama. I'll call them in from the garden...'

The publishers hope that this book has given you enjoyable reading. Large Print Books are especially designed to be as easy to see and hold as possible. If you wish a complete list of our books please ask at your local library or write directly to:

Magna Large Print Books
Magna House, Long Preston,
Skipton, North Yorkshire.
BD23 4ND

This Large Print Book for the partially sighted, who cannot read normal print, is published under the auspices of

THE ULVERSCROFT FOUNDATION

THE ULVERSCROFT FOUNDATION

... we hope that you have enjoyed this Large Print Book. Please think for a moment about those people who have worse eyesight problems than you ... and are unable to even read or enjoy Large Print, without great difficulty.

You can help them by sending a donation, large or small to:

**The Ulverscroft Foundation,
1, The Green, Bradgate Road,
Anstey, Leicestershire, LE7 7FU,
England.**
or request a copy of our brochure for more details.

The Foundation will use all your help to assist those people who are handicapped by various sight problems and need special attention.

Thank you very much for your help.